BENCH

BENCH

NICK CHOO

iUniverse, Inc.
Bloomington

Bench

iUniverse books may be ordered through booksellers or by contacting:

iUniverse
1663 Liberty Drive
Bloomington, IN 47403
www.iuniverse.com
1-800-Authors (1-800-288-4677)

ISBN: 978-1-4759-4688-8 (sc)
ISBN: 978-1-4759-4690-1 (hc)
ISBN: 978-1-4759-4689-5 (ebk)

Library of Congress Control Number: 2012916001

Printed in the United States of America

iUniverse rev. date: 09/26/2012

For those who've stuck with me
through the highs and the lows.
Especially the lows.

ACKNOWLEDGEMENTS

A debt of gratitude to Judi and Jo; Terry; Juliana & Kai; Bernie; Beattie; Becky; Debs, Phaiks & Chrissie; and Dave Naylor.

To Carol H; Carol C; Josie; Chris, Jade & Arielle; Michelle Q; cousin Andrew; Juan; Adam & Eva; Alex, Mel and the boys; Andrea, who loves D-grade horror; Jenny and the CT stalwarts, including Jason H and Andrew K; Dom and Ben; Cat of Goodputty, for the footprints; the TNG team, particularly Jac and Deb; Alisha; Alex and Jo; Kev, Rin and the kids; Alisa; Ben C; Emma, who called the Derrick storyline "a plot on crack"; Marcella Polain, for an earlier version of Derrick's tale; and the housemates in 2002 for their namesakes: Derrick, Sanjeev, Chitra and Geraldine.

A big thank you to Val, for her keen eye, and invaluable feedback and expertise in making this manuscript shine!

To Mum, for her love and support.

To Ashley, my therapy dog.

And to JD, who inadvertently made things unravel, purportedly for my own good.

PROLOGUE

THE AFTERMATH

His mouth was locked in a silent scream, and his hands were held out in front of his face in a futile attempt at warding off the impending disaster. Mere seconds ago, the sight of the old man in the middle of the road had rendered him immobile. Suddenly he saw with cruel, mocking precision the fatal consequences of his decision to detour off the road and into the field. He was unable to think or move, unable to make a sound, unable even to breathe; it was as if the act of swerving off the road had caused his spirit to become detached from his body, and he was now hovering above himself, observing helplessly, stuck in that stance with his hands held out in front of his face to fend off the impending blow—

Straight into the field, headed for the bench, for the people gathered under the tree . . .

If only he could move his arms, turn the wheel, step on the brakes, do something, *anything*—

But he didn't, *couldn't*.

He could only gape in heart-stopping panic as the car sped towards its target.

The aftermath was a scene right out of a movie. The woman frantically tugged at the car door, screaming and wailing, while her daughter tried to hold her back, crying, "Mum, Mummy, don't, *don't*—!" The vehicle itself looked as if it was trying to climb the tree, its entire front section smashed up against the trunk, headlights aimed at the sky, one still shining into the branches. The two couples stood trembling some distance away, glass, splintered wood and other debris at their feet, stunned by their near-brush with death, and marvelling that what had only moments ago been a scene of calm had so suddenly turned into one of chaos and destruction.

Residents, young and old, were rushing out of their homes, all a-twitter at the drama that had unfolded in their usually quiet neighbourhood. Some of them gathered around the old man lying bloodied and unmoving by the side of the road, while others congregated around another, younger man, also unconscious and in worse shape than the elderly gent, his leg bent at an ugly angle, clearly broken.

Next to this man was a girl in tears who called his name, and the agitated neighbours hurled questions at her—"What happened?" "Are they all right?" "How on *earth* . . . ?"—even as the emergency personnel turned up and hurried across the grassy expanse, and the media arrived on the scene to speak to the strangers united by this horrific turn of events.

PART ONE

FLYIN' REAL FAST

Matthew Leigh surveyed the area, squinting in the glare of the midday sun. Two little girls chased each other across the grass, squealing and giggling, their blond hair almost white in the sunlight. Somewhere, a dog barked a repeated pattern of three high-pitched yaps in rapid succession. In spite of the tinted glasses propped on his nose, Matthew's eyes began to hurt, and he decided he had best find a place to have his lunch or else head back to the university library, where he had been cooped up for three and a half hours that morning. But he needed a little fresh air, no matter how hot it was. If anything, the sweltering atmosphere outside was a relief compared to the mustiness of the bookshelves.

On the west side of the field a solitary wooden structure stood bathed in the shade of a tree. Matthew went over to it. Perfect. Sheltered, private enough in the open space. Made of a sturdy wood: Rough and jagged but securely constructed, stable as he sat.

The girls shrieked and giggled, thoroughly enjoying their game. *Fucking annoying*, he thought. Birds fluttered in the branches above his head, and he looked skyward warily. A lone car chugged slowly along the road that ran the perimeter of the field, separating the grassy area from the houses that lined the Square. In a quiet, suburban neighbourhood like this, there was no need for speed.

For a while Matthew sat under the umbrella of the tree, taking his time to pry his chicken sandwich from its plastic casing. In the intermittent silence, punctuated by the occasional squeals of the children and the crackle-squeak of plastic in his hand, his mind filled with thoughts of his frustrating morning in the library, with the broken-down air conditioning and hidden textbooks on subjects he couldn't give a shit about.

"Go home, Robby!" The shrill voice of one of the girls.

A little boy's voice cropped up, whiny, followed by the girl's insistent "Go *home*, Robby! Get out of here!"

And then the other girl's voice, more calmly: "Go on, Robby. Three's a crowd, you know."

The boy protested again, and Matthew heard the grating bell-like laughter of the girls gradually fade as they undoubtedly skipped away into the distance.

He bit into the sandwich and felt a spurt of warm mayonnaise on his tongue.

Somewhere behind him, there was the sound of footsteps, soft and light. He heard quiet intakes of breath, interjected with a sharp gasp and a sniffling of the nose. It did not take a genius to figure out that the boy was crying, or was on the verge of it.

There were crackling noises, and the snapping of a twig.

Then, emerging from behind the trunk, the boy stepped towards the bench, towards Matthew, a grubby hand wiping tears from his eyes. Matthew felt his heart sink to his stomach. *Don't come near me, kid*, he thought sourly, and took another bite.

Sniffling loudly, the boy made his way to the wooden seat and plopped his little behind upon it, on Matthew's right. The child snivelled, and fresh tears ran down his cheeks. He wiped at them, painting his face with grey streaks.

Matthew glanced askance at the boy. Sandy-haired, his freckled face now stained. One of those cherubic brats with snotty noses and dirt-encrusted hands with blackened fingernails. He shifted further away from the child, and took a third bite, wondering offhandedly if expiration dates on pre-packed sandwiches could really be trusted (*Prepared today*, the pack declared unhelpfully, *expires in three days*) —

"They won't let me play."

Matthew nearly choked on the sandwich. He swallowed, cleared his throat, and stared at the kid. Little Robby wasn't looking at him; his head was woefully in his hands, and he gazed at the grassy ground as if the dead leaves and foliage were most exciting to look at. Head bowed, the child whimpered pathetically, "Mister, they won't let me play."

Matthew sighed inwardly but remained quiet. Go away. Go away, go *away*.

"They won't let me play," the boy said again, and looked up at him expectantly.

Matthew exhaled. "Well. That's . . . tough," he said curtly, and chewed.

There was silence, followed by three high-pitched yaps from the dog, and the boy's sniffles.

Then: "You wanna play?"

Matthew nearly choked again. Irritation swept over him, and he turned sharply to the child. Little Robby looked up at him, his eyes red and puffy, his irises gleaming with a touching, innocent display of anticipation that failed to move Matthew in the least. His response was short, albeit not too sweet: "No."

"Oh."

Another tension-filled silence. How quickly the sweet spot had turned sour—how the solitary, tree-shadowed bench had fast become a sitting-place of contention. *Too good to be true,* Matthew thought, shaking his head as he chewed on soggy lettuce.

The boy wiped his nose audibly with a grimy arm, then looked up at the branches of the tree, where the birds chirped noisily. He said, "I wish I could fly, mister." Matthew's jaw worked soundlessly. "Mister?" Little Robby scooted a little closer to tap Matthew's leg with a dirty-nailed finger. "Hey, mister?"

It took every ounce of resistance for Matthew not to shove the kid off the bench. Instead, he shifted to the left, so that the gap between them widened. He hoped the brat would get the hint.

The brat got the hint. He remained where he was, and returned to staring at the treetops.

After a moment, he said, "Birds don't fight."

Matthew flinched.

"Birds get along very well, don't they, mister? I wish I was a bird. How come you don't ever see two sparrows fightin', mister?" The child craned his neck, looking up into the leaves. "You see two, three, four, five sparrows, all together, havin' fun and buildin' nests and flyin' around and singin', and they don't fight, do they, mister?"—oblivious to the hostility emanating off Matthew in waves. "They don't say 'go home' to each other, or—or say 'three's a crowd', do they, mister?"

"Jesus, how old are you, kid?" Matthew snapped.

"Six."

"You think too damn much for someone who's six."

The boy considered this. "If I was a bird and other birds was mad at me, I'd fly away and find new birds to be friends with. I wish I could fly. I wish I was a bird. Somethin' small, like a sparrow. Don't wanna be a vulture or buzzard. They're big, and they're scary, and they fight. I don't wanna fight, mister. My mummy says buzzards and vultures are big and scary and they like to fight. I've never seen 'em. Don't know if my mummy has ever seen 'em neither."

Matthew stuffed the remains of his sandwich back into its plastic casing impatiently, trying to think of a clever retort that would end this inane dialogue. The best he could come up with was: "If you were a bird, you'd be a crow."

Nice one, Matthew. You'd make a terrific *lawyer.*

"I don't wanna be a crow," little Robby replied, ignoring the barb, or maybe just not getting it. "Don't mind bein' a sparrow. They's everywhere, but they're nice, and they're quiet, and they get along. Or maybe a hummin'bird, 'cause they fly real fast and their wings, they go *bzzzz, bzzzz,* 'cause they're movin' really quick, y'know? But I don't like crows," he proclaimed, and folded his arms across his chest resolutely. "Crows are big and

black, and they make this horrible noise, this *awwwwk, awwwwk!*"
The boy looked at the man. "What bird *you* wanna be?"

This time, Matthew chuckled, but it was filled with
condescension. "I don't want to be a bird. Birds shit all over
you, and they're noisy, and they wake you up in the morning,
making you think the freaking planet's all bright and cheery
and everything's all right with the world, when in reality, things
sure as hell are *not*."

If the crudeness bothered him, the child didn't let on. He
mulled this over. Finally, he asked, "Why *isn't* the world all
bright and cheery?"

"'Cause it isn't!" Matthew barked.

"Seems bright and cheery to *me*."

"Well, when you grow up to be *my* age, you'll realise
the world's a much bigger and badder place than your puny
six-year-old brain could ever perceive it to be, and you'll see
that there really isn't any point in waking up all fucking cheerful
and singing at the top of your fucking lungs, all right?"

Silence.

For a while, the only sounds were the leaves rustling, and the
birds cheeping, and the dog barking from one of the buildings
somewhere in the Square, and Matthew's noisy chewing as he
disgruntledly resumed his lunch.

The boy said, "You sound like you're a chicken."

He balked. "What?"

"Chicken."

"A *chicken?*"

"Yeah. 'Cause chickens . . . they're, like, always cooped
up, right, mister? And they becomes food for us to eat, right?
So I'm thinkin' chickens aren't happy. They're thinkin' the
world's a bad place to be. And if *you're* gettin' up every mornin'
and *you're* thinkin' the world's a bad place to be, then you're
probably"—stumbling over the word—"thinkin' what the
chickens are thinkin', right?"

"*What??*"

"So you sound like you're a chicken."

Flummoxed, the older glared daggers at the younger. Little Robby's expression revealed no signs of impertinence, and suddenly Matthew felt warm in the face. Was he flushing? Did the boy really *do* that to him? Christ! He clenched his fist, only to find that he had squished the sandwich he was holding.

Above their heads, the birds flapped, and the leaves swayed, and the branches jostled in the post-noon light. Perhaps sensing that he had said too much, little Robby slid off the bench and sprinted away from the shade, leaving Matthew to stew in his hostility. A low squawk rang out from the overhanging branches, followed by the almost perceptible whistle and *splat* of bird-doo as it sailed downward and mingled with the warm mayonnaise oozing from between the tooth-marked slices of bread.

PROSPERITY AND MARITAL BLISS

Heat soared through Derrick as he ran hell for leather towards his apartment building. His heartbeat pounded loudly in his ears; his blood was rushing through him, coursing through his veins, thrumming at his temples. His teeth were tightly gritted, and he repeatedly clenched and unclenched his fists as he tried to make sense of what was happening. Two hours ago life had been perfect—and now, a mere two hours later, it was cast into a maelstrom of sorrow and despair.

How? he shrieked in his mind. *How did this happen? How? How?!*

He'd been preparing for this occasion for *ages*. He'd gone and bought the best diamond ring his money could buy. He had spoken to his friends Sanjeev and Chitra about it, and they'd cheered him on—although Chitra had added, nonchalantly, that the occasion had been long overdue. Derrick didn't think so. Twenty-seven was the best age to get down on bended knee. With Geraldine being just two years younger, it was also the right time for her.

At least, that's what he'd thought.

Derrick had always assumed the proposal would go smoothly. They'd been together for years. She had a steady and well-paid job at the local paper, a position she'd held since leaving college four years ago. She'd never spoken of going back for further study; neither had she complained about her duties as a sub-editor for *The Tribune*—a stimulating career that promised a good future, including a rise to prominent journalistic positions, if she stuck with it.

So wherein lay the difficulty? What was stopping her from accepting his proposal? It wasn't as if getting married would inconvenience them in any way—they were, after all, neighbours; he lived in apartment 2A, she in 3B. All she had to do was move in with him downstairs. What was the problem? What? *What?*

He'd planned so painstakingly for this night. The restaurant had been booked—Emilio's, the best seafood place in the city, the most romantic. Getting a table there on a weekend was no easy task, and he'd had to book several weeks in advance, pull a few strings, kiss a few asses. Then there were the flowers, and the champagne, and the car that would take them up to the Point to overlook the sights and lights of the city. If that wasn't romantic, what the hell was? And the suit. He'd gone out and had it tailor-made for the evening: A double-breasted dark-blue dinner jacket over dark pants, with a Windsor-knotted necktie and navy silk shirt. Not too fancy, but not too plain, either. Not too expensive—but not too cheap, either. All in all, the whole affair had cost him a bomb, and he'd expected it to, but he'd told himself it wouldn't be a problem, since the smile on her face—as he'd imagined it—would make up multi-fold for the expenditure. Nothing, he'd told himself decisively, *nothing* was going to stand in the way of their happiness tonight.

Except, perhaps, for the unexpected rejection of his proposal.

As he tore down the road, his leather shoes *click-clack*ing against tar and kicking up tiny pebbles that bounced off and peppered his shins, the events of the evening repeated in his mind like a film reel that had got stuck and was playing the same scene over and over and over again. *(Breathe!)* His jacket was growing heavy; his lungs were burning as he inhaled and exhaled heavily, inconsistently, breathing only because he had to. A pain had begun to creep up his left side. He ignored it. Fuck. *Fuck!*

Derrick had picked Geraldine up in the black Peugeot that Sanjeev owned. It was no limo, but it was fancy enough. They had reached the apartment at 6:45PM on the dot, as according to plan ("Not a minute sooner, not a minute later!"), and Derrick had sprinted up to Geraldine's. She'd greeted him at the door, looking absolutely ravishing in a stunning dress that flowed from collar to ankle: a dark shade of red that contrasted exquisitely with his blue, a silken sheen that accentuated her curvaceous figure as she walked. Around her neck a silver chain, complete with a crucifix. Around her wrists sparkling bracelets that, in Derrick's hopelessly romantic eyes, paled in comparison with her shimmering beauty. Her hair—dark brown, the sweet, luscious colour of honey—was done in a different way, falling down her shoulders effortlessly, shiny as her dress. She was intoxicating. She was amazing. And she was *his*.

So he'd thought.

"My God," he said, stepping backwards. "You look —incredible."

She laughed, a tinkling sound, like wine glasses being clinked together in a toast: *To bright futures! To prosperity and marital bliss! To years and years of happiness!* And she said, "Rick, what's the occasion?"—the question she'd been asking since he'd first told her about tonight, over a week ago. In response, he smiled enigmatically and offered her his arm.

Down the stairs, inhaling her sweetness. Outside, into the open, where a cool breeze sent wafts of her perfume into his every breath. Her hair brushed lightly against his face, and he revelled in the sensation of it. Into the Peugeot, where Sanjeev sat waiting in the driver's seat with a baseball cap propped backwards on his head in an admirable but less than successful attempt to emulate a chauffeur.

Then it was off to Emilio's, where their table awaited. Their maitre'd, Luis, helped them get seated, and soon they were dining on the fresh and succulent seafood that Emilio's was famous for, complete with bubbling glasses of pink champagne. Derrick struggled to maintain his composure, but as they reached the end of the meal, he felt himself growing increasingly excited. The moment was arriving. The little box was waiting in his suit pocket, ready to be presented and exposed to the whole room in its full, incandescent glory. What *was* she talking about? Something about how a foreign newspaper had come under fire for mistakenly reporting an assassination attempt on its nation's prime minister, and *honey, I still don't understand what's so special about tonight, why did we have to dress up like this, it's not like we haven't dined here before . . . ?*

Not when I'm about to propose, we haven't, he thought, casually dismissing her questions by signalling for a waiter to top up their champagne. He hoped he wasn't drinking too much, that would be a giveaway. He hardly drank—a can or two of beer if he was hanging out with his friends, a glass of wine or two at social events. He wondered if he was imbibing too much in his bid to calm his jittery nerves. He wondered if he was going to be adversely affected by the overindulgence. He wondered a lot of things.

Finally, the Moment arrived, by which time Geraldine was revealing a *slight* displeasure at being kept in the dark about the Big Secret, and by which time Derrick's heart was pumping so frantically against his ribcage that he imagined the other diners looking about in puzzlement, wondering, *What the hell's that rapid but steady dual-beat rhythm . . . ?*

"Honey," he whispered, taking her hand. His own was cold and damp, but if she noticed, she didn't show it. Curiously she stared into his eyes, and he swallowed repeatedly, his mouth too dry to speak. He managed to choke out, "I've—I've got s-something for you."

"What?" she demanded, squeezing his hand so hard it made him wince.

His other hand dug into his jacket pocket. His fingers danced about, and for a fleeting moment he panicked, thinking, *It isn't there! Dear Jesus, it isn't there, oh my God it's gone it's gone it's gone it's gone it's* and then he found it, fished it out, and gently disengaged his fingers from hers so that he could present it to her with both hands.

As he moved the box across the white tablecloth, he pried the lid open, revealing, in its aforementioned full, incandescent glory, the ring.

He heard her gasp, saw her sit more erect in her chair.

"Geri," he said breathlessly, "honey . . ."

"Oh, my God," she whispered, staring with saucer eyes at the glimmering diamond, flashing gold and white in the light of the restaurant chandeliers. "My *God*, Rick, that's the *biggest* rock I've ever seen . . . !"

"Honey," he tried again, and managed a nervous smile. "Will you . . ." His voice faltered, and he cursed himself for being so apprehensive. He powered through. "Will you marry me?"

She paled. At least, he thought she had; it was hard to tell in the light. Nonetheless, all of a sudden, the spectacular, magical Moment transformed into one of utter despair. She pushed her seat back with the silent screech of wood against carpet, and, much to his consternation, uttered a frantic and seemingly frightened "I've got to go, Derrick!" As abruptly as she'd risen to her feet, she'd grabbed her purse and got the hell *out* of there, leaving him alone, box and diamond in hand, pink champagne bubbling indifferently away, looking stupid and confused and feeling even more so.

It was only several stunned and seemingly interminable minutes later that he'd rushed to the entrance of Emilio's, pocketing the ring, while Luis had exclaimed with his heavy accent, "What ees wrong? El nino, what ees da matter . . . ?!"—and he'd shot out onto the pavement, into the cool wind that had suddenly strangely become ice-cold, to scan either direction for Geraldine.

He was too late. She'd disappeared.

And so, it seemed, had Sanjeev in his battered and suddenly unromantic Peugeot.

"Geri!" he'd shouted, causing several passers-by to jump, turn and stare accusingly at him. "*Geriii!*"

Why? Why? *Why??*

Now, as he ran in the direction of the apartment block, feeling the icy sting of the wind in his eyes and drying the sweat on his skin, he wondered where he'd gone wrong. His breath steaming up in front of his face *(Do I have halitosis? Is that it, is that why she won't marry me?)*, he pushed himself to the limit and ran, ran, ran, round the corner, down the dark and rank alleyway with its resident rats, round another corner and into the Square, where the Kiara Apartments sat.

Ignoring the glares of the few strangers and fewer familiar faces on the street, Derrick tore up the pavement to the front door of the building, punched in the security code to get the door open, and, having thrown himself through the open doorway, fumbled up the stairs. His feet thumped loudly against the carpeted steps, and for a moment he fretted that the noise might wake the neighbours — only to remember that it was 8pm, not after midnight; after midnight being, of course, the time he'd *expected* the evening to end . . . !

He pulled to a halt in front of apartment 3B. For a while he remained bent over with his hands on his trembling knees, his body racking as he gasped and panted, listening to the rapid explosion of his heart. Sweat, cold and clammy, dripped down the sides of his face. The jacket was now too constricting.

Derrick knocked on the door, three hard thuds, and waited. Waited, thinking, *Geri, have you come home? Please, please, answer the door. Please!*

The sound of footsteps made him bolt upright. He wiped sweat away from his face with his sleeve. There was a series of clunking noises as the lock was disengaged, followed by the click and squeal of the knob being turned. Then someone peered through the crack in the doorway. Derrick, licking his lips and tasting salt, exclaimed, "Hope! I've got to talk to Geri, where is she?"

Hope Brewster pulled the door wide open and looked at Derrick with a blank expression — one he suspected was reserved only for him. As usual, she was chewing gum, an idiosyncrasy that always struck Derrick as rather clichéd on a character like her. It complemented her shocking-pink hair—short, like a football helmet—and her tight clothing, and a tattoo of a musical *segno* symbol on her neck. Hope had spunk, she had attitude, she was no pushover, and, above all, she was very protective of her housemate and best friend, Geraldine.

Glaring at Derrick with one raised eyebrow, she removed the wad of gum from her mouth and said with a burst of Tutti-Frutti breath, "Geri? She ain't here. Ain't she supposed to be with you, Dick? What the hell happened?"

Derrick groaned, shaking his head. Droplets of sweat fell to the scuffed wooden floor beneath his feet. "I don't—oh, God, Hope, I don't know what the hell happened. One minute we were having dinner and everything was fine and going so well, the next she was running out of there as if she'd left the iron on and her pants were on fire." Several seconds went by before he added, "Oh, and I asked her to marry me."

Hope didn't look surprised by the announcement. She didn't look *at all* affected: her face remained blank. Popping the gum back into her mouth and chewing with an air of insolence about her, she said, "That's exactly what I figured. Figured you'd wanna tie her down, what with her getting all dolled up like that. She said no, did she?" A snort. "Well."

"She didn't say no!" Derrick exclaimed loudly. He quickly looked around to see if anybody had heard. Lowering his voice, he added, "She just upped and hopped it. I don't know why."

"Maybe you freaked her out."

"Why would she have freaked out?"

"Have you guys ever discussed marriage?"

"Well—no, but come on, isn't it obvious that I would . . . one day . . ."

"Can't assume anything these days," she said, matter-of-fact.

"We've been going out for eight years; it was only a matter of time before . . ."

"Yeah, whatever." She looked at her nails. "Listen, Geri ain't here; you'd better check her usual hangouts. That outlet she likes to go to when something's eating away at her. When you're down in the dumps, a little retail therapy works wonders, you know?"

"Down in the dumps," he said sullenly. "So *that's* where you buy your stuff."

Derrick was about to make his way back down the stairs when he heard Hope call out to him. He turned, looked sadly at her, and she said, softer now, "I'm sure everything will be fine. You probably just surprised her, that's all. Give her a couple of hours, a day or two, she'll call you, let you know."

"Why the surprise?" he retorted, throwing his arms up in a gesture of helplessness. "I don't get it. I just don't get it!"

"Take care, you dick," she said, and shut the door.

He began the slow trudge down to his apartment. At the landing, he decided that he wouldn't stop, but would head out of the building to the field in the middle of the Square. He'd always found comfort there—a space to clear his mind and get things into working order.

Tonight, there was a lot of clearing and reworking to do.

Door closed, Hope made her way into the living room of apartment 3B. Geraldine Bateman sat in the middle of their lumpy and threadbare sofa, her head in her hands, her hair mussed up. "I should have seen it coming. I really should have seen it coming."

Hope sat next to her and put an arm around her, pulling her close. "Oh, honey, I'm sorry."

"Hope, I don't want to break his heart!"

"I know." She squeezed a little tighter. "I'm sorry. That Dick's a nice guy; I don't want his heart to be broken either, you know that."

"If only I'd ended it sooner. If only I'd known . . ." Geraldine shook her head in despair. "But we've never talked about it!

We've talked about every other damn thing from here to the end of the universe, but we've never spoken about getting married, or settling down, or having babies or whatever. Jeez, Hope, I just — I don't know, all of a sudden he decides he wants to propose? And I have to accept? No!"

"Sssh. Don't. Calm down now."

"I can't." Geraldine sighed. "I can't calm down. I just . . . I don't know."

A moment of silence went by, during which Hope rocked them both from side to side: a gentle, succouring movement that Hope's mother had performed whenever Hope herself had been upset. And Hope, in her twenty-eight years, had had many things to get upset over. The offer by renowned hairdresser Frankie Marcioni to take her under his wing and whip her into a professional stylist was the best thing that had ever come her way. It was, as Marcioni liked to tell his friends, the sure-fire way of getting Hope off the streets and stopping her from sucking her mother dry of the limited income that she had.

Hope felt a surge of warmth at the thought of Marcioni, who had always been good to her. It was Marcioni who'd sourced out her apartment four years ago, and had offered to cover the rent until she could afford to pay for it herself. She'd been happy, and immensely grateful, but Hope had suddenly found herself lonely, friendless. So she'd put an ad in the paper for a roommate, and Geraldine had turned up. Later she'd discovered that Geraldine had been waiting forever for a vacancy in the building; after all, Derrick lived in the apartment below. However, Geraldine's strict and pious Catholic upbringing had stymied any prospect of her living with her boyfriend — not to mention the strict and pious Catholic *parents* who had barred Geraldine from moving in with Derrick. Heck, they had even tried to stop her from moving in with *Hope*. Fortunately, Geraldine had won the latter battle, and, three years ago, she'd become her roommate.

And now she and Hope were the best of friends. Like sisters.

Only closer.

Geraldine stopped rocking. Quietly, she said, "I guess I don't have a choice."

Hope shrugged sympathetically. "I guess not."

"Rick and I . . . we have to end it."

"I guess."

"I don't want to . . ."

"I know you don't, sweetie. But if not . . . what then?"

It was a question that Geraldine couldn't answer — and didn't want to.

Hope pulled away and moved off the sofa. Across from them, an open window allowed a cool breeze into the apartment. Hope, seeing Geraldine was shivering, ambled over to it. She was about to pull it shut when her gaze drifted to the field in the near distance, where the distinct figure of a pained Derrick Weston could be seen hunched on the bench under the tree, bathed in near-darkness. Hope knew the bench was where Derrick and Geraldine would sit when they needed to talk, or when something was troubling them, or when they simply wanted to relax and enjoy the serenity of their surroundings.

As Hope stood there, the wind blowing against her face and ruffling her fluorescent pink hair, she saw Derrick lower his head into his hands. From the shaking of his shoulders, she could tell he was crying.

Silently, Hope pulled the window closed. She turned to Geraldine, who was already making her way into the bedroom, and followed her roommate to the bed.

Hope was comfort, and comfort was hope.

Tonight, Geraldine needed hope more than ever.

And Hope was ever ready to oblige.

A Slow But Sure Disintegration

The eight committee members of the district's residents' association met once every other month for an evening of lively discussion, coffee and cake, and a couple of rounds of Gin. Tonight, as Derrick Weston lamented in the field and Geraldine found Hope in her bedroom, the committee members sat in Jessy Cooke's kitchen with half-finished cups of warm coffee on the table, and a smattering of cake crumbs in their laps.

The main issue of the evening was what was considered the "appalling state of the neighbourhood".

"The problem is the weather," Bertha Asterville from Number 23 pronounced in her mouse-like voice. "In the day, the sun comes out and it's hot as the netherworld; when evening descends, the cold winds blow and it gets to freezing." This prompted several others to nod their heads enthusiastically, as if they were all meteorological experts who had been diligently observing the climate change. "What happens is, the houses expand in the day and contract in the night, resulting in cracks in the walls, holes in the sideboards, nuisances like that."

"Well, Mrs Asterville," Jessy Cooke said calmly, "there's not much we can do about the climate now, is there?"

"No, of *course* not," Bertha squeaked. "But surely we can do *some*thing about the dreary appearances of our homes and community buildings! Mr Jensen's grocery shop, for one. Heaven knows the bloody place hasn't been done up in decades. Decades!" she declared with a vengeance. She tilted her head at an elderly man with a grey moustache and similarly grey, wrinkled skin, and crooned, "No offence, Mr Jensen. My *point* is," she plunged on, "the climate has been taking its toll on our properties, and I think it's high time that we, the members of this very esteemed association, do something about it!"

"Oh, *do* pipe down, Bertha," somebody said, and a few men chuckled. Bertha Asterville coloured and decided to sit.

"Look, Mrs Asterville, I believe the decision to do up the houses and buildings has to be made by the owners themselves," Jessy said kindly. "We've already proposed that the neighbours could rally one another to give each other a hand, but . . ." She smiled wistfully and upturned her palms. "If the owners choose not to participate, it's pretty much out of our hands. What we can continue to do is speak to those we know—those who wouldn't mind unsolicited advice—to suggest, *suggest*," she stressed, "that they take a good look at their homes. Otherwise . . ." She shrugged.

Mr Buckley from Number 41 raised his hand apprehensively, and, upon being given the go-ahead, stammered, "In—in my humble opinion—and it's just what *I* think—the climate, in itself, does not do much damage to the homes. Many countries experience horrible, sweltering days and cold, foot-numbing nights as the autumnal equinox descends upon them. Australia, for one. Um, no offence," he uttered inexplicably. "Why, I remember when I was living in Perth—that's in Australia if you don't know—not that I'm accusing you of being ignorant of your geography, that's not what I'm doing, but—in case you *didn't* know—"

"Your point, Mr Buckley," someone cut in impatiently.

"H-houses," he said tremulously, "have to be looked after. I'm sure we all know that. I fear . . ." He paused, giving the clear signal that his train of thought had derailed and he needed time to get the wheels back on track. "I fear many of our residents have not looked after their homes very well. It would be a good idea, in my opinion, my opinion only, and I'm not forcing this upon you, but it *would* be a good idea if the owners did up their houses regularly, say, every three to five years, since the heat and the cold tends to . . . *tend* to adversely affect . . . um . . . the houses." He paused, licked his lips in a fluster, and went on in his usual quasi-coherent manner: "I'm saying — I'm thinking — that many residents don't do this. They — they don't take care of their homes, don't do them up every few years, and as a result, their houses are now in a bad condition, as — as dear Bertha has very observantly . . . observed." He nodded, as if to affirm his obscure point. "Yes."

Everyone was staring at him, and, like Bertha before him, he coloured.

"Yes," Jessy Cooke repeated quickly, smiling in as placating a manner as she could. "That may well be right, Mr Buckley, thank you very much. Yes, I *do* believe the houses would look much less shoddy if their owners consistently maintained them."

"That's what I was trying to say," Buckley sputtered. "What — what you just said."

"Again, unfortunately, we cannot *force* people to look after their own homes, but can only offer suggestions," Jessy added.

"Perhaps what we could do," sixty-eight-year-old Della Rosenberg — inexplicably twice married and three times divorced, as she liked to tell people — spoke up, "is give everybody a free subscription to *Better Homes and Gardens*." She grinned widely, clearly pleased with what she thought was a suggestion of pure genius, proudly displaying her crooked and yellowed teeth for the whole room to see.

Everyone stared at her.

"I see," Jessy said noncommittally, and blinked. "We'll . . . have to try that. Moving on." She looked at her clipboard. "Now, I believe Mr Wong has a proposal for the committee. Mr Wong?"

A bald and bespectacled man stood and addressed his audience of seven. After some preamble, he stated: "Clearly, the field is a neglected space. A two-acre piece of land with three sad trees does *not* exactly promote exemplary plant conservation, even if you count the grass and weeds, which, in the spring, grow to frightening heights, and, in the summer, dry up and make the area an ideal location for a bushfire.

"And as we can all see, therein lies only one bench, just *one*, itself not in the best of conditions. The field has been left in disrepair for far too long, and as such, we have to conclude that in its current state, it is not a suitable place for recreation. We all know that more and more of our residents are venturing to the play area in the neighbouring suburb, where their residents' association has put up a play park for the kids, complete with slide, swing and sandpit." He paused for dramatic effect. "I would like to propose that we do something more lucrative with the plot that is our field. Perhaps it needs a complete overhaul, a cementing-over. That bench, for one, needs to go. We could install a new one, or a *row* of new ones, metal benches that aren't so prone to the effects of the weather . . ."

The mention of the weather sent an enthralled thrum through the crowd.

He went on for a while, and when he was done, Jessy said, "Thank you, Mr Wong, that certainly bears some consideration. Perhaps when each of us goes home tonight . . ."

"Except you, you live here," Mrs Rosenberg cut in with a giggle.

"Yes, that's right. But perhaps each of us could go back to our respective homes and think about the field. I would hasten to add, of course, that our funds are currently edging towards the red, and we would need to be able to present a clear and concise proposal and budget plan to the council. But, I trust that if we put our heads together we can come up with something agreeable and feasible that we can present to the mayor and the budget committee. Now." Jessy managed a smile, her hands on her hips. "Any questions?"

Bertha Asterville said, "Got any more cake?"

Everybody laughed heartily, and Jessy Cooke went into the kitchen to bring out another serving of her chocolate-chip

mocha cake—the one that dear Mrs Rosenberg had been
pestering her for years to provide the recipe for: a request that
Jessy Cooke consistently refused to oblige, citing it was her late
grandmother's secret, and hoping that Mrs Rosenberg wouldn't
read the boxes of cake flour and discover that Grandma Cooke's
sacred mocha cake recipe was actually printed on the back of
the packets.

When everybody had finally gone home after an exhilarating
game of Gin, Jessy Cooke shut and locked the front door,
breathing a sigh of relief. Being the president of the residents'
committee was an exhausting job, more so when she had two
teenaged children to clean up after, and when there were so
many things going wrong in her household . . .

As she swept mocha crumbs into a mound on the tabletop,
she tried to reflect on what they had discussed during the
meeting. Mr Wong's suggestion that they cement over the field
across the road, and get rid of the bench, had appalled her.
Where would she go when she needed a peaceful place to get
away from it all? As she thought that, her eyes drifted to the
dining-room clock. Ten-thirty. Ten-thirty on a Friday night,
and Paul hadn't yet returned from work. He had plans, their
son Joe had informed her. *Might go for drinks with the guys.*

Meaning, Jessy thought with a stab of resentment, *I don't
want to come home; I will go for drinks with my friends and I don't give
a damn what you think, and for God's sake, I'll be home so late you'll
have woken up by the time I crawl into bed. So don't bother waiting
up.*

Her marriage was in serious trouble, there was no denying
it. The worst part was that she and Paul were past the point
where any form of discussion would prove fruitful — Paul, who
thought it was easy for her to be the primary breadwinner as
well as the homemaker; Paul, who helped out at his family
hardware store, garnering a monthly income that was provided
by his parents (who, being up to their necks in money, didn't

need any help running the store to begin with, but who, in all selfishness, loved having their baby boy around at all times to the extent that they were oblivious of how his reliance on them was affecting his family unit); Paul—pathetic, dependent, irresponsible and complacent.

Her marriage was in serious trouble, and she constantly found herself having to put on a brave face: in front of her colleagues in the PR company, Houssen & Dwight; in front of her children, Joe and Maggie; and, to top it off, in front of the neurotic, semi-senile group that comprised the committee of the residents' association. Every day she returned home exhausted, saddened by the slow but sure disintegration of her and Paul's relationship, wishing she could do something about it before it slipped through her fingers entirely. She often wished she could seal herself in a quiet place somewhere far away from the rest of the world. But, on the other hand, being on her own meant that she would have the time and the space to *think*, and when she thought about her existence—forty-one and without much in the way of a social life, residents' group notwithstanding—she always wound up feeling more depressed and mentally drained. So she found it more cathartic to immerse herself in work of some sort, at the office, or at the kids' school, or around the house. Distractions.

She certainly couldn't seal herself off in some desolate, isolated area, not when there were so many counting on her, her children being the most important. Then again, it wasn't as if Joe and Maggie were still little. Joe was seventeen, Maggie two years younger. (*Teenagers*, Jessy thought with a sigh, as, from clearing up coffee-and-cake remnants, her eyes drifted to a pair of mud-streaked trainers left by the back door, decorating the tiled dining-room floor with spatters of dark brown.)

She couldn't seal herself off, but she *could* get away once in a while. And the best time was after driving home from Houssen & Dwight, after escaping the traffic jams and turning into the driveway, when she'd take a quick walk to the near-deserted field and drift wearily to the bench.

Very often evenings would find her sitting alone, under the leaves and branches, contemplating the meaning of life, love, marriage and other disasters, watching the shadows scatter and scuttle across the grassy floor as the boughs shook and the leaves rustled in the wind. And she'd breathe in that wild, natural odour of plant life, the fecundity of silt and soil, deciding not to think for those few, precious moments — to refrain from thought, to refrain from grief, to simply let life pass her by.

Lying with the pillow and the space next to her unoccupied, protected from the wind that whistled through the cracks in the doorjamb and under the door, she thought about Joe and Maggie, in their individual beds in their separate rooms. She remembered the days when the children used to sleep together, snuggled under the quilt of the queen-sized bed that now belonged to Maggie alone. She remembered tucking them in, kissing their sweet foreheads, brushing the hair off their faces, telling them how much she loved them and wanted the best for them.

Jessy knew the children were aware of what was happening between her and Paul. Joe especially, at that volatile age of seventeen, had become increasingly moody and broody, refusing most times to even be in the same room as either one of his parents. Jessy longed to speak to him, to tell him that everything would be fine; but she stopped herself, because firstly, she knew he wouldn't be willing to listen — and secondly, because she herself wasn't sure if it *would* be all right.

Regardless, Jessy was sure Maggie and Joe understood that no matter what happened, it was in no way due to any wrongdoing on their behalf. A part of her was tempted to tell them out loud, just to be sure — but then again, wouldn't that be jumping to the conclusion that the marriage *was* over? Surely it wasn't — was it?

If only she and Paul could talk. If only he'd be home, instead of leaving early to the Cooke Hardware Stop and staying until late, hanging out with his pals, not giving a damn about his own family. Jessy had considered speaking to her parents-in-law, but had quickly dismissed the idea. She and the senior Cookes had never been close—bringing to mind the forced smiles and shameless shows of mock affinity that marked every get-together—thanks to Paul having gone against their wishes by marrying her. (Now she could see how hindsight truly is twenty-twenty; her choice had been between Paul Cooke and another, but Jessy had gone for Paul because she'd thought, at the time, that he had the brighter future.)

On the far wall, several glow-in-the-dark stickers in the shape of stars and other planetary objects—the handiwork of her children when they had been younger—began to lose their phosphorescence. Jessy drifted off into a slumber, thinking how ironic it was that, like the stars on the wall, her marriage was beginning to lose its light. And her final thought before she dozed off completely was a deep and heartfelt prayer that her life, and all that was in it, would remain as bright as the stars she often observed sitting in the twilight under the tree in the field, on that hard and jagged-edged bench that she hoped would remain indefinitely.

DRUNKEN ECSTASY

In the next room, Maggie Cooke was writing in her diary, keeping note of the day's events. The highlight for this Friday was *the most incredible thing happened. Zack McPherson called and asked me to go out with him tomorrow! I'm, like, "oh, my God", you know? As you know* (she wrote, often referring to her diary in the second person), *I've always thought Zack was cute, and now a miracle has happened! Maybe I can finally,* finally *move on from Chris, because Zack and I are going out on a da*

The soft rapping of knuckle against wood made her pause in mid-scribble. Her bedroom door moved, and her brother peered in. "You still up?" Joe stepped into the room, shutting the door quietly.

"Yeah," she replied. "It's only eleven."

"Listen, I'm going out with the guys tonight."

Maggie shut her diary and leaned against the headboard of her bed. He quickly added, "Before you say anything, let me remind you that you owe me from the time you caused that dent in the car door and I didn't say anything to Mum or Dad."

"That's different," Maggie said. "That was an accident."

"Just leave the door unlocked and let me come in later, all right?"

She sighed. "If Mum catches you . . ."

"Mum won't catch me. Not if you don't squeal."

Maggie shook her head. Her blond curls—which she'd inherited from her mother—bounced about her face, and she rolled her eyes to the ceiling, conceding. "Whatever. But if anyone sees you, it's not my fault."

"Trust me, I'll be fine."

Maggie lowered her voice, speaking in more subdued tones: "What if Dad comes home?"

Joe paused. The clock on Maggie's bedside table tick-tocked: the only sound. Finally, he replied, with more than a trace of bitterness in his voice, "Maybe he'll be too pissed to realise I've snuck out." He turned on his heel and strode to the door, letting himself out, closing it behind him without a sound.

Maggie sat there, staring at the shut door, and it was several seconds before she returned to her diary. The word "date" stared up at her in its half-written form. She completed the word before scribbling something about how Joe needed to use the rose trellis to sneak out of the house again. His bedroom window opened to reveal a long drop to the ground below; Maggie's came with the perfect escape route, sans roses. Nonetheless, Maggie always thought that if Joe simply took the initiative to oil the hinges on the front door, he would be able to sneak in and out with less chance of being caught. But then again, the stairs creaked as well. Besides, as Joe constantly reminded her, Maggie's window was located on one side of the house, while his parents' room was in the front. The trellis, as far as Joe was concerned, was the best way to go.

Maggie finished off the entry for the day, and when she turned the lights out, moonlight came through the window, spilling across the carpeted floor in a grid of squares as the beam filtered through the trellis. She stared at the ceiling, at the glowing stars she'd insisted her mother glue on so many years ago so that they would keep watch over her during the night, and thought about Zack McPherson.

Joe Cooke inadvertently nodded off before his 2AM appointment, but he'd been wise enough to set his clock. Being a light sleeper, he immediately bolted upright in bed when the first tinny strands of the alarm began to sound. He lashed out an arm to shut the thing off before it alerted anyone. Then he rushed to the closet, threw on a jacket, slipped on a pair of sneakers, and headed out of his room to Maggie's.

At Maggie's door, he hesitated, wondering if she'd obeyed, if she'd left it unlocked. With baited breath he placed his hand on the knob—cold—and twisted it gently. It unlatched with a barely audible click, and he breathed a sigh of relief. *Good girl, sis. Way to go.* He pushed his way in and shut the door behind him. Maggie was under the covers, her head propped by one plump pillow. The room smelled of the perfume she used—a citrus scent Joe had always found rather revolting. He held his breath as he scurried to the window, where the silver moonlight spotlighted the trellis outside.

She'd left the window partially open so it would be easier for him to get out. He thanked his sister silently and pushed the frame all the way up; then he lifted one leg out of the gap, and placed his foot firmly upon the trellis. Soon he was climbing down. The structure wobbled under his weight, but he had done this so many times he wasn't worried. Within minutes he was on the ground. He took off, heading for the field in the middle of the Square, where he and his friends had agreed to meet.

The field was illuminated only by moonlight, and he could make out the silhouette of the bench under the tree, as well as the figures gathered around it. The gang awaited, and Joe's heart-rate sped up as he thought of the one person he was particularly eager to see: Carrie Taylor. Their late-night meetings in the field were very precious to him, and one night more than any other stuck out in his mind in the midst of his juvenile memories and fantasies . . .

It had happened nearly two months ago:

Joe hurried across the wide expanse of grass, ignoring the dark shadows cast by two other wilting trees that stood in the field. He screeched to a halt under their favourite shade, where Pete Wentworth exclaimed, "Cooke, you're late!"

Joe, breathing heavily, shot Wentworth a glare. "Just by a couple of minutes." He could smell beer, mingling with the sharp, sour scent of sweat that rose from the members of the group as well as from his own shirt, damp from his running. "Give me one of those, will ya?" he grunted, one hand outstretched. A flurry of movement, and Wentworth was placing a cold can in his palm.

"Come on, then," Alf Richards spoke up. "Where we headin' off to?"

"I kinda like it here," Carrie Taylor said, and her breathy voice immediately caught Joe's attention. Carrie! There she was, seated on the bench, dressed in tight-fitting black top and leather skirt that didn't stray anywhere close to her knees, dark boots on her feet. Her wavy black hair was being tossed and blown by the breeze, giving her a look that Joe found incredibly arousing. Joe had had the hots for Carrie since God knows when. And he had the feeling Carrie liked him, too. The other guys were constantly ribbing him about it. Why else would she frequently flash him a smile whenever their eyes met — like right now, as she sat with her legs crossed, revealing just a hint of dark stocking at the tops of her boots? He smiled back. She threw him a wink. *Fuck*, he thought, and immediately felt warm all over. He tilted the tin of beer to take a drink. Nothing happened — he hadn't popped the tab off yet.

"Well, if Carrie likes it here, here's where we're gonna stay," Wentworth declared.

Joe pulled the tab off and took a large swig. Cold and bitter, the beer went down his throat smoothly, a salve. Alf Richards was saying something about how the field would make a good place for football — all they needed was a couple of goalposts. Wentworth said the residents were not likely to go for it, screw them all. Carrie shifted her legs, sipping from the bottle of — what *was* that? Alcoholic cider? — and that minute movement was enough to get Joe's undivided attention. He stared at her out of the corner of his eye, growing warmer by the second, and wondered what she was wearing under her top.

"McPherson, you're awfully quiet tonight!" Wentworth shouted to the figure seated on the other end of the bench.

Zack McPherson held up his bottle of drink as if he were raising a toast.

"Zack, come on, loosen up," Joe called.

"I'm fine. I've had a couple already. Hey, Cooke, take this away from me, will you?"

Joe shook his head, gesturing to his own tin of beer.

"Go on, Joe, take it away from him," Carrie said with a hint of ridicule in her voice. "Zack can't handle his drink." A sharp laugh escaped her, and Joe found himself grinning in spite of himself.

He took the drink from Zack.

Joe wasn't sure how he had reached this point, but all he was able to think of was how the world was spinning and tilting under his feet, and how his head was throbbing, and how his cock was pressing painfully against the front of his pants. He was laughing and talking a bit too raucously—although was it just him, or were the others also bellowing at the top of their lungs? His vision was blurry, for some reason. The taste of alcohol—sweet, sour, bitter, hot, cold, all at once—was in his mouth, at the back of his throat, and he wanted more of it, and Carrie, he wanted Carrie, he wanted her so bad . . .

"Come on, Cooke!" Wentworth cackled hysterically. "One more! Just one more!"

"No more," Joe pleaded. "No more! Can't take it!"

"Sure you can," Wentworth said, and laughed. Too loud. Hurting Joe's ears.

Sprawled on the bench, Carrie Taylor let out a string of giggles, kicking her legs in jubilation. Behind the bench, leaning against the hard trunk of the tree, Alf Richards sputtered a punch line, "And then—and then the hedgehog replied, 'Don't look at me, *you're* the one with the pouch!'" Joe had not heard the earlier part of the joke.

Carrie, having just quaffed a mouthful of Stoli, spit it out and burst into peals of hilarity. "Oh, my God!" she shrieked. "Oh, Jesus, that's stupid! That's so incredifuckin'ly *stupid!*"

"*I* thought it was funny," Richards murmured, crossing his arms.

"McPherson, you wanna join the party?" Wentworth called out. "You gotta let your hair down, bro." Without waiting for Zack's response, he turned back to Joe, held out a full bottle: "Joe, come on, pal. Just one more drink, buddy, you can do it, come on."

"Yeah, come on," Carrie whooped, giggling. "You can do it!"

Joe turned sharply to her. His head spun with the movement. "I can do it?"

"Hell, Joe, of *course* you can do it!"

That was all he needed to be told.

Joe Cooke, seventeen and still a virgin, much to his chagrin, chucked his bottle of Stoli away and turned to the bench. In a deft movement he was on it—meaning he was also on Carrie. And he was shoving his lips against hers, kissing her, tasting her, wanting her so bad.

After all, she'd said he could do it.

The most incredible thing was that Carrie wasn't protesting. In fact, her hands moved to the back of his head, running her fingers through his hair, pushing his head against hers, hot lips against hot lips, tongues diving in and out, tasting sweet alcohol and sweeter saliva.

"Ohhh, Joe, you da *man,* man, you da *man!*" Wentworth hollered.

"Come on, baby!" Alf Richards shouted. He began thrusting his hips against the bark of the tree. Wentworth whooped loudly, cheering them on. Even McPherson seemed impressed.

Joe pulled away from Carrie long enough to take a breath—but she was hungry for him, it seemed, and forced him back against her and kissed, sucked, tasted.

And then one of her hands was fiddling with his fly, brushing against his cock—and he moaned, shuddered, whispered her name against her cheek, and waited for the moment of drunken ecstasy to arrive.

Joe and Carrie sat side by side in each other's arms, breathing heavily. McPherson, Richards and Wentworth were seated on the grassy ground, watching them with stupid smirks plastered upon their faces. When Carrie shivered in the cold, Joe pulled her closer to him, hugged her, stroked her shoulders.

"You guys," Wentworth said after minutes of silence, "are da *bomb*."

The world was still spinning. Joe hugged Carrie tightly. Then, wondering if he was being too forceful, he loosened his grip. Shifted in his seat, feeling the rough surface of the bench against his ass. Carrie sighed and said, "Never done something like this in an open space like this before. Pretty exciting, huh? It's, like, any moment somebody could come over and catch us, or peek out of their windows or something, know what I mean?" She laughed, and it sent a thrill of gratification coursing through Joe.

"Nobody would've caught you," Richards remarked. "Not with us bodyguards."

That had taken place two months ago—the first encounter of many. Tonight, as Joe hurried across the dark field to his friends, he looked forward to yet another round of inebriated intercourse—in both the verbal and sexual sense.

And at 4:30AM, Maggie Cooke awoke in her bed, thirsty. As she sleepily strolled over to the bathroom, she remembered what had happened the day before, and couldn't suppress the grin that crossed her face. *Zack,* she thought. He'd asked her out. They had a date tonight!

   She drank from the tap and hurried back to bed, figuring the sooner she slept, the quicker the hours would go by. Leading to the moment when she would be meeting up with the yummy Zack McPherson.

Spinning Circles

In the wee hours of the morning, when most people prefer to remain in bed, Graham Hanson would be wide awake and refreshed. He needed no more than five hours of sleep. He would be dressed in thin pyjama bottoms and an old t-shirt: his usual sleeping garb, regardless of the climate. Having survived through decade after decade of nippy autumns and frigid winters, he had developed a high tolerance for low temperatures.

Today, the cool winds that blew as the sun rose provided no bother as he slid the covers down at one corner. He turned to see Felicity still sleeping soundly. Careful not to disturb her, Graham got out of bed and placed his feet on the cold floor, then turned to look at his bedside table, at an old-fashioned clock with bells and an analogue face upon which was proclaimed the glorious hour of five AM.

Taking slow steps towards the en suite bathroom and shower, he considered the events that he had planned for the day—basically the same plans he had executed every Saturday, since his retirement nearly fifteen years ago. First, a shower—not too warm, not too icy. More cold water than hot. Washing away the dregs of sleep, revitalising his elderly body as the streams hit him. Washed with Pears soap, the translucent-brown bar that Felicity repeatedly claimed looked "good enough to eat". (He'd dared her to do it once, and she'd dared him back, and he'd bitten into the soapy block, wondering—as he sputtered—how something called a "cake" could taste nothing like it. She'd gaped at him, taken aback, and as he'd spat out the chunk and begun gurgling under the tap, she'd burst into gales of laughter, horrified and entertained, shocked and impressed all at once. "You're crazy!" she'd exclaimed, and he'd replied through a mouthful of lather: "Crazy for you, sweetheart.")

Having changed into semi-warm clothing, Graham proceeded to wake his wife, kneeling at her side of the bed and shaking her gently with a veined, wrinkled hand. "Honey," he whispered. "Fel, sweetheart." Another gentle shake. She stirred, her eyes fluttered slightly, and he whispered, "It's gone twenty past now. Time to rise and shine." A man of clichés, and he wasn't afraid to admit it.

As she got herself ready to begin the day, he ventured into the kitchen and started on breakfast, timing himself so that when she stepped out of the bedroom, she would be greeted by a succulent meal, fresh and steaming-hot. This morning it would be her favourite: poached eggs and grilled tomatoes on French toast. It was a recipe he'd learned from his late mother (she'd passed away just last year at the impressive age of ninety-nine, one year short of the centennial celebration the residents' association had been planning for her, complete with a float parade and a hundred different types of birthday cake. Oh well).

They would then go for their post-brekkie walk, which consisted of an amble across the road and into the field, into that wide-open space, to look up at the sky and see the spectrum of colours that marked the dawning of the day. Today, filled with his share of eggs and most of hers (she hadn't been hungry, she said), they walked in silence, enjoying the placidity of their surroundings. The birds, bathed in the orange glow of the rising sun, were spinning circles over their heads, and the air was crisp, fresh with the fragrance of morning. Somewhere, along one of the roads that made up the Square, a dying breed known as the paperboy chucked rolled-up tabloids, broadsheets and magazines at front doors, making loud smacking sounds as the goods hit their mark. The grass crunched softly under their feet — dry, dying, dead. And they held hands, feeling each other's fingers, leathery with age (although he swore Felicity's were still soft, soft and smooth, *that's the advantage of wearing rubber gloves when you do the dishes, my dear*), enjoying each other's company without the necessity of words.

They would sit on the bench under the tree, as was their routine. Graham silently thanked the Lord for blessing them with longevity and good health. Mother might have died at ninety-nine, but as far as he was concerned, seventy-eight was a long and blessed age to live to as well. And what a gift it was having Felicity by his side to enjoy these later years. Today, like any other day, he pondered on how marvellous she was, how invaluable, and his heart swelled with pride and affection that was seemingly boundless.

Minutes went by, during which they simply observed the changing of the dark purple sky to a gradual orangey-yellowy-red. As the sun rose, Graham raised one hand and pointed to the fading crescent of pale light in the sky—"There it is!" he whispered, breaking the quiet—such being their daily early-morning contest, trying to see who was the more observant in spotting Mr Moon before he was obscured until nightfall.

Felicity squeezed his hand. "Looks like you beat me again." She tended to speak in whispers, a quality that he still found immensely heart-warming. Seldom did she raise her voice, not even back when they'd both been teachers at the public school, a twenty-minute drive from home. During their younger days they'd taken turns behind the wheel; now, Graham was the only one who took out his 1968 Volkswagen Beetle, mostly to head down to the shops for groceries, even though they much preferred their favourite delivery girl to transport their purchases right to their doorstep.

Michelle Leigh was a sweetheart, and very much like a daughter to them—the child they never had. She'd often speak to them about her life, the trials and tribulation of being an adolescent. (*Those days, how long ago they seem*, Graham and Felicity would simultaneously think whenever Michelle spoke of her teenage travails, and they would glance at each other surreptitiously as if they were telepathically linked—which, in a way, they were.) A frequent name that cropped up in Michelle's tales was her brother Matthew, who, from the way Michelle described him, didn't sound like an altogether pleasant person, although Graham and Felicity were not one to judge, and consistently urged Michelle to invite him over sometime. (He'd never shown. They'd never met him.)

Their being childless was not by choice. Not long after they'd married—a small, intimate ceremony attended only by their immediate relatives and a handful of their closest friends—Felicity had developed ovarian cysts that required surgery—surgery that, the odds against them, had resulted in her being unable to conceive. How she'd cried when they'd told her; how Graham had held her and repeatedly consoled her, *Everything will be all right, I love you, don't cry, please don't cry,* and how she'd still wept against him every night: a twenty-something bride and groom who went to bed sobbing and sorrowful, the act of making love a grim reminder of the cruel blow that the hand of fate had dealt them. He had continuously and unfailingly reminded her *it's not your fault, it just wasn't meant to be.* The idea of adoption had come up over the years, but they'd decided against it. If God meant for them to be childless, they figured, then childless they shall be.

So there they were on that Saturday morning, on the bench. Felicity asked him about the funeral, whether or not he'd be attending it that afternoon, and he replied softly that he wouldn't be able to live with himself if he didn't. Tracing the green-blue veins that protruded from the back of his hand, Felicity whispered, "I've always liked her, Graham. She was a wonderful person."

Graham nodded, thinking of his Aunt Phyllis, a sweet, small-sized woman with blue hair who had always been there for him with her arms wide open and her kitchen aromatic with chocolate chunk cookies. He couldn't remember exactly how or when he'd learnt about her passing, but Graham believed that death was not a reason to mourn but to rejoice: after the long and hallowed lives they'd led on this earth, they finally had the honour of being with God. The idea was not in the least frightening. Phyllis had led her life well; she'd been a good woman, strong and caring. Knowing she was with God was a reason to celebrate; the funeral was just a ceremony to be carried out in accordance with the laws of the Church and the expectations of family.

"As long as you come with me," he told his wife.

Felicity smiled. Her eyes were moist. "Of course."

"Phyllis loved you so," he reminded her quietly, and she nodded. "She always had a kind word for you, Fel, remember? 'Lovely girl', she always told Mum. 'Such a wonderful wife for Graham'." Felicity laughed softly. "And so supportive," he added, and this time, the volume of his voice slipped down a notch. He thought back to how his mother and Phyllis had gathered in the kitchen of their then-new house in the Square and had hugged Felicity, telling her that there was no such thing as hopelessness, not with a firm and sound faith in the Lord. Felicity had cried, lamenting over the prospect of not being able to continue their lineage. Phyllis had been the one to wipe the tears away and produce a batch of freshly baked peanut-butter cookies topped with sprinkles. How had they known it was Felicity's favourite since she was a child? "If this doesn't cheer you up," the older woman had quipped, "*nothing will!*"

Felicity squeezed his hand again and shifted herself so that they were pressing against each other. "I'll be there," she whispered, and patted that same hand comfortingly. "I wouldn't miss it for the world."

And together they remained on the single, solitary bench, enjoying the peacefulness of their surroundings, comfortable with each other.

Watching the sun appear, confident that a brand new day lay ahead.

PART TWO

RUFFLIN' FEATHERS

Matthew Leigh stormed down the corridors of the university, his cheeks flushed with anger. The encounter in the library had not helped his already sour mood, and as he strode towards the exit, he swore in his mind, *Bitch, bitch, bitch!* — not giving a damn that the bitch had not been in the wrong. After all, she'd already reserved *Business Law in the 21ˢᵗ Century* — her name and student ID and signature were all there, prominently displayed in the Reference Book Reservation Book, so she'd had every right to take the only copy of it off the shelf. The problem was, Matthew had also wanted the book, needed it, damn it, for his latest project. Only, of course, he hadn't signed the RBRB. Now he was stuck with an assignment due on Monday afternoon and one less book to refer to.

Out of the building, into the grounds, where the sun was hot, and the glare off the pavement made his eyes and his head hurt. He moved as fast as he could, taking huge, wide strides with his long legs, thinking, *Fuck, fuck, fuck, why the hell am I studying law, I should have done something easier . . .* ! Of course, he *had* been warned that studying law would be no piece of cake, but as far as he was concerned, it was a whole lot easier than taking up medicine or pharmacy or whatever it was that his father had wanted him to, just because Leigh, senior, was a doctor with his own private clinic and was hoping that Leigh, junior, would follow in his footsteps. *Yeah, right.*

He needed a place to cool down, gather his thoughts. Surely he could dredge up more information on the Internet, and, if worse came to worst, forge the references. Who the hell really *knew*, anyway? As *if* the professors would actually look up each and every book he'd supposedly referred to, checking dates of publication and exact quotes and page numbers. As *if* they had the time or the patience, or could be the least bit bothered!

He had to calm down. Find someplace to rest, out of the heat. He remembered the bench, under the tree in that near-abandoned field. He remembered how relaxed he'd been sitting there, sandwich in hand, just minding his own business, languishing in the oxymoronic comfort of the stiff, uncomfortable bench.

That was, of course, before the kid had shown himself.

Matthew's mood blackened further at the thought of the boy. The public nuisance. The little brat, with a mouth too big and too garrulous for his face. Asking too many questions — and *stupid* questions, at that.

As he began the walk to the Square, wishing he had his car with him, he recalled that the kid had wanted to play with the girls but had been rejected. That meant, in all probability, he lived in the vicinity. What were the chances of him being there today? *Hopefully slim*, Matthew thought as he turned into the housing area.

The field was empty. Bright and white in the sunlight. No annoying girls running around, making a spectacle of themselves. No irritating boy with scratched and scruffy knees and elbows, eager to share his life story no matter how short his life had thus far been. Empty. Empty, with the shady area waiting, calling him, beckoning to him, *come and join me, come into the shade, come to the dark side!* A smile finally crept onto Matthew's face as he mentally criticised his own lack of poetry. It was a good thing studying law didn't require anything in the way of creative writing. If it did, he offhandedly pondered, he'd be failing the course for sure.

Today he didn't have anything with him to eat: The idea of stopping to buy something had slipped his mind as he'd stormed out of the university complex with his blood at the boiling point. *Stupid bitch*, he thought, immediately placing the blame on her, whoever she was, for his empty stomach.

Matthew was grateful for the shade, but the dryness of the air was getting to him. He leaned his head back, closing his eyes for a moment. Up in the branches, the birds were squawking and chortling, probably recalling their triumphant let-go the day before, *direct hit, sir!* The thought of it made Matthew snap back to attention. *Fucking bird*, he thought, and wondered if his luck was so bad that he'd be attacked with doody the second day in a row —

Footsteps! From behind him.

The brushing of feet against the grass, the dry scrape of sole against soil. The sounds of a little boy walking towards the shade.

Matthew stiffened, feeling a sinking sensation within him. He heard the soft crackle of a twig snapping underfoot; the footsteps approaching.

Then, the pitter-patter of running, approaching the bench and stopping behind the wide trunk of the tree. A brief moment of silence, punctuated by the faint sounds of breathing. Matthew, turning his head so that he could see the mottled grey-and-white tree trunk, felt a queasiness as he realised the boy was trying to keep himself inconspicuous behind the tree, failing. He wondered how long the boy would stay there, trying to catch his breath, as if the short sprint from the sunny area to the shade had tired him out. Matthew remained quiet and faced forward, waiting for the boy to go away, if he chose to. Matthew hoped with all his might that he would.

He didn't know how many seconds passed. His heartbeat thudded in his ears. A single droplet of sweat formed at his left sideburn and trickled, slowly, tauntingly, down his cheek. He moved one hand, slowly, to wipe it away.

The kid let out a soft snort, like a pig's oink, followed by a high-pitched giggle.

Matthew gritted his teeth and remained silent. It dawned upon him that this was a test of will. The boy was testing him.

Jesus, the boy was *testing* him! *The nerve,* he thought, and rolled his eyes, letting out a sigh that revealed his exasperation. *Go away. Get out of here!*

Silence: nerve-rending and heart-pounding, the anticipation thick in the air.

It was the boy who, thankfully, gave in to his own game and finally moved away from the tree. Matthew heard his approach, hoped again he would leave. The child didn't. Small feet crunched upon broken twigs and branches, and then the boy appeared by Matthew's side, his chest coming up to the jagged armrest, his face grubby and his cheeks—where there wasn't any dirt—rosy-red, painted with droplets of perspiration. Little Robby placed his hands on the armrest, and Matthew couldn't help but think of how disgusting the boy was, with his fingers streaked with mud and his fingernails crusty with soil. The boy watched him for a while, and Matthew kept his expression blank as he gazed straight ahead, his lips pursed. Another waiting game commenced. The boy was testing him again, the dickhead. Seeing who was better at keeping the silence, seeing who was the stronger of the two despite their vast differences in size and maturity.

Again, the boy gave in first. Speaking in hushed tones, he said, "Whatcha doin', mister?"

I'm ignoring you, Matthew thought darkly. *Go away.*

"Hey, mister?"

Go away!

"Whatcha doin', mister?"

Fuck off! Matthew shrieked at the boy in full silence.

"I's thinkin' about what we talked about," little Robby whispered, and paused for any flicker of acknowledgement in Matthew's face. None came. Unfazed, the boy went on: "Y'know? About the birds and all?"

Oh, God, not the birds.

"Have you ever seen battery hens?" the boy asked. Without waiting for a response, and guessing, accurately, that he wouldn't receive one: "I saw them on TV the other night.

Couldn't go to sleep after. Battery hens—they're, like, kept in these small little rooms, so small and so tight they can't move? And only their heads stick out, and it's so small and tight they can't even, y'know, peck themselves or ruffle their feavvers or anythin'. My mummy says the rooms're so small, they looks like the inside of a car battery. I've never seen a car battery, mister, but if Mummy says they're so small, then they're so small, 'cause my mummy's never wrong, right, mister?"

Go away!

"And the hens, they're, like, really in bad shape, 'cause they're always, y'know, standin' in one place and can't move. And later, the people who takes care of them, they just fling them all together and kills them, so we can eat 'em and stuff. And those that're too sick to be eaten, they grind them up, like, into tiny little bits?" Little Robby paused and wrinkled his nose contemplatively. "I's just thinkin', maybe"—and now his voice dropped a notch—"maybe I don't wanna be a bird no more." He paused and waited. "'Cause if you're a bird, then they might wanna . . . trap you and kill you, y'know? And I think . . . I think it would hurt."

"Of *course* it would hurt!" Matthew suddenly yelled, turning his head so sharply his neck cricked. "Of *course* it'd *fucking* hurt!"

The boy blanched and took a step backward.

"Go away!" Matthew hissed.

The boy gaped at him with saucer-wide eyes.

"Get the hell *away* from me! Leave me *alone!*"

There. Done.

Matthew, temper unleashed, folded his arms in front of his chest and feasted his eyes on the magnificent view that was the dry field. The boy remained where he was, several inches away from the side of the bench. It was only after several minutes that he took a tentative step forward, back to his original spot. He cleared his throat softly, and, in a trembling voice, whispered, "Why d'you hate me, mister?"

Matthew felt a fresh wave of frustration sweep over him.

"D'you hate all kids?"

A pause.

"Or just me?"

Another pause.

And then Matthew actually felt a pang of what he'd later come to realise was regret—regret at having yelled at the boy and hurting his young feelings. He felt the odd prick of—something—deep inside him, and he pursed his lips, wondering what the hell that emotion was, almost certain that he wasn't feeling bad about raising his voice—

No, he thought, and crossed his legs in an unconscious gesture of defiance and denial. *No, surely not* guilt . . . !

The boy looked at the ground for a moment and shuffled his feet awkwardly. Matthew took a glimpse of him out of the corner of his eye, and saw that small, shimmering beads of tears were trickling down the child's red cheeks. Suddenly a feeling of resentment swept over Matthew: resentment towards himself for having lost his temper, and resentment towards the boy for *causing* him to feel resentment towards himself. He let out a loud sigh—then, seeing the kid's eyes on him, drew it out, so that it became an exaggeration and a satire of all sighs everywhere.

The boy giggled in the midst of tears. "Long yawn," he said, and giggled again.

"It wasn't a yawn; it was a sigh."

"A what?"

"A sigh. You know. Like when you're fed up, you go . . ." Matthew sighed.

"A sigh," little Robby whispered, thrilled by his new word of the day.

"Yeah. You got it."

"Like . . ." Little Robby sighed, an imitation.

"Yeah. Like that. You got it. Good for you."

"Do birds sigh?"

Not again. "I don't think so."

"Why not?"

Matthew didn't know how to answer that one. He responded with: "Why should they?"

"They eats, right? And they breathe? And they poop, right?"

Matthew shook his head, letting out a snort mixed with a chuckle. Across the field, a solitary figure appeared, indistinct in the bright light of the sun. Someone taking a stroll.

"So why don't they sigh?" the boy demanded.

"They fly, don't they?" Matthew shot back. "But *we* don't."

"We fly in airplanes," the child countered, not missing a beat.

Matthew chuckled humourlessly. "Yeah, well, airplanes don't count. See, birds fly because they are meant to. Men fly because they *want* to, although they aren't *supposed* to."

Little Robby pondered on that for a while. Then: "But airplanes crash."

Matthew looked at him, curious.

"Right?" little Robby said. "Airplanes can fall from the sky and hits the ground and go *kaboom,* like y'always sees on the telly. Birds don't crash."

"Yeah. They don't."

"So I think," little Robby said, "birds're a lot more smarter than people."

"How do you figure?"

"'Cause they don't necessarily"—stumbling on the word—"*wan*na fly, they just *do,* 'cause nature *makes* 'em wanna fly, right? People—people ain't *supposed* to fly, they *wan*na, and they ends up fallin' from the sky and hittin' the ground real hard. But birds, who don't wanna fly but *have* to, don't ends up crashin'. I've never seen a bird crash—have you?"

Matthew shook his head. "Never," he conceded.

"So if I wasn't *made* to fly, I wouldn't *wan*na fly, not when I could fall from the sky and crash. But birds, they're *meant* to fly, and so they *never* crash." The different emphases, coupled with the boy's unbroken voice, rendered his speech comical, and Matthew's smile grew wider despite himself. "So birds are more smarter," the kid went on, "'cause they fly knowin' they'll never crash, while people are stupider 'cause they fly even though they know they *can* crash."

"And little boys?"

"Little boys what?"

"How smart are *they?*"

"They're people, so they're not as smart as birds."

"You're not as smart as the birds, huh?"

Little Robby appeared indignant by the question. "*No,*" he said sharply. "'Cause if I was as smart as the birds, I'd be buildin' my own home and findin' my own food."

"But only the grown-up birds do that, not the little ones. And you're still little."

"So? Grown-up *people* don't do that neither. You build your own home?"

Matthew's face froze in mid-grin.

"You find your own food?"

"Yes," Matthew replied at once.

"You go out there and you start diggin' the ground for your own food?"

"No, I go to the shops, like most people."

"But the birds *don't* go to the shops, do they? They digs in the ground and stuff."

Smartass.

"So I still think birds're better," the boy said decisively.

"But you just said you wouldn't *want* to be a bird. Battering hens, and all that."

The boy looked at the ground. Several seconds passed, and Matthew waited, his arms and legs still crossed. Just when he thought little Robby had forgotten completely what he'd been about to say, the boy responded, "I'd feel better if people don't kill the birds."

"But they do."

"Why?"

"Why what?"

"Why do people kill the birds?"

"Food, for one. Do you like chicken?"

"Yeah."

"So you eat chicken?"

"Yeah."

"Even though each chicken was once alive."

"Huh?"

"Chickens. They are living things, you *know* that, you just *said* that's what they kill the battering hens for."

"Battery."

"Whatever. So you criticise people who kill the birds, but you eat the birds anyway."

"No," the boy began, "I — "

"You're a hypocrite!" Matthew jabbed, and let out a full laugh.

"I'm not a hippo!" the boy protested, affronted, which only caused Matthew to laugh more loudly. "And I didn't *kill* the chickens!" the kid squealed.

"Makes no difference, pal," Matthew countered. "You still *eat* 'em!" Another laugh, an uproarious one. Several birds that were perching on the branches squawked loudly and departed in a flutter of feathers and wings. "You know what's sad, little boy?" Matthew demanded, turning to the red-cheeked boy. "What's sad is that you *strongly* believe in so many things, and yet you commit the very crimes that you accuse other people of. You're a hypocrite! You're a bloody hypocrite! And that's really sad, kid, it's fucking, downright sad!"

The boy's eyes were moist, and he appeared visibly upset.

"What you gonna say now, smartass? Huh? *Huh?*"

The child licked his lips, moved them wordlessly. He finally whispered, "Not as sad as a man who likes always gettin' the better of a little boy." And he turned on the balls of his feet and stalked away from the bench, leaving Matthew suddenly feeling like a jackass — while the birds, the clever birds, laughed at him from among the branches and leaves above his head.

SKEWED RATIOS

The hours were crawling by at an agonising rate.

At least, that's the way it seemed to poor Derrick Weston, who had spent all Friday night sitting on the bench, moping incessantly, pondering profusely, copiously shedding tears. Now, at a quarter past eleven on a bright and cheerful Saturday morning, he lay buried under the covers in his bedroom in his apartment, his eyes red, wet and stinging, waiting for sleep to come and relieve him of the agony within.

Geraldine! Oh, God, Geri —!

Why? The question kept pounding inside his skull like a pain-inflicting mantra. *Why? Why? Why?!*

If she'd never wanted to marry him, why hadn't she said anything in all their years together? Then again, he had never brought up the subject either; but that was only because he'd always assumed — (*Never assume! You must never assume! What have I always told you about assuming?* the ghost of his mother — who was still alive — nagged away in his brain . . .)

Deep down, he knew what the problem was: over the years, she'd gradually fallen out of love with him. But he was too bent up to accept that notion, so he kept on telling himself as he bashed his head against his soft, fluffy pillow *I'm mistaken, there's another reason, there just* has *to be another goddamn reason . . . !* Still, the underlying impression kept pushing its nasty head through the roiling thoughts that cluttered his mind: *She's not in love with me . . . she doesn't love me anymore —*

Why the hell is it so cold —?

Is there somebody else? he wondered. *Is that it? Somebody else?*

It couldn't be Jason, could it? The guy who lived one flight up from her apartment, in 4B. Geraldine had always said they were just friends, and Derrick certainly couldn't imagine the two of them sneaking around behind his back. In fact, Geraldine had always let him know when she and Jason were going out; she'd even given him Jason's mobile phone number, "so you can check on me if you get suspicious," she'd said. No, it couldn't be Jason, he was too much of a softie. A bit effeminate, really, with his rather shrill voice and tight leather pants, and the short-sleeved shirts that revealed too much forearm and *way* too much muscle. Or was it just Derrick's way of convincing himself that it couldn't be Jason? Was he *really* effeminate? Derrick couldn't remember; he'd only met Jason once, and he'd seemed effeminate, or maybe Derrick had just been hoping, feeling frightened, threatened and insecure about the relationship between him and his —

Stop it! he screamed at himself inside his head, which was now under a pillow that oddly resembled a giant marshmallow that had been stepped on. *Stop it or you'll go mad!*

Somewhere in his apartment, a rapping noise rang out: the sound of someone hitting a fist against wood. Like somebody knocking on the front door. Knocking on the front door. Yes, that was it, except Derrick was too deep in his sea of sadness and self-pity to realise it. With his head under the pillow (God, he needed to change the sheets, what *was* that smell? Curry? Why was there *curry* on his sheets?), the sound of the knocking registered but faintly, skimming on the edges of his consciousness. He dismissed it as nothing important — nothing as vital as lying there crying and wailing and writhing in self-torment.

Outside, Geraldine waited. Knocked again, feeling the butterflies dancing in her tummy, and folded her arms against her breasts *where last night she had felt Hope, warm and sweet, nuzzling against her and teasing her nipples with a moist, warm . . .*

Derrick wasn't responding. She figured he was either asleep or in the shower or had left the apartment. It also occurred to her he could simply be ignoring her, but that seemed too unlikely to be the case. Surely he would be *dying* to talk to her after last night's debacle . . . wouldn't he?

. . . Teasing her nipples with a moist, warm tongue . . .

Focus, she told herself.

She knocked again, and waited with the butterflies growing ever larger and more disorderly in her stomach.

No answer.

"Come on, Derrick," she whispered, feeling queasy, and knocked for the third time: three rapid raps, the usual pattern. When she was certain nobody was going to answer the door, she sighed, wondering what to do next.

Throughout the night, lying next to Hope, embracing her warmth in the midst of all the coldness (some of which was deep within her very *bones,* imagine that), she'd rehearsed what to say. "Derrick, you're a great guy and I'm blessed to have known you for this long, but . . ." *No,* she'd thought, *not the 'great guy' speech, that would be the* worst *way to begin.* "I hope you don't take this the wrong way, Rick, but . . ." No, just as bad. Too harsh. "It's not you, really, it's me" had been the third option, but she'd discarded it the moment it had popped into her mind. Everybody knows that when someone says *it's not you,* they really mean *it's you, it's all you!* Of course, in this case, it wasn't just him, it was both of them.

God, life was perplexing.

She decided she needed some space, some air. She headed out of the building, telling herself the sooner she let him know, the sooner they could get on with their lives. Of course, it wouldn't be easy to let go. Eight years is a long time, especially in the instance of a faithful, monogamous relationship. Except that Geraldine hadn't been very faithful. Oh, how she'd cheated on him, on *countless* occasions. And how he'd no idea — no idea of the many times she'd visited Jason, the guy upstairs, to ask him of what it was like being gay. No idea of how Jason would share his experiences and advice with her—as best as he could as a gay man, as opposed to a gay woman—after which she'd go to Hope and they'd talk, discuss, share . . . share a *lot* of things.

Sexuality, Geraldine thought morosely, *can be a pain in the ass.*

From where she stood, in the heat of the sun, she could see the bench in the distance. She squinted in the light, disappointed that there were people there, in the shade, in *their* shade, sitting on what she and Derrick had always referred to as *their* bench. A man, she made out, and a boy.

Oh, well. It *was* a public place, after all.

They'd met there, she and Derrick. She was seventeen, fresh out of high school and waiting to get into college; he was in the first year of his degree. One day, she'd walked past him in the corridor during a university tour, and he'd followed her, captivated by the vision of beauty that she was. So he said. Then she'd got into her car, and he tailed her in his own vehicle. She'd driven around, new to the area, wondering where to stop and have her lunch. By pure luck she'd come across the field, with the grass ankle-high at the time, spring. It was unoccupied. Geraldine had spotted the bench and thought, *That's it.*

Unbeknownst to her, Derrick had stopped his car further down the road, and watched in fascination as his vision of beauty stepped into the field and walked with all the grace and finesse of a swan-cum-ballet dancer towards the tree, the only one with a wooden bench under it. Its branches cast criss-crossing shadows across the ground, and the grass was littered with its little pink flowers. He watched her, his heart pounding and his mouth dry, as she glided towards the bench, and thought (as he told her later), *My vision of beauty is going to sit among the flowers!*

He'd observed her as she ate her lunch, daintily crossing her legs and concentrating on the novel in her lap. Then he'd decided to speak to her, and she looked up as he approached, her expression revealing no concern, just curiosity. He'd then uttered the words that made his lifelong-lasting first impression: "You're a bision of veauty."

Silence prevailed.

To Derrick, even the leaves overhead seemed to have frozen in mid-rustle.

Then: "Oh, *Jesus!*" he'd shrieked, and squeezed his eyes shut as she began to giggle. "Oh, *God,* I don't believe I screwed that up!"

"Not the best pick-up line, anyway," she'd replied sweetly.

"Oh, damn, damn, damn, damn, *damn!*" Humiliated. *Humiliated!*

"Calm down," she'd coaxed, and laughed some more.

"I don't *believe* I did that!" he'd wailed, and sank to his knees, *actually* sank to his knees, soiling his khakis, his head raised in a cry of utter despair, his fists clenched and his arms held up towards the sky as if he were demanding of God, *Why? Why?* Why? *Lord, have mercy on Thy servant: a humble, bumbling, blithering* idiot —

She'd patted the seat next to her: "You wanna sit down? Compose yourself a little?"

And he'd stopped in mid-mortified scream, mouth agape.

It was the start of a very interesting relationship.

"**I**nteresting", as far as Geraldine was concerned, because he'd triggered off in her one of those few instances of attraction towards men. Interesting because, as time had gone by, she'd begun to feel for him, to genuinely *feel* for him. He'd told her very early on that he loved her, and even said he'd never known what true love was until she'd come along. At least, that's what she *thought* he'd said; her head had been spinning and a high-pitched noise had rung in her ears that she'd really missed half of what he was saying.

Regardless, she'd automatically replied that she loved him too, and it wasn't a lie. She felt something for Derrick, she truly did. She knew, deep inside her, that it *was* love, but a love of a different sort. Her feelings for Hope were different from those for Derrick, which was now the source of the problem: that for years, for *eight* freaking years, she'd given him the impression that she was more than merely attracted to him, she was *in love* with him. But, Geraldine realised, it wasn't that she was *in* love with him, she only *loved* him. Like a friend. Like a sister. Like — something other than a lover or a lifelong partner (although, on a side note, she *did* desire to have children, and she figured that sex with a man would be much, much more worthwhile if it was done for pro- and not recreation).

They'd had sex, of course — although if Geraldine's strict, conservative Catholic parents found out, she'd never hear the end of it. She'd liked it enough, although sex with girls was more — scintillating. Still, she didn't mind doing it with guys, in spite of the fact that the first time Derrick had run his tongue into her mouth, she'd shuddered, thinking, *This is interesting* and *this is gross!* at the same time. She'd learned to like kissing him back, playing along and getting into it ardently. And she'd definitely had a good time when he'd tongued her *there*, and when he'd thrust himself into her. Oh, she'd moaned and groaned and laughed and panted like any girl would. She was passionate, she was.

The head-giving thing had posed a little dilemma, though. Geraldine didn't like to think about her blowing debut, because it had been awkward and she'd thought that the idea of tasting him would be *gross* but *interesting*. Still, as time went by, she'd grown more accustomed to it, even to the point of enjoying it. Oh, yeah, it had been interesting, all right. And not really gross, just — interesting.

Now Geraldine stood several metres from the occupied bench, wondering how she was going to break the news to Derrick — the news that, being in a situation where she was in a relationship with a man and was living with a woman, she wanted the woman more than the man. How would Derrick respond to that? How would he deal with it, if he were to deal with it at all? He'd get mad, she figured; he'd be pissed like hell, and then *he'd probably wonder how I could have hidden it from him for so long. He'd probably blame me for leading him on and wasting his time over the past eight years.*

Surely it isn't my *fault,* she thought, and kicked at a small pebble. It bounced off her foot and landed in the middle of the road next to the field, where it would undoubtedly be run over and crushed into a tiny mound of grit. *Surely he can't put the blame on me.*

Or could he?

Maybe she should have told him sooner. Maybe she should have ended the relationship much earlier, instead of letting it drag on. Or maybe she shouldn't have even started it, shouldn't have invited him to sit down next to her on that bench *(with his stained knees)*, shouldn't have accepted his offer to take her out for dinner and a movie. If only she'd turned him down, then she'd —

. . . Well, then she would not have been able to know so personally and intimately a truly wonderful young man; a man who never failed to make her laugh; a man who was always ready with a few wise and wisecracking words whenever she was feeling down. This was a man who didn't need to be asked twice when she needed his help. He was, for the most part, a great guy, and he was smart, and sensitive, and handsome, just —

Just not *enough.*

Not sensitive enough, like Hope was.

Not attractive enough, like Hope was.

And definitely not *sexually* attractive enough — like Hope was.

Living with Hope wasn't the easiest task in the world, either, although there was no denying it was never boring. When she'd first moved into the apartment three years ago, she'd not felt anything for Hope (although in retrospect, perhaps she'd been practising self-censorship, disallowing herself from feeling anything more than platonic). During the course of the months that followed, she and Hope had gradually learned more and more about each other, and each liked every new revelation about the other.

Geraldine soon had to face the fact that she was falling, deeply and hard, for her roommate. It was frightening, realising that the person you were developing a crush on was a person you couldn't avoid; in this instance, the only way to avoid her would have been to move out. And so Geraldine had begun acting up, acting unusually, around Hope, in the hope that she'd fall out of the infatuation: by ignoring her most of the time; acting distant, snappy, hostile, even. Because Geraldine figured that if she didn't force herself to dislike Hope, then she'd be *liking* Hope, and liking Hope was the heart of the problem to begin with.

How could she have known that Hope Brewster had been aware of what was going on — or, at least, had had her suspicions — and that she, Hope, had nothing against the idea of Geraldine falling for her? In hindsight, perhaps Geraldine would have known if she hadn't been too caught up in her determination to stop being attracted to Hope; if she hadn't obsessed about it so, and had simply opened her eyes to see the signs and the inherent messages that Hope had been signalling to her. But Geraldine had not noticed them: she'd only told herself over and over again, *This is wrong, you can't feel for Hope, it's not going to happen, she's straight as an arrow!*

Hope had certainly not helped by going out with the guy upstairs, Jason. How could Geraldine have known that their intimate little dinners were so that they could discuss the homosexual issues at hand? And that other guy, the older man of Italian heritage, Frankie Macaroni or something-or-other, who constantly flirted with Hope and physically touched her, stroking her arms, her shoulders, touching her legs, while

Geraldine had sat there and watched, thinking, *I want to do that, I want to be the one doing the stroking* . . .

How the tension had mounted. How awful it had been in the apartment, with the two girls frequently being in the same room with neither one saying anything to the other. Hope had later revealed she'd wanted to speak up, proclaiming something along the lines of *I know what's going on, and I want you to know I'm cool with it, it's not a problem, girl!*, but had felt uncertain each time. Geraldine had later revealed that she'd wanted to scream, *Talk to me, Hope, listen to me, look at me, touch me!* —and, simultaneously, had wanted to scream, *Go away, don't speak to me, don't look at me, get the hell out of my life!* —so torn had she been. It was truly awful, Geraldine often ruminated, how you can want somebody so much while knowing it would never happen, *could* never happen —so much so that there's a constant struggle within you: *Come to me, get away from me*, both at once; yearning for the other person's attention while wishing that that other person would simply disappear out of your life for good, by dropping dead or getting hit by a truck or something. Cruel thoughts. Awful thoughts, wishing that the problem could be eliminated just like *that*. Nasty thoughts, mixed with the occasional *no, I don't mean that, she's a fantastic person!* —and constantly syncopated with the harsh, wistful *she should just go to hell!*

Long story short (a little too late, Geraldine thought cynically), the whole shebang had come to an end (or had begun, rather?) when Hope had walked into her bedroom to catch her crying. Hope had asked, quietly, what the matter was. Geraldine had refused to answer, in spite of the fact that her aching heart was thumping rapidly against her ribs. But eventually Hope had broken down the wall of non-communication between them, and Geraldine had spilled her guts like a sack of beans thrown to the ground. Hope, much to Geraldine's surprise, had responded in exactly the way Geraldine had always dreamed and prayed she would but never thought would happen.

Now, whenever Geraldine looked back on it, she could see how it had seemed very much like a sitcom or a teen drama, in which the characters sit down and have awkward, heart-to-heart conversations. It is frightening how real life tends to emulate fiction.

This morning she had to tell Derrick the whole story, and it was clearly not going to be an easy task. "Easy" was a word that didn't apply at all. She supposed she would start with the theory that all people in the world were bisexual. It was what Hope believed, and Geraldine supposed she believed it herself, although she wasn't altogether certain. (Then again, who can elucidate with absolute confidence the workings of human sexuality?) Regardless:

"Everybody in this world has the inherent ability to swing both left and right," she planned to say. "It's an inbuilt trait within all animals, and we human beings are not excluded. *Every single person* is bisexual; it's the 'ratio'—for lack of a better word—of sexuality that determines your preference.

"For example, most 'straight' men would probably have a ratio of, say, 90:10. These numbers are a rough estimate and a general guide; it really is quite difficult to pinpoint the exact figures," she'd say. "So the average 'straight' man's attraction towards women would be very strong, and the attraction towards the same would be minimal. Using the same example, because the ratio of *homo*sexual attraction is only 10%, it would take *very* specific characteristics in a man to be deemed attractive to the average 'straight' guy. Suffice it to say, the average man would probably go through life not meeting the other man who can fulfil that 10%—I mean, what are the chances, right?—and, as such, he'd think of himself as perfectly straight, without the need to acknowledge that small proportion of homosexual attraction."

She'd probably have to pause at this point to see if Derrick was comprehending any of this. She could imagine he would be, but would also be wondering what the hell this was leading up to.

"The same applies to women," she'd go on, "except in many cases, the ratios would probably be geared differently—let's say, 75:25, whereby 75% of attraction would be towards men, and 25% would be towards the ladies. This could explain why women are more comfortable expressing their feelings to and for other women, and why one woman is able to look at another and say, 'Wow, she's beautiful', while you seldom, if at all, see a 'straight' man look at another man and say, 'Wow, he's hot'."

("What the hell are you trying to tell me?" she could imagine him cutting in.) She'd continue: "Now, in the instance of gay men and women, the ratios are clearly inverted. We could say that in many gay people, their ratios are geared at, oh, say 80:20, with the bigger figure aimed at people of the *same* gender. So that's why many gay men can still appreciate the beauty of a woman, but fail to find them sexually attractive. Or vice-versa: a lesbian would appreciate the good looks of a man, but would find sexual appeal a bit lacking, you understand what I'm saying?

"Then, of course, we have those who claim to be bisexual. They are the ones who have ratios of, ooh, I don't know, 60:40? I dare say that the chances of a person being 50:50 are very slim; after all, these quotients are shaped according to a myriad of factors as a person is growing up. Hence, because of elements such as his environment, his upbringing, his education and life experiences, a guy might find himself having homosexual tendencies during his teens, but might grow out of them as he enters young adulthood. That's why you can hear of a lot of people—adolescents and young adults, particularly—being 'curious', experimental, wanting to know what it's like, because their ratios have not been set yet.

"And who's to say that the figures are actually 'set', per se? I mean, you might think you're straight or gay now, but when you're older, something you experience might change the way you feel, the way you think, the way you react to others around you. It's possible that there's no permanence to a person's sexuality ratio," she'd suggest—although the last statement could easily jeopardise the whole situation as it would allow Derrick the chance of a rebuttal over *her* preference.

"The most important thing," she would conclude, "is to understand that a person's ratio is *biologically* driven, and hence it isn't something that would register in one's consciousness. In other words, regardless of the factors influencing your ratio, the *gearing* in itself bypasses the brain. It's something that *happens*, without conscious thought or decision. It is *not* a state of mind."

They'd actually had a debate on the topic before. A couple of years back, she and Derrick had walked into a friend's house, only to catch him watching a gay porn video. Not that it was a big deal, they'd both known the guy was gay. But Derrick had actually seen the images on the screen, and his reaction had been just the *tiniest* bit insensitive towards their friend's feelings: "Oh, my God, that is so *sick!*"

That had led to a dispute between him and Geraldine, with her clearly supporting the rights of homosexuals, bisexuals, lesbians, transsexuals, transvestites and other similar people out there. Derrick had insisted vehemently that while he appreciated and respected his friends being what they were, he had no intention of approving it, and would definitely not be *encouraging* it. For Derrick's point of view was that people are capable of doing anything (read *anything*, with heavy emphasis) as long as they put their mind to it.

"Nothing's impossible with the human brain," he'd insisted. "I believe that gay people can turn straight if they want to!"

She'd been indignant, perhaps overly so: "What the bloody hell are you talking about, Derrick? So are you saying that if *you* really wanted to, you could turn gay?"

"Yeah," he'd replied at once.

"Give me a break. You don't know what you're talking about."

"Look, I believe in the power of the mind," he said, "and I believe that if I really chose to — not that I would in a million years — I could easily turn myself gay. I could go up to another guy and make myself like him, even force myself to be sexually turned on by him. Sure, there would be the initial reaction of disgust, but when you do something often enough, you become *desensitised*: you get used to it, and you'd learn not to let it bother you. Hypothetically speaking."

"Far out," she'd uttered scornfully, rolling her eyes.

"It's like eating raw garlic," he went on, although for the life of her she couldn't relate having a sexuality crisis to eating raw garlic. "You might hate it the first time, it might make you gag and vomit, but if you keep doing it, keep forcing it in, keep forcing it down, your body eventually gets accustomed to the taste and you stop retching. You might even start to enjoy it. The same thing applies to a person's sexuality," he'd declared matter-of-factly. "You can change. You can adapt. You can adjust. You can assimilate."

Not impressed by his vocabulary, she'd countered, "That's a load of crap. First of all, why would a person have to put himself through all that shit, forcing himself to do something against his natural being?"

"Because being gay isn't natural," he'd retorted.

Oh. Okay. "Go to hell," she'd told him, although she could understand his perception. At one point, Geraldine herself had thought the bisexuality theory implied that being gay wasn't a natural phenomenon, based on the postulation that external factors played a part in determining one's sexuality ratio. But then Hope had reminded her that if one's sexuality ratio was innate, then it *was* natural, and an inclination towards the other or the same would in any case be *stemming* from the natural. "Ergo, a faction of the natural cannot be deemed unnatural," Hope had declared. Made sense to her.

"It isn't," Derrick had replied, dismissing her rejoinder. "And I wouldn't *want* to be gay, not when there are so many things at stake. My reputation, for example. And my religious beliefs, if I had any. If I were to have children—through adoption or whatever—how could I subject the poor child to a lifetime of uncertainty and the threat of scorn from other parties, those who know that, oooh, little Benny or little Genevieve has two daddies or two mommies who're ramming dicks and dildos up each other every night—"

"For God's sake—!"

"And don't even start to tell me God won't punish those who are gay because it is He who *makes* them gay. If there really *is* a God, He'd do no such thing. Sexuality is but a mental state, *meaning,*" he'd said loudly, lest she were to cut him off, "it is changeable, it *can* be determined by the individual, and it *should* be adjusted according to the rules and norms of society, otherwise we'd have a social order overrun with queers left, right and centre, and all hell would break loose!"

Geraldine had sighed. "That's not fair at all, Derrick. Why would a person have to change just to cater to society's expectations? If two people of the same gender can find love and warmth in each other, why should that be, in any way, inappropriate or wrong or sinful?"

"Because man and women have a *purpose* being together, to breed, to bring on the next generation. Man and man, or woman and woman, have *no* purpose, they *shouldn't* be together. Physical relations were made in order to reproduce, not to satisfy the cravings of the flesh."

"What if they're two really close individuals who aren't *in* it for the sex?"

"Then it's called a friendship," he'd answered, not missing a beat.

"And not a relationship?"

"Geri, a relationship—in romantic terms, at least—implies there would be a natural coupling. There can be no relationship without physical interactivity *somewhere* along the line, whether it's at the start or at the end. A relationship entails both the emotional and the physical, and, as such, no two people of the same gender can or should have a 'relationship'. If two guys get along really well and start sharing their emotions and stuff, it's okay, it's a friendship. But if they start getting raunchy and doing it, then it's wrong, it's sinful, it's sick, it's unnatural. It should be terminated. A *friendship*, yes," he stressed, "but *not* a relationship. No way. Uh-uh."

"And you believe it's all in the mind," she'd murmured wearily.

"Yup. It's a . . . brain matter," he'd said, and laughed at his vague joke.

"What makes you so sure?"

"Scientists, psychologists, experts from all over the world have been exploring queer phenomena for a long, long time. Many renowned psychologists have concluded that sexual preference is all in the head, not in the genes. We don't even need to talk about Freud here; my point of view is based on *modern* scientific findings, because the world, as you know it, revolves on the basis of science today."

"Then you shouldn't have mentioned religion, because religion and science clash."

"Whatever the case, if our friend chooses to watch gay porn, that's his problem. If he's okay with it, I'm okay with him being okay with it. But if you ask me, he should seek psychiatric help so that he'll turn straight and become a normal, functioning member of our community."

At that, a surge of fury and resentment had shot through her. "Fuck you!"

"Yes," he'd replied calmly, "indeed you can."

Geraldine had turned away, ending the dispute there and then.

And here I am, she now thought, *ready to bring it up again.*

She headed back to the complex, steeling herself for the moment.

Tired with wondering why, he decided to get out of the apartment.

They ran into each other at the entrance of the building.

ROOTED

When Jessy Cooke woke up at nine, the first thing she did was reach over to the other side of the bed to feel for her husband's body.

She didn't find him.

Bolting upright, she stared at the space next to her. She touched the sheets, feeling for vestiges of her husband's body heat to indicate that he'd, at the very least, come home.

The covers were cold. Unslept in.

She looked at the floor to see if his sneakers—the ones he usually wore to work, and which he usually brought into the bedroom with him despite the numerous times she'd told him to leave them outside—were there. With a further sinking of her stomach, she saw that they weren't.

She glanced at the chair on the right side of the room, the one Paul usually threw his faded and creased leather jacket on. The jacket wasn't to be seen.

Suddenly she was inundated by a sadness that surpassed the despondency of the past days. Her marriage had been on the brink of ruin, she'd known, but this seemed to push it over the edge. Paul Cooke had not come home last night, hadn't left any messages, hadn't even taken the time to call. Which made stronger the impression that he didn't care, couldn't give a crap about his own family.

The only thing that could make her feel worse was the thought that possibly, just possibly, Paul Cooke hadn't spent the night at his parents'.

Jessy decided she wouldn't be getting out of bed just yet.

Joe Cooke awoke at around noon with a splitting headache. Yet he could still remember how Carrie had felt beneath him, and how she'd tasted as he'd screwed her under the boughs of the tree. Just thinking about her was making him hard again. He grinned to himself stupidly in the midst of his tangled sheets and rumpled covers. If he headed back to Carrie's now, would she allow them to have another go at it? Why wouldn't she? He knew she enjoyed their little escapades almost as much as he did. Earlier that morning, when he'd met up with the gang and got sloshed, he'd fucked her while their friends had kept their eyes averted and alert for signs of passers-by, and she'd squealed and whimpered and moaned so loudly that the others had to urge her to shut up for fear she would attract the attention of those living nearby.

Joe, beaming with pleasure at the memory, was certain it hadn't been her drunkenness that had caused her to shiver in pleasure as he'd done her.

He reached for the telephone next to his bed.

She agreed to meet him at one.

That left him with only a half hour to get ready.

She met him at a pizza place in the city, a twenty-minute drive away.

She said last night had been the best sex she'd had yet.

She said she didn't mind if it happened again.

They didn't stay for lunch.

While Joe Cooke was having the time of his life with Carrie Taylor, his father was busy groaning under the sheets in his old room at his parents' home. With the senior Cookes away at the hardware store, Paul Cooke had taken it upon himself to introduce himself to Maria, before introducing her to the meaning of pleasure, coaxing her—without much effort—into his bedroom and into his bed. Even as he led her into his bedroom, he wondered fleetingly if Joe and Maggie were awake yet, and if Jessy had prepared anything for them to eat, and if Jessy herself had even —

The thought didn't get a chance to complete itself, for she was pulling down his shorts and putting him into her mouth, and he silently thanked his parents as he moaned and throbbed for having hired foreign domestic help.

And Jessy Cooke, vacuuming the living room at three in the afternoon after having called the store only to be told that her husband wasn't there, decided she didn't have to be the victim here. Why should she be the one to suffer when *Paul* was the one throwing their lives away? If he didn't care about her, about any of them, then they didn't have to care about him, either. Tit for tat, an eye for an eye, that kind of thing. She would let go. She would carry on.

A half hour later, she called her in-laws' home, praying he would be there.

At the Cookes' residence, the phone rang, but nobody picked up. The only persons home were Paul and Maria, but they were in the swimming pool, her arms wrapped around his neck, his arms around her waist. The phone rang and rang. Maria asked in her heavy accent whether they should answer it; Paul shook his head, kissed her, and told her in short, simple sentences that nothing was as important to him as the woman in his arms right now. Flattered, Maria snuggled against him, brushed her knee (on purpose? By accident? Who could tell?) against his groin, feeling him harden again.

It wouldn't be his first time doing it in his parents' pool.

The sheets were rumpled beneath them, the air thick with the smell of sex. He looked at her appreciatively, admiring the droplets of perspiration that dotted her shoulder blades and her cleavage and her breasts. Her breasts. He couldn't get enough of them. As he scrutinised her slender, curvaceous body, he found himself eager to taste them again — the warm, sweet saltiness of her. He put an arm around her waist and drew her closer to him so that he could smell her: perfume with a hint of women's scent. Sweet. Arousing.

She was midway through a sentence, but he hadn't paid attention to what she was saying until she whispered, "My mum's always spoken highly of you. Well, actually, she's always spoken very highly of *your* mum, what with her being the president of the residents' association and all that. I think mum might like the fact that I'm going out with Jessy's son."

Why was she talking about their mums right after *sex?* Joe wondered. The mention of his mother's name made him think of what his parents were going through. Not like it was any big surprise — the signs had been there for a while, but it was only recently that Paul had started pulling his vanishing act on them. Still, his mum and dad had been giving each other the silent treatment for months. They'd be in the same room together, but would never speak directly to each other. If Joe or Maggie was present, it'd be "Joe, tell your father he needs to fix the garage door", or "Maggie, tell your mother I won't be home for dinner".

Earlier, at half past four that morning, Joe had (drunkenly) observed that the garage was empty, and at a little before one that afternoon, his father's car was still not to be seen. Which, of course, could have meant Paul had come home and left again, but Joe didn't believe it. He was certain Paul had not returned last night. His mother must be frantic. Frantic, or depressed. Or both.

It was clear to Joe that his father was the problem. His mum, he'd observed, was trying hard to maintain the role of a patient and loving wife, a role Paul had increasingly taken for granted and now didn't seem to even give a damn about. Joe felt a prickling of anger towards his father for treating his mum—and not just his mum, but he and Maggie, too—with such disrespect. How irresponsible could one man be, to neglect his own family? Was Paul feeling guilty over the hurt he *surely* knew he was causing? Did he even *care?* Or was he simply going to let everything collapse—walk away, just hide behind the wealth and status of his parents, and let the whole world think that Paul Cooke was a great man when he was far from it?

And what could Joe do? *Nothing,* he thought, and sighed. If he were to bring it up with either of his parents, they'd say, *It has nothing to do with you. This is just between us, we'll sort it out. Let us grown-ups deal with it.*

Joe decided that when he got married, he would never treat his wife that way. He would always appreciate the good deeds she performed, and let her know that she was well and truly loved. *Never,* he thought resolutely, *will I end up like my father. Never.*

Carrie rolled over and whispered, her breath tickling his ear, "What're you thinking?"

"Nothing," he replied, and managed a smile.

She ran a hand through his hair, and the look she gave him told him that she was ready for another round. *Am I up for it?* he asked himself.

Oh, yeah, he was up for it, all right.

Paul Cooke had, in his forty-five years, slept with many women. Most of them had been before he'd met Jessy—and a handful of them after.

With Maria whimpering as they thrashed about in the water, Paul found himself thinking, *She could be the one.*

The one with whom he could spend a few weeks fooling around, having endless sex.

Yes, she could be the one. Jessy, try as she might, didn't excite him anymore—in fact, she had long failed to turn him on. Their lovemaking sessions were a bust, with him usually forcing himself to think of the other women he had fucked while his wife paraded in front of him in her nondescript lingerie that failed to accentuate her virtually non-existent figure. He'd get a hard-on thinking about the others — and Maria now added to the list — so Jessy would be fooled into thinking she still excited him. The stupid woman.

What Paul intended to do was invite Maria to be his personal housekeeper, his abode being the spacious pool house behind his parents' home that he planned to move into shortly. And there, they'd engage in hours, days and nights of mindless sex; no commitments, no responsibilities, no bothersome wives telling you to fix the plumbing or mow the lawn or pick her up from work because she was hesitant to drive during rush hour. No kids demanding money from him (not that he was short of it, courtesy of dear ol' Mum and Dad) or whining for him to play a game of football, or to attend a boring school play one of them was involved in. Not that he wasn't fond of Joe and Maggie, he still loved them, really; it was just that ever since they'd hit puberty, they were increasingly becoming pains in the butt. They were old enough, he figured, to survive being loved by their father from afar.

The issue was that Paul had always been the philandering type, had never been one to stay rooted to one spot for extended periods of time. The close to twenty years he'd spent with Jessy definitely qualified as 'extended'. *Way* extended. It was time to go, and his pool house was the best place to hide out at until he was sure of his future plans. Jessy and the family hardly set foot into the senior Cookes' home. Jessy, Paul knew, was not well-liked by his parents, and the invitations were sparse.

Looks like Mum and Dad were intuitive, Paul thought coldly as Maria held him tight and moved up and down against him, the water, smelling of chlorine, splashing and forming ripples and waves all around them.

Inside the house, the phone rang.

Jessy listened as the ringing tone bleeped on and on. Nobody was picking up.

She put the receiver down and stood where she was, her hand on the telephone, the vacuum cleaner by her feet.

Where *was* Paul? Why hadn't he called to let her know where he was? It wasn't the first time he'd disappeared from home overnight, but he'd usually leave a message with one of the kids . . .

And the kids—where were *they?*

She'd earlier checked around the house for messages left in their usual places: the refrigerator door, the dining table, the little blackboard in the living room that she and Paul had bought for the kids when they were younger.

Maggie had left a note on the fridge. Joe hadn't.

A part of Jessy couldn't help but wonder at her son's lack of consideration. Surely he knew she'd worry, not knowing where he was! Somewhere in the back of her mind, the thought began to surface that Joe and Paul weren't far off from each other—a terrible and terrifying notion that, as soon as it began to reveal its ugly head, she quickly tried to suppress.

But it was too late.

The apple, she thought in spite of herself, *doesn't fall very far from the tree.*

STAINED

"I hope you understand."

Silence. Seemingly tactile silence.

"Derrick?"

He'd been staring at the carpet forever. And he kept on doing it.

"Derrick, are you . . . ?" She paused, licked her lips apprehensively. Tried again: "Derrick, look, I don't mean to hurt your feelings, I don't mean to offend or upset you, I just . . ."

He kept looking at the carpet, at a little brown stain on the beige fabric. *What* was *that?* he asked himself, trying to come to grips with the situation but feeling it rapidly and unnervingly slither through his fingers. *Red wine, that's it. Red wine.* He and Geraldine had been sipping it—oh, how many years ago? Two. And she'd slipped, spilling some of it onto the carpet. She'd yelped as if the spillage had hurt her, wailing about how sorry she was. He'd calmed her down, told her it was just an accident, and the carpet was due to be cleaned anyway. No big deal.

How easily he'd forgiven. How easily she'd let herself be forgiven.

Now it was almost as if she'd taken his nature for granted, and was seeking his pardon for a wrongdoing much bigger and more repercussive than a mere splash of red wine—a stain that would leave an impression on the carpet of his heart . . . *forever!*

He groaned silently at his lack of lyricism.

"Derrick, talk to me?" She said it as if it was a question. "Talk to me, please?"

He never did get the cleaners round, he realised as he ran the toe of his sneaker against the brown splash. Maybe it was time to perform a complete clean-up. Not just of the carpet — the mess that was his entire life . . . !

Why was she still standing there? Didn't she know he wanted her to get the hell out? Couldn't she read the signs? What the hell was she, *blind?* He wasn't looking at her, right? He wasn't acknowledging her. He wasn't saying anything in response to the fucking *large* bombshell she had dropped upon his head — not so much a bombshell, now that he thought about it, but a mountainous pile of *turd* —

Get out of here! he wanted to yell. *Get the hell out!* But he couldn't produce enough spittle to wet the insides of his mouth, couldn't dredge up the energy to speak a single word. His heart was pounding like a sledgehammer against his ribs *(Broken heart! Aching heart! Heart, stop, I command thee to* stop!*)*, and his breathing was constricted, his nose blocked with snot. A high-pitched ringing was in his ears. Through the barrier of sound everything else was garbled: the hum of his refrigerator, the dripping of a leaky tap, the birds chirping and flapping outside, Geraldine's annoying, butch-fucking-lesbian voice, *get out! Get the fuck out!*

"I was hoping," she said, and now her voice trembled with the threat of an onslaught of tears, "that we could . . . you know, talk about this? Like, come to an — an understanding?" She was suddenly speaking like a ditzy chick, the kind of bubblehead you'd find in teen movies and American TV shows. "Rick?" she tried again, her voice squeaky and frail, "can't we, like, go out? Find a place to sit and chat? How about the field? We could, like, you know, go out to the field? And, and maybe just . . . just discuss . . . what I . . . what I told you?"

The ankle bone's connected to the — shin bone, he sang in his head. *The shin bone's connected to the — knee bone. The knee bone's connected to the — thigh bone . . . !*

She waited, holding her breath without realising it. The carpet seemed to be the most attractive object in the room to him. Wasn't his neck hurting from craning it like that? Stuck in one perpetual spot, with his head bent forward and downward, watching the carpet, staring at —

Oh, sweet Stain;
  See how it
    Dances and shifts
  As the foot
    Plays with it
On the beige textile.

She was going to go mad. The indication was there: the inane construction of hackneyed poetry in her head. Suddenly she had to leave. She struggled to hold back tears as she stumbled and staggered across the room to the front door, grabbing her purse off a chair on the way out, leaving Derrick to gaze so raptly at the stain on the carpet in front of him, increasingly darkening from the dirt off his shoe.

Till Death Do Us . . .

The crowd was dressed in dark, sombre clothing as they gathered around the mahogany casket. Graham Hanson thought it magnificent, and pondered on the macabre irony that the most beautiful bed a person lies in is most likely to be a coffin.

The service, too, had been beautiful, and Graham was touched by the eulogies that had been presented. *Phyllis was loved by many of the townsfolk*, he thought, stepping back as the pallbearers prepared to move the coffin to the cemetery outside St Mary's Cathedral. Graham had heard the most wonderful stories about his late aunt. A certain Martha Cunningham had gone up to the podium, a damp wad of tissue paper against her cheek, and had spoken of how she and Phyl — as everybody called her — had gone way back. "We met nearly fifty years ago," the crotchety Cunningham — who liked to tell people she'd been a regular character on the old sitcom *Happy Days* — had croaked into the microphone. "And oh, the fun times we had. Right up to the day she died, she was a truly warm and fun-loving figure . . ."

Graham had been duly surprised when his cousin Jacob had asked if he was going to say a few words. "You're certainly not *expected* to," Jacob said, "and it's entirely up to you, but . . ." No, of course I'll say something, Graham had cut him off; it would be my honour. And he'd sensed, rather than seen, Felicity nodding in agreement by his side.

So he'd managed to deliver a short but poignant eulogy. "Phyl," he'd said, going along with the rule, "was somebody who'd been there for me through thick and thin. She . . ." He paused, feeling a wave of sadness wash over him. "She was a remarkable woman, who was very supportive of the difficulties that have taken place in our lives. While we've been unable to have children of our own, Phyl has always been . . . well, she was always a beacon of hope, saying, 'There is no such thing as hopelessness. Everything has a purpose, and if you have faith in God, then there will be a way.'

"Today," he spoke into the microphone, wondering why his voice was booming so loudly throughout the cathedral despite the fact that he was whispering, "I don't believe Phyl would have wanted us to grieve over her passing. No . . ."—blinking tears out of his eyes—"I am strongly of the conviction that Phyl would have wanted us to *rejoice,* to celebrate this momentous occasion. Because Phyl, as I'm sure all of you know, was a very strong and staunch believer in our Lord, and . . ." He managed a weak smile. "She's with Him right now. If being with the one you love for the rest of eternity isn't a cause for celebration, then what is?

"Clearly," he whispered, and now his voice trembled with emotion, "we'll miss her very much. She lived a very long and fruitful life, and she will always live on, I'm sure, in our minds and in our hearts, as a woman full of love, strength and compassion, who is now at peace in the warm embrace of our Creator." He paused to let the message sink in. Then: "Thank you," he murmured, and moved away from the podium.

Back in the congregation, Felicity moved to his side, her eyes moist and her voice trembling. "That was beautiful, Graham."

"Thank you," he whispered, and drew her close. "Thank you."

Now the crowd was dispersing to head to the cemetery, and Martha Cunningham (who actually had no affiliation whatsoever with *Happy Days*) found her way to them. She fell in line with Graham, flashed him a toothless smile, and gently slid her hand through his right arm, his left occupied by Felicity's. "That was beautiful," Martha whispered, unknowingly echoing

Felicity's words just a few minutes earlier. "That was truly, truly beautiful. She was blessed," she said, *"blessed* to have had you. Graham"—and she stopped, forcing him to stop with her—"I know this will be a very difficult and trying time for you, but you've got to remember we're all here for you. We know how much you loved Phyl, and how much she meant to you, and . . . we want you to know we're very proud of you, and that you're not alone. You're never alone."

"Thank you," Graham said sincerely, touched. "Thank you, Martha."

Martha smiled and moved away.

They watched as the casket was lowered into the ground, and the priest concluded the service with the last rites. Graham stood slightly apart from the rest of the crowd, observing the mourners who ventured forth to throw flowers and other keepsakes into the grave. An elderly man Graham didn't recognise dropped a silver bracelet in with the coffin, looked up, nodded at him, and turned away.

"Who was that?" Graham whispered.

"Who was who?" Felicity asked.

"Him." He pointed inconspicuously at the man, who had made his way back into the crowd.

Felicity gasped softly. "Jim!"

"Jim?"

"Jim Williamson."

"The Jim Williamson?"

"The Jim Williamson." Felicity nodded. "I've told you about him."

"What's he doing here?"

"I don't know. I must have introduced him to Phyl at some point," Felicity replied. "Nice of him to come."

Looking in the direction Williamson had wandered in, Graham saw a number of people glancing over at him. He nodded sympathetically to them, and they returned the gesture.

Jim Williamson seemed to be staring at him the hardest, the most intensely. It made Graham a bit insecure and vulnerable, but he shook off the feeling, telling himself it was fine. Just because Williamson and Felicity had dated many, many, many, many, *many* years ago ("It wasn't *that* long ago, Graham," Felicity would bark), it didn't mean there was anything wrong with them remaining friends. Though it was interesting that, as far as Graham knew, Jim Williamson had never shown up in their more than fifty years of marriage. He didn't know if Williamson and Phyllis had kept in touch. Jim could simply have seen the obituary in the paper, and had decided to pay his respects.

When the first dollop of earth was dropped into the grave (why did that awful *plopping* sound make Graham grind his teeth? He figured it was because it was official: Phyllis was gone and now she was going to be buried forever), he saw Williamson walk over. After the preliminary introductions, Jim shook Graham's hand. "I'm really, really sorry for your loss," he said quietly, as if talking any louder was forbidden.

"Thank you," Graham replied earnestly.

"How have you been, Jim?" Felicity asked.

Jim sighed and looked at the dispersing crowd. "I'm surprisingly sad about all this. I mean, I know she lived a long and fruitful life, and she and I only knew each other for a short while, a long time ago, but—I'm nevertheless deeply affected by her passing." He turned back to Graham, his eyes revealing a sadness that Graham wasn't certain he himself was feeling. "I'm truly sorry," Williamson said again, and bowed his head, as if to confirm his words were sincere. "You were obviously a lot closer to her, Graham. I pray you find peace during this time of difficulty."

Graham cleared his throat awkwardly, and nodded with an expression he hoped looked genuine. "Thank you, Jim, I really appreciate that. But to tell you the truth, I'm . . . I'm coping really well. I mean, she *was* old. A good life, like you said. She's . . ." And the sentence trailed off. A pause ensued, during which Jim stared mournfully at the grassy ground and Graham clutched Felicity's hand, wondering what to say next. The quiet was quite palpable.

"How did you know her?" Graham asked after a while.

Jim raised his eyes, looking surprised. After a moment's hesitation, he managed an awkward laugh. "Why . . . we — well, we met each other so long ago, it's . . . well . . ." Again, he left it hanging.

"Well," Felicity whispered after a beat.

"Well," Graham repeated, and another silence followed.

A woman standing near the grave squinted in their direction from under the brim of her hat. As she moved towards them, Graham thought this would be a good way to end the increasingly discomfited conversation with Jim Williamson. Holding out his hand, he said, "I appreciate your coming over, Jim. And for taking the time to come to the service. I know Phyl would have been very grateful."

"Thank you." Jim smiled, and the men shook hands.

"Take care," Felicity said softly, almost shyly, from her husband's side.

"I'll . . . see you around," Jim added, and turned away, just as the woman with the hat stepped up to them.

"Bertha," Graham said.

Bertha Asterville took Graham's hand and patted it. In her squeaky voice she whispered how sorry she was over Phyl's passing, and how important it was for them to be strong: the general sentiment of the sympathetic masses during such a time of loss.

"I know it's going to be hard," Bertha peeped, "but I want you to know you can always come over, you can talk to me, anytime at all, you hear?" He and Felicity nodded. "After all, we're not just friends, we're neighbours." She lived on a different street in the Square from them, but, being one of the more vociferous members of the residents' association, considered everyone a friend and neighbour.

"That's really kind of you, Bertha," Felicity said gratefully.

"Well, if you need anything at all," Bertha crooned, and it seemed to Graham like the woman was holding his hand far too long for comfort, "don't hesitate to give me a tinkle, you hear?" She patted said hand affectionately. "We all have to go sometime, it's only a matter of when the Good Lord decides to call us home. Don't be too upset, dear. Be strong in Him." And with another flash of old-lady teeth, she gave his hand a final pat before moving away.

Graham turned to his wife. "Was she flirting with me?"

Felicity chuckled. "Don't flatter yourself."

"No, you saw that, didn't you? She was flirting."

"She wasn't, she was just being kind."

"I'm telling you, she wants me!" Graham exclaimed.

Several others came up to offer their condolences, and Graham for the life of him couldn't figure out who they were and where they had met before. He answered them politely, and, after a while, sensing his detachment, they went on their way.

Michelle Leigh, who was like a daughter to them, came over, her eyes red and puffy. Graham opened his arms to greet her, and she stepped into his embrace. He felt Felicity's arms slide around them both. Michelle sobbed against the front of Graham's shirt, and he stroked her hair, whispering that it was going to be okay. Another figure hung back in the distance—taller, masculine—but Graham couldn't make out who it was as the glare of the sun rendered the person a silhouette.

Michelle pulled away, sniffling. "I can't believe she's gone," she said. Graham remembered she had frequented Phyllis's home in her duties as delivery girl for the supermarket. Wiping her nose with the back of one hand, Michelle gestured to the man in the distance. "My brother, Matthew."

Matthew Leigh stepped forward, his arms folded across his chest. "Hey." He ignored Graham's extended hand.

Graham took the siblings in with one glance, noting how similar they looked. Both had the same dark hair, wavy, except that Matthew—whose body language clearly implied he had been forced to come to the funeral—had his short and neatly cropped, while Michelle's tumbled down to the middle of her back. They were both young and good-looking, with green eyes. Green eyes, Graham deliberated, that would certainly attract girls' attention if Matthew would stop pulling that sour face.

Michelle, on the other hand, was a beauty. No contest there.

There were more exchanges of condolences as Matthew watched from a distance, keeping a wide berth, not wanting to get involved in something that had absolutely nothing to do with him. He'd not wanted to come to the funeral at all, but Michelle had told him off. "It's a *funeral*, Matt!" she'd practically yelled. "I've been wanting you to meet them for months, but you've never given a damn . . . can't you get off your high horse just *once*, just *today*, for me?"

Fine, Matthew had responded insolently. *Whatever.*

Now he stood there as the embracing went on. After a while, fed up with the emotional display, he turned and walked away without a word.

"He likes to sit on that bench," Michelle said, as she helped herself to a steaming cup of herbal tea. "At least, I think he does. Matthew and I don't talk very much, but I was in the neighbourhood earlier and I saw him sitting there, under the tree, looking all contemplative."

"It's a nice place," Felicity said softly, and patted the girl's hand.

Michelle sighed. "I'm really embarrassed that he walked away like that. I'm sorry. He's just . . ." She shook her head. "He's always had a short temper, this incapacity to get along with other people. I've told you that before, right? Yeah." She nodded, answering her own question. "And with Dad harping on and on about how he should have gone into medicine, it's horrible back home."

Felicity shook her head and *tsk-tsk*ed. "He just needs someone to talk to him — and to *listen* to him."

Michelle sighed. "At twenty-four, he still acts like a spoiled brat."

"Now, sweetheart," Graham said gently. "You don't mean that."

"You *saw* him, Mr Hanson! You saw how rude he was." She shook her head in exasperation. "It was just so embarrassing, the way he refused to even shake your hand, as if — as if — he — "

"It doesn't matter," Felicity said. "He has other things on his mind. Don't worry, honey, we understand; twenty-four can be quite a difficult time in a young man's life."

"You know what I really love about that bench?" Graham changed the subject. He pushed a platter of sliced fruitcake across the table. Michelle looked at it glumly, didn't touch it. "Go ahead, eat," Graham urged, before continuing: "If you get up early and spend some time on that bench, you'd be surprised at how much it relaxes you. It's cool in the mornings, and it's very quiet, very soothing. I'm not surprised Matthew has taken to sitting there, and I think you, my dear, would greatly benefit from taking some time off to calm yourself and collect your thoughts. Spend some time alone on that bench one morning — it's a great way to prepare yourself for the rest of the day, what with your having examinations and all that."

"How's that going, sweetheart?" Felicity asked. "Your exams?"

"I'm not really focusing on that right now," Michelle replied, and shrugged. "It's the weekend, anyhow. And one of my friends called me earlier, said she wasn't feeling too good, so I'm going to drop by her place later. All this has messed with my study schedule, but . . . I'll survive."

Felicity patted her hand again. "Don't you neglect your studies, you hear?"

"We want you to do your very best in everything you do," Graham agreed.

"Don't worry," Michelle said, and managed a wan smile. "I'll be fine." She looked at Graham with concern. "How about you . . . ?"

"We'll be fine, sweetheart," Felicity reassured her.

"What are you going to do . . . you know, for the rest of the week?"

"Probably the same things we do every week," Graham replied. "Head down to the children's shelter, help out at the church. Tomorrow I might tend to the garden most of the day. Sweetheart," he said, seeing her pained expression and stroking her hair gently, "please don't worry. Everything will be fine, just you wait and see." He gestured to the cake, rich with the fragrance of fruit and spices. "Eat, eat."

She jabbed at the cake with her fork, but she was still too upset to put the food into her mouth. She hoped she wouldn't hurt his feelings by not eating it.

GIDDY

Maggie Cooke stood in front of the full-length mirror behind her closet door, gazing at her reflection, at the light-blue top that she'd been saving for a special occasion such as this. But her mind was not on her clothing; instead, she was thinking about her father, wondering how she would react if Paul Cooke were to vanish once and for all. Would she be able to deal with it? She told herself she probably would. She and her father had not been particularly close—at least, not in recent years. Sure, she'd miss him dreadfully, but time heals all wounds—doesn't it?

Maggie shook her head, telling herself to stop thinking this way. She made herself realise that if anything, she ought to pray that relations between her mother and father would mend, that there wouldn't be a separation or divorce or whatever.

But in the event that her father *did* get out of the picture permanently . . . well . . .

Some of Maggie's schoolmates lived with single parents who had broken up due to "irreconcilable differences", whatever that meant. If they could do it, surely she could.

Right?

Forget about it, she thought. *Just focus on the task at hand*: getting ready for the big date with Zack McPherson. They'd planned to meet under the tree in the field, and although she wondered what was so special about it, she wasn't the type to question—especially when the request had come from somebody as wonderfully delicious as Zack.

Seven twenty-five, and she was standing under the tree, tapping her foot nervously against the base of the trunk. When she'd left the house, her mother had been in the kitchen, stirring a pot of pasta. "I'm going out," Maggie had said, and her mother had nodded, seemingly without interest. Maggie knew it was a sign that her mother had other things on her mind, and it didn't take a genius to figure out what.

"Will you and Joe be okay?" Maggie had asked, and her mother had shrugged with a semblance of a smile. Maggie had then realised that her mum was probably going to be eating alone that night, and a stab of guilt had struck her. She had briefly contemplated staying home to keep her mother company, but Zack would be waiting, and she'd been waiting for Zack for*ever*, so . . .

Zack was to meet her at half-past, and now the minute was almost approaching. Maggie told herself to calm down, take a few deep breaths. A date with a much-liked boy didn't mean that she had to constantly be on her toes, high-strung and jittery. She couldn't recall ever feeling this apprehensive with her ex, Chris Hardman. Her heart was pounding a rapid tattoo in her chest, and she was practically giddy with excitement. For a brief moment the giddiness turned to nausea, and she had to fight the urge to throw up. But that wouldn't do, throwing up when Zack was due to arrive—what if he *saw* her do it?? She breathed deeply, willed the nausea to subside, and it did, thankfully. And not a moment too soon—she saw him in the distance, ambling across the field towards her.

EYES BLOWN WIDE OPEN

Sanjeev and Chitra rushed to Derrick Weston's apartment, wondering what the emergency was. Derrick had called them fifteen minutes ago, sounding distraught as they'd never heard him. He answered the door almost immediately, and when they were seated in his messy living room, he nearly went into conniptions telling them the story. Sanjeev and Chitra listened, engrossed, giving him their undivided attention. When Derrick finished, his eyes bloodshot and puffy and his cheeks streaked with tears, he opened the floor to let them have their say.

Their say was not what he'd expected.

Sanjeev burst out laughing, a high-pitched, donkey bray that reverberated in the confined apartment space. Chitra, too, giggled hysterically, kicking her legs. Derrick stared at them with his mouth agape, wondering what the hell was so funny. Sanjeev playfully slapped Chitra's arm, and she countered the action. Feeling a wave of red-hot anger sweep over him, Derrick took a deep breath and bellowed, "What the *hell* are you guys laughing at?!"

"We've suspected it all along," Chitra said between giggles.

"*What?*"

"Geraldine," Sanjeev said, snorting through tears of hilarity. "Oh, God, it's about *time* she came to acknowledge the truth. Self-denial can be such a burden."

"Whoa," Derrick exclaimed, rising to his feet unsteadily. "Whoa, whoa, whoa, whoa, whoa! Are you telling me —"

"Come on, buddy," Sanjeev said, grinning. "She's always been . . ."

"You know," Chitra said, and they both left it at that.

Derrick squeezed his eyes shut in frustration, and there was much wailing and gnashing of teeth. "She's always been what? What? *What?!*"

"Well, she's always been a little bit . . . how do I put it?" Chitra pondered.

"Butch?" Sanjeev suggested.

"Well, no, not 'butch' per se, but . . ."

"Tomboyish?"

"Tomboyish, maybe, but a little less to that effect . . ."

"*I can't believe what I'm hearing!*" Derrick shrieked. "My girlfriend—my former girlfriend—my *whatever*-she-is!—she's *not* butch!"

"Butch isn't a bad thing," Chitra said kindly.

"No! She's not! She's the most feminine, most girl-like girl I know!"

"Only because you're in love with her, and you choose to see what you *want* to see," Sanjeev reasoned. "It's like that old sitcom, the one with the nanny? When ol' what's-his-name fell in love with her and he didn't even realise that she had that *voice*? That's how in love he was, and that's how in love *you* are, and it's perfectly natural for you to get accustomed to or block out certain things when it comes to someone you really care about, and we're not really helping, are we?"

"No," Derrick seethed, and began to pace back and forth, scuffing his feet against the red-wine stain. "No, no, no, no, *no!*"

"Seriously now," Chitra said, and stopped smiling.

"Seriously," Sanjeev repeated.

"Derrick, come on, sit down," Chitra urged. "Let's discuss this seriously."

"I can't believe you two walk *in* here and tell me you've known all along—!"

"Not known, suspected," Chitra corrected.

"All right, *suspected*," Derrick spat. "Suspected, suspected, suspected!"

"You're getting hysterical, sit down," Chitra said, gesturing to the couch. "We're not going to solve anything if you're going to get all wound-up and upset about this."

"*Wound-up and upset?!*" he raved, his voice reaching a pitch nobody had thought possible. "For the love of God, my girlfriend of eight *fucking* years—that's eight years of *fucking!*—has just confessed that she's a goddamn *lesbian,* for crying out loud, and you're telling me not to get 'wound-up and upset'? *Jesus!*"

Chitra turned to Sanjeev, who looked unperturbed, and said, "I think he's wound-up and upset."

"You know what, you guys are a great help!"

"All right, we're sorry we laughed," Sanjeev said calmly. "It's just that there were always these signs that Geraldine might be swinging more heavily to one side than the other, and you've never noticed them because you care very deeply and strongly about her—and there's nothing wrong with that!" he hastened to add. "It's just that, as third-party observers, Chit and I have seen—or sensed—some things, and we've never thought it appropriate to tell you, because . . ." He shrugged. "Well, because, at the risk of repeating myself, you care very deeply and strongly about her."

"Oh, God," Derrick moaned, and plopped himself down heavily upon the couch. "Oh, God, what the hell am I going to do?"

"Seriously?" Chitra asked.

"*Yes,* seriously!"

"Seriously, I think that . . ." She glanced at Sanjeev, who shrugged slightly. "I think you'll just have to respect her decision." She saw Derrick's mouth move and his eyes widen in protest, and she quickly cut him off: "You've got to think about how difficult this must be for Geri, too, okay? I know right now, what she's done, what she's said, must seem very selfish and hurtful, but I think it's only fair that you stop and think about what she's been going through."

"Struggling with her sexuality can't be easy," Sanjeev said.

"And I think, *seriously*, that you've got to . . ." Chitra paused.

"Got to what?" Derrick demanded weakly.

". . . Come to terms with this . . ." Another pause.

"Cut out your fucking dramatic effects!" Derrick yelled.

". . . And come to accept it," she finished.

"Come to—*come to accept it?*" he squeaked. "For God's sake, I *love* her!"

"Well, if you really do, all the more reason for you to accept it and let her live her life the way she wants, and the way, perhaps, it's meant to be," Sanjeev reasoned.

Silence went by, thick and suffocating—to Derrick, at least—during which Chitra helped herself to his half-finished can of Coke on the coffee table and slurped loudly. Eventually, Derrick hissed in a condescending tone brimming with rage: "'Meant to be'? This kind of thing is *never* 'meant to be'."

"Oh, boy." Sanjeev sighed.

"How can it be 'meant to be'? Like, God *wanted* it this way? I don't think so! Oh, no, I don't think so!"

"You're getting wound-up and upset again," Chitra said. "We know this is hard for you. We understand that, but it's important you give yourself some time. You should get out of this place for a while. Get away from your cramped, stuffy apartment, away from work, away from all *this*. Take some time off, clear your head, organise your thoughts."

"Yeah, that's a great idea," Sanjeev agreed. He and Chitra beamed at each other.

Derrick sighed, long and loud. "I don't know . . ."

"You're too close to you-know-who upstairs," Sanjeev said.

"You need a change of pace."

"A change of scenery."

"Bunk over at Sanjeev's, that should help. You don't mind, do you, Jeev?" Chitra asked, and went on before her friend could respond: "You've seen the place, Rick. It's a lot more roomy than this hovel of yours, and it's right next to the beach! You can wander along the shore, listening to the beat of waves against the sand. You'll have all the privacy and freedom you need to think things through and get things straight." She paused, before adding jovially: "No pun intended!"

Derrick shook his head.

"The door's wide open," Sanjeev said, and patted his friend on the shoulder. "Anything you need, anytime you want to come over, spend the night, you're more than welcome, you know that."

More silence. Chitra slurped loudly from the can of Coke, while Sanjeev twiddled his thumbs and began to hum quietly to himself, a showtune.

Then Chitra said, "Should . . . one of us . . . talk to . . . Geri?"

Derrick didn't respond.

Sanjeev said, "That might . . . be . . . a good . . . idea."

"Don't bother, I think she's already got somebody to talk to," Derrick cut in. The idea of Geraldine and Hope—together? Holding hands? In bed?—touched a nerve. With his hands behind his head, he bent forward until his face was practically touching his knees. "Oh, *God!*" he moaned, and let out several loud groans of frustration. "Nnngh!" he grunted, and began to punch ferociously at the empty air in front of him. "Nnngh, nnngh, nnngh!"

They watched, half-fascinated and half-afraid, as Derrick attacked the nothingness in front of his face. They watched, in part amusement and part nervousness, as Derrick lashed out with all his might, moans akin to one caught in the throes of orgasmic passion bursting forth from his twisted lips. They watched, in an equal quotient of intrigue and horror, until, satisfied and spent, Derrick flung himself against the back of the sofa and bellowed an uptight cry to the Almighty—*"Gawd!"*—then seemed to deflate, bushed. They waited patiently as he panted and gasped for air, until he finally whispered, "I need to get out of here."

"Attaboy!" Chitra cheered.

"Need to go and get pissed fucking drunk."

"Attaboy!"

"Hey," Sanjeev said, "anything for our friend, eh, Chit?"

Chitra beamed. "Yeah." She slung an arm around Derrick's shoulders, and drew him close. "Anything for our friend."

WHETTING THE APPETITE

Zack McPherson's idea of a good time on a Saturday night wasn't exactly the most original in the world, but it was more than enough to keep Maggie Cooke on a high: a light dinner at the nearby fast-food joint, and a trip to the movie theatre to watch a romantic comedy. Seated in the darkened room, she tried to keep her eyes on the screen, but found herself constantly glancing at the boy—two years her senior, and cute like hell—sitting next to her.

Would he put his arm around her? She sure hoped he would.

Would he kiss her?

Her first kiss had happened three years ago when she was twelve. Who had it been with? She tried to remember as the images flickered on the big screen. Billy. Of course. Billy Dale, then thirteen years old and filled with raging hormones and an active dancer in his pants. They'd been at a mutual friend's birthday party and he'd pulled her from her seat, saying—and she could still hear his voice clearly in her head—"Come on, Cookie, dance with me!" She'd not been very fond of boys at the time, despite the signs that had been developing: the small breasts (which her mother insisted coaxingly would grow to an impressive size in time, even if Jessy's own breasts didn't provide much reassurance), and the monthly bloody packages that visited her (her friend Tina used to insist rather gratingly that she'd had her first 'visit' at the age of ten and three-quarters, thank you very much!). And so she'd been rather distraught that Billy Dale (who later related to all the boys at the party that he'd had his first wet dream two nights before, and had his father to thank for his abundant crop of body hair) had chosen *her* to dance with. Her. Unknown little Margaret Cooke, with her fine head of golden curls tumbling wildly about her face in an oxymoronically orderly fashion. So she'd danced with Billy Dale despite the fact that she hadn't really liked him (pimples were beginning to sprout on his face at the time, and oiliness was not a particularly attractive characteristic in both the physical and behavioural sense); and when the song had ended, she'd murmured an awkward "thank you" to the boy, who'd replied "you're very welcome" with his shirt damp and underarms stained with perspiration—and he'd suddenly drawn her close to him, much too close for comfort, oh boy, and she could smell his deodorant (much too heavy, as was the case with many boys of that age, masking the nastiness with an equal amount of nastiness), and he'd said something along the lines of "I've always wanted to do this with you", and she'd wondered *what, what?* as he'd drawn her closer still and pushed his face against hers, mouth-to-mouth, oh, my God, oh, my God, *Doritos* and salsa breath. *Dear Lord in Heaven!* she'd thought, her mind screaming as he continued to press against her face in spite of, or because of, the number of guys and girls who were gaping in alarm and amusement and awe (the boys, especially, were clapping and cheering their oleaginous heads off, those testosterone-drenched bastards!); and then he'd done the unspeakable and the unthinkable and the unbearable and had run his tongue into her mouth, just like that, one quick and clean *slooop*, wet and slippery and thick with the spicy fragrance of cheese and tomato dip. She'd pushed him away (hurting him in the process? She definitely hoped so), screaming bloody murder and sputtering and spitting and going "oh, God, gross, that was *disgusting!*" while Billy Dale, thirteen and suddenly transcended into a shining hero in the eyes of his other boy-buds, slapped his puerile group of friends high-fives, friends who were practically worshipping the very soda—and alcohol-spattered ground he walked on as they screamed "you da *man*, man, you da *man!*"

After Billy there'd been a handful of boys, none of whom she'd been particularly serious about. Then, of course, had come Chris, her first steady one. Chris Hardman, who had been a great kisser and much more, but whom she didn't like to think very much about since it really hadn't been that long since they'd ended their relationship. Chris and his family had had to move out of the country about a month ago, and Maggie was naturally still nursing a tender broken heart. They'd decided that they should see other people — God only knew when they'd meet again — and tonight, she was with Zack, having been introduced to him by Tina during a party. She'd taken to Zack instantly. Somewhere deep within her, the thought had crossed her mind that she was probably on the rebound, but so what? She missed Chris like crazy, but life had to go on. At fifteen she was already all too aware of the complexities of relationships, and she vowed never to become jaded or embittered by the past, the present, and the future.

Anyhow, tonight she was with Zack, who was just so adorable and handsome and sweet and kind and polite and a myriad other mindless positive adjectives, so much so that the thought of him being as infantile and annoying as the guys during her Billy Dale days was just inconceivable, and the thought of Billy Dale's tongue made her queasy. Looking at him out of the corner of her eye, she couldn't see, couldn't envisage, the adorable and handsome and sweet and whatever Zack McPherson pumping his fists in a childish display of triumph, exclaiming, "You da *man*, man, you da *man!*" — no, not Zack, who was so adorable and handsome and whatnot.

She smiled at him in the near-darkness. He didn't smile back; he was too busy staring at the screen, bathed in the flickering grey light of the movie projector. After a while he offered her his popcorn (if *that* wasn't sweet, *what* was?). She declined with a polite shake of her head, and he put the tub down on the empty seat on the other side of him. Then, be still her beating heart, he grinned that boyish grin and moved his arm so it was sliding warmly and gently around her shoulders. Thank God for movable armrests between the seats, she thought daftly, unable to believe he was doing it, drawing her close, drawing her closer, squeezing her shoulders lightly, almost as if he were testing the waters, and when he didn't sink, squeezed her more tightly. Dear God. *Don't throw up. Don't throw up!*

The next hour or so of the movie went by without her seeing or hearing much of it; she was too caught up in the mist of euphoria that surrounded her as Zack McPherson's arm grew warmer and warmer against her skin. By the time they filed out of the cinema—*too soon, much too soon*—they were comfortable with each other's touch, and he kept his arm there all the way out of the building. He said something but she didn't hear him, so spellbound was she as she floated on her ninth cloud. Only when he repeated it did she start and go, "Huh? Sorry? What?"

He chuckled. "I asked if you liked the movie."

"Oh, yeah." She nodded enthusiastically, wild hair tumbling neatly. "Liked it. Much. I mean, very much. Yeah."

"Which part did you like the best?"

She had to think about that one, and uttered intelligently, "Ummm . . ."

"Hey," he said, as they approached his car. He looked at her, into her eyes, which were merry with excitement. "I hope you've been having fun so far."

"Fun, yes," she said, nodding again. "It's been great, Zack, it really has."

"I'm glad," he said, and kept on looking at her until she began to feel just the slightest bit uncomfortable. And just when she thought she wasn't able to bear it anymore—he was so kissable; the idea of leaping at him and plastering one big smacker on his lips the way Billy Dale had done to her flashed unremittingly across her mind—he gestured to his Corolla and said, "I was just wondering, since it's still early . . ." What time was it? Half past ten? ". . . Whether you'd like to go someplace, maybe we could sit and talk, and . . ." Shrugged shyly, a gesture she found incredibly endearing. "You know, get to know each other . . . better."

Sure, she answered, and then realised she'd only thought it, hadn't said it aloud. "Sure," she said, and her voice cracked. She blushed heavily, thanking her lucky stars that it was dark and he couldn't see.

He laughed. "You thirsty?"

"Yeah, a little," she said, grateful that he'd saved her face.

"Maybe we could drop by the 7-Eleven, grab a drink before we talk."

"That sounds good," she said breathlessly. "Really . . ." No other word could come to her mind quickly enough, so she repeated lamely, ". . . good."

They got into the car and he drove to the nearest convenience store. There, he parked in front and told her to lock the doors, he'd be back in just a minute. She waited for him, her heart all a-flutter, her palms sweaty. She wiped them against her skirt repeatedly, wondering if palms could smell like armpits. She rolled her eyes scornfully at her silly reckonings. *Just relax, you've been jittery all night. Zack's a great guy. Just sit back and have a good time. Who knows,* she told herself, *if things go well, he might ask you out again.*

That *Zack* might be the one hoping for a second date didn't even cross her mind.

She found herself feeling more nervous, instead of less, when Zack decided the ideal place to sit and chat was directly across from her house. She glanced at her wristwatch: almost 11PM. Would her mother still be up? Was she likely to see them if she were to glance out of the bedroom window upstairs? *No,* Maggie told herself; the bench was too far away in the distance, and it would be too dark. The thought comforted her. And then Zack's hand was gently pushing against the small of her back, guiding her forward, crunch-crunch-crunch across the branches and dead leaves and grass on the ground, towards the darker area where the bench sat under the tree.

They sat, cold wood against warm skin. Zack held the brown paper bag containing the drinks, and he reached into it and pulled out a chilled can of diet Sprite for her. His own drink came in a bottle; she couldn't see the label, but figured it was also a soft drink of some sort.

She tilted the can to her lips, swallowed, and announced, "It might rain this week."

He looked at her, so handsome in the moonlight, with one eyebrow raised. *Stupid, stupid, stupid!* She could have kicked herself. *Of all the things to talk about —!*

"It might, huh?" he said, and grinned. "That'd be cool."

She smiled back, relieved he'd responded.

"Hey, move a little closer, will you?" he said softly. The invitation was too tempting to turn down. She obeyed, her heartbeat loud in her ears. He slid his arm around her shoulders. "I'm having a really good time tonight."

She stammered back in a voice that was barely above a whisper, "M-me, too."

"Maybe . . . we could do this again sometime?"

She dared herself to make eye contact. His face was inches away from hers; she could smell his breath, pungent with the odour of — what was it? Something or other. Sweet. So close, his lips within tasting distance if she were to simply dart her face forward —

"M-maybe," she replied, all nerves.

He darted his face forward and caught her square on the lips.

It wasn't anything like Billy Dale's kiss. It was almost as good as Chris Hardman's. Warm and slightly moist and delicious. This didn't involve any exchange of fluids, just a pleasurable pressing of lip against lip, a sample to whet the appetite. This was different and pleasant and wonderful.

When he pulled away, she was stunned. And eager for more.

He smiled shyly, looked down at the ground in the darkness. "Sorry. I didn't . . ."

"No," she cut him off, "it was—that was . . . fine."

He looked up. "Really?"

"Yeah."

Eye contact. And he moved forward again and pressed his mouth upon hers, his skin hot and smelling of the cologne that he wore. One of his hands moved to the side of her face, touched her cheek gently, swept back her curly locks. The kiss got a little more passionate, more forceful, and she found herself responding to this marvellous new sensation that was thrumming through her—a deep, enthralling feeling that ran to her very core and made her feel hot and cold and dreamy and wide awake all at once.

So much for being on the rebound.

It was a little past midnight when Maggie stepped through the front door. She was greeted by a heated argument taking place in the kitchen at the back of the house. She turned to Zack, who stood on the porch behind her with one eyebrow cocked, and gave him an embarrassed and apologetic look. He nodded, understanding it was time to go. He gave her a final goodnight kiss before leaving, and she braced herself for the war within.

"Why are you being so unreasonable?" Her mother's voice was harsh, cold and angry. "Stop and *think* of other people for a change! Why the hell can't you just, for once in your life, be more considerate?" There was the scrape of a chair against the floor, and the sound of rapid footfalls, followed by her mother's yell: "Don't you walk away from me, Joseph! You get back here right now!" More movement. Maggie stared at the kitchen door, uncertain if she should announce her presence.

"*Joseph!*"

"For God's sake, Mother, stop treating me like a child!"

"You're *acting* like a child!"

"I'm seventeen, Mum, give me a fucking break!"

"Watch your language with me, don't you dare—"

"I'm a grown *man* now!"

"When you're a grown man, I'll be the first to let you know!"

Perhaps she should intervene, perhaps not. She was the youngest, after all; they might tell her it was none of her business. Then again, could issues involving family members truly be none of her business? Undecided, she headed for the stairs and gingerly made her way up. The steps creaked under her weight, and she winced.

The next thing she knew, her mother came storming out of the kitchen, Joe tailing her sullenly. She shouted at her, "Maggie, has Joe been sneaking out of the house at night? Tell me! Yes or no?"

Maggie flashed Joe a look of confusion. She deemed it best not to say anything, but Jessy was moving towards the stairs, one arm reaching out to grab her wrist to pull her down to where her brother was standing. "Does he or does he not sneak out of the house, Maggie?"

"I—I don't know," she stuttered.

"What do you mean—?"

"Maggie has nothing to do with it," Joe snapped.

"Shut up, Joseph, you're in big enough trouble as it is!"

"Stop yelling at me!"

"I'll yell at you all I want, I'm your *mother!*"

"Mum, Joe, please," Maggie whispered. "Don't."

"If your father was here—" Jessy began, but Joe cut her off:

"*If* he was here—but he's not, is he? He doesn't give a damn about any of us, and I don't see why the hell *you* have to care so much either! Why can't you be more like Dad, *Mother?*" he spat. "He doesn't care! He doesn't give a shit! He's out there living his own fucking life, doing whatever the hell he wants. Well, *I want that too!* For God's sake, let me live my own *life!*"

"Joe," Maggie started weakly.

He rounded on her: "*What?*"

She turned and ran up the stairs, her feet pounding against the creaky wood.

Jessy's face took on a pallor, and she moved a hand to her forehead, massaged her temples. When she spoke, her voice was forcibly controlled: "Joseph, you can *live* your own life . . . all I'm asking is that you show us a little bit more consideration. *Please,*" she said, seeing he was about to protest, "just a note. Surely that's not too much to ask, one note? Just tell us where you are, or call, or whatever. Don't stay out all night. Don't *not* pick up your phone. I worry."

Joe sighed, the fire in his eyes turning to embers. "Fine."

"Okay? Please?"

He sighed again, turned away from her, giving in. "Okay. Fine. Whatever."

"And about your father . . ."

"I don't want to talk about him."

"I do," she said.

"Well, I don't!"

"Joe, your father and I are going through a rough spot . . ."

Joe snorted derisively. "A *rough spot.*"

"Joe . . ."

"I'm tired, Mum," he said wearily. "I want to go to bed. And I don't want to talk about Dad. He's—he's a dickhead."

"Joseph, that's not—"

A voice rang out from the kitchen doorway, low and gruff but familiar, cutting off her reproach midway: "That's all right, Jess. Let him be."

Jessy stiffened. She turned to gape at her husband standing in the doorway, having come in through the back door.

An expression of embarrassment crossed Joe's features, but it passed as quickly as it had appeared. He turned away and sprinted up the stairs, leaving his mother to battle it out with their father on her own.

"Jess."

"Dear God, Paul . . ."

"We have to talk," he murmured, and sauntered, unsteadily, into the kitchen. Jessy took a few tentative steps backward and realised, from the way her husband smelled, he had been drinking again. Drinking still. Whatever. This wasn't new. At all.

"Paul," she said, struggling to fight back tears, the emotions that roiled within her. "Paul, where have you been?"

"I've been—here and there," he said dismissively.

"Why didn't you call, you should have called, I was worried, we all were."

He laughed, a scornful sound. "I don't think my son was. Worried, that is."

"He—he was," Jessy said weakly. "He really was. And Maggie . . ."

"I'm not here to talk about the kids, Jess," he cut her off, and glared at her with watery, bloodshot eyes, his lips cracked, the stench of booze lingering in the air around him. "I'm here to talk about you and me."

Four AM, and Joe sat up in bed upon hearing a knock on the door.

The doorknob rattled softly. Then Maggie popped her head into the room. "You awake?"

"Yeah. What do you want?"

She came in, shut the door silently behind her. Whispered, "Something's wrong, Joe. It's 4AM, and Mum's in bed, crying."

Joe looked at her.

"She's in bed, Joe," Maggie repeated, and he saw her eyes were also moist. "She's in bed, and she's alone, and it's 4AM and she's crying."

BIG GUYS DON'T CRY

Matthew Leigh thought it uncanny that little Robby always showed up when he was sitting on the bench, as if the boy had nothing better to do with his time than wait for him. Today, Monday noon, the boy wandered over, his eyes puffy as if he'd just awoken, his bare feet crunching upon dead grass and brittle branches. Matthew sighed, but he had to admit he was mildly curious as to how their conversation would take shape. Last week, he'd been pissed off by little Robby's comment about him getting the better of the boy. But looking back, Matthew begrudgingly thought the comeback had been pretty spot-on. So although he had come to the bench for some solitude while having his lunch, a part of Matthew was interested to see what the topic of the day would be, the child being the chatterbox that he was.

"Hey, mister," little Robby greeted him sleepily, rubbed at his eyes with dirty hands, and yawned loudly.

Matthew replied, "What are you, some kind of psychic freak?"

"Huh?"

"How the hell did you know I was here? You don't wait around all day for me to turn up, do you? Hell, it's past noon, don't you go to school?"

The boy looked at him, and for a moment, it seemed to Matthew that an expression of indignation flashed upon the child's face. Then Matthew blinked and it was gone. The boy scuffled his bare feet against the soil, kicking up a small cloud of dust, and muttered, "I don't go to school, mister. My mummy says I don't need to."

"You don't go to school," Matthew repeated incredulously.

A little shake of his head. "No, sir. Mummy says it's a waste of time. Everythin' I gots to learn, I learns from my mummy."

"How extraordinary," Matthew commented, thinking, *You freak.*

"I'm pretty smart."

"That's for sure. Pretty smart-mouthed."

"Yeah," the boy agreed, missing the insult.

"Look at your eyes, they're all red," Matthew said, seeing the kid's bloodshot whites, teary from rubbing.

"You can't look at your own eyes."

"Don't be a smartass. You still half asleep? Or have you got conjunctivitis or something?"

"Huh?"

"Pink eye."

"No. Don't think so."

"Then you're just sleepy?"

"Yeah. I guess."

"How come?"

"Why d'you wanna know?" the boy shot back, not harshly.

Matthew feigned offence. "So it's all right for you to ask me questions, but not all right for *me* to do the asking? Give me a break. What kept you up?"

"I couldn't sleep."

A pause. "Are you playing the fool with me?" Matthew asked.

"Depends," the boy said. "Are you a fool?"

Another pause. Matthew looked at the boy, whose expression remained blank.

"You trying to be a comedian, boy? Is that it? A funny man, huh? Think you're so hilarious, do you?" Matthew snorted. "You should just go home and go to bed."

"Maybe," the boy replied.

"Well, if you don't, you're just going to keep rubbing your eyes, then you know what will happen? Your eyes will dry up. Like two raisins. They'll shrivel in your eye sockets, and one day while you're having breakfast, they're gonna fall out of your head and into your cereal. And you'll be scooping them up with your spoon and eating them."

The boy giggled, his first strain of laughter. "That's funny," he said. "How do you spell 'blind pig'?"

Matthew had heard this countless times before, but he went along anyway.

"Wrong!" little Robby exclaimed. "It's 'b-l-n-d-p-g'. If it had two 'i's . . ."

". . . It wouldn't *be* blind," they finished together.

"Aw!" The boy shook his head. "You heard it before."

"No, I just guessed the ending."

"Liar."

"Am not. Wanna know how I guessed?"

"How?"

"I'm a psychic freak," Matthew replied.

The boy took great delight in this small act of self-derogation, and began to bounce up and down on his tiny feet, clapping his hands with glee. "Psychic freak! Psychic freak! Psychic freak!" he chanted, his words garbled by high-pitched giggles that revealed how much he was enjoying himself, and just how young he truly was. Matthew watched him and grinned despite himself. The boy bounced up and down, up and down, scattering particles of sand and dust all around them until Matthew had to ask, beg, him to stop.

Winded, the boy said, "Think I should go nap?"

"I think you should."

"Will you be here tomorrow?"

Matthew hesitated before telling him, "I might."

"I'll keep lookout," the boy said.

And, giving the young man an exuberant wave, the child sprinted off in the direction from whence he came.

Tuesday, and Matthew didn't make it.

The boy watched the field from the balcony of his house, waiting, glancing at his Mickey Mouse wristwatch, wondering if his new friend would show.

His new friend didn't show.

Little Robby remained on the balcony until the watch beeped to let him know it was three o'clock. Three PM, and Matthew hadn't shown up. It was official. He wasn't coming.

The boy felt a pinch of sadness and disappointment, but figured, somewhere in the back of his six-year-old mind, that a glass of diet orange soda with whipped cream would fix the problem.

"You didn't come yesterday."

"Nope."

"Why not?"

"Why do you want to know?"

"Only stupid people answer a question with another question."

"Funny," Matthew said, "*you've* done it yourself. Answered my question with another question."

"Have not."

"Have too. Don't deny it. I'm older than you, I can remember more."

The boy's forehead wrinkled in thought. "Naw—older you get, less you remember. S'why you sees old people on the telly not bein' able to remember stuff. Always forgettin'."

"Yeah, but I'm not old."

"You're older. Means you remember less."

"But I *know* more."

"Still, you *remember* less," the boy insisted. "I turned six two months ago. I can remember what I was doin' on my birthday. Can you remember what *you* was doin' on *your* sixth birthday?"

Fuckwit, Matthew thought, and had to give in: "No. I think—I think my dad bought me a Garfield cake, but that could've been another birthday, I don't know."

Little Robby grinned smugly. "I remember *my* birthday."

"That's not a legitimate example," Matthew pointed out, ignoring the boy's puzzled expression at the use of the word 'legitimate'. "You remember it because it was recent. By the time you're *my* age, you won't remember your sixth birthday anymore, either."

"I will now, 'cause we're talkin' about it."

"What?"

"I bet you when I'm—how old are you, mister?"

"Twenty-four."

"When I'm twenty-four," little Robby proclaimed, "I will remember what I did on my sixth birthday 'cause I'll be remindin' myself from now 'til then."

"You've got to be kidding."

"No. Every day for the next . . ."—he started counting with his fingers, his lips moving soundlessly as he concentrated—". . . fourteen years, I'll be tellin' myself, 'Think of the cake, and the floatin' balloons', and-and-and . . ."

"You got the math wrong."

"Do *you* remember what movies you were watchin' when *you* was six? No? Well, I promise *I* will when *I'm* twenty-four."

Matthew snorted. "Fine, you win."

All this time, the boy had been standing next to the bench; now, he braved himself and sat down on the hard seat next to Matthew, making sure they were at least a couple of inches apart. Matthew's tub of yoghurt—dessert for the day—had begun to grow warm, and he dug his spoon into the carton and scooped out a big, white, fruit-chunky glob. "You know what this is, kid?" he asked, gesturing to the blob on his spoon.

"Yoghurt?"

"Yeah, yoghurt, but do you know what yoghurt *is?*"

The boy admitted he didn't.

"Have you ever drunk sour milk?" Matthew asked.

The boy made a face, screwing up his freckled features and sticking his tongue out between his teeth. "No! But I've *sniffed* it before! My mummy, she tooks the box out of the fridge once, and she shooks it, and it was all lumpy and chunky, and she told me, she said, 'Robby, the milk's off, don't you touch it', but I didn't know what 'off' means, so I sneaked over and I took the box and I opened it and I sniffed it and it was *eeewww*, it was really yucky, it was really, really gross."

"Well, here's some news for you." Matthew gestured to his spoonful. "This stuff . . ."—a pause for dramatic effect—" . . . *is* . . . really . . . *sour milk.*"

The boy grimaced, and the face he pulled was hilarious. Matthew found himself cracking up as he shovelled the spoonful of yoghurt into his mouth. "No!" the boy screeched. "No, you'll be sick! You'll be sick! My mummy said she drank sour milk and she had runny shits day and night!"

Little Robby was so overwrought, and his last statement was so comical and unexpected that it made Matthew choke. He coughed and coughed and coughed until little Robby, his face contorted in genuine concern, reached over to pat the big guy on his back with his little six-year-old hand.

"**H**ey, mister?"

"What?"

"What do people call you?"

"Huh?"

"What do people call you? Do you have a name?"

"'Course I do. Take a guess."

"Um . . . Jonah?"

"'Jonah'?"

"Like the guy in the Bible."

"I don't read the Bible, boy."

"You've never read the Bible?"

"I didn't say that. I've *read* it, I just don't *read* it anymore."

A contemplative pause. Then: "The guy in the Bible gets eat up by this big fish."

"It was a whale, and whales aren't fish."

"Oh. Okay. So it's not Jonah?"

"No, it's not Jonah."

"Um . . . Ronald?"

"Ronald?"

"Like the clown at McDonald's."

"Aw, gee, thanks a lot, kid."

"It's not Ronald?"

"No, Robby, it's not."

"You know my name?"

"Yeah. I do."

"How do you know it?"

"I'm psychic."

"Psychic freak," little Robby said, and cracked up.

"**M**atthew . . . like one of Jesus' friends? The one who . . . who wrotes the godspel?"

"Gospel. Yes. Matthew, that's right."

"Nice. I wish my mummy named me after one of those friends who wrotes the godspels."

"Well, Robby's just fine. Is it short for Robert?"

The boy shook his head. "Robson."

"Robson? Cool. What's your last name?"

"How'd you know my name?" the boy asked in turn.

"I heard those girls say it. Remember? When you met me last week. They were telling you to go home. Now what's your last name?"

A dark look crossed the boy's face, and he folded his arms. "They aren't very nice."

"Who?" Matthew raised his eyebrow, reaching into a brown paper bag for today's lunch. "The girls?"

Little Robby nodded. "They're mean. I don't like girls." A pause. Then he looked up at Matthew curiously and asked, "Do you like girls, mister?"

"You know my name now; you can call me Matthew."

"Do you like girls, Mister Matthew?"

He pulled out a banana. His sister Michelle had brought a box of fruit home from work. He figured she'd probably swiped it from the supermarket. But then again, probably not: she was too good, too straight an arrow, to pull a stunt like that. "Girls?" he said, when little Robby prodded his right thigh with a little finger. "Yeah, I like girls." He peeled the fruit and stared at it for a moment before offering it to the boy. "You like bananas?"

The child took it, and his little face lit up in an ear-to-ear grin that looked almost painful. "More than I like girls!"

"I've always thought bananas and girls go together." Matthew cackled.

The boy didn't get it, but that was okay. He took a small bite of the fruit, chewed, and pondered on Matthew's response to his question. "I don't like girls," he repeated after a quick swallow. "They're all . . . giggly and curly-haired and yucky."

"Trust me, buddy, you won't feel the same when you're older."

"What's so nice about girls?" the boy asked, looking up at the man with an angst-ridden expression on his face. "They don't like playin' with . . . with robots or football or cars. They wear stupid dresses with stupid ribbony thingies. They don't—they don't talk like me, or sound like me, or—or smell like me, or look like me. Girls are—" He seemed at a loss for words, and he took another tiny bite of banana. "Girls," he tried again, his little forehead furrowed, his hair damp with perspiration.

Without realising he was doing it, Matthew reached out and brushed the boy's hair away from his forehead in a gesture that he would later realise, with a mild jolt, was a vague show of affection. "Different?" he suggested.

The boy looked at him. "Different. I think so. Yeah. Different."

"Well, you'll come to realise when you're older that it's the difference that makes girls very nice."

"I don't get it."

"You will." Matthew grinned. "Trust me."

"Explain," little Robby said, and reached out to grab Matthew's wrist, almost as if he were afraid that Matthew was going to leave. "Please?"

"Aw, come on. It's not easy, kid, it just—is."

The boy continued to stare at him, uncomprehending.

"You know how you just said girls don't talk like us, or smell like us, or look like us? Well, when you're older, you'll learn that *because* they don't talk like us, or smell like us, or look like us, girls are . . . very nice. Especially the 'look like us' bit. And *thinking!*" he exclaimed abruptly, startling little Robby by tapping the boy's left temple with his free hand. "Believe me, girls don't *think* like us, and it can sometimes be very tiring trying to understand what goes on inside their heads, but once you understand them and do whatever crap it takes to make them happy, you'll realise that girls can be very, very, *very* nice."

The boy thought about this for a while, as he did with so much of Matthew's wisdom. Half-eaten banana in hand, he looked straight ahead, into the distance, where the shadow of the tree ended and the bright sunlight dried the already dry ground. Looking at little Robby, Matthew could practically hear the cogwheels of the boy's mind whirring in motion, trying to digest this new, mysterious information, attempting to make sense of it all.

Matthew waited, and ate his lunch.

The boy frowned in apparent incredulity, and muttered under his breath, "I don't like girls."

"Will I see you tomorrow, Mister Matthew?"

"Please. Just Matthew."

"Will I see you tomorrow, Matthew?"

"Well . . ." Tomorrow he needed to do more research on another law paper. He wondered if the girl he'd had a spat with last week had returned the book to the library. The previous assignment had been handed in on Monday; now he had another one, and *Business Law in the 21ˢᵗ Century* might still come in as a good reference. Nevertheless, tomorrow he needed to do some research, even if it meant having lunch in the cafeteria filled with his noisy, smart-aleck contemporaries who always seemed to know a lot more about *everything* than he did.

Little Robby was looking up at him expectantly.

"Sorry, pal, can't make it," Matthew replied.

The boy's disappointment was evident.

"I've work to do," Matthew explained quickly, and later he'd wonder why the child's look of disappointment had affected him so much. "It's school stuff, a lot of—homework," he said, using a word the boy would understand. *Except the child didn't go to school, did he? No, little Robby's mum seemed content with him being educated at home, for whatever reason . . .*

"You still go to school?" little Robby asked, sounding awed.

"Well . . . university. You know what university is?"

"Sorta. It's, like, after school, right?"

"Yeah. I'm studying law."

The boy looked at him uncertainly.

"I'm going to be a lawyer," Matthew said, suppressing the idea that it would only happen *if* he saw the whole course through. "You know, like you see on TV?"

The boy's expression remained.

"Look, all you have to know is, lawyers help people."

"Kids, too?"

"Well, depends. There are lawyers who help grown-ups, and there are lawyers who help kids. So I don't know yet. But I'm thinking I'll probably be the kind who helps grown-ups."

"Not kids?"

"Uh-uh."

"Why not?"

Without thinking: "I don't like kids."

A pause. A dark look crossed the child's face, and it struck Matthew that he might have made a mistake there. "Except you," he said quickly. "You and . . . many others," he added, although it was clear this wasn't a good save.

In a quiet voice: "Why don't you like kids, mis—Matthew?"

Great. Just great. Just when he thought he'd been establishing a rapport with the boy, the boy just *had* to transform into a brat. "Because," Matthew answered, and sighed, folding his arms across his chest. How could he explain it? Kids were—annoying. They were whiny, and too nosy for their own damn good, and too *clingy*. However, Matthew had begun to think of little Robby as being set apart. Sure, the kid was nosy, but he wasn't *too* whiny. And as for being clingy . . . well, sometimes interesting things could be learned if you allowed yourself to be clung to. But what irked Matthew now was that the kid seemed to be sensitive. Yes. *Too* sensitive, which could lead to the assumption that the kid had a *propensity* for whininess. Damn.

The boy was silent for a while. Finally, he said, "I wanna be a doctor."

Silence. Anticipatory.

Matthew asked, "Why a doctor?"

Silence. Anticipatory.

The boy answered, "I want to help other people."

"Really."

The boy nodded solemnly. "Many, many sick people out there. Not just here, but . . . all over the world. Many, many sick people, not enough doctors."

"Yeah. I guess."

"Y'know, I sees on TV all these sick people, makes me wanna cry," and suddenly he sounded very much like the child he was: innocent, ambitious, vulnerable. "Makes me feel all sad and stuff, inside."

Matthew continued to nod, his arms crossed. He felt an unexpected flash of—what felt like *guilt*—as he thought about how his father had always been pestering him to join the guild of doctors, to take up medicine as a profession. "To help people," Jonathan Leigh would persistently urge. "Think of how you'd be contributing to the greater good." But Matthew was well aware of the numerous messages that were not being stated: "Keep up the family tradition!" "Make me a proud father!" "Make us tons of money!" *Sorry, Dad, but you'll have to keep urging Michelle on, because I'm not going to do it . . .*

"You ever cry when you sees these sick people?" the boy asked, jolting him out of his reverie.

Matthew chuckled, but there was very little humour in it. "I don't cry."

"You don't cry?"

"No. Big guys don't cry, kid."

The child looked at him unblinking. Then: What happens if you're sad?"

"You just deal with it."

"Huh?"

"Just deal with it. Get over it. Solve the problem. Whatever. Just make sure you don't cry. It's not good for you; it makes you soft inside. Big guys don't cry."

"But—"

"But what?"

Again, the boy frowned, obviously mulling this new advice over. Matthew expected him to pursue it, but was surprised when little Robby reverted to the original thread of the conversation, saying, "You ever thought of bein' a doctor, mister?"

"Yeah," Matthew replied, eyebrows raised. "I have."

"And?"

"And—I'm sticking to being a lawyer."

"Why? Don't you wanna help people?"

"Lawyers *do* help people. And it's strange how you wanna be a doctor when you grow up, considering how last week you said you'd like to be a bird."

The boy gave him a long, inscrutable look.

"You know," Matthew said, suddenly feeling silly, "because birds . . . don't . . . study . . . medicine."

"Birds help other birds."

"True."

"Doctors help other people."

"Yes."

"And lawyers help other people?"

"That's right."

"But not how doctors help people."

"No, not in the same way, no."

"Do lawyers make people get better?"

"Um." Matthew pursed his lips. "I guess. They help people get out of trouble."

The boy thought about this for a long while. Eventually: "You're not comin' here tomorrow?"

Disconcerted by the abrupt change of subject, Matthew replied, "I—guess not."

"Then I won't be waitin' for you," little Robby replied, and slid off the bench.

As he disappeared behind the tree into the distance, Matthew remained with his lunch bag in one hand and the other on the seat next to him, wondering if he'd said something to piss the child off. Because—unless he was being as oversensitive as he'd earlier accused little Robby of being—he could have sworn the conversation had been cut short by an unexpected mood swing in the boy.

Fuck it, he thought after a moment's hesitation, and got up to go, leaving the banana peel on the seat to blacken in the heat of the day.

BETTER LEFT BURIED

Alone in the house, Graham Hanson sat in his favourite hardback chair at his desk in the living room. The desk's surface was littered with envelopes and colourful pages of writing paper, most of them faded with age, the once-white sheets a monochromic shade of yellow. The sweet, if somewhat musty, scent of Felicity's perfume, with which she had sprayed each letter, lingered in the air, rising from the open envelopes in front of him.

It had been a tiring week, and Graham had only now realised how truly saddened he was by the events that had unfolded. The memories of all the good times he'd had with Aunt Phyl had finally caught up with him, and, as he sat gazing at the old letters, he wondered if, perhaps, he should have spent more time with the woman before she'd moved on. Then he reminded himself that he'd been with her for most of his younger years, and had remained a filial relative despite the distance that had gradually grown between them: the natural rift that germinates, even if imperceptibly, between extended-family members who do not live together. Still, everybody needs to mourn, no matter how one chooses to do it. For Graham Hanson, catharsis lay in the form of spending some quiet time alone in his own home.

It had been a tiring week because everybody he knew had learned of Phyl's passing, and had taken the (frequently unnecessary, in his opinion) time and effort to approach him and express their condolences in one way or another. On Monday, for instance, he and Felicity had driven up to the children's shelter where they helped out, and Marguerite Dumont had greeted him with a suffocating embrace. "She was a very, very special part of our family here at the shelter," Dumont had gushed, near tears with emotion. "And we're all very, very sorry for the loss." A lot of verys—too many.

Graham breathed a sigh of relief that the younger children had likely been spared the news, judging by how they hadn't reacted any differently towards him. No need for the young 'uns to learn about death before they needed to. Some of the older children, however, expressed how sorry they were over Phyl's passing. Graham had even been startled by the tears some of them had shed, until Felicity reminded him that Phyllis used to help out in the children's shelter as well and the children had cherished her. In fact, Phyllis had been the one who'd introduced him and Felicity to the establishment.

Now, sitting in his favourite chair, Graham picked up a sheet of scented paper at random. The faint whiff of sandalwood floated up from the leaf, and he breathed deeply, inhaling the spicy fragrance. The paper was brittle with age, but the words—a neat fountain-pen scrawl in black ink—were still clear. It was the (extremely) brief message he had sent to Felicity during his college days in London to obtain his doctorate in Education. At the time, they had been engaged—the wedding was to take place once he returned.

> *Dear Felicity,*
> *I miss you.*
>
> *With lots and lots of love,*
> *G*

"I was touched by the effort," she'd later told him dryly.

"I couldn't help it," he'd replied. Each time he'd thought of her, he'd missed her so intensely that it had been hard to go on with the day. So it'd been easier to temporarily push her out of his mind; hence the short letter, written quickly so that he wouldn't have to spend too much time thinking about her. It might be nauseatingly sweet, he acknowledged, but such was the depth of his love for her: crippling.

Graham put the envelope down and scanned the surface of the desk. So many letters, so many memories, but they weren't all there: naturally, some of the writings had gone missing over the years. But for what remained, he was grateful neither he nor Felicity had had the bad sense to throw them out. He was planning to start work on his memoirs, and these documents would come in useful.

Especially the pink envelope that lay on the far left-hand corner of the desk—the one with the faint imprint of children's building blocks on it. The letter that had made him shed tears when he'd read it; the letter that must have taken Felicity all of her courage and fortitude to write. She'd sprayed baby cologne into the envelope before folding the flap down, unsealed, and placing it under a loose floorboard in the living room—the floorboard that could still be lifted up, if not for the rug they had decided to place over it. Graham had accidentally come upon it when he'd desperately searched for a lost stamp that had gone missing from his philatelic collection. Prying the floorboards apart, he'd discovered the loose plank—complete with the letter secreted underneath. He'd supposed Felicity had not intended for him to find it, but that hadn't stopped him from pulling the note out and reading it.

He'd cried. How he'd cried.

My darling child,

You might not have been born, but that doesn't mean I don't love you. You might not be here, but that doesn't mean that your Daddy and I don't think about you. You will always be alive in our hearts. I am so sorry. Please forgive me for not being able to bring you into our beautiful world.

I try not to cry, but please understand it's not always easy for Mummy to be strong. You are a treasure that we, for the time being, are not meant to possess. Although I am of the conviction that it is the will of the Almighty, I still shed tears thinking of how precious and wonderful you could have been and you are, and how I regret not being able to share our profusion of love for you, with you.

Maybe one day you will come into our lives, but until then, I can only keep on praying and thinking of how beautiful your little nursery shall be, with its light-blue walls and the vintage cot I used to sleep in, which you shall sleep in. Your grandmother kept so many of my old toys, and I look forward to the day I can share them with you: old Bronson, my rocking horse; my Jack-in-the-Box; the alphabet blocks with which I learned to read. So many toys, my sweetheart, my darling. All waiting for you.

One day I know I will come to an understanding of why you are not a part of our lives. But until that day, your Daddy and I cling to each other in the hope that we will see you, and you will know us, and you will be part of the love that your Daddy and I share for each other, copious and overflowing, waiting to be shared with that special little person who is a part of our very flesh and blood and spirit.

I love you, my precious darling. I love you, and your Daddy loves you, and I am so, so sorry. Please forgive me, my love. Be here soon.

> *With lots of hugs and kisses,*
> *Your loving Mummy.*

"*Why? Oh, my dear Jesus, Felicity—*"

"*It was—it was a prayer, Graham. Just a prayer.*"

His face was buried against her belly, the belly that would remain flat, would never bulge with the treasure they so hoped to create. He shed tears of grief, in mourning for the child they so wanted to have but could not. She put his arms around him as he held her and sobbed and wailed and cried like a baby. He cried and cried as she comforted him and loved him. And, with the instincts of the mother that she was never meant to be, she cried, too.

The memory of that day still brought tears to his eyes. It had been a day of sadness, but also a day of self-development, as Graham had found a way to confront his deep, hidden feelings of loss, and the denial he had previously been living in, treating the lack of a child as "no big deal".

He picked the envelope up, but just to place it at the bottom of the desk drawer where all their written memories were kept.

Some things were better left buried.

SCREWING WITH THE CONCEPT

The week seemed to have gone by in a complete blur for Derrick Weston, who had, for the time being, moved out of his apartment and into Sanjeev's beachside home. If anybody asked him what he'd done over the week, he would mumble, "I dunno." Because he'd spent most of his time sitting on the sand by the ocean, watching the push-and-pull of the waves, trying to stop his badly broken heart from breaking into even smaller pieces. He had even gone to the extent of requesting a fortnight's leave from work, taking up most of his remaining days of leave. Geraldine had to be pushed out of the picture, he kept on telling himself. But actions proved harder than words. Subsequently, he began forcing himself to get as much sleep as possible, because slumber meant relief. Assuming, of course, that he didn't dream about Geraldine *and Hope, having Hope, doing Hope —*

"I hate you!"

He didn't realise he had uttered the words aloud, but when he looked down the sandy shore, he saw a little girl with a tiny bucket and three miniature sandcastles staring at him in dismay. Derrick blushed and broke eye contact, feeling stupid and feeling indecisive and feeling great anguish in his heart.

Who exactly did he hate, he wondered — Geraldine or Hope? Or both of them? After all, it takes two to tango, as the adage went. *Damn them*, he swore, and began to comb the beach with his hands, squeezing tiny mounds of sand tightly before letting them trickle through his fingers. *Damn them, those go∂∂amn le∫bo∫, fin∂ing comfort in each other an∂ playing with each other an∂ ∫inning, ∫inning,* sinning—*!*

"Fuck you!" he shouted aloud.

"Come on, darling, he might be dangerous," the little girl's mother urged, dragging her daughter away.

Derrick felt another surge of heat to his face. Sighing, he looked at the sun setting on the horizon, but couldn't come to appreciate the beauty of it. In fact, none of the panoramic beachside views registered in his mind; all he could think about was the girls, the girls, the girls. How bloody unfair this situation was. Things had been going so well—why did God have to screw things up like this? (He'd never been a big believer until he'd met Geraldine. Since then, he'd found it a lot easier to blame God when nothing was going right. Isn't that what most people did when things got topsy-turvy? Blame God. That's okay, He's big enough, Geraldine had once told him. Well, okay then.)

He wanted to lie there and gaze into oblivion. He wanted to start wading into the ocean and never stop. He wanted to shut his eyes and sleep forever. He wanted to pound his head against a brick wall until his skull caved in. He wanted to go out with Sanjeev and Chitra and get drunk, as he had that Saturday night nearly a week ago. He wanted to stab Geraldine and Hope in their little gay hearts over and over and over again. He wanted to hold Geraldine in his arms the way he always used to, and kiss her. He wanted to tell her how much he hated her. He wanted to tell her how much he loved her. He wasn't sure what the hell he wanted.

Sanjeev had been a good friend as always. He understood that Derrick needed his space and didn't bother him very much, although he wandered down to the beach every now and then to ask if Derrick was in need of anything—a drink, some lunch, some Prozac. Derrick would usually wave him away, not wanting any attention. But a couple of days ago, on Wednesday, they'd entered into a very interesting, heated and controversial discussion: religion versus human rights and personal desire. It was a subject that Derrick had very fixed opinions on. Sanjeev had known it and had been hesitant to engage in such a dialogue, but he hadn't been able to get away. So he'd decided to stay and let Derrick thrash it out, knowing Derrick needed an outlet. And so they'd wandered along the shore, the roar of waves in their ears failing to drown out Derrick's rage:

"She's Catholic! She's God-fearing! She reads the Bible! She knows what's right and what's wrong, how the *hell* can she possibly even *think* that *this* is what God wants of her? Jesus!" he profaned at the top of his lungs, causing Sanjeev to thank the Lord that they were in a wide-open and virtually deserted space at eleven o'clock on a weeknight. "Who the hell is she trying to fool here? How the hell can she *live* with the sort of guilt that these kind of sick, twisted sexual activities must rouse in her? And for the love of God, *Hope* knows all about Geraldine's religious background—how can she condone this? It doesn't make sense! It just doesn't make any fucking sense!"

As Derrick raved, Sanjeev drew little circles in the sand with his big toe. Light shone down from the oblate moon high in the sky, reflecting in the waves, illumining the shoreline. It was beautiful, even if Derrick's outburst wasn't. "And Geraldine's parents, for crying out loud—isn't Geri *thinking* about them at *all?* What the hell are they going to *say* about this? Are they supposed to accept this—this perverse fornication that their daughter is committing on a daily basis, and just let it go? Fuck, no! She's so selfish, so unbelievably selfish, and Hope is so goddamn selfish as well, why the hell can't they *see* that this is wrong, wrong, wrong, wrong, *wrong!*"

"Okay, calm down now," Sanjeev murmured.

"Can't," Derrick responded, his voice cracking with emotion. "I . . . I don't know, I just can't bear the thought—" He sobbed softly, and abruptly laughed. The sound was ugly, filled with irony and frustration and resentment at his ex-girlfriend and the entire world and the Almighty. "I just don't know, Jeev, I'm falling apart. I can't eat, I can't sleep, I can't think about anything else . . ."

"On top of that, your hair's falling out," Sanjeev contributed.

"What am I going to *do?*"

They'd finally decided to sit. Their butts were made damp by the wave-washed sand. "Listen to me, Rick," Sanjeev said gently. "I honestly think you have to stop beating yourself up about this and try to think a little more rationally. Wait, let me finish. I know this is incredibly hard, but you've got to try and give Geri a chance to explain herself, you know? I mean, like Chit and I said the other night, this must be driving her crazy as well. I'm sure she has a lot to say to you, if you only you'd give her a chance. Hear her out, that's my advice. It's not going to be easy, but if you put your heart and soul into it, you can do it. Just let her talk. But not now. Only when you're ready to see her again."

Ready to see her again, Derrick now thought, as the sun began to disappear into the water. *What a joke.*

Will I ever *be ready to see her again?*

The night was chilly, and the three figures huddled under the tree, dressed in warm clothing. Hope had her arm around Geraldine's waist, and they were seated in close proximity. Next to Geraldine, Jason Marcel, their upstairs neighbour, rubbed his gloved hands together and blew at them.

"It's been a week," Geraldine spoke up softly, as Jason muttered something about having sat on somebody's discarded banana peel. "He still hasn't called. Chit told me he's at Sanjeev's place, but I just—I just wish we could talk."

"Screw him," Jason remarked.

"Aw, thanks, Jase, that really helps," Hope said sarcastically.

He grinned. "No, I meant, could I? He's cute."

"Screw you," Hope snapped, shaking her head.

"Intelligent conversation," Geraldine muttered. "You gotta love it."

Hope caressed Geraldine's back. "Come on, Ger. I'm sure Dick just needs his time and space is all. Jeev's a pretty smart dude, he'll talk some sense into him."

"Yeah, but Derrick's — Derrick," Geraldine said, and didn't elaborate. She sighed, rubbed her face with her palms. "I feel — I don't know, I feel pissed off, and upset, and frightened — a whole *multitude* of things, and it's awful."

"You talk to God, don't you?" Jason asked. "Doesn't that help?"

Geraldine sighed a third time. "God's another problem."

"How's that?"

"He makes me mad."

"Oh, honey, now, listen, I'm a good old-fashioned free-thinker myself — love and respect, that's my creed — but the last thing you wanna do is be mad at God."

"Too late."

"Well, personally I'm glad," Hope spoke up. "I don't think I want to believe in a God who causes such distress to His people." She shrugged. "My life has been a hellhole since day one, and the only good thing I've gotta be thankful for is that I finally found myself somebody to love."

"Come on," Jason said. "How about how that Italian guy who gave you the job at the salon, huh? Pulled you off the streets, stopped you pumping all that shit into your body, shaped you into a working member of society again, didn't he? That's what you're always telling us, anyway. What was his name? Melancholy something?"

"Marcioni."

"Marcioni, that's right. *He* seems like a godsend."

"Yeah, but was he sent by God?" Hope shot back.

Geraldine sniffed. "You know the Bible . . ."

"I've read it," Jason said. "It was really long."

"It has so many passages about homosexuality and how it's wrong and you'll be thrown into the pit of fire and stuff like that, it just makes me think that — well, if God were so all-knowing and all-loving, He'd realise the delicate situation that people like us are in. But it firmly states — in the Old Testament *and* in the New — that homosexuality is wrong, wrong, wrong. Condemnation! Punish the sinners!"

"Ah, but the concept of Christ was that He would be freedom from sin," Jason said.

"I'm surprised at you, Jason. If anything, I'd think the verses in the Bible about homosexuality apply more to *men* than to women," Hope said pointedly, even though it wasn't necessarily an accurate point.

"I like to think the word 'men' applies to 'mankind', not just the gender group," Jason countered. "And so what? I wouldn't take every word in the Bible literally. I don't think it's *meant* to be read literally. Like the whole thing about Adam and Eve, and how many people think they were the only two people in the Garden at the start of time. But I read somewhere that 'Adam' is Hebraic for 'man', and many theologians believe the Adam in the Bible symbolises all males, while Eve symbolises all females. So you can't take every word in the Bible at face value, I think."

"So you're saying the Bible is wrong," Hope said.

"I didn't say that."

"But it is, isn't it?"

"No, I just think—whether it's the Bible, or the Torah, or the Koran or whatever—you've got to read deeper than what's there. And anyhow, who knows for sure how many people there really were when Adam and Eve existed? The person who wrote *Genesis* wasn't present at the time."

"You're contradicting yourself, honey," Hope rebutted. "So now you're saying the 'Good Book' isn't necessarily accurate?"

"Not 'accurate' in the sense that *we* know it. I mean, the works in the Bible *were* written by people, and people make mistakes, too."

"Right, but shouldn't God have inspired them? If God inspired them, doesn't that mean the Bible is absolutely accurate? And shouldn't that mean that the whole homosexuality thing is, as it says, a sin? After all, the Bible *is* the Word of God, and if the Bible is flawed, then isn't *God* flawed? No, God cannot be flawed, that's what everybody says—and therefore, the Bible *isn't* flawed either, is it? Because if the Word of God was written by God-inspired people, then it has to be right—because God cannot be wrong, right?"

"Yeah, but . . ."

"So homosexuality's wrong. As it clearly states."

"I don't know . . ."

"And so if we were to go by the Biblical standard, we're all sinners. We're all going to hell because we're committing foul transgressions each and every day, in our thoughts, in our words, in all that we fail to do, isn't that right, darling? We're all going to burn for all eternity, aren't we?"

"Hope, this isn't helping," Geraldine groaned wearily.

"I think it's pretty much set in black and white that we're all committing hideously wicked things and we're going to be punished," Hope went on heedlessly. "So where's this all-loving, all-forgiving God we're talking about? The God who is slow to judge but quick to bless? If the Bible says we're damned because of our sexuality, where's this deliverance? Where's the pardon? Or is God *truly* all-forgiving, and the Bible is wrong, which, ultimately, one way or the other, makes *God* wrong?" She snorted loudly. "If you ask me, somewhere along the way mankind has screwed with this concept of God so much that it's all a pile of mumbo-jumbo now. And I think the best thing to do is to just forget it. Don't believe. Don't believe in the Bible, don't believe in God, don't believe in anything. If you don't believe in something, it ceases to exist in your world, and that's good enough for me. So I don't feel wrong about what we're doing . . . it's wrong according to *whom?* Not God. God doesn't exist," she said, rubbing Geraldine's back again.

Geraldine uttered a cry of frustration. "But it's wrong to *me!*"

Hope pulled her arm away, sighing.

"It feels wrong, even though it's wonderful, but I just can't help but wonder . . . how . . ." Geraldine shook her head, trying to untangle the mess of thoughts and feelings within. "I wish I could somehow *stop* believing in God, so there's no conflict of the flesh versus the spirit. This sucks! But I can't simply stop believing, I've been Catholic since I was born; my mum still calls me every Sunday to make sure I go to *church*, for the love of God! It's so easy to think maybe God made me this way, and this wonderful thing between us is meant to be, but the Bible says *this* and we're thinking *that*, and nothing makes sense, and I'm just so fucking tired of the whole goddamn sexuality issue! I'm all sexed out!"

In her mind, she began to construct poetry out of the situation, as she tended to do when her stress levels got high:

> *Oh, God,*
>> *Why do You*
>>> *Taunt and tease*
>> *Us, the*
>>> *Lesser*
>>>> *Mortals*
>> *Of Your*
>>> *Creation?*

"Honey, honey, calm down," Hope said soothingly. "Please. I'm sorry."

"I think of sin as something that hurts other people," Jason said softly, patting Geraldine's shoulder. "What we're doing—it doesn't hurt others, so where's the sin?"

"Haven't I just hurt Derrick?" Geraldine responded dejectedly.

They stopped talking momentarily, listening to the cool wind rustling the leaves in the trees, and a cicada or two chirping in the distance. Hope returned to stroking Geraldine's back; Jason unconsciously rubbed at a tattoo on his arm. Then came the sound of footfalls, and they turned to find a couple, silhouetted in darkness, standing on the edge of the field to their left. The couple had obviously intended to sit on the bench, but they stopped and turned around, seeing the three of them occupying the space. As they disappeared, Jason said, "I think it was a boy and a girl. Damn, have *they* got it easy. If only they knew."

Geraldine sighed for the umpteenth time that evening. "If only he'd talk to me."

"He who?" Jason asked quietly. "Derrick, or God?"

She looked to the skies. "Whoever," she replied, exhausted. "Whoever."

FERTILITY CAN YIELD
UNEXPECTED FRUIT

They walked away from the field, his arm across her shoulders, warm and pleasant. "We can just sit in my car and talk," he suggested.

Maggie Cooke smiled wanly as they headed back to Zack McPherson's Corolla, parked at the edge of the field. They got in and sat in darkness. For a moment neither of them spoke. Maggie turned to glance out the passenger window at the row of houses across the road—at her own house in particular. Zack touched her arm gently, bringing her attention back to him. "You okay?"

"Yeah," she lied.

"Come on," he said, and smiled that amazing smile of his. There was empathy and concern in his expression, and suddenly she felt the urge to spill everything. But she hesitated. *No need to saddle him with my troubles,* she thought, in spite of his prompting. And how to tell him that—probably because of everything that was going on at home—she'd been feeling sick to her stomach all day, had even thrown up that morning? Not exactly prime date conversation, she thought.

"Talk to me."

"It's . . . it's really nothing."

"Doesn't seem like nothing. You've been distracted all night."

"I'm sorry."

"No, don't be. We all have troubles, but . . . sometimes it's good to talk about them."

"Well," she said, and stopped there, thinking.

After Paul Cooke's late-night appearance last Saturday, Jessy had told Maggie and Joe that they wouldn't be seeing their father for a while. While it wasn't unexpected, Maggie had nonetheless been stunned by the news. It had come true: her parents were breaking up. "We are *not* breaking up," Jessy told her, seeing the tears in her daughter's eyes. "We're just — taking a break. A break from each other. Every couple does this once in a while."

Right, Maggie thought dolefully. *Of* course *they do.*

"If you think about it," Jessy added, "it really is for the best."

Right. Of course *it is.*

Then there was her brother. How often over the course of the week had Joe been out with that girlfriend of his? He spent almost all of his waking hours at her place, and sometimes — *most* times — stayed over. Didn't the girl have parents? Didn't they wonder what she was doing with a boy practically every night of the week? Or did this girl, whoever she was, live on her own? More importantly, didn't Joe realise how inconsiderate it was of him to stay away from home, taking advantage of their mother's preoccupied state?

"You know you can talk to me anytime, Mags," Zack spoke up softly, and she was thrilled to realise that he had called her by a new pet name. *Mags.* "About anything," he said earnestly. "I mean — I think . . ." He paused, seemed to gather his thoughts, and whispered, "Joe has mentioned — some things — about your mum and dad, and I'm . . . I'm sorry."

Oh. Maggie blinked, working her jaw without making any sound. *So he knows about that. Thanks, Joe.*

After several seconds, she managed: "*I'm* the one who should be sorry, Zack. This was supposed to be a fun night, but I'm bringing it down . . ."

"Hey, no, don't think that," he cut her off. "Look, it's hard for you to have fun when there're these kinds of problems hovering all around you, you know? I've—I've been there, too. My parents . . ." He paused, and now it was his turn to become reticent. He licked his lips and stared out the windscreen before going on: "They got divorced a long time ago. I live with my dad. I miss my mum a lot, but I don't get to see very much of her. She's—far away. So . . . yeah, I know what you're going through, and it's tough, it's really shitty, but you're—you're going to pull through, you know? I know *I* did. And I think . . . you're strong. You're a strong person, you can get through this, no problems."

A moment of silence went by, with Zack continuing to look out the windscreen, and Maggie gazing at him from the passenger seat.

Finally, touched, she reached over and squeezed his hand. "Thanks, Zack."

He smiled at her. "You're very welcome." And he reached for her. She slid towards him as he put his arms around her shoulders, held her there protectively, and lowered his face to kiss her tenderly on the lips.

"It's a lot more comfortable in the backseat. What do you say?"

She hesitated.

"Come on," he whispered, and began to climb out of the car.

She waited, wondering, unsure.

And then she made up her mind.

The house was dark by the time she made it up the driveway and onto the front porch. Then she was inside, and she made her way into the kitchen, feeling thirsty and warm in spite of the coolness of the night. As she stepped through the kitchen doorway, she stopped short, seeing a dark figure seated at the dining table. It took a moment for her eyes to adjust to the darkness, but once they did, she realised it was her brother, nursing a mug in his hands. He didn't look up when she entered, didn't acknowledge her as she stood there, staring at him. A few seconds passed before she cleared her throat and whispered, "Hey."

He nodded, barely perceptibly. "Hey."

She reached for the light switch, flipped it. Joe groaned loudly as the light filled the room, and he shook his head, squeezing his eyes shut. When he opened them, she saw his panda eyes were bloodshot. He looked exhausted. He looked dreadful. Joe was still dressed in his day clothes—scruffy jeans, much in need of a wash, and a faded grey stonewashed t-shirt under his cracked leather jacket. He smelled faintly of booze, and she wondered what was in his mug, although there was the hint of coffee about him.

She filled a glass with tap water, then moved to sit across from her brother. "You all right?"

He shrugged, a vague movement.

"Is Mum . . . ?"

"She's asleep."

"Yeah, but is she okay . . . ?"

"I think so. I don't know. Don't care."

"Don't care? Jeez, Joe, she's—"

"*Don't,*" he said sharply, holding out one hand to stop her in mid-sentence. "I know, okay? Just—don't."

A terse silence ensued, and she broke it by slurping at her tepid water. Placing the glass on the table, she whispered, "Are you missing Dad, Joe? Is that it?"

"I don't want to talk about it."

"Joe, if you're missing Dad, that's okay."

"I *said*—look, just leave me alone."

"I miss him, too. But you know how he is, and how he's been treating us and all . . ."

"It has nothing to do with—"

". . . I think maybe Mum was right, maybe we really are better off . . ."

"You're with Zack," Joe cut in abruptly, and now he was looking her in the eye. "Aren't you?"

She stopped, taken aback. "Well, we've been going out . . ."

"How's he been treating you?"

"He's been—okay."

He laughed, a disdainful sound. "If he's been trashing you . . ."

"He hasn't. He wouldn't do that."

Another laugh. Short and scathing. Scornful.

"He wouldn't do that, right?"

He shrugged. "I don't know. But he better not mess around with you, Maggie, because if he does . . ." He smiled then, a simulacrum of a smile, letting the statement hang in the air.

She glanced at the tabletop, suddenly awash with uncertainty. "I—I can take care of myself, Joe."

The smile faded. "I hope so."

"No, I *can.* I mean it."

"I really hope so."

"I mean, I'm—you know. And Zack—he's not a bad guy, right? He's really nice and sweet and all, so what have I got to be afraid of, right?"

"Well . . . if you think he's nice, then he's nice, I suppose."

"What about *your* girl?" she returned. "Is she nice?"

"As nice as you can get."

"So what's the problem?" She laughed, unwarranted, with absolutely no trace of humour in it. "If it isn't Mum or Dad that's bothering you, that only leaves . . . her."

"There's no problem."

"Really."

"Yeah. Everything's cool. Now get lost."

She sighed and finished off the last of her water. Wanting more, she headed back to the sink and refilled, then returned to the table, where Joe was sipping from his mug. The smell of coffee was stronger now, mixed with the stench of booze—a cloying combination. Sitting down, she asked, "So, *do* you miss Dad?"

Joe brought the mug down upon the tabletop with a loud *clunk*, and Maggie winced. He snapped, "He was never really around, anyway, so what's there to miss?"

"Still, he *used* to be around," she ventured.

"Whatever, I don't care."

"Really?"

"Really. I don't."

"You don't care."

"No, I don't. Now will you just leave me alone?"

"This is Dad we're talking about. And Mum."

"Well, I don't *want* to be talking about Dad and Mum, okay? Lay off."

"I mean, jeez, Joe, Dad—"

"I don't want to talk about him!" This time, he raised his voice, then quickly lowered it when he remembered their mother was in bed upstairs. He sighed and shook his head angrily. "Look, Maggie, I've got more important things on my mind, more pressing matters, and I really don't want to be thinking about how Dad has screwed us all up, and how easily he thinks he can get onto his horse and ride off into the sunset without looking back. I don't want to be talking about how Mum's crying her eyes out every night, and how I'm suddenly expected to become the man of the house just because our irresponsible father has taken off, being the fucking chicken shit that he is!" Now his eyes were wide, intense with fury, and she saw him gripping the handle of his mug so tightly that his knuckles were chalk-white. "Got it?" he hissed.

Maggie looked at the tabletop again. There was a discoloured circle in the wood caused by a bowl of soup that had been too hot for the table without a coaster, a lighter patch of brown that stood out against the rest of the furnishing. She'd caused it—unintentionally, of course—how many years ago had it been? Four? Five? Her mother had let out a protracted sigh of exasperation when Maggie had lifted the bowl to reveal the pale scorch mark, but Maggie had known she was only teasing her. Their father had not been at the table at the time, oddly enough. *Oddly enough.*

"Is that what you're worried about?" Her voice was small, kittenish. "That you're suddenly the man of the house?"

Silence.

"I think — I think we can all cope if we work at this together, you know?" she said.

"I don't know," Joe mumbled. "And what the hell do *you* know?"

She looked at him, a little stung. "I'm old enough to understand a lot of things, Joe."

"Huh. Yeah, well . . ."

"I mean, I'm going to be sixteen."

"Sixteen, schmixteen."

"I know a lot more than you think."

He gazed into his coffee cup, the corners of his lips upturned in a cynical smile.

She sighed. "I'm not sure I want to keep leaving the window open for you."

Joe looked up and smirked. "That's fine. I'll just head out the front, no big deal." Another beat, and Joe tapped the tabletop once with his fingernail. "I mean, it's not as if Mum's in any state to tell me off about going out anyway, not with her mind so transfixed on . . ." He didn't complete the sentence. They seemed to be doing a lot of that lately. "And for Christ's sake, don't tell me off about how I shouldn't be taking advantage of Mum's situation. Because as far as I'm concerned, you have no right to be staying out after midnight with Zack McPherson either."

"That's none of your business, Joe," she said, and regretted it, knowing what he'd respond.

He did: "And *my* life is none of *your* business, Maggie."

She opened her mouth to refute, but did a double take and said instead, "I was just worried, that's all."

"Well, thank you, but I think I can cope perfectly well without your concern. And FYI, you going out with Zack McPherson *is* my business, because I know Zack. And I know you. And I know that Zack's the kind of guy who can—who will—screw you over. Or you might screw *him* over, I don't know." Maggie frowned. Her brother shook his head and snorted derisively. "Whatever the case, you and Zack? It's my business. Me and my chick? You don't know her. She doesn't know you. It's not *your* business."

"Fine, whatever," she replied, definitely stung. "Excuse me for caring." She gazed into her glass of water, suddenly preoccupied with some invisible thing that had begun to swim in it, and realised her vision was blurring because she was about to cry. But she didn't want to cry in front of Joe, not in front of Big Brother; she had too much pride for that. So she waited, and pushed her lips tightly together, feeling her lower jaw tremble with tired emotion, and prayed for the hurt feelings to pass.

Joe must have felt guilty, because, after a seemingly interminable round of silence, he whispered, "I'm angry at him. Are you angry at him?"

"Who?" she asked. The tears dribbled down her cheeks anyway, damn it. "Who are we talking about? Zack?"

"No, silly," he said, and chuckled feebly. "Dad."

"You're mad at him?"

"It isn't fair of him to leave. I know his running off is long overdue, but . . ." He shrugged. Maggie perceived in the gesture more tumultuous emotion than he probably realised: betrayal, hopelessness and desperation exposed in that brief, ambiguous movement. "I sometimes think he should just drop dead, you know? He and whichever cheap trash bimbo he's fucking. I mean, screwing. I mean—you know." He let out an inappropriate laugh, much like she had earlier. "He's never been much of a father, anyway, sis," he whispered, and his words caused more tears to spill from her eyes. *Damn, damn, damn, stop crying, please stop crying,* she prayed, as he went on quietly, "It's always been Mum, you realise that, don't you? It's always been just Mum. Dad's just—he's just . . . a guy. A guy who's been causing nothing but trouble, you realise? I think—I think this *is* for the best, don't you?"

She struggled against the blitzkrieg of tears that threatened to erupt. "Who are you trying to convince, Joe?" she choked out. "Me, or you?"

"God, I don't know." He sniffed once, ran a hand over his face, across his red-rimmed eyes. "Maybe you. Maybe me. I really don't know. But—we'll pull through, right?"

She didn't reply. She didn't think the question needed a response.

A little while later, she got to her feet, wiping tears away with the back of one hand. "I'm going to bed. Want me to turn the light off?"

He nodded, holding the mug of spiked coffee to his chest. "Yeah, thanks. Good night."

She replied, "Sleep easy," and winced at how trite it sounded.

Sleep easy, Joe thought, and cringed in the darkness of the kitchen. *What a stupid thing to say.*

How could anybody in his position 'sleep easy' after a night like this?

First, there had been the latest argument with his mother earlier that evening. Well, *yesterday* evening, since it was already after midnight. He couldn't even remember what they'd fought about. Jessy had raised her voice, which in turn had caused him to raise his, and not before long they were yelling at each other in the living room, with the dirt-filled dustpan and the broom Jessy had been using lying inert and apathetic on the floor. It had something to do with Mum suspecting that Joe had been spending too much time with Carrie, and how if he wasn't careful, he was going to end up "just like your father".

That had hurt, and Joe had shouted a profanity at his mother before storming out the front door.

He'd got into his mother's car and had driven circles around the block before finally deciding to stop at Carrie's place. When he entered Carrie's granny flat, he gave free rein to his pent-up emotions and cried against her shoulder, sobbing nearly incoherently about how fucked-up life was, and how things never should have happened this way. Then, in an effort to shift his mind away from the nightmarish circumstances surrounding his life, he'd pushed himself against Carrie, hoping to taste her once again, hoping she'd be able to satisfy his desires as she had in the past. Sex therapy.

But she'd pushed him away, much to his surprise.

"Carrie—what—?"

"Joe, please, don't."

"I don't—did I do something wrong?"

"No. I—I guess I'm just not in the mood."

He laughed uncertainly. "Don't tell me you've got a headache."

"I've got more than a headache."

"Carrie, come on. What's the matter? Tell me."

She crossed her arms, looked at the far wall of the granny flat, at a nondescript painting of a beach.

"I mean—you let me cry. Let me do the same for you."

"I don't think it's any of your concern," she said, but the look in her eyes betrayed her words, and he could tell it was *definitely* of his concern.

He reached out to cup her hands in his. "What's the matter?"

"I don't want to talk about it, Joe."

"Carrie—"

With sudden vehemence, she pulled away: "I said I don't want to talk about it!"

He reeled in surprise. "Carrie—"

"Joe, I think —"

"What? What is it?"

And now her voice trembled with emotion: "I think I'm pregnant."

Somehow the news didn't shock him as much as he'd imagined. He ran his tongue over his lips, swallowed hard. "Okay," he said tentatively, and managed what he hoped was a smile. "No problem. This isn't a big deal, Carrie, we'll handle this." A pause. "Are you sure?"

"I'm late," she replied, and her hands were at her belly, as if she were already round with child. "Like, nearly two weeks late."

"But you're not sure."

She shook her head. "No. No, I'm not, but I feel — different. Like, there's something . . . I don't know."

"Okay, okay, let's just calm down here," he said, and made his way across the room to put his arms around her. "I think the first thing we've gotta do is get a pregnancy test." She stared into his eyes, almost as if she didn't comprehend him, and he managed a feeble chuckle. "I mean, that's what they always do on TV, right? When a girl thinks she's pregnant? Get a pregnancy test?"

"This isn't TV, Joe."

"I know. I know, I just meant . . ." He shook his head and decided to broach the subject from a different angle. His heart was thudding rapidly in his chest, and he had to remind himself to keep breathing, keep breathing, *this isn't the end of the world, Joe* — and although he felt as if the world were crumbling to pieces, he told himself he had to stay calm for Carrie's sake. If she were pregnant, and if the baby were his — *no reason for it not to be, I mean, how many guys has she been screwing?* — then they could handle this. They were virtually grown-ups. Young adults. Responsible. They could do this. "We just need to be sure, Carrie. I mean, we don't wanna be freaking out for no reason here, right? I don't know much about—your—women's cycles and stuff, but if you're two weeks late, it doesn't mean you're pregnant—necessarily—does it?"

"We've had sex, Joe," she said, and for some reason uttered a high-pitched, near-hysterical giggle.

"I know. I know, but that doesn't mean—could it just be you're under a lot of stress, or you're, I don't know, you're . . . missing your period for some reason, not pregnancy, could it be possible? At all? Possible?"

"Joe," she said softly, and looked up at him with a look of imploring in her eyes. "I think this might be real."

Deep breaths. "Why don't we get it checked out? We'll drive down to the pharmacy, we'll grab a kit, we'll check it out."

She nodded. She began to make slow, faltering moves towards the door. Halfway there, she quietly asked, "And what if I am, Joe? What if I'm pregnant?"

Then—we'll have to get rid of it.

He placed a hand on the small of her back, guiding her forward. "We'll . . ." A pause, and he moistened his lips nervously. ". . . We'll figure it out."

Blue.

"**I**'ve got to go. I—I'm sorry, I've got to go."

"Joe. Joe, don't, please, you can't leave, you said we'd deal with this together!"

"I'm sorry," he said, all a-fluster, rushing to the coat tree, where his leather jacket hung. "I'm sorry, I'm really, really sorry, but this just too much, okay? Just too much, I'm sorry, I've got to go." Rambling. Drenched with cold sweat, his heart pounding like a bullet train against his ribcage. Too much. Too much. Too much.

"Joe! Joe, please!"

"I've really got to go, Carrie, I'm sorry." So many apologies, repeating himself.

"Joe, you can't do this to me. What am I going to do?"

He put the jacket on, moving quickly, missing the left sleeve hole, having to fumble around with it until he had it on properly. "I don't know, Carrie," he gasped, all breathless and frightened and bordering on full-fledged panic. "I don't know, just deal with it, I'm sorry, I've got to go, okay?"

"For God's sake, Joe!" she screamed.

He stopped moving and watched her, his eyes wide, mouth agape, breathing hard. Fists clenched, she glared at him with rage. "We're in this together! You said so yourself, you said we'd deal with this together, now you're acting like a big chicken, *what the hell, Joe!*" She slammed her fist against the wall. Let out a cry of pain and grabbed her fist with her other hand, while Joe hyperventilated, wondering how it'd got this bad, how his life had spiralled into this cesspit of perplexity and misery. "Fuck!" she screamed. Tears ran down her red-flushed cheeks. "Fuck you! Fuck you, Joe!"

"Carrie, I'm sorry," he managed to choke out.

"You've said that," she uttered, her voice strangled. "You've already said that, but sorry isn't going to cut it."

He ran a hand through his hair, blinking repeatedly as he tried to think. *Think.* "Can't you—can't you tell your parents?"

"Are you crazy?"

"No. No, you can't, I'm sorry, I just—I'm sorry . . . oh, God, I'm just—freaking out, that's all, I'm sorry." Babbling.

"Well, we've got to do *something,*" she cried, and wondered why people tended to say such stupid and helpless things in times of distress. *What a lovely funeral it was,* that kind of thing. Stupid and helpless.

"Get rid of it," Joe said.

"What?"

"Get rid of it. Do it discreetly, nobody has to know, get rid of it, just get it out of you, and we'll act like it never happened, okay?"

Her eyes glazed over with tears, and her hands returned to being fists. "Joe, I've never — I can't."

"Carrie . . ."

"I can't, Joe, I . . ."

"What are you, *stupid?*" he shouted, and flinched at the anguish that marked her features. "Please, please, please, for the love of God, just do it. Get out there, go to a doctor or gynaecologist or whoever and get it done, all right? I'll even pay for half the procedure, whatever it takes, just get *rid* of it!"

She stood there watching him with tears running, her lips apart, salt dribbling into her open mouth.

"Don't tell me this is about principles," Joe seethed. "If it is, you shouldn't have let yourself get into this mess in the first place. I mean, how stupid can you get, fucking around without any form of birth control, and then getting torn up because I'm asking you to get rid of it? It's your fault. Fuck this shit, Carrie, it's *your* fault!"

"No," she choked out.

"No?"

"No. It's *our* fault."

"Don't blame me for this," Joe said, feeling another wave of panic sweep over him, his chest tightening. "You should have been more careful."

"What about *you?* I warned you about — !"

"I didn't know you were going to get pregnant!"

"That's absolutely ridiculous, Joe! *Jesus!*"

"I'm getting out of here." He stormed over to the door, reached for the doorknob. "You — you do whatever the hell you want, okay? I don't have time — I don't have the time, or the patience, or the energy to cope with this, you understand me? There's too much for me to deal with now, and I can't —" He gestured vaguely in her direction, a motion that revealed how lost, how out of control he was feeling. "You're on your own, all right? Just — make up your mind and let me know. Please?"

"Joe." Desperate. Pleading.

"I'm sorry, but I've got to go."

"Joe. Joe, please? Don't?"

He opened the door.

"Joe, don't go, please," she whimpered, quivering, her whole body racked with frightened tremors. She wrapped her arms around herself and sobbed and wailed, a low moan punctuated by sobs: "I can't . . . do . . . this . . . alone . . ." Another wail, louder this time, tearing through the very heart of him. ". . . *Joe* . . . !"

He stepped out and shut the door behind him.

As he walked away from the granny flat, out through the side door that bypassed the house where Carrie's parents were probably asleep, and out of the Taylors' yard, Carrie's sobs and distraught keening continued to echo in his ears, in his mind, in his very heart. In the driver's seat of his mother's car, he broke down and sobbed against the steering wheel, mourning the destruction of his own family and the obliteration of his and Carrie's innocence, and the horrible way he handled every single lousy situation in his screwed-up life.

Back in the kitchen, Joe continued to sit in the darkness, filled with remorse at the way he'd reacted towards Carrie, feeling like a complete bastard.

Just like your father.

While in the bedrooms upstairs, Maggie was filled with both sorrow and joy, a conflicting duet of emotion that deprived her of the respite of sleep.

Her father was gone, but she had a new, blossoming relationship with a warm and caring guy.

The Lord giveth, and the Lord taketh away . . .

And Jessy Cooke lay in bed with her eyes open, having been under the covers for over an hour, immensely worn out but unable to sleep thanks to her aching heart and racing thoughts. She was missing Paul, missing his warmth, his touch. And she reminded herself that she was better off without him, that they *all* were — repeatedly, until the words became completely and irrevocably banal.

TOO LATE FOR REGRETS

Despite the roughness and hardness of the bench, Graham and Felicity Hanson were content as they watched the sun rise, a brilliant, orange ball of flame. The morning light played over the grass, starting from the far end of the field across from them, and gradually shifted, expanding, illuminating the span of the ground as the sun moved higher in the sky, dispelling the chill of the night. Sitting side by side without any space between them, they remained in silence, enjoying the simple pleasure of watching the splendour of nature, and basking in the beautiful wordlessness of the dawn.

As they watched a flock of birds circling in the sky, Felicity whispered, "I've been thinking, sweetie . . ."

"I thought I smelled brain cells frying," he cracked.

She pulled a face and playfully smacked his cheek.

Chuckling, he said, "Okay, what have you been thinking?"

"Well, with Phyllis's passing and all that, I was just thinking that . . ." She stared off into the distance, and Graham waited, knowing she was trying to construct her thoughts properly. "It's not going to be too long now, is it, Graham?" she asked, lowering her voice to a near-whisper, as if in reverence for the exquisiteness of the sunrise. "You know what I mean? We've lived happy, long lives ourselves, and I'm wondering what would happen if . . ." She gestured vaguely with one hand, and Graham understood her meaning entirely. "When," she said, accenting the word, "you know?"

He slid an arm around her shoulders. "I know."

"Because—I don't want to go without you."

"Well, me neither, honey, but that isn't really our call, is it?"

"I guess not."

"Well, then," he said, as she nestled against him, "I think whatever happens, it wouldn't be a sad occasion. I mean, we'd be with Jesus, won't we? In the kingdom of the Almighty? I think that sounds wonderful, and it'd only be a matter of time before we meet again, assuming one of us goes first." He paused for a moment, taking in the view. Then he said, "You know I'm happy about the way things turned out, even though we don't have any children or grandchildren. I've got no regrets — except, perhaps, that I might have waited too long to start writing my memoirs." He chuckled. "Which reminds me. I'm going to ask Michelle to help me with it. She's always said she enjoys writing; I think she'd really enjoy helping us gather our stories, our experiences, our lives."

Felicity nodded thoughtfully. "That sounds excellent. Think we should give her a call, ask her over for lunch?"

"Good idea. We'll bait her with food, get her stuffed and vulnerable, and when she least expects it: *bam!* I'll hit her with the memoirs!"

They both laughed, clutching each other's arms like lovesick teenagers. Graham believed that despite their age, the two of them were very much young at heart. They'd moved with the times, absorbing the new information, apparatus and appliances that had come their way, even though their home only comprised a washing machine and a TV with an old VCR as instances of their keeping up with technological advancement. No, they weren't living in a backward world, in spite of their adherence to tradition and routine — like their early-morning walks and the semi-cold showers that Graham insisted on having.

They wandered leisurely across the field to their house, and Felicity proceeded to tend to the rose bushes in their garden. Inside the house, Graham stood by the window overlooking the yard, watching as his wife, despite her age, bent over and began to prune away at the plants. Once more he thought about how much he loved her, and he prayed that when their time came, they would go together.

Because, as much as he knew that moving on meant meeting up with their Creator, he couldn't bear the thought of either of them being alone, even if for a short while.

Michelle Leigh wasn't home to receive Graham's phone call. She had an appointment with a friend, her mother said, so Graham left a message with Mrs Leigh, asking Michelle to pop by anytime she could.

Michelle waved goodbye to her brother and made her way into Nick's Place, the popular café located on the ground floor of the shopping centre. On this Sunday afternoon, it wasn't particularly crowded, and Michelle let her eyes scan the thin throng before seeing her friend sitting alone in the far corner.

Gripping her purse, she walked over to the booth. Her friend had sounded so troubled over the phone that morning, and had pleaded with Michelle to meet with her. Michelle had agreed, and her brother Matthew—who planned to meet up with his own friend to discuss a university assignment on torts or tarts or whatever it was—had grumpily agreed to drop her off on the way.

Her heart thudding, she uttered a greeting and slid into the booth.

She wondered what this was going to be about.

"Chelle, don't freak out, but I'm pregnant."

Michelle froze, her glass of iced chocolate raised halfway to her lips. Stunned, she set the glass down, stared at the other girl in the face, and said, "Say again?"

"Pregnant." She gestured helplessly, a strange, gauche movement, a variation of the common shrug. "I took a pregnancy test, and . . . yeah, it's—it's for real. This is really happening."

"Oh, wow," Michelle gasped, and for a moment didn't know what to say. How does one respond to this kind of news, especially when it comes from a friend, a friend who couldn't afford to have a baby just yet? "Who's the father? Is it . . . ?"

"Y-yes."

"What are you going to do? Does he know — ?"

"I don't know. I mean, yes, he does, but — it didn't go too well. I called him this morning, but — he hung up on me. I'm so . . . oh, God, I'm just so screwed up, I don't know what to do! I can't tell my mum or anything, she'd freak out, you know how she is. Oh, Jesus, Chelle, what am I going to do?"

"Do you want to keep the baby?" Michelle asked softly.

"Do I have a choice?"

"Yes, you do."

A moment of silence. Then: "No, Chelle, you know how I feel about . . ."

"Honey, I know, but this is — this is really serious. You have to think about a lot of other factors, not just your values. I mean, you're — I'm sorry, but I can't see how you're possibly ready to be a mother, not at your age, with so much more ahead of you! And seeing how the father doesn't want any part in it, how are you going to . . . ?" Michelle shook her head. "What about your own family, what are *they* going to think?"

"I don't know, Michelle." The girl was sobbing now, quietly, so as not to draw attention. "I could give it away, maybe? I mean, you know, to a shelter, or to an adoption . . . whatever . . ." The sheer weight of the issue took its toll, and her voice cracked. She buried her face in her hands. "What am I going to do?"

A skinny, tired-looking waitress came up with a tray of food, their lunch, but the girls didn't have any appetite left. As she placed the plates on the table, the waitress muttered, "Y'ask me, you best get rid of it, unless y'wanna be saddled with a heavy burden for the rest of your pretty young life."

And she turned and sauntered away, leaving the two girls to numbly wonder exactly how loud they'd been talking.

Happy Are Those Who Do Not See . . .

<hr width="20%" align="left" />

"Turning into a regular cradle-snatcher, aren't we?" Patricia Ash tossed her head back and let out a hoarse, throaty laugh: loud, infectious—and bloody annoying to those who craved a little peace and quiet. "Or a paedophile?" she taunted, letting out another loud crow.

Matthew Leigh, resting his chin wearily in one hand and staring through half-open eyelids at her, waited for her to get over the joke that only she found amusing.

"You done?" he said when she calmed down. "Satisfied?"

"I've had better."

"We're supposed to be studying."

"Hey, *you* brought up the little brat."

"He's not a brat," he said sharply, and then wondered why he was defending the brat. "He's just a kid. And he's really intelligent."

"Intelligent, huh?" She giggled. Everything seemed to tickle her, as if she were one big funny bone. "*Intelligent* is a word you use to describe animals, baby. Now dogs, they're intelligent. Dolphins, more intelligent. People are *smart*. Not 'intelligent'. *Smart.*"

He rolled his eyes.

"What was his name again?"

"Robson. Robby. I never got his last name."

"When on earth did you start liking other people, especially kids? You're a misanthrope of the highest order." She gestured to the textbooks. "Can we get on with it? Or are we done?"

"We've hardly started."

"Oh, come on, Matt, look outside, it's a freaking nice day. I don't wanna be cooped up in the house all day staring at words."

"Fine. What do you want to do?"

"Let's go for a movie."

"There'll be nothing on until the matinee."

"Okay, let's go bowling."

"I didn't bring my bowling shoes."

"They rent 'em out at the alley, you know."

"I'm not wearing socks. They want you to wear socks."

"You can buy 'em."

"No, thanks."

"Oh, you're a barrel of monkeys, you know that?"

"Hey, let's go over to the Square," he said.

She blinked rapidly, her thick eyelashes flashing up and down. "Say what?"

"I'll introduce you to him."

"To who?"

"To the kid! Robby."

"Matty, you know I love little ankle-biters just as much as the next broad, but to give up this wonderful opportunity to fill my mind with random and meaningless law terminology so I can acquaint myself with some peculiar youngster you've met on a butt-rest under a tree in a dying potato patch? Tempting, but no thanks."

"Look, we'll study there, okay? Under the tree. It'll be cool."

"That's because of the shade," she shot back, and cackled. "Wait 'till winter sets in, then we'll see how cool it can get."

"You're a regular bundle of laughs, aren't you?"

"Beats being a barrel of monkeys."

"**H**ow do you know he'll show?"

"He'll show. I think."

"Does this kid not have a life?"

"I don't know. But if we're here, he'll show."

"What *is* he, psychic?"

Matthew shrugged and sat down. "Sit. Enjoy the shade."

Ash, as she preferred to be called ("Patricia's such a boring, *saintlike* name," she constantly griped. "It makes me sound like a nun—Sister Patricia of the Order of the Sacred Heart of Jesus"), sat with her feet tucked under her, as if she were doing yoga. "Gotta admit, this place is kinda nice. But I betcha this is the kind of place teenagers come to in the middle of the night to fuck. Look around, you'll find used rubbers lying about the place."

They sat there for a good half hour—books in their laps, not one word read—before there came the sound of footsteps. They listened attentively and heard the shuffling of feet against the ground, the snap of a twig from behind the tree. "It's him," Matthew said, and they waited.

The boy approached them hesitantly, and Matthew figured it was because there were now two people on the bench instead of one. Little Robby lingered by the trunk for a few seconds, his hands on the bark, his fingers tapping the wood lightly as if he were playing the piano. Matthew looked at him. "Hey, you're here."

"Hey, mister," the child returned shyly. "I mean, Matthew."

"I wanna introduce you to somebody."

"What you doin' here on Sunday?" the boy asked, coming closer, taking small steps.

"Just thought we'd visit you. This is my friend, Ash." Matthew gestured to his companion, who wiggled her sausage-like fingers in a parody of a wave, and flashed the kid a big, toothy grin. "Hey, Robby."

The boy said, "Did you go to church today, Matthew?"

Matthew glanced at Ash, surprised by the question. Turning back to the boy, he said, "No. Remember, I told you, I don't read the Bible—and I don't go to church."

"Why not?"

"Why should I?"

"'Cause your name is the same as one of Jesus's 'sciples . . ."

"Yeah? So?"

". . . And one of them godspel writers."

"Gospel. Yeah. No big deal."

"Matty, Marky, Luke and Johnny. That's how my mummy helps me remember 'em. Matty, Marky, Luke and Johnny."

"Hey, that's catchy!" Ash exclaimed, and laughed uproariously.

"Don't you ever call me Matty," Matthew told the boy.

"And don't call me Patty, 'less you wanna die young," Ash chortled.

The boy said, "Have you ever *been* to church before?"

Matthew laughed, although a little knot of discomfort was building up inside him. He loathed religious events and absolutely despised religious discussions. "Of course I've been to church before," he answered.

"Which?"

"Um, that big stone one."

The boy seemed satisfied with that. "Didya like it?"

"No," Matthew answered immediately.

"Why not?"

"Well, I don't believe in God."

The boy's mouth dropped open in shock. "But Mister Matthew sir, you *gots* to believe in God!"

"And why is that?"

"'Cause what happens when you die if you don't believe in God?"

Matthew laughed contemptuously. "I become fertiliser for the ground."

The boy's forehead lined in thought, and he blinked, evidently not understanding Matthew's response.

"*I* believe in God," Ash piped up.

Matthew shot a look at his friend. "*You* believe in God?"

"I do."

"I find that hard to believe, *Sister* Patricia."

"Shut up, Father Matthew."

"I think," little Robby said ponderously, "it's better to believe than not believe." He looked up at Matthew, his expression solemn — solemn, like so many of those dull services Matthew had attended from childhood until his late teens. He no longer went. No point in partaking of a series of mundane rituals just to make other people happy when there wasn't a modicum of faith left in him.

Little Robby continued: "I mean, if you don't believe in God, then you ain't gonna go to Heaven, and if you ain't gonna go to Heaven, then you're not meetin' up with anybody's gone before you, you know?"

"That's fine with me, I don't know anybody who's gone before me who I wanna meet up with again anyway." Matthew shifted in his seat. "Why, do you?"

The boy looked into the distance, at the row of buildings across from them, and he shrugged his little shoulders slightly, a barely perceptible motion had Matthew not been staring so intently at him. It dawned upon Matthew now that little Robby had mentioned his mummy several times, but had never hinted at a daddy. *Maybe Daddy has moved on to the* (non-existent, as far he was concerned) *other side*, he thought, and gently tapped the boy on his shoulder. The boy jumped visibly and turned to look at Matthew with his eyes wide and serious. "Hey," Matthew said. "You okay, kiddo?"

"I believe in God," the boy replied softly.

"Well, good for you."

"If you don't believe in God," the boy said, and now his voice took on a softer, sadder quality, "then we won't be able to meets each other in Heaven."

"Well, I don't think you have anything to worry about," Matthew answered, and looked at Ash, who shrugged.

Abruptly the boy slid off the bench. "I think Mummy's lookin' for me." He moved away from them, then turned back and addressed Matthew: "See you tomorrow?" Hoping. Hopeful.

"Yeah, sure," Matthew replied, "just as long as we cut out the God talk, okay?"

The boy paused to consider this, and nodded. "'Kay." And he took off in a gallop, away from the tree. Matthew shifted in his seat and strained to look beyond the trunk, but it was too wide for him to see past without getting off his seat.

He turned back to Ash. "Told you he was intelligent. A little too grown-up, that's what I think."

"Was it just me," Ash said, "or was he ignoring me?"

They headed back to Matthew's car, with Matthew thinking he had, somehow, again upset the kid. On the previous occasion, he'd dismissed the notion of the boy being offended as paranoia, and denied any feeling of anxiety within himself for having potentially affected the child in such a way. Today, however, the notion was back. He would later find himself wondering if and how he'd upset little Robby—and would subsequently wonder why this upset himself so much.

A DESPERATE DISPLAY OF PERSUASION

Sanjeev and Chitra knocked on the door of Hope and Geraldine's apartment, and waited for a response. They heard footsteps, followed by the rattle-scrape-clunk of the door being unlocked. Then Hope, with her shocking pink hair seemingly brighter than before, stood before them, chewing gum as usual, her expression bland and unsurprised by the unannounced visit. "Hey-lo," she said, and raised an eyebrow at the two. "I take it you're here to see Geri?"

"Well, yes," Sanjeev said, "but also to see you."

"What's up?"

"May we come in? Where's Geraldine?"

"That depends. How's Dick, the Sad One?"

"Still sad."

"Aw." Just a trace amount of sympathy. Hope stood back and held the door open for Sanjeev and Chitra. They entered. She shut the door and accompanied her visitors into the living room, where Geraldine was sitting on the couch, staring at a television that wasn't turned on. Next to her, flipping through a magazine, was a good-looking, muscular young man with a trendy crew cut. He turned to look at the newcomers inquisitively.

"Hey, Geri." Chitra plonked herself on the other side of her and gave her a hug. "How you holding up?"

"I'm holding up," Geraldine replied. "How's Rick?"

Sanjeev answered, "He's still hanging around the beach, staring into the sea. Sometimes I fear he's going to try and drown himself, but I don't think he's brave enough to try it." He paused. Geraldine nodded, and he added, "He doesn't seem to be feeling any less angry about the situation, I'm sorry to say. He keeps on raving about God and how unfair it is, and I don't really want to say much more because I probably wouldn't help, would I?"

"No," Hope answered him, "I don't think you would."

"Because I'm confused, too," Geraldine said softly.

"Now, honey, don't bother yourself," Hope urged.

"Look, I'm confused, okay? Come on, Hope, just because *you're* comfortable with . . ."

"Geri, please, not now. Let's not talk about it."

Mr Crew Cut interjected: "Have we met?"

"Oh!" Geraldine gestured to her two friends. "Jason, this is Sanjeev and Chitra. Guys, this is Jason. From upstairs."

They exchanged pleasantries. Then Sanjeev nudged Hope's side, whispering something about having Jason leave the room because they had to discuss private affairs, but his whisper must not have been too quiet because Geraldine said aloud, "Don't worry about Jase, he knows what's been going on. We've bonded," leaving Sanjeev to look embarrassed and flustered.

"Listen, guys, we've got to talk," Chitra said. "It's about Derrick." She shot a glance at Sanjeev, who nodded encouragingly. "He's all upset, that's no surprise; but from the way it looks, he appears to be sinking deeper and deeper into this state of hurt, not the other way round. I mean, in the past week, he's grown more detached, more irritable, and even more violent. Yesterday he stomped on a kid's sandcastle, squashed it flat, destroyed it, and when the poor kid cried, he actually snapped: 'For God's sake, you think *you've* got problems?!' and stormed away!"

"It's true," Sanjeev said. "I was there. I saw it. I sympathised. I pretended not to know him."

"Sounds rough," Jason mused.

"Yeah," Chitra said. "But then again, we can't blame him. I mean, Geri, the two of you were together for so many years, he's bound to be hurting. But we think that we need to expedite the process of healing, or of acceptance, before he does some *real* damage. You've seen him when he's angry, Geri—he can sometimes fly off the handle and do things he'd later regret."

"I'm getting a little frightened of talking to him," Sanjeev confessed. "In just one week, he's turned into a different person. He's moody, he's broody, and growing . . . crudey and lewdy."

"Nice." Jason grinned.

"Thanks."

"I know it might seem like we're acting too rashly," Chitra continued. "I mean, it's only been a week, and God knows we usually need a lot longer than that to deal with a broken heart. But Sanjeev and I are worried that this might be more than just a broken heart—this is a broken heart *coupled with* a deep, unreasonable antipathy towards Geraldine's decision to be who she is. I've studied psychology, and—well, this doesn't necessarily have to happen, but Derrick's situation could lead him to act irrationally. And if he were to come over to confront you girls"—gesturing to Hope and Geraldine—"it could be dangerous. Especially if he's being controlled by his emotions."

"God knows he's easily controlled by his emotions," Sanjeev put in.

"So we think he needs to get out more," Chitra said. "He needs to meet new people, to be surrounded by others, so that his mind isn't on Geri, Geri, Geri, twenty-four hours a day. He needs a means of moving on, and I think we need to take him out tonight."

A pause. Everyone stared at her.

"Why can't you and Sanjeev take him out?" Hope asked.

"Because we need you and Geri to be there."

"Wait. How would Geraldine being there help take this dude's mind *off* Geraldine?" Jason asked.

"Excellent question, Jason."

"Why, thank you, Chitra."

"Because we're going to try and get him interested in somebody else," Sanjeev said, and his eyes glinted with mischief. Everyone turned their attention to him, and he elaborated: "We'll set him up with somebody, and we'll push him to get to know her better. When the time is right, Geraldine and Hope, you two appear. Chances are, he'll feel so upset that he'll want to show you girls up by purposely getting *closer* to his new date. You know, to comfort himself, or even to make you jealous, Geri."

"But I wouldn't be jealous, I'd be happy," Geraldine objected—and then it seemed to make sense. "Aaaah. So maybe this *could* work."

"You want him to move on, don't you?" Sanjeev said.

"Yeah."

"But would he really be moving on?" Jason questioned.

"Sure he would," Sanjeev said. "He'd be meeting somebody new, getting closer to her, and when the girls show up, it'd give him an excuse to try and get to know her *more.*"

"Sounds to me like he'd simply be using the girl, but he'd try to get together with Geraldine the moment Geraldine's alone," Jason replied. "Sorry, dear, but this plan of yours doesn't make any sense. And it *is*, after all, too soon. Shouldn't we give him more time and space?"

"Oh, I think he's *had* his time and space," Sanjeev told him.

"Yeah, but just a week? That's hardly anything."

"That's plenty," Sanjeev rebutted.

"I don't think so, not when it comes to a broken heart."

"A week is a lot of time," Sanjeev insisted, adamant. "It's—what's twenty-four times seven? One hundred-something hours!"

"Have *you* ever had a broken heart, hun?" Jason asked.

"*Yes*, and I took only three days to get over it."

"Well, maybe it wasn't genuine to begin with."

"Hey—"

"Sorry, but it seems to me that if you're getting over a broken heart after three days . . ."

"Who is this guy?" Sanjeev asked the room. "Seriously, who *is* this guy?"

"You were probably dealing with a one-night-stand kind of romance . . ."

"Oh, shut up, I don't like you."

"Be that as it may, I think we should give him more time."

"No more time."

"Why not?"

"Just—no more."

"It's only been a week."

"It's *already* been a week!" Sanjeev insisted, his voice rising.

"Okay, fine. I'm just saying—"

"One *freaking* week!"

"Please don't yell."

"If you think it's easy spending one week with him in this state—"

"Honey, if you're going to yell, I'm not listening."

"—Then *you* try looking after him—"

"I'm not listening. I'm not listening!"

"Oh, God, ladies, *please*," Geraldine begged.

"—Because *I* sure don't want to deal with him anymore!" Sanjeev bellowed.

Silence reigned, and everyone fixed wide eyes on Sanjeev. Hope, leaning against a wall with her legs crossed at the ankles, chewed and popped her gum loudly. "Ha, *now* we seem to be getting to the point."

Sanjeev sagged. "All right, all right." He sighed. "I know it's awful of me, but I'm the kind of guy who needs my own space, and right now, Rick's being too much of a pain in the butt, and not in a good way. I need him to move along, move *out*, and I don't know how to tell him without pissing him off and making him think that I don't want his company anymore. I mean, I *don't,* in a way. Want his company. Not seven days a week of moping and griping and hoping and . . . wiping."

Jason snorted disdainfully.

"So this is the real deal, isn't it?" Geraldine said softly from the couch. "You just want Derrick out of your life."

"No, not out of my life, just out of my *house.* There's a difference."

Chitra put in, "*And* we feel he could do with some shoving in the right direction, you know what I mean?"

Nobody answered her, but she figured they did.

"So what do you say?" Sanjeev asked, looking at the others. "Chit and I will talk him into joining us for a night at the club, and when we're there, we'll set him up with someone."

Hope popped her gum loudly, chewed for several seconds, and said, "I don't mind going out, if Geri's up to it."

"I'm not up to it," Geraldine said at once.

Everyone stared at her.

". . . But I'll do it, if it's going to help Rick," she added.

Sanjeev cheered, and Chitra clapped her hands enthusiastically.

"In fact," Geraldine said—and now she broke into a smile—"I think I have the perfect idea of how to go about doing this."

A Cruel and Unreasonable Ultimatum

Jessy Cooke wrapped the apron around her waist, her fingers fumbling as she tried to tie the ends of the strings together. When she couldn't do it—she was trembling, that was the problem—she let out a soft cry of frustration and flung the apron across the kitchen counter, where it landed in a heap on the floor. She pressed her hands flat against the countertop, stretched her arms, keeping her head low between her shoulders. Stared at the grease-streaked tiles (*Somebody made breakfast and didn't clean up, do I have to do everything around here?*) and forced herself to take deep breaths. Again the thought crossed her mind that *everything's falling apart*—and then it struck her that it had *already* all fallen apart.

So maybe the worst of it was over. Her husband had declared he no longer loved her and had no intention of staying with the family. It had become a cliché, a clichéd cliché, but *this is all for the best.*

Still, why was it so hard to accept? Why did her heart feel as if it had been smashed into smithereens? Why did she keep feeling as if Paul were right there in front of her, with his face decorated with five o'clock shadow and his top buttons undone, revealing the curly chest hair she used to enjoy running her fingers through, looking at her and laughing at her and mocking her and stamping on the remains of her broken heart so that they were broken *and* crushed to a fine dust? And, dear God, why did she feel the strongest urge to grab the carving knife out of its holder and wield it like Zorro or one of those Three Freaking Musketeers and slash Paul sonofabitch-lying-cheating-bastard Cooke into equally tiny—tinier!—pieces?

She had to let go. She had to move on. With him gone, she could finally focus on all that she had a penchant for: her work, her children. Her life. She didn't have to worry any longer about where Paul was, or why he hadn't called when he'd finished work over three hours ago, or why he hadn't been there to pick up his own children from school. She didn't have to get all suspicious and paranoid whenever he came home smelling faintly of another woman's perfume (*"Jesus, Jess, it's my mother's! I work with her eight hours a day, it's bound to get on my clothes!"*), or if she found a strange strand of hair, light-coloured, on his comb (*"Jesus, Jess, I keep the comb in my back pocket, my dad uses it every now and then, will you lay off?"*).

Now she was liberated, she'd been emancipated, freedom had come at last!

At least, that's what she kept telling herself.

But her poor, aching heart didn't believe it. It kept reminding her how she'd been used and abused—although never physically—by the man she'd fallen head over heels for over twenty years ago, who no longer gave a damn about her. That hurt. It really did. It made her feel undesired, and undesirable. Unloved, and unlovable.

She'd spoken to her older sister Josephine over the phone. Jo was a very good listener and adviser, but her location in England made it hard for her to be a real comfort. It was in times like these Jessy wished her parents were still alive; but her mother had succumbed to cancer over twenty years ago *(approximately around the time Paul and I got together)*, and her father had reunited with his wife just three years ago. *(But it was okay, because Paul had been here for me, he'd been very reassuring, even though I guess he hadn't cared as much as it seemed . . .)*

To top it all off, Paul had not expressed a desire to see his children after they were separated, but had, in the spirit of callous commiseration, agreed to send money regularly, "so they won't be wanting for anything once I'm gone," he'd said. Jessy wasn't sure whether they'd actually be receiving any of those cheques.

She largely blamed herself for the increasing lack of communication between her and the kids. Over the past few weeks, she'd grown more and more distant — or so it felt — from Maggie and Joe, and she told herself she had to do something before she cut herself off from them entirely, or vice-versa. She had become so irritable and short-tempered that a normal conversation with Joe had become virtually impossible. Twice they'd got into screaming fights, and the second time he'd actually cursed at her, something he'd never done before. It had left her flabbergasted. Sure, he was seventeen, an age when young men chose to display their independence and their presumed maturity, but she'd never imagined he'd actually say such an awful thing to her. It still hurt to think about it — another hurt on top of the big slice of hurt her husband had generously dished up. It made it hard for her not to think Joe and Paul were so frighteningly alike. She and Joe had to talk, Jessy told herself; they had to talk rationally and maturely, like grown-ups, with equal and mutual respect. And they had to do it soon, so they could get on with their lives and attain a sense of normality, whatever that meant, sooner rather than later.

As for Maggie — her daughter was going to be sixteen at the end of the year, and she, too, was at that point where she sought a sense of self-sufficiency and independence. Jessy tended to think of her daughter as still a baby; but now, she realised she had to do the same with her as she would with Joe: treat her like a grown-up. A woman. A person with troubles and feelings and wants and needs and desires. No longer a baby to be mollycoddled and handfed.

Jessy hadn't seen her children in a few days, hadn't *really* taken a good look at them, held them and told them it would all be okay *(this is all for the best)*, the way a good mother was supposed to. On the divorce and separation sites she'd forced herself to investigate on the Web, she'd come across several analyses of the newly separated parent, and failure to fulfil domestic responsibility was a frequently highlighted issue. She'd thought it absolutely ludicrous: no way would she stop being a good mother just *because* . . . and yet, it was increasingly apparent it *was* happening.

Still, it wasn't too late, right? She could still do something about it.

Being a good parent, she had to make sure her children didn't go hungry. Dinner. Yes, dinner sounded right. Maggie and Joe had always looked forward to their Sunday dinners, so why not prepare something tonight?

Jessy took another deep breath, then pushed herself upright and decided she'd head onward with no regrets. So her bed contained one person fewer now—big deal. More room for her.

"Joe, dinner will be ready in about ten minutes."

"I'm not hungry, Mum. I'm going out."

"But it's almost done. Why don't you eat first?"

"I said I'm not hungry."

Jessy pursed her lips together, feeling a surge of anger. The goulash was simmering nicely, the chunks of beef cooked to perfection, the buttered rice that accompanied the stew ready. *No. Wait. Don't get upset again.*

Joe stood by the kitchen table, watching his mother. She glimpsed him out of the corner of her eye. He was wearing his cracked leather jacket again—and was that the same pair of jeans? She mentally debated whether or not to comment on his appearance. She decided not to.

"How are you coping at school, honey?"

He didn't answer her. Instead, he quietly said, "I'm sorry I yelled at you yesterday, Mum."

She looked at him, surprised.

"I was just—upset."

"It's okay," she managed. "I'm sorry, too."

"Okay," he murmured.

She turned back to the stove to stir the bubbling gravy. "Won't you eat with us, Joe? Please? There's plenty, and it's beef goulash, your favourite," she said, and chuckled because she thought it necessary to punctuate the statement with a frivolous tinkle of laughter.

"I'm full," he replied, and quickly added, "I'll be with the guys," before rushing out the back door.

Wishing they could've had a longer and less tedious chat, she continued to stir the contents of the pan, her own emotions swirling within her. Joe truly was becoming more and more a stranger. She figured he wasn't meeting his friends; it was more likely that Carrie girl. *And if Joe is anything like his father,* she thought, but cut herself off with the admonishment: *That's not fair, stop thinking that of your own son . . .*

Maggie spooned the thick gravy around, but Jessy noticed she was hardly putting any of it into her mouth. The silence between them was thick, almost asphyxiating. Jessy wished she could say something that didn't sound entirely trite. Small talk tended to sound too much like small talk, but serious discussions were not exactly appropriate for the dining table, either. Jessy reached for the bread basket. "Another roll, honey?"

"I'm fine," Maggie murmured, and took a mouthful of stew.

Jessy put the basket down, feeling rejected. *I'm just being too sensitive,* she told herself, and used the same hand to sweep back a lock of her hair *(limp and lifeless; I've got to start conditioning again or I'll end up looking even worse than I already do . . .)*

The room was filled with the aroma of spicy stew, and the penetrable silence was intermingled with the sporadic *tink* of cutlery against crockery.

"Mum?"

Jessy looked up, momentarily startled by her daughter's voice.

"I think — I think I might take tomorrow off school. Would that be all right?"

Her voice, so soft and frail and vulnerable, struck a deep chord within Jessy's heart, and she found herself nodding assent without even considering the request. "Yes," she said, and managed a smile that she supposed was too wide and unnecessary. "Yes, that would be fine, sweetheart, I'll write you a note." She waited a beat. "Okay if I ask why?"

Maggie shrugged. "I guess I'm just — tired. You know? I — I haven't been sleeping very well, and . . ." She gestured indistinguishably with her hands, and Jessy nodded in understanding. "I guess I just want to spend less time thinking, more time resting?" she said, forming it in the style of a question. "And — and maybe spend some time talking to some friends, just to — just to share, get some feedback on what's going on . . . ?"

You can talk to your own mother, you know, Jessy thought wistfully as she reached out with her free hand to pat her daughter's. "I know," she said.

Maggie managed a smile. It warmed Jessy's heart, the upward curl of the lips transforming her daughter's face, so weary and strained by circumstance. "Thanks, Mum," Maggie whispered, and squeezed her mother's hand gently.

It was all Jessy needed to know that life could go on.

On his way over to Carrie's, thoughts tumbled through Joe Cooke's mind. His mother had asked about school. Sure, he'd been going, but he'd been drifting through every class like a zombie. Somehow the teachers knew about his father and had been sympathetic, even to the extent of offering counselling, which he declined. Gossip moved quickly in a place like this, especially with the yentas who attended the residents' association meetings.

As he pulled into the Taylors' driveway, he wished he could stop the prick of tears in his eyes, the bile creeping up the back of his throat.

Carrie opened the door to her granny flat, and stopped short upon seeing him standing on the doorstep. Her first impulse was to slam the door in his face, but she also told herself he might be there for a good reason.

"Joe. What do you want?"

"May I come in?"

She hesitated. "Depends on what you want."

"Look," he said, dropping his voice to a low murmur, "I'm sorry about the way I acted yesterday."

"Okay," she said, and waited.

"And, now that I've calmed down a little—maybe I could come in and . . . we talk about it."

She stepped back and gestured for him to enter.

"Thank you," he mumbled, and stepped in.

The cordiality didn't last long.

"What are you saying?"

"You *know* what I'm saying."

"You bastard!"

"Call me what you want—my decision stands."

"Fuck you!" she yelled, and grabbed the nearest object to throw at him. Unfortunately for her, and fortunately for him, the only thing within grabbing range was a cushion in the shape of a heart. It bounced off his chest, and she looked around furiously for another object to throw.

"Stop!" he shouted, raising his hands in defence as she grabbed a vase from the coffee table. "For God's sake—Carrie, you're acting crazy!"

"You make me crazy!" she cried, and quickly lowered her voice—no need to alert her parents, in the main house. The last thing she wanted was for them to find out she was pregnant with her boyfriend's child (ex-boyfriend, no way were they together anymore), and that he was telling her his cruel and unreasonable decision—that regardless of whether she got rid of it or kept it, he'd not be involved in any way.

"I'm out of your life from now on. You're responsible," he'd told her just minutes ago. "Entirely. I'm out. You want it, you take care of it. I'm out. All the way out."

"You fuck!" She let out a frightened, frantic sob.

"It's entirely your decision . . ."

"It *shouldn't* be! For God's sake—"

"I'm going to go," he said, and moved towards the door.

"Joe! Joseph Cooke, you fucking bastard!"

"Goodbye, Carrie."

"You're just like your father!"

He froze in his tracks, a red-hot rage burning inside of him. Suddenly his hands balled into fists, and he was pushing his tongue into his right cheek, the way he always did when something truly pissed him off. And she'd truly pissed him off, making the forbidden comparison between him and Paul Cooke. He was in no way like his father! He took several deep breaths, inhaling noisily through his nose, feeling the rage boil within him. "You're just like your useless shithead of a father!" Carrie yelled through her veil of tears. "You're running away! That's what the two of you are so fucking *good* at!"

He spun around and glared at her with a formidable look of wrath. She knew, somewhere in the back of her mind, that continued provocation might lead him to hurt her physically, but she didn't care, and she continued hurling obscenities at him, especially the *vilest* obscenity of all that Joseph and Paul Cooke were one and the same. *"Shut up!"* he yelled, and if he was concerned that her parents would hear him, he didn't show it.

"Go!" she screeched at him. "Just go! Run away, Joe! Be just like your father!"

"Shut the fuck up!"

"No wonder your father chose to run, with a bastard son like you!"

That did it. That really did it.

He stormed over to where she stood, his fingers squeezed so tight that his nails cut into his palms. He swung his arm back to smash his fist into her big fat mouth, but, at the last minute — just as a look of horror crossed her features — he changed his mind, and instead shoved at her with his other hand, making her cry out and stumble backward over an ottoman. She fell to the floor with a crash, crying out in pain, just as the front door flew open and Carrie's father bulldozed his way in, his eyes wide as he demanded to know what the hell was going on.

Joe ran, pushing past the bearlike Mr Taylor, getting the hell out of there.

When her father later asked what happened, Carrie replied it was just a fight that had got out of hand, and convinced him not to call the cops.

Her father barred her from seeing Joseph Cooke ever again.

"You're just like your father!"

God, Joe thought vehemently, and stomped on the accelerator, switching into fourth gear, then fifth. *Stupid bitch!*

"You're just like your father!"

"No," he told himself loudly.

"You're running away!"

"Shut up!" he bellowed through the tears that had begun to stream down his face, blurring his vision as he pressed down ever harder on the accelerator. "Shut up, *shut up!*"

The traffic light in front of him changed to red, but he was mindless of it. He soared past, too caught up in his fury to realise how lucky it was that he would make it home in one piece.

PARTY TILL YOU CAN'T
PARTY NO MORE

The time: 8PM. The place: Sanjeev's beachside home. The Enforcers: Sanjeev and Chitra, best friends of the Target. The Target: Derrick Weston, wallowing in Self-Pity and needing a Good Shove in the Right Direction.

Sanjeev said, "Come on, Derrick, buddy, we're getting out of here."

"No."

"Buddy, you've been moping around for the past week. Get out, get some air into your lungs."

"We're right next to the beach."

Sanjeev sighed. "Rick, let me be honest with you. There's not much point in your hanging about around here twenty-nine hours a day, thinking that's going to rectify the situation with Geri. If you ask me—and I know you didn't—you need to get out there. You want her back? Go talk to her, try to understand her side of the story. You want to forget her? Get out there, meet someone else."

"We're quite certain you'll get someone's attention, handsome fool like you," Chitra said.

Derrick, sitting in a leather-upholstered reclining chair, stretched his legs out so he was practically lying on his back. "I don't feel like it."

"Honey, please," Chitra pleaded. "Get up. Get up, get up, get up. You're going into the bathroom and you're going to take a nice, long shower . . ."

"You need a nice, long shower," Sanjeev put in, and didn't elaborate.

". . . And you're going to get dressed and we're going to go out."

Derrick, in a long, drawling moan: "I don't waaaant tooooo."

Chitra, legs parted, arms akimbo: "It wasn't a suggestion. It was an order."

"God," Derrick groaned, and sat up, forcing the chair into a normal position. "You two will be the death of me."

"No, I think staying here will be the death of you," Chitra stated.

Sanjeev put in, "Not like this place hasn't been blessed by your presence."

"No, not like it hasn't," Derrick muttered ambiguously, and shook his head. "I really don't feel like doing this." He planted his feet on the floor and shifted so that he was sitting on the edge of the leather seat. Letting out a sob-sigh, he whined, "I know you guys are trying to help me, but—*must* we? I don't feel like it, I really don't. I feel—I don't know, I'm feeling really sick. Think I'm going to throw up."

Chitra began to cave. "Well . . . if you're not well, then . . ."

"*No!*" Sanjeev yelled, startling them both. "We're going *out,* and that's *that!*"

He grabbed Derrick's hands and pulled him to his feet. Derrick groaned and moaned, and when Sanjeev let him go, he stumbled wildly. Apparently the breakup had caused him to lose the ability to keep his balance. Derrick wailed about how queasy he was feeling, and how cruel it was for them to force him to go out beyond his will. "You're sadists! Sadists, you are!"

"We're sadists who don't want to hurt you," Sanjeev retorted, and stopped to wonder at his statement.

Chitra said, softly now, "Honey, we're just trying to help, and we're sorry if it seems like we're pushing you, but—everybody needs a push every now and then, you know?"

"In the right direction," Sanjeev added.

"Don't talk to me about right or wrong directions," Derrick snorted, as he finally caved and staggered towards the bathroom, shaking his head of days-old unwashed hair.

The club was called *Interreactive*, and it was surprisingly packed for a Sunday night. As they shoved their way through the horde of people towards the bar, Sanjeev cried, "Dear Lord, don't these people have to *work* Mondays?!"

It was a bitch trying to find vacant stools for the three of them, so when they spotted just one that was unoccupied, Sanjeev and Chitra forced Derrick to sit, and they flanked him like two unlikely bodyguards.

"Two Scotch and Cokes!" Chitra yelled at the bartender, who cupped his hand around his ear, trying to hear over the thumping bass and percussion that tore out from the club's massive speakers. "Two Scotch and Cokes!"

"What?"

"Two Scotch and Cokes!"

"Two crotch and cocks?"

"Scotch and Cokes! *Scotch and Cokes!*"

"Get me one, too," Sanjeev said.

"Three! Make it three!"

"What?" the bartender yelled above the row.

"Three! Three, *three!*"

"This was a great idea, guys," Derrick muttered, shaking his head. "Really fantastic."

Unfazed, Chitra said, "Thank you. We thought so, too."

"Dance?" Sanjeev asked cheerfully.

"I just sat down!" Derrick exclaimed.

"I wasn't talking to *you*, silly," Sanjeev retorted, and punched Derrick's shoulder playfully. "Man, lighten up! Chit, you wanna dance?"

"With you?"

"Yeah, who else?"

"No," she said, and grinned.

"Three Scotch and Cokes," the bartender announced. Batting her eyelids, Chitra took the drinks from his tray, and slid him some money. The bartender took the cash and walked away. She passed one of the glasses to Sanjeev, who was laughing uproariously at her failed attempt to get the bartender's attention. "He's gay," she shouted, and when Derrick looked at her miserably, whispered, "Oops."

"Drink up," Sanjeev said, raising his glass in a toast. "To having fun!"

"To having fun!" Chitra repeated, and waited for Derrick to raise his glass. "Come on, Rick!"

Derrick sighed and clinked the edge of his glass with theirs. "To having fun," he said dully.

"Get into the spirit, Rick!" Sanjeev exclaimed.

Derrick took a tiny sip.

"That's hardly the spirit, Rick!" Sanjeev exclaimed.

"Guys, give me a break!" Derrick cried, slamming the glass down. A splash of brown alcoholic fizzy drink plopped onto the bar and exploded into a several mini puddles. "What's the matter with you two? You've dragged me here. Fine—now back off a little! Why the hell are the two of you trying so hard to get me up and about? Let me take my time! Let me find my own way!"

Sanjeev took another mouthful of his drink and placed the glass next to Derrick's. He leaned forward, his arms outstretched, one hand on the bar, one hand on Derrick's shoulder. "Listen," he said, and Derrick looked at him with his eyes flashing with impatience, "we're just trying to get you to have some fun, okay? We're thinking the longer you remain in this funk, the harder it'll be for you to climb out of it. We're sorry if we're being pushy, but you've gotta realise—" He stopped and looked up at Chitra, who shrugged slightly, a *what-are-we-to-do?* expression on her face. "Derrick," Sanjeev resumed, "buddy, we're sorry, but the thing is, Geraldine has made up her mind. Okay? She is what she is, and you've got to accept that."

Derrick exhaled loudly and seemed to deflate. He slouched forward in his seat, resting his head in his hands. "Aw, shit," he mumbled, and shook his head in glumness.

"We're really sorry, honey," Chitra added quietly, "but you've gotta move on."

"How can she do this to me?" Derrick moaned.

"Oh, boy," Sanjeev muttered under his breath.

"How can she—oh, Jesus, how can she be—?"

"Honey, honey," Chitra said hurriedly, grabbing his hand, "dance with me."

"I don't wanna dance, I just wanna curl up and *die* . . ."

"Come on," she urged, and pulled, trying to get him to his feet. He was heavier than she realised, because she kept on yanking and he wasn't budging.

Finishing the last of his drink, Sanjeev said, "You'll meet someone else."

"I don't want someone else, I want *Geri!*" he wailed, and shook his head again, once, twice, three times. "I want Geri, 'cause I *love* her!" Derrick howled, and Chitra looked around furtively, cautious of the impending scene. "Why doesn't she love me anymore?" Derrick squalled, as Sanjeev's eyes darted back and forth between Derrick and the people around them, who stole curious looks at them before swiftly turning away in embarrassment.

"Rick, buddy, calm down," Sanjeev crooned into his ear.

"She *does* loves you," Chitra said. "You've got to understand, Geri loves you and has *always* loved you, it's just that—she's come to a decision on which direction she wants to take in her life, and I think it's very, very important that we—all of us—learn to respect that. Sweetie—sweetie, don't cry like that, it's very unbecoming . . ."

"Derrick, she wants to stay friends with you," Sanjeev said. "I've been telling you that all week: *she still wants to be friends.* I think it's vital for you to grab the opportunity to remain mates with her, because if you don't, then you won't even have a friendship with her, much less a *relationship.*"

"It's — it's just so *unfair!*" Derrick bemoaned loudly.

The bartender, whose eyes had been dancing in their direction over the past few minutes, moved towards them with a glass containing a blue-coloured drink, and placed it in front of Derrick. "Hey," he said, his voice gruff, masculine, "what's the matter, sugar? Tell Daddy all about it."

"Oh, *God!*" Derrick shrieked, and stumbled off the stool, pushing himself away from the bar, leaving the bartender looking befuddled and mortally wounded.

"Thank you *so* much!" Sanjeev barked at Daddy. He hurried after Derrick, who was blindly making his way onto the dance floor, elbowing his way past indignant patrons, shoving his way through the massive throng of throbbing, sweaty bodies, snivelling, sobbing, wanting Geraldine, wanting to hold her, wanting to touch her, wanting somebody to save him from this never-ending journey of wretchedness. Sharp voices called out to him over the thumping, pulsating music, creating a discordant cacophony of slamming drumbeats, pumping electronic bass notes, synthesised drones and angry voices: "What the fuck?" "Watch it, dumbass!" *"Hey!"* "Well, *excuse* you!" "Oh, I'm *so* sorry, I'm in *your* way!" He barged through the crowd, ignoring the outraged cries from the battered and bruised partiers, blinking out of his eyes hot tears of distress and stupefaction —

— And collided into the Other Girl.

"**A**w, you *klutz!*"

"Oh, God, I'm sorry," Derrick cried tremulously.

Somewhere in the crowd behind him, Chitra called his name. In counterpoint, Sanjeev's voice rang out, lost in the mélange of flesh and noise. Derrick turned back to the girl he'd bumped into, wiping his eyes frantically, trying to clear his vision. She'd dropped her purse, and he uttered something that was supposed to be an apology. He squatted, reaching for the purse strap. As he started to stand, his eyes fell upon the dark heels she was wearing; stayed glued on her legs, long, curvaceous and well-toned; and then his eyes were on her mini-skirt, which was like a good speech: long enough to cover the subject but short enough to arouse interest; her top, glittery with something that reflected the multi-coloured lights spinning and shining into every nook and cranny of the dance club; and her breasts (*Good God*, he thought, as he rose in more ways than one) —

"Derrick!" Chitra caught up with him, helped him to his feet. She seemed to notice the Other Girl. "Oh, hello!" she greeted cheerfully. "Derrick, did you run into her? Say you're sorry."

The Other Girl smiled, slinging her purse over one bare shoulder. "That's okay, it was just an accident." To Derrick: "Sorry I called you a klutz."

"N-no," Derrick replied, "I *am* a klutz."

"Derrick!" Now Sanjeev caught up to them, gasping and panting. He slapped Derrick on the back, bending over at the waist to catch his breath. Then he, too, noticed the Other Girl, and he stood upright at once, exclaiming, "*Hel*-lo!"

"Hello," the Other Girl returned, and continued to smile as Derrick ogled her. "Well, well. Three's company. Is there a fourth?"

"No," Derrick said almost at once.

"Just us three," Sanjeev confirmed.

"So let me see," the Other Girl said huskily, "there are three of you. Two guys — one, two — and one girl." She giggled. "Seems to me like you're in need of one more . . ."

And suddenly she was standing in close proximity to Derrick, so close he could smell her perfume and the sweet smell of mint from the mojito she'd probably been drinking. "Hi there," she drawled. "How you doin'? They call me Dawn."

"Dawn and Derrick," Chitra piped up gleefully. "That sounds so cute!"

"Derrick and Dawn," Sanjeev stated, as if correcting some sort of mistake.

Derrick's mouth moved soundlessly for a few seconds, and for a moment the others wondered if he was actually saying something that was being drowned out by the loud music. "What?" they all exclaimed, and Derrick blinked rapidly—inhaling the intoxicating aroma of Dawn's scent—before coughing out, "H-hi, Dawn. I'm—I'm Derrick."

"Well, this has been fun, we've got to leave the two of you alone now!" Sanjeev exploded. A startled look crossed Chitra's face, and she nudged him in the ribs without Derrick noticing. Sanjeev turned to stare at her questioningly, and she shot him a cold *look* that warned him not to be too hasty. "Oh!" he exclaimed, understanding the *look*—just as he always understood most of Chitra's *look*s without her having to say anything: such being the physiognomic strength of the bond between them.

"Did you guys come from the bar? I'm parched," Dawn said, linking her arm through Derrick's. "Let me buy you a drink."

Derrick blinked. "S-shouldn't *I* be buying?"

"Honey, you look blue," Dawn replied, and she wasn't referring to the psychedelic lights that tilted and twirled from the ceiling. "I think," she said, reaching for her purse, "you could do with a nice, relaxing beverage, what do you say? My treat."

"I . . . I don't know—"

"What's the problem?"

Derrick managed a grin, pathetic as it was. "It's just—I'm the guy."

"Oh, don't you start on all that P.C. baloney with me," Dawn replied, rolling her eyes and batting her lush lashes. "Now you listen, gorgeous, I'll be doing the buying tonight, okay? You feel sucky about it? Too bad, take me out some other night. Tonight is entirely on me."

Chitra and Sanjeev stood back as the two of them made their way back to the bar. The dance floor was filled with the mass of moving, dancing, twisting, turning bodies of all shapes and sizes, and the smells of booze and cologne and sweat were high in the air.

Sliding her arm through Sanjeev's the same way Dawn had with Derrick, Chitra sighed happily. "So what do you think? If all goes well . . ."

"Dawn needs to get a few drinks in Rick first," Sanjeev pointed out. "But, yes, if all goes well . . ." A smiled lit up his face, and Chitra chuckled, sidling up against him as the dazzling and technicoloured lights splashed across them and danced away.

Simple Pleasures

The phone rang as Graham was sifting through his bounteous collection of personal writings.

"Hello?"

"Hello, Mr Hanson?"

"Michelle! Hi."

"How are you?"

"I'm good, and you?"

"Good. I mean, a lot better. My mum said you called earlier . . ."

Graham laughed. A cool breeze blew through the window on his left, threatening to mess up the sheets of paper on his desk. He placed one palm flat upon the surface, keeping the notes in place. "Yeah, I was hoping you could come over for lunch," he said. "Feli and I, we thought we would make you your favourite meal, fatten you up."

"Fatten me up?" Now it was Michelle's turn to laugh. "Oh, I don't think so, gotta watch the waistline."

"Sweetheart, trust me, enjoy your food while you can before your digestive system starts to reject certain things. I actually have a proposal for you, something I was hoping you might be interested in helping me with."

"Oh? What is it?"

"Do you think you could drop by tomorrow? Say, after school? Have a late lunch?"

There was a pause. Then: "Oh, no, tomorrow's not good for me, I'm going to be busy . . . I have to be at the supermarket after school. How about Tuesday?"

"That sounds good," Graham said, and jotted it down on his notepad on the edge of his desk, away from the other writings that he'd compiled over the years: journal entries, accounts of his experiences, the upturns and downfalls over his long and eventful life. He was hoping to get it sorted out into some sort of order so that it would make things easier for Michelle once she started on the project. *If* she decided to start on it. It was going to be an arduous task, chronologising the past and adding in new, more recent escapades and words of wisdom. Being in her final year at high school, she might decide not to take up the extra work.

Oh, well, we'll see what happens on Tuesday. He'd get Felicity to cook up the carbonara then.

When he hung up, he wandered into the bedroom, where he saw his wife was already under the covers, reading. She was such an avid reader, Graham reflected. Even back when they'd first met, she'd been picking up paperbacks by then-renowned authors. It was a very good habit to cultivate, he'd always thought, despite the fact that he wasn't very much into reading for leisure. Being a former teacher meant Graham's passions had always lain in textbooks and academic journals. But he didn't scorn those who chose to read fiction; whatever pleasures people could get out of life . . .

Bertha Asterville, for example—the feisty, dim-witted resident of Number 23, who spoke through her nose and who, Graham believed, was infatuated with him. She seemed to find great joy in baking. Just earlier that evening, she'd left a cake on the doorstep. When Graham had stepped out for some fresh air, he'd nearly stepped on it: a rich, moist fruitcake "with 27 different dried fruits and nuts", Bertha had claimed in an accompanying note. On the back of it, she'd written: *To comfort you in this hour of sadness. Yours lovingly, Bertha.*

The presumptuous old biddy, Graham had thought good-naturedly, taking the cake into the house. He'd shown it to Felicity, who'd laughed and insisted they at least eat some of it. "Bertha's the kind who'll call tomorrow to find out how you liked it, and if you don't give it a taste, you'll never hear the end of it." So they'd cut themselves each a slice, and it *was* good, he had to admit, although he doubted there really were twenty-seven different types of fruit and nut in it.

The point was, everybody enjoys doing different things, and Graham was of the belief that as far as you weren't hurting anybody, there ought to be no limit on what you want to do. If spending hours playing the piano makes you happy, then by all means, do it. Such was Graham Hanson's philosophy, and it was one that he stuck to keenly. Life is short, so enjoy it to the full, and don't live in regret, for if regret and self-pity were at the fore of your life, you wouldn't achieve much out of it. He and Felicity had been severely affected by their inability to have children, but if they had held on to that hopelessness all the days of their lives, he was certain they wouldn't be here today, content despite their shortcomings, with friends and family who, despite *their* shortcomings, were never a liability.

As Graham got into bed, he realised that, as much as the woman was a pain in the proverbial behind, Bertha Asterville meant well. He decided to repay the favour by bringing a cake to *her* doorstep tomorrow morning. Graham chuckled to himself, which made Felicity look up from her book curiously.

"I'm going to pay Bertha back," he chuckled.

She raised an eyebrow, her expression deadpan. "You do that."

"I'm going to give her a cake. You know, in return for the one she baked."

She put the book down. "You're going to bake, sweetheart?"

"I'm going to get it from the supermarket," he said, and chortled as if it were hilarious, leaving Felicity to shake her head.

"You're getting senile, old man," she remarked, as he turned out the light.

Vodka Oranges and Odd Jobs

"**S**he's gay."

"Aw, honey."

"A lesbian."

"I'm so sorry."

"She likes the ladies."

"Oh, sugar."

"She loves the boobies."

"I get it."

"What's a guy to do, huh?" Derrick chortled and emptied the last of the drink into his mouth. His fifth.

"Yeah," Dawn said, looking positively forlorn on his behalf.

"I'm sorry. The guys—Chit and Sanjeev—they tell me to just forget allabout'er, move on with my life, but it's not so easy, y'know? Y'understand me?"

"I understand," she said, nodding, blond locks falling across her eyes. She pushed them out of the way with one hand, a quick, fluid movement that Derrick found incredibly titillating.

He tilted his head back to receive more of that delicious orange drink, but found he had already finished it off. Damn. He wanted one more. "Hey, another vodka orange!" he shouted to the bartender, who shot him a dark look and turned away.

Dawn watched Derrick with those intense doe eyes, eyelids batting under those long lashes, the tip of her pink tongue sticking out of one corner of those red, red, ruby red lips. Looking at her made him grow hard again, and he told himself to calm down, because somewhere within the fogginess of his mind he knew it was most probably the alcohol that was making him yearn for her, for just a taste—

He forced himself to look away, feeling a flush of warmth in his cheeks, a stab of guilt. It took him a moment to realise he had nothing to be guilty about. Geraldine had turned away from him, they were over and done with, kaput, no more! That meant—

That meant—

"Hey," he said aloud, and Dawn looked him curiously.

The bartender sauntered over, his expression sulky, and placed a sixth glass of vodka orange in front of him with a loud thud. Startled, Derrick stared at him, and the bartender grabbed his empty glass, grunting, "You know, I can dress up for you if you want me to."

Derrick gawked at him. Dawn slid money across the counter and smiled at the bartender lethally. "Go away, sweetheart. He's mine." The man stalked away.

Derrick turned to Dawn, his mouth agape. "What kind of club *is* this?"

"Why, a gay club, of course."

"A *what?*"

"A jolly, merry, gay club, darling."

"Why the hell would Chit and Sanjeev bring me to a *gay* club?"

Dawn looked at him. "To get you to accept, perhaps? Your ex-girlfriend's decision?"

"So—are you—gay, too?"

She startled him by tossing her head back in a hearty laugh. "Oh, darling, please, don't be ridiculous!"

"Then—what are you doing here?"

"Sweetie, this is the one place a girl can come to to make good male friends, and not be bothered by horny men who simply want you to suck their dick and move on."

Derrick's mouth opened and closed like a fish out of water, and it took several seconds before he choked out, "But I'm not gay."

"That's okay," she said, unperturbed. "Sometimes a girl *wants* to suck a little dick."

It took several more seconds for the implication of *this* message to hit Derrick, whose brain was now numb as it had never been before. Swallowing hard and finding he hadn't any wetness to swallow, he gulped down the vodka orange and shifted agitatedly in his seat, wondering what to do now, what to say next, how to erect—*react! How to react!* "Dawn," he began, and licked his lips furiously, his mind racing with thoughts such as the weather and how his mother's next-door-neighbour's laundry line proudly displayed knickers that were large beyond description—thoughts that were in no way connected to his current situation and were in no way of any help to him—"Dawn," he tried again, thinking *knickers, knickers, knickers,* and Dawn looked at him curiously, a faint smile on her fair, lovely face, as he wondered how he could tell her that *dear Jesus, I'm a man, you're a beautiful woman, I'm in mourning over the loss of my ex, I want therapy, I need to take recuperative measures!*

"What is it, Derrick?" she asked, her smile widening, as if she knew and was trying to lead him to say the words.

"I was . . . um . . . just wondering, if you'd like to—uh . . ." *Knickers, knickers, knickers! Knickers the size of an elephant's ass!* "Would you like to . . . ?"

Suddenly, a couple across the bar from them caught his eye—not because they were doing anything to attract attention to themselves, but because *he recognised them all too well.* The girl with the long, honey-brown hair and the other girl sitting next to her, with that *shocking pink* boyish haircut and a mouth that was repeatedly chewing, chewing, chewing, as if she were a cow. A great pain stabbed at his chest as he watched Hope pluck the wad of gum from her mouth, stick it onto the surface of the bar, and grab the back of Geraldine's head. Then he felt his gorge rising as Geraldine shot her head forward and kissed

Hope right on the lips. They pushed against each other, mouth to mouth, glued together for what seemed to Derrick like a freaking eternity.

Dawn must have noticed the direction of Derrick's gaze, for she, too, turned to observe the girls. "Derrick," she began quietly. He continued to gawk. They were going at it long and hard, not breaking apart, not even taking a moment to breathe. They were so revolting, it made him sick!

"Derrick," Dawn tried again—

—As Derrick shot off his stool, his face twisted with determination. He grabbed Dawn's hand and gave it a sharp tug. "Let's get out of here!"

Together they strode, hand-in-hand, to the end of the bar, towards the exit.

After Derrick and Dawn had barged out of the club, the girls pulled apart. Geraldine smiled at Hope, who, in turn, gestured to Sanjeev and Chitra hovering nearby. The four of them gathered and grinned, thrilled by what they believed was victory.

When it was over, Derrick found himself in a further state of bewilderment. Dawn had been amazing, although she hadn't allowed him to go all the way with her. With his pants down, he'd asked whether she wanted to adjourn to the bedroom, and she'd stopped what she was doing long enough to say, "Not tonight, honey, tonight I'm happy enough doing this," before returning to it, making him writhe in pleasure, hot with desire, surprised and proud that he could still get it up after all he'd drunk that evening. He'd wanted more, but she'd been content with just the job, which suited him just fine.

Later, lying on his bed alone, he felt the tiniest trace of guilt at having done what he'd done. But he told himself it wasn't a big deal; it wasn't as if he'd cheated on Geri. She'd made her bed, as the saying went. Yet he felt guilty, and he reprimanded himself in his drink-addled, post-orgasmic stupor: *Screw it all, if I live to regret this for the rest of my life, I'd at least have had this experience, instead of dying without having experienced it at all.*

It occurred to him a few minutes later, as the darkness of sleep began to tint the edges of his already blurred vision, that Geraldine also deserved to think that.

BIG, FAT FISH AND
SMALL FAVOURS

Jessy Cooke woke up at 7am and got ready for work, despite her boss having urged her to take some time off. After she got dressed, she headed down to the kitchen, wondering if her children were ready for school. They were usually at the table when she got downstairs, halfway through their breakfast. This morning, she found the kitchen empty. She stopped at the doorway and stared at the vacant chairs around the table. Then she remembered that Maggie had wanted to sleep in and recuperate, and Joe . . .

Well, Joe was old enough to look after himself, and if he was going to be late for school, so be it. He had to clean up his own messes. Which wasn't to imply that Jessy was, as those dreadful websites on single parents had warned, "giving up her matriarchal duties"; Joe had made it clear he didn't want her involved in whatever he was having to deal with at this time. The night before, he'd come home all upset and in an absolutely hellish mood. She'd asked what was wrong, and he'd shouted at her to butt out and stormed up the stairs, slamming his bedroom door so hard it had virtually shaken the entire house. Jessy had then decided her son would have to wipe his own ass if he were to soil his pants. In a cruel, ironic way it was just as it had been with Paul: if he needed her, she would, of course, be there for him; otherwise, he had free rein to do whatever he wanted and face the consequences.

That she was eager to go back to work was a good sign. Jessy was certain most of the obstacles had already been thrown her way, and the path that lay ahead was, if not smooth-sailing, then considerably less bumpy that the road already travelled.

She fixed herself a quick breakfast. Afterwards, she headed to her car. As she climbed in, she saw the left rear bumper was dented, and quite badly, too. It hadn't been there earlier, which meant Joe had, sometime over the past couple of days, got into an accident and hadn't told her. *Another fish he has to fry.* She sighed. If he didn't bring it up, she'd have to confront him with it—and God knew it wasn't exactly high on her keen-to-do list.

Joe squirmed and thrashed, his dreams plagued by horrid images of his supposedly pregnant ex-girlfriend. It was a dreadful montage of lurid and disturbing imagery, including one that featured Carrie Taylor, her tummy bloated like a grotesque, pillow-sized Easter egg, waddling about and pointing her fingers accusingly at the bulge, shrieking, "It's all your fault! You're just like your father!" Then it flashed to another series of distressing scenes, pieces of the jigsaw that made up his life. The last image right before he awoke was of Carrie, sitting up in a hospital bed with her legs parted and blood staining her entire lower region as well as half the mattress. A doctor was hollering that she had to push, it wasn't going to be long now, just *push!*, and Carrie was screaming at the top of her lungs. Suddenly her legs, bent at the knees, jerked upwards to form perfect, blood-streaked Vs, and her dilated vulva was visible for Joe to see. He saw fingers prying out from within her, deep scarlet and oozing, forcing her apart, tearing her open. Joe let out a wail of horror and despair—for it was his father's face peering out at him through the slick red wetness, his glare accusatory and his ghastly lips seemingly mouthing *you're just like me, you're just like me . . .*

He bolted upright in bed, drenched in a freezing cold sweat, gasping and panting. The final, dreadful image of the nightmare replayed in his head, over and over: the parted labia, those bloodied nails tearing her open, his father's grisly, abhorrent visage . . . He pushed himself into the bathroom, lurched towards the toilet bowl, and vomited.

When he was done and the spasms subsided, he made up his mind that whatever decision Carrie made, he was not going to be part of it. He didn't want to see her ever again.

He stumbled back to bed, saw that it was already after eight AM, and realised it was a Monday. He was in no state to go to school today—or the day after, or the day after that. He knew the school authorities would eventually call his mother, but he'd cross that bridge when he came to it.

Carrie Taylor walked into class late, having slept in. She'd actually awakened when her mobile phone alarm had gone off, but had remained in bed, her mind clogged with perplexed thoughts, her heart weighed down. She'd fallen back into an uneasy sleep, only to jerk awake twenty minutes later. She knew she wouldn't make it to school on time, and contemplated playing truant altogether, but if she did, Wentworth, Richards and McPherson would start asking questions. She could tell them she was sick, but the last thing she wanted was for them to fawn over her with concern. She didn't think she had the strength for confrontations, especially since her father had practically interrogated her to death after the fight with Joe the night before. She had refrained from saying too much—if she were to reveal she was pregnant, that would've been the end of her life as she knew it. So she'd remained quiet until her father had left, and she'd slunk into bed, crying.

Carrie was a risk-taker, and always had been. At age four she'd climbed onto the roof of her house to see what the view was like from there. Her father had spotted her and had nearly had a coronary. At eleven, she'd gone trekking through the woods with a bunch of friends from school and had taken the dare of wandering through the dense wilderness on her own. She'd eventually got lost, and they'd had to send out a search party after her. They'd found her sleeping, perfectly content, under a berry bush, her fingers smeared with pulp and juice, but her mouth empty of any traces of the unknown fruit—she was young, but she wasn't stupid.

In short, she had always been a daredevil, but she'd always injected a bit of common sense into everything she did or planned to do.

Except for this.

She'd been so sure nothing would happen. They had not used any contraception, and now she had to deal with the fallout. Alone.

Lying in bed, she'd wondered if the horror stories about abortions were true, that they sucked the foetus into a vacuum-cleaner-like thing with spinning blades at the end so that it would be hacked and chopped and sliced and diced into bloody ribbons. One of her friends had undergone the procedure and had later battled with the ethical issues surrounding it. Was the thing growing inside of her, feeding on the food that she consumed to keep herself alive, alive or not? Was it just a mass of lifeless tissue, cells formed together without any capability of thought or expression—or was it to be considered a living being that deserved to be given a chance at life following its conception, regardless of the much-debated point that a foetus without a central nervous system and brain was technically *not* living yet?

She wasn't religious, nor was she the type who believed anyone had a right to impose their beliefs on someone else, especially when it came to what they should or shouldn't do with their own bodies—but her friend's accounts of internal conflict were enough for her to be hesitant about going through with the process. On the other hand, could she really let it live, let it grow, let her body expand and let the whole world know she was with child, *without* a father, *without* a husband? In this day and age it was hardly considered a dishonour, but that didn't change the fact that her entire future, her entire life, would be dramatically altered based on one decision: to live and let live, or to die and let die.

Carrie reached the school a half-hour late, and she walked into class, trying to lift her head high in spite of the crumbling emotions within. Her teacher reprimanded her for being tardy, and she barely nodded her head in apology or acknowledgement. She sauntered to her chair, while Richards, Wentworth and McPherson looked at her curiously from behind their desks.

As she had hoped, Joe wasn't there.

Thank heaven for small favours.

A STRANGE SORT OF FEELING

For once, Matthew didn't have to wait for the kid to show. Even as he parked his car on the edge of the field, he could see the small figure sitting on the bench, feet not even brushing the ground. Matthew stepped out of his vehicle, shutting the door on the reference books he'd taken out of the library, and made his way across the field with his brown paper bag containing today's lunch. The sun was high in the sky, but there was a slight nippiness to the air. The grass and leaves rustled and little pink flowers danced across the space.

He reached the bench. "Hey. How you doing?"

"Hey, Matty," the boy replied, and patted the seat next to him. Matthew sat down. "Whatcha bring for lunch?"

"Well, I've got a ham sandwich," he said, rummaging into it, "and a couple of apples."

"I like ham! Don't get to eats it much, though."

"Why not?"

"My mummy don't let me. Gimme!"

"Whoa!" Matthew yanked the bag away from the boy. "Who said I was going to share?"

"Aw!" the boy exclaimed, looking hurt. "It's good to share. Sharin' means carin'."

"Spare me. I was just kidding anyway. See? I sliced the sandwich into halves, so you could have one."

"Does it have mayo in it?"

"Sure does."

"Lots?"

"A fair amount."

The boy took his share and bit into it, chewing enthusiastically. Matthew wondered if the boy had had lunch—if his mummy, whoever she was, had fed him. The kid was tucking into the sandwich as though his life depended on it. Maybe he was just a big eater, Matthew thought, and quietly bit into his own sandwich.

"Hey, Matty?" the boy said, with his mouth full, cheeks bulging. "Where do babies come from?"

Matthew let out a sharp bark of laughter. At the same time, his mind was filled with inane images of cabbage patches and long-beaked storks. Choking on the remnants of his sandwich and chuckling, he said, "Taiwan."

"Taiwan," little Robby repeated incredulously.

"Yeah. Taiwan. They make them in the factories and ship them across the world."

"So I comes from a factory?"

"You and me both, kid."

The boy frowned, looking dubious. "Are you teasin' me, mister?"

Matthew grinned, ear-to-ear.

The boy said, "You got bread stuck in your teeth."

"Smartass," Matthew retorted, and picked at it. The boy smirked and bit into the sandwich. Matthew conceded: "Okay, okay. Babies. Hmmm. Let's see . . . well, there comes a time when big boys, like myself, get together with big girls . . ." The boy made a disgusted noise, something that sounded like "ewe", and pulled a face. "No, no, hear me out. Big boys and big girls get together, and they—well, they have sex," he said, and guffawed at the top of his lungs. Brilliant! A lesson in sex education—never too young to learn!

"What's that?" the boy asked.

"What's what?"

"Sacks."

"Oh, sex? Well . . ." Matthew laughed again, and the boy glared at him, seemingly not sharing the older guy's amusement. Matthew wondered how much he ought to share. Children were learning about it at an increasingly younger age these days, on TV, on the Internet, in school. But little Robby didn't *go* to school—so maybe he needed to learn about it from some other source. He certainly couldn't see little Robby's mummy telling the boy where he'd come from—so maybe the responsibility fell on Matthew's shoulders!

"Okay," he said, making up his mind as the boy yawned widely, "you know how girls are different from us, right? Like, they have to sit down when they pee because they don't have a . . . well . . ."

"A pecker?"

"Yeah. Yeah, that. Oh, this is going to be hilarious."

"I'm getting bored," the boy said.

"Okay, okay," Matthew repeated, and made some bizarre gesture with one hand that made no sense whatsoever to the boy. "Say, this is the boy's pecker. And say *this*"—making another weird gesture with his other hand—"is the girl's . . ."

"Pillow case," the boy said.

"Pillow case?"

The boy shrugged.

"Uh . . . okay, pillow case. So," Matthew said, and made another series of strange gestures, "if you can imagine the pecker and the pillow case moving to combine as one . . ."

The boy's frowned deepened.

"Okay, I know! Imagine the boy's pecker as the pillow. When grown-ups have sex . . ." He made further queer gesticulations with his finger formations while the boy stared at him, bewildered. "It's kind of like, if you can imagine it, putting the pillow into the pillow case? You know what I mean? It's sorta like, moving in and out of the pillow case . . ."

"I don't understand," the boy said in an annoyed tone. Then a look of shock crossed his features, and his mouth dropped open. "OhmyGod! You know, my mummy sometimes says she wants to change the pillow case—does it means she wants to do sacks?"

"Have sex," Matthew corrected him, and laughed uproariously. The boy stared at him, and he sputtered, "Oh, you know what? Just forget it, kid. You'll understand when you're older."

"S'always when I'm older," the boy grumbled, and yawned again. "I'm sleepy."

Between chuckles: "Didn't you sleep well last night?"

"No. Had bad dreams."

"Aw, that's too bad." Another burst of tittering, and the boy gave him a look that clearly said *get over it*. "You wanna tell me about them? The bad dreams, I mean?"

The child shook his head. "Can't. Mummy says I shouldn't."

"Why not?"

Little Robby hesitated, and then his eyebrows furrowed as his lips twisted into a frown. "'Cause Daddy was in the dream."

Matthew stopped laughing. "And you can't tell me about Daddy because . . . ?"

"'Cause Daddy's a bad man."

"Oh. Okay."

A pause. Then: "Daddy didn't like me much."

"Yeah, well, that's not uncommon," Matthew retorted bitterly.

"He didn't like me. Which is okay, 'cause I didn't like him too much neither."

"That's—your right, I guess."

The boy gazed into the distance, his eyes glazing over, and Matthew wondered if the kid was going to cry. Little Robby's hands trembled slightly as he looked off into oblivion. Matthew watched him and waited, figuring the boy needed the silence.

Finally, the kid murmured, "So sleepy." He seemed to lose his grip on the sandwich, and Matthew reached over and caught it before it fell to the ground. The boy looked at him through half-open eyes. "Can I sleep now?"

Suddenly uncertain, a little anxious, Matthew replied, "Sure."

Little Robby's eyes fluttered shut and he leaned against Matthew, who wasn't entirely comfortable with the proximity, but he let the child be, wondering how awful a man had to be to not be liked by his own six-year-old, and to create nightmares that caused a child to stay awake at night.

The boy dreamed again:
His mummy, with the sugar-free vanilla ice-cream . . .
In the bedroom, changing the pillow cases . . .
And him falling. Falling. Falling down the stairs —

"Hey. Hey, Robby, pal, wake up."

The boy mumbled something under his breath and fidgeted against him, but didn't awaken. Matthew gave him a little shake. "Come on pal, it's time to get up."

The child's eyes parted slightly, and he blinked.

"Kid. Robby—whatever your last name is, wake up."

The boy glanced up at Matthew without recognition. Then the glazed look passed and alertness registered. He croaked, "What happened, mister?"

"You fell asleep. You were really tired, huh?"

"Asleep . . . ?" The child pulled away, and Matthew felt the coolness after the warmth of the boy's body. Matthew also felt something deep within—an emotion that he would later look back upon and identify as *concern.* For the moment he was preoccupied with making sure the boy came fully awake so he could get home safely. They'd been sitting on the bench for nearly a half-hour—a half-hour during which Matthew had slowly nibbled on his lunch and finished it.

"Hungry," the boy murmured.

Matthew held up the child's half of the sandwich. "Still have the ham."

The boy shook his head. "Shouldn't have ham. Mummy says . . ." He shook his head again. "I should go home, mister. Mummy might worry."

"Okay. Can you get home okay?"

"Yeah."

"You want me to help?"

"No."

"Come on, pal, I'll see you across the street."

"That's okay, Mister Matty, I'll be okay. God will see me home safely."

Matthew put the sandwich down on the seat next to him. "Fine. Then we'll let God do that."

The boy looked at him through sleepy eyes. "I got guardian angels, mister."

"Really."

"Yeah. They look after me."

"That's good, kid. Very good."

"Do you believe in guardian angels, Mister Matty?"

Matthew laughed, but it sounded more like a derisive snort. "No."

"Why not?"

"Why should I?"

"Because they looks after you. Make sure you're okay."

"I'm okay, but it's not because of guardian angels."

"Naw," the boy said, shaking his head, and all of a sudden the drowsiness in his eyes vanished. "It's 'cause of 'em, all right. God looks after all of us, and He sends His guardian angels to protect us. S'just the way it is."

"In case you've forgotten, I don't believe in God. So I don't have any guardian angels."

"Just 'cause you don't believe in 'em don't mean they not there."

"Just because *you* believe in them doesn't mean they *are*."

"Don't you wanna go to Heaven when you go, Matty?"

"We've had this discussion before, and I told you, I don't want to talk about God, or about guardian angels, or about anything to do with religion, okay? We can talk about other things. Like your mum, tell me about your mum."

The boy had to think for a while before replying. "She's okay. She takes care of me. And she cooks good. She cooks lots and lots of yummy stuffs for me."

"Yeah? Like what?"

"Spaghetti with lots and lots of cheese."

"Hmm. Sounds yummy."

"Cheese and butter."

"With *butter*," Matthew repeated with mock incredulity. "Well!"

"And cream. Lots and lots of cream."

"Hmm. Sounds . . . fattening. You do know that's not good for you in the long run."

The boy didn't seem understand this statement.

"It's bad for the heart," Matthew said.

"Mummy says it's good for me," little Robby replied.

"Fine, whatever."

"My mummy lets me eat it every day."

"What?"

"Yeah. Sometimes it's somethin' else, like—scrambled eggs. I love scrambled eggs. Mummy cooks 'em with heaps of butter."

"Every day?"

"Almost."

Matthew stared at the boy. The menu sounded delicious, but it also sounded unwholesome. Surely it wasn't good for a little boy to be eating like this on a regular basis. Curious, he asked, "What about fruit and veg and all that? The healthy stuff?"

"Salad," the boy said, after thinking about it for a good half a second.

"Ah, that's not too bad then."

"With mayo."

"With mayo," Matthew repeated, and blinked thoughtfully.

"And ice-cream. For dessert. My mummy lets me have ice-cream, almost every time."

"Aw, man. Seems to me that you're on the fast road to disaster, kid." But then again, Matthew told himself, he was just a child, and didn't most children grow up on diets such as the one little Robby's mother was advocating . . . and worse? Weren't children supposed to have high metabolisms anyway? Maybe there was nothing wrong with the way the boy was being fed. Matthew was no expert. On the other hand, if such a diet were the norm for children, he figured every child would grow up obese and overweight. But that wasn't the case.

Which brought him to another notion: if little Robby were telling the truth, and he lived on a diet of such unhealthy proportions, why wasn't the kid plump? The boy was small-sized, and, now that Matthew focused on it, he looked *underweight.* He didn't look unhealthy per se, but—but there was something about him—something Matthew had never noticed before—that didn't seem right. Or was he just imagining it . . . ?

Maybe I'm wrong, Matthew thought. *Maybe there's nothing wrong.*

Maybe he's just kidding about what he eats.

"What d'you mean?" the boy asked, referring to his last statement.

"It means what you eat could badly affect your heart. In the future, I mean."

The boy frowned, uncomprehending.

"Too much butter and cream and stuff ain't good for your heart, kiddo. Put your hand right there . . ." Matthew moved his hand to his left pectoral, and the boy mirrored the movement, placing his palm flat on his own chest. Matthew said softly, "You feel your heartbeat, buddy? That's what's keeping you alive, you know that? And it's no good for it to stop, because then you won't be alive anymore. Too much butter and cream and cheese might cause it to stop. I mean, not now, but after many, many, many years, when you're a big man, it might not be healthy. Mummy might be taking you down a dangerous road."

"You mean if I keep eating like this I could die?" the boy asked solemnly.

"Well, your heart could stop, and . . ."

"And I could die?"

"No. I mean, yes, everyone has to die someday—but . . . well, yes. If your heart stops, you die. Or you *could* die."

"That means I gets to see God," the boy said.

"Aw, Jesus." Matthew rolled his eyes.

The boy's face lit up with a wide smile. "I gets to see God!"

"Not if He doesn't exist!" Matthew exclaimed.

"What d'you mean?"

"Not if He's not *real.*"

"Of *course* He's real!" the boy said loudly. "He's real! And He sends the guardian angels, who have wings just like the birds!"

"Oh, no, *not* the birds . . ."

"So if I was like the birds and I could fly just like the birds . . ."

"Then you'd be an angel?" Matthew let out a scornful laugh. "Give me a break, kid."

"I'd be an angel," the boy said, sounding awe-struck. He swung his legs back and forth in excitement at the idea. "I'd be—like, one of them angels who looks after other people. And—and hey, mister, maybe if I'm an angel, I could be *your* guardian angel and I could looks after you and make sure everythin's okay and make sure you're fine and all, isn't that great?"

"No, because *you wouldn't be real.*"

"I would, I would!"

"Come on, buddy, don't kid yourself."

"Maybe Mummy wants me to meet God. Maybe that's why she keeps feedin' me, 'cause she wants my heart to stop and she wants me to die so that I can go and meet Jesus! Maybe—maybe my heart *should* stop, and I *should* die!" The boy's voice was shrill with eagerness and intrigue, and Matthew gaped at his little friend with more than a little disbelief. What the *hell* was this kid talking about? Just how naïve *was* he? How could a kid so intelligent *(smart* — animals *are intelligent, people are* smart) be so stupid at the same time? Incredible!

"Kid, listen to me . . ."

The boy began to sing, tunelessly, a hymn Matthew knew too well from all his wasted years in Sunday school. *"Jesus loves me, this I know . . ."*

"Robby, wait, listen . . ."

"'Cause the Bible tells me so . . ."

"Robby, listen to me . . ."

"Jesus loves me, this I know," the boy repeated, evidently not knowing the rest of it.

"Rob — hey, Rob, listen — !"

"'Cause the Bible . . ."

"Listen!" Matthew shouted, and the boy flinched, stopping in mid-croon. Little Robby looked up with his eyes wide and his face taking on a shade of pale, obviously startled and frightened by Matthew's outburst. Seeing this, Matthew swallowed hard, felt a stab of what felt like guilt, and softened, lowering his voice to a normal volume. "Listen," he repeated, and the boy kept his eyes on him, "don't you be doing anything stupid, like killing yourself or trying to die or something just because you have this ridiculous notion that you're going to see God afterwards, okay? Because that's not going to happen."

"B-but," the boy replied, and his voice was almost inaudible, "God is real."

"Fine. Whatever. But if you kill yourself, He's not going to love you."

"I — I never said I was gonna kill meself."

"Good." Matthew nodded. "As long as we've got that clear."

The boy nodded slowly. "Yeah."

"Good," he repeated, and exhaled loudly. His pulse was thudding loudly in his ears — so loud he thought the boy would've been able to hear it, or the bench would've been shaking with each beat — and a cold sheen of sweat had covered his forehead. Matthew wiped his face, suddenly aware that his friendship with the little guy had unexpectedly taken a morbid turn, and he wasn't feeling at all at ease with it. He had to wonder about a little boy who had been taught — erroneously or otherwise — that death was a good thing because it meant reconciliation with God. As far as Matthew was concerned, there *was* no God, even if this was a fact that was hard to escape given the district's number of church, mosque-, and temple-going citizens; and even if there *were,* a boy of six was too young to be aware of the fact that death could lead to the (much-conjured) afterlife. *Six,* Matthew thought, shaking his head, exhaling loudly a second time. *He's only six. Shouldn't he be with the other kids, having fun? Living the life of a six-year-old?*

For the first time since he'd met the boy, Matthew began to wonder, seriously, about what was going on in little Robby's life. As far as Matthew knew, he didn't have any other friends, although the two girls he'd seen and heard two weeks earlier had known the child by name. Didn't the boy have any other playmates, anyone around his age who — *who, I don't know, play with army figurines or destroyer trucks or video games?* What about his schoolmates? No, the boy apparently didn't go to school — which brought up the question, why not? A boy of six should be in his first year, and yet little Robby was bumming around, day after day, his only buddy a man more than fifteen years older. Why didn't the child's mother send him to school? Why didn't his mother make sure he played with the right group of people? And who *was* his mother, anyway — why didn't she ever come out to check on him? Didn't she care about her boy? Didn't she wonder if he was safe? The boy had to cross a road to get to the field; it was the way the buildings were constructed, separated from the field by four roads forming the Square. Didn't the mother worry about the kid crossing roads in the middle of the afternoon all by himself? The boy, today, had spent more than forty minutes away from home — wasn't she concerned? Why did she think it fit to keep the boy at home and teach him everything herself, and yet let him roam free without supervision? Why did she think it fit to — purportedly — feed the boy unhealthy, fattening foods that were ultimately detrimental to the kid's health? Where was the boy's father, and why did the boy declare that he didn't like him? How many kids of six proclaimed their fathers didn't love them, and that they, in turn, didn't care about their fathers? Something was wrong here, and Matthew realised he should have noticed it right from the start, only *I didn't care at the start, he was just a little brat; now he's —*

He was still a little brat, but he was also more than that. They'd bonded. They'd formed and forged a bizarre kind of friendship. And that meant, no matter how much Matthew tried to deny it, he cared for the little twerp. He had a strange sort of paternal feeling towards the boy, even if the kid's constant ramblings about God tended to drive Matthew up the wall.

Maybe he ought to follow the boy home, meet his mother, see if what the boy had been telling him was true. But a part of Matthew was reluctant to get *too* involved. Meeting the parent would imply he was getting too attached to the kid, and attachments were not something he was a fan of. No. If he were to do that, he'd be just like his sister Michelle, incessantly fussing over every one of her friends, caring too much about them, tending to get too involved. Little Robby had lasted so far without Matthew's interference; there was no real reason for him to start now.

"I'm sorry I yelled," Matthew said under his breath.

"'Sokay," the boy replied, just as quietly. "Sorry I mades you angry."

"I wasn't angry. I was just — annoyed. A little bit."

"Sorry."

"'Sokay," Matthew said, and the boy managed a smile.

"Psychic freak," the kid said, and Matthew grinned in return.

They sat in silence for a few seconds, with the leaves whispering overhead as if talking among themselves about the two strange people sitting on the bench below them; with the sky a brilliant blue decorated with swathes of moving cloud, blown by the wind; with the birds, little Robby's much-adored birds, flying in fascinating formations high in the sky, black in the midst of all the blue.

"Why do they do that?" the kid asked, pointing at the birds.

Matthew looked. "Do what?"

"Fly in that funny shape?"

"I'm not sure . . . I think it's because the bird flying in the lead creates a wind in its wake. So the birds fly in a 'V' so that the one flying behind the other doesn't get the wind smack in the face. It's hard to fly with the wind in your eyes."

Little Robby giggled. "They're so smart."

"True, but we have brains that are over a hundred times bigger."

The boy replied, "So why aren't we as smart?"

Matthew could only look at him and blink stupidly.

BEAR WITH A SORE HEAD

Derrick awoke with an awful hangover. Sitting up required small, calculated steps. He sat on the edge of his bed, feeling like he was going to throw up, and wondered what the hell he'd done to deserve this. He couldn't dredge up much memory of the night before and the wee hours of that morning. He told himself that if he couldn't remember it, it was probably for the best.

He shuffled, inch by inch, towards the shower, and accidentally knocked the telephone off the edge of his desk. It hit the floor with a crash, and he cried out as his head pounded as though it were being struck by sledgehammer. His outburst caused another savage bout of pain. It was a bitch bending over at the waist—all his joints were aching—to pick up the telephone. Somehow, he did it, and he placed it back on the edge of the desk.

It was then that he saw the scrap of paper with scribbling on it. It was on the desk next to the phone, lying atop a reminder from the phone company that if he didn't pay the bill within the next three days, they'd disconnect the line. He had to squint through blurred vision to make out who had written it and what it said:

Call me—92416561
Hugz, Dawn

Dawn?
Derrick shut his eyes, trying to recall.

The phone rang, exploding in his ears. He screamed in pain—worsening the blow—and reached for it, groaning and moaning. He yanked the receiver towards him, but the cord wasn't long enough and he ended up pulling the entire instrument off the edge of the desk again. It hit the floor with another sickening crash, and a fourth explosion of excruciating pain in his skull. Derrick groaned further as he bent to pick it up. He barked into the mouthpiece, "What?!"

"Rick?"

Geraldine.

He instantly sobered. "Oh. Hey. Hi. How are you?"

"I'm good." A pause. "I was just wondering if you were all right."

Derrick chuckled weakly. "As fine as I can get, I suppose." Strange, he wasn't sure if it was the vestiges of alcohol in his bloodstream, but he didn't seem as affected by Geraldine as he previously had. The idea of her having broken up with him was still infuriating, just—not as much. His listened to her breathing over the phone, and realised *it didn't seem so bad.*

Dawn. Who the hell *was* she . . . ? He couldn't recall . . .

"Would you—be available to . . . chat . . . sometime?" Geraldine asked.

He swallowed. His throat was sore. He exhaled, and that hurt, too. "Sure. I guess."

She sounded relieved. "Oh. That's good. That's very good, Rick—I'll be down in . . . say, a half hour?"

He shut his eyes, and the indistinct image of a woman *with long, shapely legs and short mini-skirt and sequined top* popped into his mind. He opened his eyes, and the image vanished, Was it just him, or was there a strange, faint scent of—of something sweet in the air . . . some sort of perfume . . . ?

"Derrick?"

"Yeah?"

"Half an hour okay with you?

"An hour would be better."

"Okay. I'll see you then."

"Hey?" he said.

"What?"

"I —" he started, and stopped. "Never mind."

"What is it?"

He licked his lips. His mouth was dry, and his tongue felt thick, as if he had a mouthful of cotton. "I — saw you last night."

There was silence on her end.

"Last night," he repeated after a while. "At *Interreactive.*"

"I know. I looked up, and — you were walking out that new girlfriend of yours."

Derrick's response was immediate: a sharp, mocking laugh. "My what?"

"Your girlfriend. Don't you remember?"

"Remember what?"

"You and Dawn. You two met last night, and you hit it off really well."

"We — we did?" Those long legs. The shapely curve of one pantyhose-sheathed thigh. It dawned on him that the obscure images in his mind had to be those of the mysterious Dawn. Licking his lips again and wishing to God he had a glass of cold water in his hand so that he could either drink it or pitch it into his face, he stammered, "H-how do you know this? And why would you assume she was my girlfriend?"

"I ran into her as she was leaving your apartment. She said you'd asked her to be your girlfriend, and she accepted."

"*What?* I did no such thing," he exclaimed, but he didn't know that for certain. Everything was so fuzzy that he couldn't recall if he and Dawn *had* had such a discussion. But it didn't make sense that he would ask Dawn to be his girl after having known her for just a few hours. It *had* been just a few hours, hadn't it? He couldn't remember, although now he could almost recall what she looked like, and the note next to the telephone proved she *had* been in his apartment. He could also vaguely recall reflecting on the choices both he and Geri had made.

Something about experiences . . . *experiencing everything once,*
instead of dying without knowing . . .

"I — I think I was drunk when I asked her," he murmured.
Geraldine was silent.

"I mean, if she said I asked her, then I *must* have, right . . . ?
I just . . . don't remember."

"Well, she seemed happy," Geraldine said softly. "If she's
taken a liking to you, it might be a bit of a bummer if you take
back what you said."

"What I *purportedly* said," he corrected her, thinking
offhandedly that 'purported' was the weirdest-sounding word
he'd ever uttered.

"Yeah," Geraldine concurred. "Still . . ."

"She — she left her phone number."

"I think you promised her you'd call."

"Did I? I don't — I don't remember that, either."

"That's what she told me."

"When?"

"When we met each other on the stairs," she reminded him.
"She was heading out, ready to go home. Hope and I had just
come back from *Interreactive.* You also promised to take her out
tonight, Rick."

"I did what?"

"You asked her out," Geraldine repeated. "She said you
asked her to be your girl, and you asked her out tonight, and
you told her you'd call to confirm your plans for the evening."

Derrick *really* couldn't remember any of this. He silently
cursed the phenomenon of selective memory, and the fact that
he had grossly underestimated how much the alcohol would
affect him. He shut his eyes again, pushed himself to ignore the
throbbing of his head and focus on recollecting more about last
night and this morning. Bits and pieces of what had taken place
began to filter into his mind, and they didn't seem so bad: The
full-busted, leggy blond with that gorgeous smile; the beautiful,
sexy-as-hell woman who was a good listener and a good hugger
and a good kisser and —

Oh man! Something *had* happened with Dawn that morning. He had no doubt about it now.

"Derrick," Geraldine said, snapping him out of his reverie.

"Yeah?"

"I said I'll see you in a while."

"Oh. Oh, yeah, okay. I'll see you then."

After she hung up, he stood there with his hand still on the receiver, wondering at the strangeness of it all. New developments had taken place so suddenly and unexpectedly over the past few hours. New feelings and emotions were rousing within him. Coupled with the hangover, he was experiencing a strong sense of vertigo, throwing everything into a massive state of disorientation. He headed to the bathroom, thinking that a hot—or cold—shower would do him a world of good, awed by the hard-on he'd got during his conversation with Geri about Dawn.

LOONY-BIN CANDIDATE POTENTIAL

It was a carrot cake with a cream-cheese frosting. The great thing about carrot cake, Graham Hanson thought, was because it was technically made of vegetable, Bertha Asterville could consume it with less guilt than she would a red velvet. The thought made him chuckle as he pushed his grocery-filled shopping cart, placing the cake on the top of the pile so the other items wouldn't squash it. He whistled as he moved along, his eyes scanning the shelves.

"Graham?"

A woman's voice, from behind him. Graham spun around, manoeuvring the cart dexterously, and found himself looking at a blur. It took him a moment to realise it was a fingerprint or smudge on his glasses. He cleaned them with his shirt-tail, and, when he put them on again, found himself looking at a small woman with honey-brown curls and a round, rosy face. She was smiling at him, her eyes crinkling at the corners. She looked vaguely familiar, and yet he wasn't sure they'd met before.

"Graham, it's me," the woman said, coming closer. She held a filled shopping basket in one hand. He squinted through his glasses, unable to figure out who she was. "It's Sarah," she said, and stopped, now looking as uncertain as he felt.

"Sarah?" Graham frowned. He didn't know a Sarah. Oh, wait—he knew *two* Sarahs, but one of them was his colleague who'd long ago passed away, and the other was Felicity's younger sister, the sweet thing who had once had an interest in him. It used to worry him back then that his girlfriend's sister liked him, but Felicity hadn't been bothered by it. "She's a teenager, it's a hormonal thing. She'll get over it." Indeed she had, and Sarah had landed herself a nice man and had three lovely children.

Sarah, Felicity's little sister, was *not* this woman.

"How are you?" the woman asked him guardedly.

"I'm okay. I'm . . . I'm really sorry," he said, and managed a weak chuckle, "but I'm not sure we've met."

"What are you talking about? Graham, it's me." She stared at him questioningly. "It's Sarah, honey," she said again. "Sarah Robertson?"

Graham shook his head, confused. What was she trying to pull? She wasn't Sarah Robertson! Sarah had straight, silver-blond hair, and an angular face. This woman's features were completely different. Suddenly apprehensive, he said, "I'm so sorry, you must have me mistaken for somebody else. Good day", and began to move away, turning the cart around and heading towards the checkouts.

"Graham!" the woman who claimed Sarah Robertson called after him, bewildered.

He kept walking, whistling softly, trying to act nonchalant. She called his name again, and he saw several other shoppers turn curiously in her direction. *I don't know her,* he told himself, and proceeded to the checkout line, number twelve. He froze when he saw the girl behind the counter, passing the items over the barcode scanner. It wasn't Michelle. Graham tentatively approached her. If this girl claimed to be Michelle, he would check himself into the loony bin that afternoon itself.

"Hi, how are ya?" the girl trilled gaily.

"I'm good. How are you?" His eyes fell on her name tag. *Elizabeth Mann.* Elizabeth. Not Michelle.

"I'm well, thank you."

As she rounded up the items, he asked, "Is Michelle here?"

"Oh, I'm sorry," the girl replied cheerfully, "she took the day off."

"She did?"

"Yeah. She was supposed to come in, but she said she couldn't make it. I'm covering for her."

"I see."

As he walked to his car with the bags of groceries, he wondered why Michelle had lied to him. She'd said she couldn't make it over to his place because she had to work. But apparently she'd taken the day off. How strange, he thought, deciding he would probe, gently, to find out more when Michelle visited the following day.

Bertha Asterville lived across the field from Graham's house. He parked in his own driveway and ambled across, the carrot cake balanced in both hands. When he reached her house—a pleasant, double-storey building with white walls and vines decorating the façade—he knocked, once, twice—and then noticed the doorbell. He pushed it with his elbow and heard *Waltzing Matilda*, which was funny because nobody in the Asterville clan was Australian.

The door opened a crack and Bertha Asterville peeked out. She beamed with delight, swung the door wide open. "Graham! Well, hello! Won't you come in?"

"Thank you, Bertha," Graham replied warmly, and wiggled the cake in his hands. "But I just came over to drop this off."

"Oh, Graham, you shouldn't have!" she squealed. She took it from him delicately. "It's gorgeous. Thank you so much."

"It's the least I could do after your wonderful gift yesterday."

"Did you bake it yourself?" Bertha asked. "Oh, you don't bake, do you? If memory serves me, you love to cook, but baking has always eluded you for some reason, isn't that right?"

He laughed. "Bought it from the supermarket."

"Well, it's the thought that counts. Let me put this in the pantry. Why don't you sit down? Something to drink, perhaps? I've got milk, juice, gin . . ."

"My dear!" Graham faked a shocked gasp. "At this time of day!"

She laughed heartily. "Darling, at our age, we really shouldn't give a darn, should we?" She headed into the kitchen. Graham lingered in the foyer, hearing her putter blithely in the back of the house. When she re-emerged, she held a tall glass filled with an orange-pink beverage. He accepted it, sipped tentatively. Guava, mixed with orange or mango, he couldn't tell which. "Come, sit, sit," she urged, gesturing to the living room, to her plush, overstuffed couch.

Graham shook his head politely. "Thank you, Bertha, but I think it's best I go."

"Please, don't feel you have to leave, you're very welcome to stay."

He laughed and waved his free hand at the doorway. "I've got groceries in the car, milk and whatnot . . ."

"Tell me," she said, sitting down on couch as if he hadn't protested, "how are you coping, darling?"

"Coping?"

"You know," she said, and looked sad for him.

He chuckled. "Bertha, I'm perfectly fine. Phyl was old, it was just her time to go."

She looked surprised.

"And, you know, she and I weren't as close as we used to be."

She looked even more so. With one hand pressed against her bosom, she whispered, "Why, I had no idea."

"It was just how things turned out, you know? It was bound to happen over time, and it did for us."

"So," she said, and stopped, looking flustered for a moment.

"So," he repeated, and stopped as well.

"So," she said a second time, "you *are* okay?"

"Yes," he said, and took another swallow of funny juice.

"It's just—I would have thought—well, when a loved one passes on, it's difficult. I've been widowed twice, I should know." She paused, and Graham watched her. In an even softer voice, she said, "It's just that *I* sometimes feel incredibly lonely . . . and . . ." A vague shrug, a slight rise and fall of her shoulders. ". . . I was just wondering, if you were feeling lonely, too, we could . . ." She let out a sudden giggle, and her cheeks took on a rosy shade. "Oh, listen to me, I sound downright pathetic!"

Graham, feeling disconcerted, managed a wan smile. "Well, I'm definitely not lonely, Bertha. I mean, I still have Felicity."

She looked at him, long and hard. "You still have Felicity," she said. "Of course. You still have her. Why *would* you feel lonely?"

"I should get going. Thank you for the drink, and we truly appreciate the cake . . ."

Suddenly she bounced off the sofa and patted the front of her dress, smoothening it as she replied, a little too loudly, "Yes, the cake, it's nice of you to bring me one in return, you definitely didn't have to do that." And she bounded to his side, taking hold of one arm, her grip light. "It was nice talking to you too, Graham, and you come over anytime, you hear?"

"Yes," he said stiffly, and stepped out the door. "Thank you."

Before she shut the door, her voice dropped back to a whisper. "Tell Felicity I'm thinking of her," she said.

Graham blinked behind his glasses. "Yes. I shall. Thank you, Bertha."

"You take care now." And she closed the door gently, leaving him on the front stoop, puzzled, thinking it was time Bertha Asterville got herself checked into the nearest loony bin.

You Gotta Have Friends

"Carrie! Wait up!"

She shut her locker door with a bang and closed her eyes, counting to ten. *Give me strength* . . .

Zack McPherson ran up to her, his knapsack bouncing against his back. "Hey. What's going on?"

"What are you talking about?"

"Are you okay? You look tired."

"I am. Tired. It's been a long week."

"Carrie, it's Monday."

"No, I meant *last* week. It was . . . difficult." She began walking, taking wide, brisk steps, headed for the main doors of the school. She prayed Zack would lose interest and back away from her; she was in no mood to speak to anyone about what was on her mind.

"What's that on your arm?" he asked, matching her strides.

"What's what?"

He pointed. "That. It looks like a hickey or something."

"Yeah. That's what it is." No need to tell him how she'd got that dark, black-and-blue patch on her left forearm—falling over in her granny flat after Joe Cooke had swung his fist at her.

"You've got more than one," Zack observed, his brow wrinkling in consternation. "Hey, these—these look more like bruises to me."

She kept walking, pushed her way out the doors, marching stiffly down the steps into the parking lot.

"Is everything okay?"

She ignored him and headed for her car. He stopped and grabbed her arm, but not roughly. "Carrie." She tried to pull away, but he tightened his grip ever so slightly, and she sighed, flashing him a look that conveyed how frustrated and furious she was. "Carrie, what's going on? I know something's wrong. Talk to me."

She took a few deep breaths, trying to maintain her composure. "Everything's fine, Zack. Let go of me."

"Look, if something's bothering you . . ."

"Nothing's bothering me. Please. I have to go, I'm in a hurry."

"Can I be honest? You look awful."

"Zack . . ."

"And these bruises, they look —"

"Zack!" she exclaimed angrily, and pulled away, hurting herself as she did. Wincing and rubbing at the spot on her arm where he'd held her, she snapped, "Everything's perfectly fine, and I'd appreciate it if you didn't stick your nose into my business, especially when it doesn't involve you in any way."

He took a step backward, looking hurt.

"Leave me alone, Zack. I mean it."

"I was just trying to help," he said in a small voice.

"Well, I didn't ask for it."

"I'm trying to be your friend. I thought that's what we were."

"Go away, Zack," she said wearily, ignoring his stung expression. "I really have to go home, okay?"

He sighed. "Fine. It's just that I always thought we could tell each other everything." He hesitated before adding, "That's what we used to do."

"Well, that was before we broke up."

There was a long pause.

"And now things have changed," she said pointedly.

Zack nodded. "Yeah, well . . ." He shrugged. "We were practically kids. Back then. I mean, it wasn't a *real* relationship, right?"

She started walking again. He followed her. "Don't think I enjoy it every time you and Joe get it on on that bench."

She stopped as the words struck a chord deep within her. She didn't want to be reminded. "Well, I'm just glad *we* never did it." *Otherwise it might be* your *baby that's growing in me, Zack.*

"Ouch. Thanks a lot."

"Forget it," she muttered, and continued towards her car.

"Seriously," he said, following her, "if there's anything you'd like to talk about . . ."

"I'm fine."

"You always say that, but you keep it all bottled inside, and one day you're going to explode . . ."

"Zack—"

"I'm just saying . . . I'm here, okay?"

"That's very noble of you, Zack. See ya."

"Did Joe do that?" Pointing to the bruises on her arm.

She stopped. Glared at him. "No."

"I don't know how serious the two of you are, or what's going on between the both of you . . ."

"We're not. And nothing." She started moving again.

This time, Zack didn't tail her. "If he's been hurting you . . ."

"Zack, leave me alone! Stop worrying!"

"I can't. I care about you."

"Go home!"

"Carrie—"

"Thank you for being so protective, but I really can take care of myself!" She reached her car. "Why don't you get yourself a girlfriend and fuss over *her*, for God's sake?"

"I *have* a girlfriend," he shouted.

"Yeah? Well, good for you! Hope it all pans out!" She got into the car, slammed the door and started it up, revving the engine.

Zack watched, feeling annoyed and anxious and helpless, as the tyres screeched against the tarmac and the car swung out of the parking lot. As it vanished into the distance, he sighed and said aloud, "I was just trying to be your friend"—speaking to Carrie, speaking to himself, speaking to nobody.

Two's Company,
Five's a Bitch

Derrick had just changed into fresh clothes when there came a knock on the door. Figuring it was Geraldine, he pulled the door open. She walked in, followed by Hope, Sanjeev and Chitra.

"I thought you were going to be alone," Derrick grumbled to Geraldine.

She shrugged. "They wanted to come along."

"Why?"

"Because we're your friends, silly!" Chitra replied jovially.

Derrick shook his head, carefully. "Whatever. So what's up?"

Geraldine looked Derrick in the eye. "How are you, Rick?"

He made a face. "Okay, I guess. Whatever."

"Not 'whatever'. Tell me." She reached for his hands, but he pulled away. "How do you feel?"

"I'm hung-over, how do you *think* I feel?"

"No. No, right *now* — I meant, how do you feel . . ."

"In general," Chitra helped out.

There was a moment of silence as Derrick's eyes flitted to Chitra, Sanjeev and Hope, and then danced back to Geraldine. "You mean," he said — and now his voice took on a bitter edge — "how do I feel about *you?* I'm still angry. I'm still hurt. I'm still confused. I'm a lot of things right now, so *forgive* me if I'm not exactly affable."

"But you're talking to her. That's a start," Sanjeev piped up.

"Mm," Geraldine said contemplatively. "Well, Hope and I—we were just thinking that . . . you and Dawn make a nice couple."

Derrick stared at her.

"And . . . maybe some time alone with her would be good for you."

"The two of you *are* cute together," Sanjeev said, grinning toothily.

"She's gorgeous," Hope concurred, and smiled. "I mean, take it from me, being gay and all? She's a real stunner."

"A real stunner," everyone said, practically in unison, and nodded their heads like some kind of bizarre, grinning puppet show.

Derrick took a step away from the group. What was going on here . . . ?

"We were all thinking," Geraldine went on, "that it might be really, really good for you to go out with her again. I mean, she said you'd call her tonight. We feel—and *I* especially think so—you should go for it. Call her. Call her and make plans, take her to a nice place . . ."

"Like Emilio's," Sanjeev put in.

"Or wherever you wish," Hope added quickly.

Derrick's frown deepened into a full-fledged grimace.

Geraldine said, "Treat her to the best dinner you can buy."

Chitra added, "Get her flowers, she likes flowers, baby's breath, especially."

"And chocolates," Hope pitched in. "Buy some nice chocolates for her. But nothing with coconut. She doesn't like coconut."

"Don't forget the limo driver," Sanjeev said, giving him a thumbs-up. "I'll dress up this time around. Heck, I'll even polish the car!"

"I'll chip in for the gas," Chitra offered.

Derrick, growing increasingly confused by this unexpected barrage of gusto from his friends, took a step back with each eager statement, and another, and another. Then Chitra declared she would make reservations for a private booth in a fancy restaurant downtown, and his incredulity gave way to downright indignation.

"I know what you're doing," he hissed through gritted teeth.

"Maybe a bottle of champagne . . . ?" Sanjeev proposed.

"Yeah, champagne, on me!" Hope enthused.

"I *know* what you're *doing.*"

Geraldine suggested, "Or a nice white wine."

"Oooh, good idea maybe a Chardonnay from Marcioni's vineyard . . ."

"*Stop it,* I *know* what you're *doing* . . . !"

". . . To go with the fish at Emilio's. Order their oysters. You know what they say about oysters."

"Or if you're not in the mood for seafood, perhaps a robust red . . ."

"A mellow Merlot to go with your meat . . ."

"I *know* what you're *doing,* so *shut up!*" he yelled.

The foursome fell silent, and stared at him with saucer-wide eyes.

He clenched and unclenched his fists repeatedly, his face—normally fair—taking on an alarming shade of crimson. "You're trying to get off the hook! You're trying to assuage your guilt by treating me real nice and setting me up with somebody else! You're trying—you're trying to get me to quickly get *over* you by pushing me together with that girl Dawn, and *oh, my God,*" he exclaimed as a new thought struck him like a poker in the eye, "you guys probably set last night up, didn't you? Got me all upset and drunk like a pig and then shoved the girl in my direction knowing full well we'd hit it off, didn't you?! It was all a ploy, wasn't it? Some kind of sick game you're playing in the hope of making me get over you and Hope, *isn't* it?! And all the things you've been telling me—about meeting her this morning, about my asking her to be my girlfriend, and my supposed promise to call her tonight—they're lies, aren't they? Lies, *all* lies!! You think you're so smart, don't you? No, you don't—you think *I'm* the stupid one, don't you?! *Don't* you?! Oh, Jesus!" he swore, and shook his head, aggravating his hangover five hundred percent. "Oh, Christ!"

Pure silence reigned from his quadruplet of observers.

Pure silence that roared, like Niagara Falls, in their ears.

Pure silence that was broken by Sanjeev's tiny voice: "Busted."

"I was right, wasn't I?" Derrick let out a disgusted sound and rounded on Geraldine. "You're so incredibly selfish! God, I don't believe you're doing this to me, Geri! After eight dating years of fucking, you decide to drop me on my head and ditch me for somebody else, and you try to get off the fucking hook by pairing me up with somebody else—but you're not doing it for me, you're doing it for *yourself*, so that *you* can be happy with your lesbian girlfriend, not because you give a *shit* about *my* happiness!"

Pure silence, again.

Pure silence, broken by Sanjeev's confused whisper: "Eight dating years of fucking?"

"Fucking years of dating!" Derrick shrieked. *"Eight fucking years of dating!"*

"Derrick, please." Geraldine sighed. "Look, I'm not going to lie to you. Yes, I'm thinking of my happiness. Yes, I want to be happy and guilt-free with Hope. Yes, I want you to find somebody else. But this is where you're mistaken: if you think I'm only doing this for myself without a second thought about your feelings and your future, then you're wrong. You're dead wrong. I care. I care so much that I want to see you happy with somebody else, and I won't be happy until *you're* happy. Think about it—if I didn't care about you, Rick . . . if I didn't *love* you, I simply would have said, 'I'm a lesbian. I have Hope. I don't need you. *Sayonara.*' But I'm not doing that. Instead I'm saying, 'I'm a lesbian. I have Hope. But I still need you in my life. Please

be my friend and accept me for who I am.' Otherwise," she said,
and now her voice softened and began to quiver, "otherwise . . .
I wouldn't be truly happy. I'd never be."

Derrick shut his eyes and took a deep breath. Exhaled
audibly, and whispered, "So what are you saying? That if I
don't accept you for who and *what* you are, then I'm no longer
your friend?"

Geraldine took a moment to reply. "Yes. Yes, that's exactly
right." She shook her head. Tears welled in her eyes. "Rick, I'd
like to think that my true friends accept me as a person, based on
who I am. If you can't accept me and my decision, then . . . you
can't be a real friend of mine, can you? I mean—friends . . . they
accept one another without question, without . . . judgement.
And I don't think any true friend of mine would be happy with
me sacrificing my own happiness just because he can't deal with
the decisions I make."

Derrick turned away.

"I want to be your friend, and I need you to be my friend,"
Geraldine whispered, tears cascading down her cheeks. "But
if you're not going to be sincere about me, then"—she shook
her head helplessly and blinked rivulets out of her eyes—"then
we can't be friends at all. And *that* would be sad. Really, really
sad."

For a long time nobody spoke. Derrick let out a soft sob.
They waited until he was ready to speak again, and when he
did, his voice was distorted by emotion: "I—I want to be your
friend, Geri, I do, but I . . . I still love you. After all we've been
through, I've grown to love you as my girlfriend, my companion,
my *soulmate*, and this hurts, your dumping me—"

"But I'm not dumping you; we can still be as close as we've
always been."

"It wouldn't be the same."

"What wouldn't be same?"

"I . . . I wouldn't be able to kiss you anymore."

"Why not?"

"And I wouldn't be able to—to hold you anymore . . ."

"Why not?" she repeated, as Hope stepped up to her and slid an arm around her waist. "Rick, why not? You can still do that! You can still kiss me, and hug me, and hold me, and tell me you love me. You and I can still go out for movies together, or have dinners, just the two of us . . ."

"We wouldn't be able to make love anymore," he lamented.

Hope and Geraldine looked at each other, and an understanding passed between them without the need for words. As Sanjeev and Chitra watched, the two girls stepped forward, and Geraldine put her arms around Derrick. She drew him close to her, wrapped him in her embrace as Hope looked on. As he whimpered and snivelled against her neck, she whispered, "Hope and I would love to have a child someday. We can't do that without you."

Derrick picked up the phone and began pushing the buttons, seeing the reminder on his desk from the phone company and ignoring it, reciting the numbers in his head: *9-2-4-1-6-5* . . .

UNPERTURBED BY THE CONGESTION

Maggie Cooke walked up the stairs, hearing them creak beneath her. She passed Joe's bedroom, saw the light under the door, and for a moment considered talking to him. But then she thought about his moodiness and decided against it. No need to open any cans of worms tonight. She was not in the mood. In fact, she was feeling extremely drained, and needed to lie down and rest for a few good hours.

It was half past six in the evening. The sky outside was already dark, and the wind had slightly more nip to it than before. Her mother wasn't home from work yet, and that was a good thing. Maggie entered her room and shut the door behind her, locked it. Then she crept into bed and snuggled under the covers, trying to clear her mind of the torrent of thoughts that rushed through it. *Sleep,* she thought, and blinked tears away. *Just go to sleep.*

In the next room, Joe sat on the edge of his bed, wondering if he could run away from home. With his mother in a funk and Carrie giving him shit about the baby, he was thinking that, perhaps, the best step to take would be to leave. But he dismissed the idea when Carrie's words came back to haunt him: *You're just like your father.* No, he wouldn't run away. He wouldn't pack up and leave his mother and sister in the lurch.

Sitting in near-darkness, he thought about how he was to go on living his life as normal *(normal? what's that?)*. The first step, he figured, would be to go back to school and act as if everything were fine. He would avoid Carrie, though she would very well be the one doing the avoiding. He considered telling a couple of his friends, but decided against it. Alf Richards and Pete Wentworth were good mates, but they could be so immature. News on Carrie's pregnancy would not go down well with them. And Zack McPherson was going out with Maggie, for God's sake, which could really blow up in his face.

No, it was best to keep quiet, pretend everything was fine. He could do that, no problems—after all, he'd been doing it since he'd first realised his mum and dad weren't getting along. He'd kept going through his father's prolonged absence. Indeed, Joe had had a lot of practice. All he had to do was keep it up.

Jessy Cooke was stuck in a traffic jam, a bumper-to-bumper hold-up that would have made any driver cranky and impatient. Nonetheless, she remained unperturbed by the congestion. She'd had a pretty good day at work—her colleagues had been kind and sympathetic without being overbearing—and it looked as if everything were falling, slowly but surely, back into place.

She reminded herself that if she didn't start working on rebuilding her life, she'd never do it. And the next step, she knew, was to have that overdue talk with her children, to let them know she was okay, and, more importantly, to reassure them that *they* would be okay. *The only time is now,* she thought, as the car in front of her crept forward half an inch and she remained stationary.

DAUNTED BY THE PROSPECT

Michelle Leigh knocked on Graham Hanson's front door and waited for the old man to answer. She heard the plodding of his feet against the wooden floorboards. Then the door swung open and Graham smiled at her warmly. He greeted her, invited her in, ushered her into the kitchen, past the living room, which, she noticed, was messier than usual. The smell of carbonara sauce was fragrant in the air, but a slightly different odour also hit her nostrils—faint, but familiar; so faint that when she breathed again, it was gone.

Graham urged her to sit down, told her to relax. She smiled and tried to obey, but too many thoughts were racing through her mind that relaxing was difficult. She unwrapped her sky-blue scarf from around her neck and slung it over the back of her chair. Graham placed a plate of linguini coated with the delicious sauce in front of her.

As she ate, her brother, who was increasingly cutting himself off from the family, crept unbidden into her mind. Her parents had virtually washed their hands of the idea of him becoming a doctor. He was becoming more and more estranged, and while she'd never truly been close to him, she didn't like the idea of him straying ever further from home. The other night, his friend Ash had called the house and left a message—something about Matthew "probably out cradle-snatching again", at which Michelle had laughed without comprehending. She wished she could dredge up the courage to talk to her brother, but he was the kind of guy who closely guarded his privacy and didn't like anyone encroaching upon his territory even one bit.

Somehow, that led her to think of her friend's pregnancy, and Michelle semi-consciously cursed the fact that she was just too damn *caring*. They'd decided in the diner that day that an abortion was the best way to go, despite the fact that neither of them really supported it. It was more a matter of not having a choice: there were simply too many factors that had to be taken into consideration, and the cons of keeping the baby far outweighed the pros. Even as she thought this, her mind was filled with rebuttal, notions of adoption and other alternatives. Michelle wondered if she'd made the right decision advising her friend to go for it.

So as all these preoccupations swam through her mind, she ate and listened while Graham spoke, seeing food stains on the tabletop and nodding her head when it was appropriate.

"**H**ow's the linguini?" Graham asked.

"Delicious." It really was.

"You've got Felicity to thank for that," he said, and smiled at his wife.

Felicity sat down next to Graham and put an arm around his waist. Graham took a deep breath: the sweet scent of her bath soaps, mixed with the faint odour of herbs and garlic from the carbonara. Not unpleasant.

She said, "You had something to ask Michelle . . . ?"

Michelle looked at him expectantly.

Graham cleared his throat. "Ah, yes. Well, Michelle, I was wondering if you'd be interested in helping me out with a pet project of mine."

"What is it?"

He told her about his numerous notations and writings. "I'm hoping to pass these things on to my next generation, but since we don't have one, the general public will have to suffice." He laughed. "Seriously, though, I'm hoping to get published. It's my way of leaving something behind, something to inspire others."

Michelle nodded thoughtfully. "That sounds good."

"Mind you, it will be a lot of work. There will be rewrites, and I have some thoughts that will need transcribing."

"And you'd probably need to be here more often," Felicity added.

Michelle nodded again, her expression contemplative. Sensing that she might be daunted by the prospect, Graham said quickly, "You need not start straightaway if you need to centre your attention on other things, but I thought I'd put out a feeler, see if you might be interested . . ."

"I'm interested," Michelle cut in. "Definitely."

"Oh, good," he replied, and Felicity smiled widely. "Good."

Observing her, Graham could tell Michelle had things on her mind. He wondered if he should say something, even though he knew she would ask if she needed his help. But the fact that she'd not been at work the day before when she'd said she would piqued his curiosity. He ended up asking her, "More pasta?", and when she shook her head politely, he had no doubt something was causing her to fret—she'd never turned down a second helping before.

He took the plate from her and wandered over to the sink. Felicity was putting on her rubber gloves to do the cleaning-up, and he turned the tap on for her. Moving back to the dining table, he said, "We've got ice-cream, would you like some of that?"

"No, thank you, Mr Hanson," Michelle replied. Her eyes darted to the sink, and Graham followed her gaze to see Felicity starting work on the dirty dishes.

Something was definitely on her mind, he thought, and felt a wave of paternal affection come over him. He put one hand on her shoulder gently and whispered, "Honey, is everything okay?"

She looked surprised. "Everything's fine, Mr Hanson."

"You just seem a little . . . distracted . . . today."

"No, I'm fine. I'm just tired. I think I shall go home now."

He walked her to the front door, and another indication of her being anxious was that she didn't want to stay. She'd usually linger awhile, to chat or watch television or read; today, she was clearly eager to get going. Not wanting to be cruel, but at the same time hoping for more information, Graham probed gently, "How was work yesterday?"

He looked to the kitchen and saw Felicity standing at the doorway, frowning her disapproval. He'd earlier told his wife about the weird encounters in the supermarket—the Sarah he didn't recognise, Michelle being missing in action. Felicity didn't look happy over his query, giving him a *don't be a pain* look. Too late he wished he could undo his prying, but Michelle's forehead was already creasing in thought, her mouth working soundlessly as she tried to formulate a reasonable response. "It was fine," she finally said, forcing a smile. "Busy, very tiring, but good."

"Good," he said, and smiled back, hoping it didn't look put on. "That's very good, making a good amount of pocket-money, aren't you? Good, very good," he said, and realised he'd repeated "good" too many times.

When she left, promising to call within the next couple of days, he returned to the kitchen. Felicity immediately reproached him. "The poor dear's obviously very stressed out by whatever's going on. We should respect her privacy and let her come to us when and if she wants. She's a teenager, hon. You remember those days; they aren't easy."

Graham nodded. "I remember." His thoughts went out to Michelle, their surrogate daughter. Maybe it was as she had claimed, that she was tired and stressed from schoolwork. Or maybe something really *was* the matter. He prayed that whatever it was, she'd find a way to overcome it.

As Michelle Leigh walked away from the Hanson home, she had no way of knowing she was being watched by a stranger in a parked car—a stranger who observed her confounded expression and decided she had to be spoken to before it was too late . . .

ANAL RETENTION CAN BE A PAIN IN THE BUTT

Little Robby's declarations, as told to Matthew Leigh:

i)   *That the world should have more cartoons, in the papers and on TV, so that people have a reason to laugh and be cheerful all the days of their lives;*

ii)   *That he would like to work in the cartoon business when he grows up, although that would clash with his dream of being a doctor who helps people; so maybe he could be a doctor full-time and draw funny cartoons on the side;*

iii)   *That everybody has guardian angels, and the great thing is that the angels believe in you, regardless of whether or not you believe in them;*

iv)   *That if he was to be born again, he would like to come back as a bird, something wild and free, not a chicken or a duck or turkey or whatever gets eaten; and definitely not an emu or an ostrich or a penguin, because he'd want to be able to spread his wings and fly. However, reincarnation, as Matthew had explained, isn't subscribed to by those of the Abrahamic faiths (whatever those are), so he cannot come back as a bird;*

v)   *That every person of a different skin colour is the same in the eyes of God, who loves without discrimination (a big word taught by Matthew) —never mind that there's a song (Matthew says) about everybody being a little bit racist;*

vi)   *That battery hens should be released, and everyone should hug a puppy;*

vii) That Jesus sits at the right hand of God, so God must be left-handed;

viii) That trees should be kept warm in the winter as they are also living things, although putting them into the fireplace is just plain cruel;

ix) That a man and a woman change pillow cases in order to have a baby, and that you can have a baby just by getting married, so if he were to get married today and change his pillow case, his wife would have a baby tomorrow;

x) That lawyers should be outlawed because they help law-breakers;

xi) That fathers are not and cannot be perfect, except for He who is in Heaven; and

xii) That girls are gross, an imperfection created by God, although Jesus was born of a woman who was perfect and free from Original Sin, which means that even God's imperfections are perfect.

"Fascinating," Matthew muttered, with questionable sincerity.

"Hey, Mister Matty?"

"What?"

"The other day I saw two dogs stuck together."

Matthew blinked.

"Was that changin' the pillow case?"

He grinned. "Yeah. Yeah, that was."

"Why they gots stuck?"

"Just the way it is, I guess."

The boy looked alarmed. "Do people gets stuck?"

"No!" Matthew answered, laughing. "Well, not usually," he amended.

"Ewe," the boy said, and pulled a face.

"Just the way God made 'em," Matthew said, and froze, realising he'd just uttered the G-word, which would likely make the boy further question his beliefs.

True enough: "I thought you don't believe."

"I don't."

"Why not?"

"I just don't. There's no need for a reason."

"But there *has* to be a reason," the boy replied logically.

"There isn't. Not in this case."

"Don't believe you."

"Well, I don't care if you believe me or not."

Again, as had occurred several times before, a dark look crossed little Robby's features—disappointment? Exasperation? Anger? All three? And, as usual, Matthew didn't say anything, simply waited until the boy was ready to resume chatting. When the look finally faded, he whispered, "God is real, and God is love, and in Him there is no darkness at all."

Matthew didn't say anything.

"Love is patient and kind," the boy quoted.

"What're you doing?"

"Love is not jealous or conceited or proud."

"Hey." He prodded the boy's side with one finger. "What are you doing? What's that you're saying?"

"Love is not ill-mannered or selfish or irritable," the boy replied. "First letter of Paul to the Corinthians, chapter 13, verses four to—"

"Why are you quoting the Bible?" Matthew demanded, irritated.

"Love doesn't keep a record of wrongs, it is not happy with evil . . ."

"Hey," Matthew repeated, sharper now, "why are you *doing* that?"

The boy looked at him. "'Cause you don't believe."

"Yeah, I don't believe. So what?"

"But you believes in love, don't ya?"

Matthew hesitated.

"And love comes from God."

"Says who?"

"The Bible tells me so."

"Cut it out," Matthew snapped crossly. "What's the matter with you, kid? Stop being so annoying."

The child looked affronted at this. "I'm not—I'm provin' to you God exists."

"Why the hell would you want to do that?"

"So you'll know what's right," the boy replied.

Matthew lost it. "I *know* what's right, and what's right is that you let me go on believing in whatever the hell it is I want to believe in, without you trying to alter my perceptions or change my mind. What's *right* is for you to shut up about this whole God thing and let me go about my business, and what's *right* is for you to go on home to your mummy, because, after all, won't she be worried about you?"

The boy stuck out his lower lip and folded his arms across his chest.

Sighing, Matthew said, "I'm going to go home now."

The boy looked at him out of the corner of his eye. He didn't reply.

Matthew grunted, "I'm serious."

Still nothing.

"Maybe I'll see you tomorrow, or maybe I won't. We'll just have to see."

Nothing.

"I'm gonna go," Matthew said, and got up to leave.

When he was halfway across the field, he turned to see the boy still sitting there, on one side of the bench, unmoving, seemingly not breathing. Matthew didn't slacken his pace, kept walking, and, as the cool wind blew around him, he wondered what had gone wrong, why the child seemed to be ever more bent on telling him about God, and why Matthew's own refusal seemed to spark resentment and moodiness in him.

Matthew didn't want to hear about God—God had done nothing for him. All those years going to Sunday school and attending church had come to nothing. His father was still a pain in the ass with his constant griping about the whole medicine issue; his mother was a pain in the butt with her constant queries about his refusal to follow in his father's footsteps; and his sister was still—well, she was okay, if it weren't for her incessant requests for him to get acquainted with all the old fuddy-duddies she met at work.

Matthew Leigh was the type who liked to be away from the nagging and the niggling of others. His ex-girlfriend Rachel had been a fusspot, and had eventually driven him up the wall with her anal-retentive demands—*the books aren't arranged according to height, Matt . . . the table's not in line with the pattern of the carpet . . . do this, do that, don't do this, don't do that, believe in this,* don't *believe in that . . .* ! If God was supposed to get rid of one's problems, why couldn't He get rid of all those who drove him up the wall? Once upon a time, Matthew used to pray, a long, long time ago—why had his prayers gone unanswered? *Because God didn't exist* was Matthew's conclusion. After all, he'd asked, he'd knocked, he'd sought—and found nothing. God didn't exist, and never had.

So he wasn't going to listen to anything the kid had to say about God, and neither was he going to sit there and let the little brat tell him what to do. Not after Dad, and Mum, and Michelle, and Rachel. Not after schoolteachers and girls in the library who always told him *you've got to sign the Reference Book Reservation Book if you want a text kept for you . . .* ! No more. No more!

But . . .

Something tugged at Matthew's heartstrings as he walked away. He begrudgingly acknowledged he felt upset over having hurt the boy by not listening to him, and unease over having left the child so abruptly. That he'd had a disagreement with a six-year-old—whom he had to confess he'd grown mildly fond of—made him feel even worse. Matthew was tempted to go back to the bench and finish the debate, hear out what little Robby wanted to say. But he didn't.

He kept walking to his car, leaving the child to sit there in his melancholy, the entire issue up in the air.

HITTING THE FAN

Joe Cooke walked alone along the quadrangle in front of the main school building, keeping his gaze on the ground, avoiding eye contact with those who passed him by: the teachers, the other students, and his peers, laughing and joking and pushing one another. He'd feel the occasional stab of bitterness and wonder at how every other seventeen-year-old got to enjoy his or her life without having to deal with the shit *he* had to deal with. He'd taken two days off school—on Monday and Tuesday—and had scribbled a convincing-enough note to hand to his teacher, even though he believed there wouldn't be a fuss since the faculty probably knew what his family was going through. News—especially gossip—spread fast in this town. They'd assume he needed time to clear his mind, he figured.

Earlier that morning, Pete Wentworth and Alf Richards had come up to him, acting like everything was cool. Alf had held a football, and had asked if Joe was interested in a quick game before school. Joe had muttered something about a hurt foot before walking away without even bothering to hobble to add some weight to his excuse. They'd stared after him, and he'd just moved on.

Twice he'd encountered Carrie Taylor. The first time, he'd turned around without her seeing and walked away in the direction from whence he'd come. The second time, it was she who'd spun around to avoid him.

Now, walking the perimeter of the quadrangle, he sought a lonely, secluded corner where he could have his lunch. He found none; every spot was occupied by carefree, happy people. He decided to head home, where he could at least sit in the silence and privacy of the kitchen and eat in peace.

Carrie Taylor sat alone in the school cafeteria, picking through her egg salad, occasionally spooning some of it into her mouth. She wasn't feeling well; her stomach was queasy and she felt nauseous, although she wasn't so sure it was morning sickness. Her mind was filled with confused, frightened thoughts. The idea of abortion was again at the fore. Despite what she knew, she wasn't certain if she was going to go through with it. She liked babies; she thought they were adorable, and the idea of being responsible for one wasn't entirely unappealing. Every time she walked into a shopping centre or family establishment, she'd see them being pushed in prams or cradled in the arms of mums and dads, and she'd feel all gooey inside, which was a sign she actually possessed maternal instincts. So the idea of keeping the baby was tempting. It had triggered the alternative solution she was considering: to simply let her parents know. The shit would hit the fan, but that's what happens, doesn't it? Shit happens. She'd deal with her parents, and they, in turn, would have to deal with it.

After that, she vowed to go over to the Cookes' and let Joe and his family know about her decision. Assuming, of course, she actually kept the child.

The quandary was enough to bring tears. She blinked, reminding herself that she was in public view, and besides, hadn't she cried enough already over the past . . . how many days had it been? How many hours of sobbing against her pillow, how many sleepless nights on end?

She told herself that if Joe Cooke ended up buried under the excrement she was going to hurl at the spinning blades, he deserved every single reeking drop of it.

Joe stepped into the kitchen and froze upon seeing his sister sitting there, a sandwich on a plate in front of her. For a moment they stared at each other. Then he broke the gaze and went to the fridge. With his back to her, he said, "You didn't go to school?"

It took a while before she answered him. "I wasn't feeling well."

"Does Mum know?"

"No," she said. "I don't think so, unless they called her, but I don't think the school's going to do that. Not yet, at least."

"How many days have you missed?"

"Three."

He reached for a carton of milk, turned around and saw his sister's face was pale and her eyes were red-rimmed. She'd only taken one bite of the sandwich. Maggie didn't look too well, and he wondered, momentarily, if the same look was reflected on his own face. Quietly he asked, "Is everything okay?"

"Yeah."

"What's going on?"

"Just . . . stuff."

"To do with Dad?"

She fidgeted. "Yeah. Mostly."

"Mostly." He took a gulp straight from the carton, knowing if his mum found out, he wouldn't hear the end of it. He swallowed, and said, "What makes up the rest of it?"

"Nothing."

He shut the refrigerator door and walked over to the table. Pulled out a chair and sat down.

"Did Mum talk to you last night?" she wanted to know.

He smirked, but there was no humour in it. "Yeah. She did. You, too?"

"Yeah. But at least we know she's all right, all things considered. Did she ask you how you were coping with Dad? She asked me," she said, without waiting for his response, "and I'm glad she did, that way she doesn't have to worry about us so much, wondering what we're thinking . . ."

"How honest were you?" he cut in.

She smiled, humourlessly as well. "Seventy percent?"

"Not bad."

"You?"

"I'm cool with Dad," he said, and shook his head. "He's a fuckwit, anyway."

She looked at her sandwich and exhaled air through her nostrils loudly.

"I mean, that's how *I* see him," he murmured.

"He's still Dad."

"No. No, he isn't. Not to me."

"But to me . . ." she began, and stopped.

He waited. "What?"

She laughed cynically. "I don't know. He's still Dad, and he's not, I don't know. Whatever. I don't care."

"So what else is bothering you?" he asked again.

"I told you. Nothing."

"You're lying."

"Am not."

"No? I don't believe you."

She scowled. "Well, I don't care."

He screwed the top back onto the bottle and pushed it aside. "I hope it's not Zack. If he's been treating you badly . . ."

"It has nothing to do with Zack," she said tensely.

"You should know that Zack's not the right kind of guy for you . . ."

"I didn't ask," she snapped. "Stop it."

"I'm just looking out for you."

"I said *stop it.*"

"He spends time with me," Joe said self-deprecatingly. "He's bound to be nothing but trouble."

She stood up abruptly and glared daggers at her brother. "Believe me, Joe, I've got more important issues to worry about. And it has nothing to do with Zack, or with Dad, or with Mum, or with you. So lay off. Leave me alone. If I want your opinion or your help or your advice, I'll ask for it!"

He relented, taken aback by her outburst. "Okay, okay. I'll butt out."

"*Thank* you," she hissed, and hurried out of the kitchen, leaving her half-eaten sandwich sitting forlornly in the middle of the plate, and Joe sitting forlornly in the middle of the room.

Zack McPherson listened with concern as the ringing tone went unanswered in his ear. Maggie hadn't come to school today — the third day in a row — and he was genuinely concerned something was wrong. He feared that her father's departure had affected her more deeply than anybody realised.

He made up his mind to drive over to the Cookes'.

As he headed towards his Corolla, he thought about how shitty it was that some people could simply walk away from their families. The idea of hurting somebody so deeply and irreversibly was inconceivable. And when he thought of sweet, beautiful, innocent Maggie Cooke having to endure this kind of hardship, he felt his heart breaking for her over her loss.

ON THE SUBJECT OF LOSS . . .

The woman was standing in line without any items. The customer in front of her walked away, fumbling as he tried to balance the paper bags of groceries in his arms. But still this woman—with straight, silver-coloured hair and a sharp chin—stood at the checkout counter with nothing to check out. Michelle Leigh smiled and greeted her as she did with every customer. "Nothing of interest today, madam?"

The woman smiled warmly and leaned in close to peer at Michelle's nametag, read her name out loud. "That's a very pretty name."

"Thank you," Michelle said, and glanced at the next shopper in the queue, a man with a fully loaded trolley and a puzzled expression. "I'm sorry, madam, but if you're not making any purchases today, could you kindly make room for the next customer?"

The woman said, "Do you have a minute?"

Surprised, Michelle glanced at the man behind her, who not-so-subtly pointed at his wristwatch. Turning back to the mystery woman, she said, "I have a break coming up in ten minutes. But . . ."

"That's fine," the woman said quickly. "Can I meet you there, by the meat counter?" She must have noticed Michelle's anxiety, because she quickly added, "I'd like to talk to you about one of your elderly friends . . . Graham Hanson?"

Mr Hanson? "Oh. Uh—sure," Michelle said, confused and more than a little apprehensive.

When she moved away, Michelle realised her heart was thudding rapidly in her chest, and she had to force herself to take a few deep breaths. Who was this woman, and why did she sound so intense? On the other hand, she *did* look vaguely familiar. Maybe she was a regular customer, she told herself, as she looked up and apologised to the impatient man. She ran the man's selections through the barcode scanner, thinking about what she'd been observing in the Hanson home, and wondering if this mysterious woman knew of the goings-on as well.

After ten minutes, her colleague Dan Michaels relieved her, and Michelle made her way to the meat display. Huge Styrofoam cut-outs were plastered on the wall behind the counter, grandly proclaiming *MEATS*, while a smaller sign informed that they were *non-halal*. Michelle looked around for the mysterious woman and for an instant did not see her. Then she spotted her approaching from one of the aisles.

The woman introduced herself as Graham Hanson's sister-in-law, Sarah Robertson.

"I'm worried," Michelle admitted, as Sarah Robertson watched her with kindly eyes. "Mr Hanson—Graham—does and says some pretty funny things. To begin with, he doesn't seem torn up at all. You know, over . . . her death." Sarah nodded. "And the thing I've been noticing is that he tends to talk in the first-person plural—it's always 'we' this, or 'us' that. It's never just 'me', you know? And that's scary. Plus, the house is more cluttered than it should be, almost as if he's given up cleaning it. I even saw pieces of food on the floor, and there were cracked plates and dishes everywhere . . .

"The oddest sign," Michelle said softly, and tears came into her eyes as she said these words, "was when he placed the plates in the sink yesterday and left the taps running. He just put them there and walked away without touching them, as if—as if he expected the dishes to wash themselves. I was so bothered by it, on top of—of other things going on in my life—that I had to leave, you know? It was too scary and too worrisome."

"I know," Sarah said softly. "I saw you."

"You saw me?"

"Yes. I was planning on dropping by, but then I saw you leave, and I recognised you from here." She gestured in the general direction of the checkout counters. "You looked troubled, so I thought I'd speak to you first, to make sure *I'm* not the one who's losing my mind."

Michelle sighed. "I don't think he's losing his mind, Sarah. He's just . . ." She shook her head and looked at the ceiling, at the harsh fluorescent lights. "I suspect he's in denial, and—and he doesn't believe that Felicity passed away nearly three weeks ago. I think he still believes it was his Aunt Phyllis who just died—but she's been dead for a long time now." She blinked, and tears rolled down her cheeks.

Sarah reached over and stroked her arm. "I know. This is what I've suspected, too." She recounted the day she'd run into Graham in the aisle of the supermarket, and how he'd been unable to recognise her, insisting she'd been mistaken. "I don't know how it's happening, but I'm thinking he blocks out every single association with Felicity. It's as if his *subconscious* knows my sister passed away, but it puts up a barrier each time he comes into contact with anyone or anything that might not gel with the idea of her still being alive. That's why he didn't recognise me, I suspect. And I was there at the funeral, of course"—Michelle remembered now where she'd seen Sarah before—"but he didn't even acknowledge me. Like I was a complete stranger to him." It was Sarah's turn to get teary-eyed, and Michelle found herself doing the patting of the elderly woman's hand, a strange and sad reversal of roles.

"Jim Williamson spoke to him," Sarah went on after a while. Seeing that Michelle didn't know the man, she explained, "Jim was once madly in love with Felicity. He was there at the funeral. Graham knows who Jim is, but Jim later told me he didn't seem to recognise him at all.

"On top of that, I often go past that field in the Square, you know the one?" Michelle nodded, and Sarah went on, "Once, at the crack of dawn, I drove past, and I saw Graham sitting all by himself, pointing to the sky. It looked as if . . . he still carries out his usual routine—taking long walks in the mornings, sitting on that old bench . . ."

Michelle sniffled and glanced towards the direction of the counters, where Dan Michaels looked back at her, gesturing to indicate her break was over. Turning back to Sarah, she whispered, "What are we going to do?"

"I don't know," Sarah replied. "I've been thinking about it, but . . . I don't know, how can we . . ." She let out a bitter, confused laugh. "Can we just tell him? Will he be able to accept it? Or will he not even recognise us anymore, and choose to see somebody else—someone he *doesn't* know—in our place?"

"**O**ne more thing," Michelle said, as she got up and signalled apologetically to Dan, "when did you run into Mr Hanson here?"

The woman thought about it briefly. "A couple of days ago. On Monday."

"Monday . . . ?"

"Yes. You weren't here."

"No," Michelle whispered, "I wasn't." But if Mr Hanson had been here, he would have noticed she hadn't been at work when she'd *told* him she would be. She'd had other plans to attend to. Then she recalled that Graham had asked her during dinner about Monday, and she'd lied. She sighed as she headed back to her counter, hoping the old man wouldn't inquire further, knowing she'd be forced to be evasive—or to make up more lies.

Sixty-eight-year-old Della Rosenberg—who, as she liked to tell people, was inexplicably twice married and three times divorced—peered out the kitchen window to see her next-door-neighbour Bertha Asterville leaving her house with another of her fabulous home-baked cakes. Della figured Bertha was heading over to Graham Hanson's. The poor dear had *such* a massive infatuation on the man that it was both funny and pitiful at the same time. Bertha and Della often met up for coffee and cake and hours of delicious gossip, and Bertha had once expressed her interest in pursuing a relationship with Graham, especially since he probably needed somebody in his life right now. Della wasn't too sure—she was of the opinion that people need a bit of space after such a time of sadness; but Graham had always had a strange sort of self-suffering tolerance for Bertha that could also be construed as affection, and maybe it wouldn't be so bad if he and Bertha stepped back into the dating game.

As she watched Bertha leave, Della knew her neighbour would probably leave the cake on the doorstep and run away (run? The woman could barely walk!), like a shy teenager. Della made a mental note to accompany Bertha to Graham's one day to kill two birds with one stone: to give Bertha the confidence and support she needed to chat the man up, as well as to give herself, Della, the opportunity to convey her belated condolences over Graham's wife's death.

BIG BEYOND COMPREHENSION

Bertha Asterville made her way to Graham Hanson's house via the usual route, cutting across the field, going past the bench under that gnarly tree. Distantly the memory of their last residents' association popped into her mind, but she paid it no heed, because she had a task to fulfil. Today, she balanced a homemade Black Forest in her hands, filled with real cherries and topped with lots and lots of cream. Unhealthy, but at her age, she figured it was okay to indulge every now and then.

She was walking past the bench when a movement caught her attention. She turned and saw a little boy sitting on his own, his feet dangling off the edge of the seat, his head bent low, tears dripping into his lap.

"My dear," Bertha said aloud. She made a detour, steering herself, and the cake, towards the boy. She recognised him; he lived several houses down from hers, with that single woman nobody knew much about. As far as Bertha knew, the boy didn't have a father. When they'd first moved into the neighbourhood, Bertha had tried acquainting herself with the boy's mother, but her efforts had gone unappreciated. In fact, once, the mother had actually returned Bertha's home-baked chiffon sponge cake with vanilla crème frosting—untouched. Bertha had been insulted by the gesture, and swore not to bother with the woman again. Now, as she approached the boy, the memory of finding her uncut cake waiting for her on her front porch entered her mind, and she scowled at the flashback. She wondered if the woman's next-door neighbour, Mrs Coulsen, had made any progress at breaking the ice. Probably not, since Mrs Coulsen's two blond-haired little girls had once told Bertha that little Robby was not to be played with. *Robby,* she told herself, *that's the boy's name.* A peculiar little thing.

"Hello," she said softly, stepping up to the bench.

The boy didn't acknowledge her.

"Your name's Robby, isn't it?"

Still nothing.

"Dear child," she said, "why are you crying?"

The boy didn't look up, didn't let on that he was aware of her. Unfazed, she sat next to him, watching as his tears ran like little tributaries. He sobbed and ran a dirty arm across his face.

"Oh, no," Bertha crooned, and put an arm around the boy's frail, convulsing shoulders. "No, no, no, don't cry, honey, I'm sure whatever it is, it can't be that bad." She waited for acknowledgment, and when she still didn't receive any, looked at the Black Forest cake on the seat next to her. It probably wouldn't hurt to spare the boy a slice to cheer him up. Of course, that would mean she couldn't give it to Graham as she'd planned, but baking was her favourite activity, so she'd just have to make him another. She'd give the rest of the cake to Jessy Cooke, in return for the desserts she'd plied them with during the residents' association meetings over the years, even though her Black Forest was infinitely better than the stodgy pre-mixed stuff Jessy always prepared off the back of the packets. Bertha would blame the missing slice on herself, she decided: "I couldn't resist helping myself to a piece." Jessy would buy that.

Bertha had included a little plastic knife in the box, and now she reached for it. "Tell you what," she said to the boy, "will you stop crying if I give you a piece of cake?"

The child sniffled loudly and looked up at her.

She smiled triumphantly and placed the cake on her lap. "Look at it, doesn't it look delicious? It's a Black Forest—very rich, very fruity."

The boy rubbed his nose with the back of one hand, blinked, and whispered, "Creamy?"

"Yes!" she exclaimed, delighted by the breakthrough. "Yes, it's creamy, very creamy. Would you like a slice?"

"Yes, please," the boy said, and snuffled.

She cut him a piece and handed it to him on a paper napkin. He took it from her and gave it a critical inspection. Then he took a large bite. Blobs of cream clung to his lips. Bertha beamed. The boy, odd as he was, was a sweetheart, and it made her happy to see him stop crying. "Do you like it?" she asked.

"Yes, it's yummy," he replied, swallowing and taking another large bite.

She waited for him to finish half the slice before she probed, "Why were you crying?"

The boy looked at her, and his eyes clouded over.

"Did somebody do something naughty to you?"

He shook his head sullenly and took a smaller nibble.

"You can tell me," she whispered conspiratorially.

He shook his head again and murmured, "Mummy says don't talk to strangers."

"I'm not a stranger. I'm Bertha. And you're Robby, right?"

The boy didn't answer.

"Now you know me, and I know you. We can be friends."

Nothing.

"Friends help each other. If something upset you and made you cry, it's always good to have a friend you can talk to about it."

He took another bite, his small jaws moving slowly, as if chewing had become too much of an effort.

"It's okay to cry, but it's also important to know what *caused* you to cry," Bertha advised. "And, as a friend, I'd like to help you out in any way I can."

He swallowed this mouthful and whispered, "Not 'portant."

"Not important?"

"No."

"Okay, but it made you cry, so it must've been a *bit* of a big deal."

He shook his head dourly. "Don't matter."

"Right. Well, just remember, whatever the problem is, there's nothing too big that God cannot handle, so you can always talk to Him, okay?"

That was the key that opened the floodgates of communication.

"**Y**ou believe in God?"

"Yes, I do." And why not? Her time could be up any moment now, and she wanted to make sure there was someplace to go to after this life . . .

"You believe in Jesus?"

"I do. Do you?"

"Yes!" Enthusiastic nodding, sending blobs of cake and cream flying from the edges of his mouth. "And I believe in guardian angels, do you?"

"I do. I really do." That was a bit of a half-truth; she didn't believe in guardian angels with wings and harps that flew around your shoulders and made sure you were protected from harm, but she was quite convinced that *people* could be angels, sent to look out for and help one another in times of need. She liked to think that she herself had been chosen by a divine power to help and comfort others—Graham Hanson, for one.

And now this little boy, Robby.

"**H**eaven is someplace where there's no pain. If you's always full of pain and sufferin' here, when you get there, everythin's cool, and the pain will be all gone. That's why—that's why s'important"—stumbling over the word—"for people to believes in God and angels and all. So when you go to Heaven, Saint Peter at the Girly Gates will let you in and you feel no more pain at all."

"Pearly Gates, sweetheart."

"Yeah," he said, smiling, his teeth smeared with chocolate. He shifted closer to his new friend and looked up at her with newfound admiration. Then he lowered his voice dramatically and said, "D'you believe when you gets to Heaven, you gets to meet those who're there oready? Like, if your grammama died, you gets to see her in Heaven?"

Her grandmother had died *eons* ago, and she couldn't help but to smile. Speaking truthfully, Bertha replied, "Yes, I do. I believe that." Deep in her heart, she imagined it would be wonderful to meet up with her own parents again, who'd gone to God so many years ago. And Graham, poor Graham—for him to reunite with Felicity . . .

The boy's smile faded and a look of consternation replaced it. She waited for him to speak further, and when he did, he murmured, "I dunno if that's a good thing."

"Why?"

"What if you don't *wan*na meet up again?"

The boy Robby shifted uncomfortably in his seat, and a feeling of sadness came over him. He hesitated, wondering if he should tell this new friend—a gentle, sweet woman with a really delicious cake—about his worries: that when he went to Heaven, he was less than excited about the idea of seeing his Daddy again.

"What do you mean?" she asked, and he looked at the ground, at his feet, dangling off the edge of the seat. If only Mister Matty had been ready to listen to him. He was comfortable talking to Matty, and what really hurt was that Mister Matty wasn't interested in discussing God at all. That was why he'd been crying—he'd been truly hurt by Matty's constant refusal to listen to what he had to say about Heaven and the angels. God was such a big deal for him; if God didn't heal, and if He didn't grant him strength to go on day after day . . .

"Robby?" his new friend whispered, seeing the tears come up again.

He sniffed loudly and muttered, "Mister Matty didn't want to talk about it."

"Who?" she asked, confused.

"Mister Matty. My best friend." He blinked, letting the rivers flow. "He don't believe in God," he said tremulously. "And he don't wanna talk about Jesus."

"Oh, I'm sorry, honey," she whispered. "But you know, not everybody is going to be a believer, and sometimes, as strange as it sounds, we have to respect their decision."

"Mister Matty says God don't exist," little Robby lamented, "and there's no guardian angels and no Jesus."

"Well, Mister Matty is wrong, sweetheart."

"If you don't believe," he said haltingly, "does that mean when you die you won't go to Heaven?"

Bertha had to consider that one, but in spite of her thinking, she couldn't come up with a simple enough response. So she decided to be as honest as she could. "I think . . . if you don't believe in God, then it's very hard for us to know where we'll be going. We don't know what God has to say about it, or what He has in mind for us who believe and for those of us who don't. It's hard to understand the mind of God," she said quietly, "although we get to be *closer* to Him through prayer. That's what I believe."

"Why can't we understand God?" he asked softly.

"I think it's because we're only human, and we're only limited to our five senses—our sight, touch, smell, taste, hearing. Beyond that . . . it's all beyond us, do you know what I mean? And God—being God—is big, *so* big, that to understand Him would require the use of *more* than five senses, which are all we have. I believe that for you to fully understand God, you'd have to be *with* Him in Heaven."

The child thought about this for quite a long time, nodding his head and moving his cake-dotted lips slowly and soundlessly. Eventually he whispered, "I'm scared when I die, I can't see

Mister Matty anymore if he don't believe in God, and he won't go up to Heaven. I'm scared that when I die, I'll go up to Heaven and be meetin' someone I *don't* wanna meet no more, and I'm scared that that person won't like me and tries to hurt me."

"No," Bertha answered at once, perplexed by the strange revelations that the boy was spouting. "To get into Heaven, you have to be a very, very good person. Nobody in Heaven is going to hate or hurt anyone, because God wouldn't allow people like that to get there in the first place."

The boy seemed to cheer up a little at the idea. "Oh. Thank God."

"Why is this so important to you, Robby?"

The boy pursed his lips together, stuck out his lower one. He fell silent again, kicking his legs back and forth as she waited.

"Because I don't wanna meet my Daddy, he don't like me."

Her mouth worked, but she seemed to have suddenly lost her voice. She managed to let out a slightly strangled "oh".

Little Robby looked at the napkin in his hand, decorated with tiny crumbs of Black Forest. He squeezed his fingers shut so that the paper was crushed in his fist, and, avoiding eye contact with the woman, said, "Thank you for the cake, t'was real yummy. I gots to go—Mummy might be wonderin' . . ." And before she could reply, he pushed himself off the bench and ran off across the field with the napkin balled up in one hand, leaving Bertha with the partially consumed cake in her lap.

FAITH, HOPE AND GERALDINE

Geraldine sat at her desk in the office of *The Tribune,* where she worked from 4pm to midnight, editing the various news copy that came into her in-tray. Usually she'd be vigilant for typos, grammatical mistakes and other sloppiness. But today, her mind wasn't on the job, and she was tempted to walk over to one of the other editors' desks and slip the slug sheets into his in-tray.

Her mind was cluttered with the same old debate: she still found that being religious clashed with her relationship with Hope. Derrick's words echoed in her head—words he'd uttered months ago—that homosexuality was wrong; that the Bible clearly stated it, and that there was no way for her to justify it. For someone who wasn't usually all that bright, Derrick had the verbal prowess of an orator when it came to this subject. "Any form of justification would simply be an attempt to override the so-called Word of God," he had declared pompously, prompting her to clench her fist. "To justify homosexuality would be to twist the words of the Bible to fit one's own needs. That, in itself, is wrong."

Wrong. Wrong, wrong, wrong. That was the word that was causing the dilemma. *Being gay is wrong.* Especially in the eyes of religion. *It wouldn't be God's will.*

Thanks a lot, she thought, staring into the computer screen at her desk.

The words on the screen began to blur as she thought back on more of Derrick's preaching on the issue. The theories are out there, online, he had informed her. Among them the notion

that "gayness", as he put it, is born out of an emotional void
in a person's life. For example, if a boy grows up without a
father or any close male role models, then he'd be missing that
emotional connection with a masculine figure, and would grow
up seeking the attention or approval of an older male. "That's
all right," Derrick had said. "There's nothing wrong with the
human need to seek approval from others. We all have that
yearning. But it's when a man in that situation—growing up
with an emotional void—starts to confuse this yearning with
lust, that's when the difficulty and conflict begins.

"In today's world," Derrick said, sounding as if he were
presenting an academic lecture, "we are increasingly exposed
to so many corrupted ideals, notions and images. The media,
for instance, exhibits so much sex and sexual behaviour that
no matter where we turn, it's there, in one form or another.
Images you see on the television or on the movie screen;
explicit lyrics in the songs you hear on the radio; pornography
on the Internet—all of these cloud your mind and blemish your
thoughts. The more you open yourself to images and ideas of
this sort, the more you desensitise yourself, and the easier it
becomes to accept that these things are right and are a natural
part of living the human life.

"So there you go . . . the man, or the woman, with the
emotional void ends up yearning and seeking the attention
of another man or woman. But because they're so exposed
to the notion of sex and sexual activity, their minds become
corrupt, and they start to confuse what they feel with the need
for physical intercourse. That's where most gay couples get
it wrong," the expert had expounded; "they feel strongly for
another person of the same gender and start to think, because
of their perverted thoughts, that getting physical is an integral
part of the relationship, when in reality, it isn't even necessary.

"A relationship is not based on physical actions, but
emotional. The act of getting physical is reserved for the
married husband and wife, wherein an emotional relationship
is already established, and sex becomes a physical symbol of

the oneness of man and woman, the ultimate act of love. Sex becomes acceptable here in order to procreate."

She'd interrupted at this point: "But—*we've* had sex!"

"My *point* is," he went on without missing a beat, "homosexuality shouldn't be condoned, especially if you claim to be religious. I've thought about what you once told me, about Saul and Jonathan in the Old Testament possibly being gay. They were *close friends*. There's nothing wrong with being close friends; but once you allow ideas of covetousness to come into the picture, that's when it all spirals out of control. What's written is written—clearly, hard-fact, black and white—and there's no zigzagging your way around it!"

Geraldine had felt like giving him a hand—in more ways than one.

Now, sitting in front of the computer, the thoughts swam through her mind, and she wondered if she would ever be truly comfortable with her sexuality. Maybe it was true that Geraldine had an emotional void in her life: she had no sisters, and her mother hadn't truly been the most affectionate woman in the world, preferring to show love through Catholic teachings and the occasional punishment. Maybe she *did* crave the attention and approval of another female. Whenever she thought back on her early girl crushes, it had been a desire to spend time with them, get to know them, and not . . . anything more. She'd not known much about sex; it was only after exposure to adult videos and websites that the whole thing had come into play. Which, of course, Derrick said proved his point entirely. And which, of course, ticked her off like crazy.

What had he always said? He'd always believed that most gay people could snap out of it simply by admitting that they had an emotional void that needed to be filled, and by realising that sex was an unnecessary trajectory they'd chosen to throw into the picture. *Meaning,* Geraldine told herself sadly, *if you choose to believe in what he says, then you should be happy being with Hope* without *the need to kiss her or make love to her.* But then again—everybody craves human touch . . . *although it depends on*

what form *of touch you're talking about; a simple hug wouldn't be sinful,
although lips on nipple would probably constitute a transgression . . .*

Could Derrick really be right? Could it really be as
simple — and complex — as that: the need for human validation
from someone of the same gender, diluted and tainted with
misrepresented idealisms? And did he really believe that the
key to "becoming" straight would be to realise this basic fault in
the human heart and take steps to cleanse oneself of perversion
in order to deal solely with the emotional emptiness within?

She'd spoken of Derrick's philosophies with Jason Marcel,
and his response to the view that homosexuality was born out
of the aforementioned "sentimental vacancy" had been one of
scorn and cynicism. "What the fuck does that dickhead know,
anyway?" he'd guffawed, dismissing the theory, which hadn't
helped Geraldine any. "Listen, babe, being gay is an entirely
natural thing; we don't *choose* to be it, we just *are*. It's like asking
a straight guy to be attracted to another guy, to *knowingly*
and *purposely* be attracted to him. It doesn't happen that way,
darling! We don't *choose* this, it just *is*. God, I'd love to be able
to get a hard-on every time a girl spreads her legs, but honey, it
just doesn't happen, and that's not my fault!

"Do you actually think I would knowingly decide to
become part of a minority group within society, alienated and
segregated, subject to the risk of scorn and rejection and hurt?
Do you really think I *want* to have to decide how to tell my
parents that their only son is likely to bring a son-in-law into the
family, and have to deal with the threat of being disowned by
the people I love the most? Do you think I deliberately prefer
to have to go around hiding my true nature and to forsake the
chance of growing old with my own family, my own wife, my
own children? Fuck, no! Being gay is just who we are, sugar,
and you should really stop killing yourself over it and embrace
it. Embrace it! Embrace who you are!"

She'd shared Jason's thoughts with Derrick, who'd replied:
"That's my point exactly: why have to struggle with the decision
to tell your parents you're gay when you don't *have* to be gay?

Why be a part of society that is considered marginal, subject to debasement and humiliation, when you can easily acknowledge the fact that you're craving emotional support from someone of the same gender without the need for fornication, and simply *reject* the notion of being gay altogether? You're not gay unless you choose to accept the gay lifestyle—the *distorted* lifestyle. If you don't accept it, then you don't affix a label on yourself. Don't talk about denial; don't talk about missing out on what you really want in life; don't talk about not being honest with other people; because ultimately, whatever decisions you make in order to fulfil yourself or the others around you are temporary. You can't bring your sexual happiness to your Heaven, you can't engage in homosexual intercourse once you're dead. Being sexually fulfilled now means absolutely *zilch* in comparison with the lifetime of wealth and happiness you'll supposedly be experiencing on the other side, if you go with the Word of God and not against it!"

And Jason, upon being told of Derrick's opinion, had rebutted: "He doesn't know what he's talking about. It's easy to say 'what's so difficult about being gay' when the sonofabitch isn't gay to begin with. It's like saying, 'Oh, what's so hard about quitting smoking?' when a person hasn't even tried a cigarette!"

So what was right and what was wrong? Geraldine wasn't sure, and she wasn't sure she'd ever *be* sure. Whatever the case, as difficult as it was to balance her spiritual life with her everyday life, she was determined to keep working at it. Even if it meant struggling for the rest of her days, she was determined to find a way to be happy and content with her decision. With her friends supporting her, it should only get easier.

Especially if the plan with Dawn and Derrick worked . . .

QUICK TO JUDGE

Making sure he didn't step on the Black Forest cake — minus a slice — on the front step, Zack McPherson rang the bell and hoped Maggie would answer the door. He was almost sick with worry. He wondered if she'd not enjoyed his company and had no intention of ever seeing him again. The thought was just unbearable. He'd grown to like her so much, to care for her; if she didn't feel the same way —

The door opened, and Zack found himself staring at Joe Cooke. There was a moment of awkwardness. Zack was almost certain something bad had happened between Joe and Carrie, even though it was conjecture on his part. And Joe, he figured, was probably wary because he, Zack, was going out with Maggie.

"Hey," Zack said, trying to sound cool and collected. "How y'doin', Joe? Haven't seen you around for a while."

"I'm cool," the other boy replied, although Zack thought he sounded and looked anything but. "What're you doing here?"

"Is Maggie in?"

"No, she's not," Joe replied, too quickly.

Zack hit Joe's shoulder playfully, the way they used to. "Come on, buddy, it's me." He laughed uncomfortably. "Honestly, man, is Maggie in or not?" When Joe didn't reply, he added, "It's just that she's not been to school, and I was just wondering where she is, is she all right, that kind of thing, you know?"

"She's all right, but she's not home," Joe said edgily.

"No? Where is she, then?"

"I don't know."

Zack nodded tersely, and Joe just stared at him. Sighing, Zack murmured, "Come on, man, you don't have to do this to me. I know you're worried about her going out with me, but I wouldn't hurt her in any way, man, you know that."

"Do I?" Joe replied flatly.

Hurt and anger flashed in Zack's eyes. "Why would I be here if I didn't care about her?"

A pause. Then: "I don't know," Joe conceded, "but I'm just . . . protective, I guess. Just looking out for her. I mean, you know my dad's run off and my mum's going through shit, so . . . I'm just trying to be the best big brother I can be, know what I mean? No, you wouldn't," he added quietly, and looked behind him, at the stairs. "She's upstairs, but I think she's asleep. I could let her know you dropped by, if that's okay with you."

"I'd rather see her in person."

"What if I said no?"

"Then you'd be a real shit-ass of a friend."

Joe laughed grimly. "Yeah, well . . . I guess that's what I am."

Zack threw his arms up in the air in disappointment. "I don't get it—what's the big deal?"

"Nothing's the big deal. She's asleep, and you shouldn't disturb her; she needs her rest."

"Right. She does," Zack said sarcastically, and let out another loud breath. "All right, fine, whatever, I'm gonna go. You take care, Joseph."

"I will."

Giving Joe an exasperated look, Zack turned to leave—only to mis-step and plunge his left foot into the gift left by Bertha Asterville. Groaning, he pulled away from the misshapen cake and stormed off the porch, heading for the bench in the field, wondering why Joe was being so difficult and why he didn't want him near Maggie . . . leaving behind him a messy trail of chocolate sponge and soiled cream.

SLOW TO BLESS

Derrick Weston led Dawn through the grass, pulling her hand gently as they walked towards the vacant bench under the tree. The night was quiet, the buildings around the field dark. He pointed this out, and she reminded him that it *was* two in the morning. Across from where they sat, a streetlamp sputtered, its orange light blinking sporadically. Derrick put his arm around Dawn's shoulders and drew her to him, inhaling that wonderful perfume again, getting high on her scent. Her blond hair tickled him pleasantly as he nuzzled against her neck, relishing the warmth of her skin against his face. As he kissed her below her earlobe, she let out a soft purring noise from deep within her throat, a contralto note that caused an excited stirring in his pants. "Dawn," he whispered, and kissed her again. "Oh, Dawn . . ."

"Derrick," she whispered, and her voice was a little rough, which sent shivers of exhilaration down his spine. He wondered as she turned her head to kiss him on the mouth if they'd go all the way tonight. It was something he'd been thinking about since he'd gone out with her that Monday night after the intervention in his living room.

It was their third official date in as many days. They'd wound up at his apartment on Monday night, and they'd fooled around again—although the big difference compared with the night they met was that Derrick could remember what they'd done, with great elation, the following morning. On Tuesday night, it'd happened yet again. And tonight, there was a new thrill—being out in a public place, an open space. It'd been a fantasy of his to do naughty things where they could easily be caught, the risk being part of the adventure. Of course, these fantasies had never been realised because he'd never dared to do them, and Geraldine hadn't been very enthusiastic, either. But tonight, it was going to happen—because Derrick had changed. It had been a slow evolvement, a "coming out", in his own way, from the closet of sexual oppression and repressive self-discipline, an intrepid venture into a whole new world of excitement and lasciviousness. He was becoming a new person, a new Derrick Weston, and while his heart still ached for Geraldine, he knew, ultimately, that she had a point. He had to get over her, one way or another, without losing her friendship for good.

On a more superficial level, this new relationship with Dawn was not moving as quickly as he'd have liked. Dawn, while being very enthusiastic about giving Derrick a blow job, was rather hesitant to get naked. Even taking her shirt off caused her to get flustered, which Derrick found surprising, since he'd figured she was the kind who wouldn't have a problem exhibiting herself. Which wasn't to say he thought her to be a slut; she just exuded so much sexiness and raw femininity that he'd imagined her to be more open to sexual escapades than she'd thus far demonstrated.

Goes to show you can't judge a book by its cover, he thought, as he slipped his tongue into her warm mouth and tasted her sweetness. Gently he placed his hand on her breasts and waited for her to ease his fingers away as she had the previous nights. Tonight, she let his hand linger a little longer before finally shifting her body, letting him take the hint by himself. He kissed her harder, deeper, and savoured the smoothness of her tongue against his. This was so exciting, so new to him! All those nights of dreaming and fantasising, letting his imagination run riot—Derrick wasn't going to feel any more guilt about it.

He breathed, then buried his face against her warm neck, taking in the smell of her hair and skin. "Hey, Dawn," he whispered into her ear as he nuzzled her. This was going to be a risky venture, but he went for it anyway:

"When can I make love to you?"

The time: 2:20AM. The place: Apartment 3B. The position and intention: Looking out the window at the silhouetted couple under the tree. The snoopers: Sanjeev, Chitra, Hope and Geraldine. The equipment: Four pairs of binoculars.

"What do you think he's saying?" Sanjeev said.

"I don't know," Chitra replied, "it's hard to tell . . ."

"I can't read his lips," Hope murmured. "Dawn's hair's in his face . . ."

"And it's dark," Geraldine added. "I told you we should've gone with the infra-red."

Sanjeev protested, "They were expensive."

"And hard to get our hands on," Chitra reminded her.

Hope said, "I think . . . he's . . . trying to go all the way with her."

"All right!"

"Yes!"

"Whoo-hoo!"

"'When do you think . . . I could . . . '—dammit, her hair's in the way again . . ."

Sanjeev, impressed: "Wow, when did you learn how to lip-read?"

Hope shrugged. "Ah, it's just something y'pick up when you've been on the streets like I have."

"Uh-oh! She's backing away from him," Geraldine said.

Sanjeev sighed. "Oh, no! How much longer can she do this . . . ?"

"He's going to lose interest if this keeps up—"

"But it's not *her* fault that he keeps asking her!" Chitra objected. "*She* has to propose sliding into fourth-base when the time is *right*, dammit!"

"Calm down now, calm down," Geraldine said. "Derrick won't be giving in that easily. I know him; he'll probably keep pushing her until she caves."

Sanjeev joked, "It's all your fault, Geri. Your lack of interest in sexual relations has caused him to become desperate and hungry for more."

"On the other hand, her lack of 'interest in sexual relations' is what we're counting on to make this plan work," Hope replied, coming to Geraldine's defence. "And this plan *has* to work. Derrick's—and *our*—entire future depends on this!"

"Let's hope he's the persevering type," Sanjeev murmured.

"He'll persevere," Geraldine said. "I know he will."

"Otherwise," Hope added, "he'll never learn the truth."

The others nodded, sheathed in the darkness of the apartment, agreeing wholeheartedly with Hope's statement.

"I hope," Hope said softly, "she plays the ex-boyfriend card."

They were strange figures gathered in the dark, illuminated only by the faint glow of the moon shining through the window, wide-awake despite the fact that some of them had jobs to go to in the morning, nodding their heads simultaneously, agreeing that the ex-boyfriend card was probably the next best thing.

"**W**hy not?" Derrick asked softly, trying to stem the frustration that washed over him.

She shook her head. "I . . . I guess I'm just not ready."

"But . . . why not?"

"Look," she said, and drew her jacket tighter over her shoulders as the wind rustled the leaves above them and sent a few dead ones drifting down to the ground below, "I'm sorry, Rick, but—I went through a really bad time with one of my previous boyfriends, and . . . he used me real bad." She stopped and licked her lips, her voice drawing softer, more tremulous. "He was a real asshole. I thought he loved me, but—in the end, all he wanted was the opportunity to hop into my bed and into my pants and into my . . . well, you know." She drew in a deep breath, let it out slowly. "I thought I was over that horrible experience, but . . . I'm not. I'm not ready. I need a little more time before . . ." — she glanced at him, saw the disappointment on his face — " . . . you know," she whispered, "before we actually get round to doing it."

Derrick struggled to maintain his composure, telling himself that this wasn't such bad news. "I'm sorry, Dawn." He sighed, reached over and took her hand, squeezing her fingers lightly. "I'm really sorry. I guess after all these years with Geraldine, I'm really eager to try something new. I didn't mean to come on so strong. I'm sorry about what you went through, and I hope you and I . . . one day, when you're ready . . ." He squeezed her hand again, and she looked up at him with glistening eyes, smiling appreciatively.

And then — like a bolt from the blue — he was certain what he felt for Dawn went beneath the surface, that it wasn't just a desperate attempt to get over Geraldine. Looking at her in the dimness of the surroundings, he realised his heart was hurting, filled with anger at the idea of some asshole ex-boyfriend playing the fool with Dawn and treating her bad. All at once he knew he wanted to look after her and make sure she never felt such pain ever again. He wanted to protect her and watch out for her and love her, and the realisation of this was stunning, causing him to momentarily experience a sense of vertigo.

Then she leaned over and kissed him on the mouth, and there wasn't any more disorientation, only sheer bliss and a clear understanding of what he was going to do the rest of his life. It was a most profound moment, one that was almost epiphanous, and it was a pity it was shattered by the wailing of an ambulance in the distance.

Derrick pulled away, smiled at his date, and decided it was time to see her home.

INTO THY HANDS,
I COMMEND . . .

At half past seven in the morning, Graham Hanson believed he and Felicity were sitting side by side on the bench, holding hands as they watched the sun rise. He drew her close and imagined, without realising it, the warmth coming from her body. He heard her talk as if she were really there. Somewhere in the distance, a young woman looked out of her bedroom window to see the old man sitting on his own in the middle of the bench, one hand positioned as if he were holding another person's.

Together, Graham and Felicity Hanson spoke of what they'd be doing for the rest of the years to come, as he fantasised about them growing ever older together and leaving the world as a couple still very much in love.

At half past nine, Graham drove them to the children's shelter. It was so fulfilling giving a helping hand to the little ones, and it made him realise how immaterial it was that they didn't have their own children: it didn't make them lesser parents. They would play around and supervise the young ones, and it didn't matter if Graham mentioned Felicity's name aloud, because not many of the little kiddies fully understood death.

But Marguerite Dumont, the children's shelter coordinator, had observed a thing or two, and was wondering when the timing would be right for her to have a chat with Graham. She supposed the man needed some time to process his loss. But if one of the children were to run to her complaining that Mr Hanson was talking to nobody, she'd have to do something. It hurt her to think it, and she hoped it wouldn't come to that.

Graham, accompanying the orphaned children to the playground where they shrieked and tumbled over the swings and roundabouts, continued to think he was squeezing Felicity's hand, as happy as a septuagenarian could be. Looking at her beautiful face, he could see tears sparkling in her eyes—tears that reflected his own thoughts: no regrets, no sadness, only sheer gratitude for the time they had together and the fact that the Lord God had blessed them so munificently. Again it struck Graham that while the Lord might seem unkind at times—the memory of Felicity lamenting her barrenness coming to mind—the abundant blessings He poured forth far exceeded the curses. *No*, he corrected himself, there were no curses. Some of the blessings were abundant and teeming with grace; some were less so; but they were *all* blessings to be cherished and accepted with appreciation.

"They're all so vibrant, so happy," he heard Felicity say, smiling and waving at one of the children, who was staring in their direction fixedly.

"It's strange, isn't it?" Graham said aloud, as Marguerite Dumont watched from her office window in the distance, observing the old man's outstretched hand clutching at nothing and his lips moving in a conversation with empty air. "These children don't have any parents, or their parents aren't around to look after them, and yet they're so happy. They don't seem to be sad at all. It's almost as if they realise, at their age, that God's gifts come in all shapes and sizes, big and small. They don't have their moms and dads, but they have people like us, like Marguerite, like James and Ashley," he said, referring to the young married couple who frequented on the weekends.

Then one of the children called to him, and he laughed, disentangled his fingers from Felicity's, and hurried towards the child.

Marguerite Dumont spun around in her swivel chair when there came a knock on the door. "Come in," she called, and Sarah Robertson walked into the room.

Moments later, Sarah and Marguerite were both standing by the window, observing the old man. Sarah's hand was raised to her chin, which was trembling with emotion.

"Do you want to talk to him?" Marguerite inquired softly.

"No. I mean, yes. I don't know," Sarah replied, and sighed. "It seems so heartless, but what choice do I have, honestly?"

Marguerite looked back out the window, where Graham wrestled playfully with the children, surprisingly energetic for a man of his age. It was as if the illusion of Felicity being alive kept him alive, drove him onwards and maintained his youth. No, Marguerite thought—it *restored* his youth. The man was more cheerful and brisk than she could remember.

"I don't know," Marguerite whispered, "but it seems to me the longer we let this be, the further from reality he's going to get. He's already openly talking to the air; if we stand back and allow this go on . . ."

"I know. But I just don't see how . . ."

"If you want me to be with you," Marguerite began, and stopped, clearly not wanting to finish the sentence.

"I don't know," Sarah said, and thought, absurdly, that the two of them seemed to know and not know an awful lot of things. "I'm thinking if I were to go alone, he might not be convinced. But if I brought someone with me, he might think we're ganging up on him, and that might make him angry and defiant." She paused. Graham was chasing a little girl, who was laughing audibly as she toddled along. "I was thinking I could move in with him for a while, but he wouldn't be able to recognise me. His mind would refuse to acknowledge who I really am because it would betray the unacceptable truth about my sister.

"And then I thought he should get away for a while. Maybe if he weren't here, he wouldn't think so much about Felicity, and the images of her might fade. Surely it can't be helpful being in the neighbourhood day after day, where all the memories of her remain." She paused again, and Marguerite Dumont waited.

"Then again, if he were to go away, he might believe he's going away with Felicity, and that wouldn't help either," Sarah said quietly, almost as if she were talking to herself. "So I really don't know what to do."

"Maybe we *could* just let it be," Marguerite suggested, changing tack. "The opposite could happen, too — in time, Felicity might disappear."

Sarah laughed, but there was little amusement in it. "Do you really think that?"

"Well . . ."

"I don't know," Sarah said before Marguerite could say anything further. "I really, really don't know."

Marguerite reached over and touched the other woman's arm gently. "Whatever you decide, Sarah," she said, "just know that we — every one of us here at the shelter — will be standing behind you one hundred percent. Graham Hanson is a wonderful man, an extremely efficient and caring guardian. He's kind, he's gentle, he's responsible, and the last thing any of us want is for him to not be able to move on with the rest of his life. So whatever you decide, we'll be with you."

Sarah looked back at the coordinator and smiled back, touched. The two of them returned to gazing out the window, where Graham was hefting the little girl on his shoulders. The child was ecstatic, and Graham himself looked like he was having a ball.

Give him more time, Sarah thought as she left the shelter. *Just a couple more days.*

Tears began to roll down her cheeks.

How can I break his heart when he's never been happier?

PART THREE

No Presence Without Absence

Lunchtime — a little past one — and Matthew Leigh returned to the usual spot. He'd packed a big lunch, thinking the boy — with his supposed heavyweight diets — would appreciate a good home-cooked meal.

As he walked across the field, he hoped their conversation for the day would be brighter, less morbid. *No more God stuff*, he prayed, and realised he had no idea whom he was praying to.

He sat and waited for the boy.

Waited.

And waited.

Half past three, and he had to get back to the university by four.

Half his container of noodles had been eaten; the other half he'd rationed, hoping the boy would turn up. But he hadn't, which was somewhat surprising, since he'd not broken an "appointment" since they'd met nearly three weeks ago.

He wondered what they would've talked about today. Why birds should be allowed to vote, or something ridiculous like that. Or why God didn't give humans wings so they'd be able to poop on their enemies' heads. Matthew found himself smirking at his ludicrous thoughts, and at the same time feeling a little ambivalent because the kid hadn't bothered to turn up today.

It would take him a little while to realise that the ambivalence
he was experiencing was actually disappointment.

Somewhere on the other side of town, a much-encouraged
Derrick Weston picked up the phone in his work cubicle and
dialled Dawn's number. His colleagues — some of whom were
aware of his break-up with Geraldine — had been keeping
a close watch on him, concerned he would break down and
cry halfway through his work. But, to their surprise, Derrick
seemed more buoyant than they could recall him ever being.
So when he started dialling the phone, they kept their eyes on
him, their ears straining as they anticipated his lips forming the
name of his former girlfriend.

Dawn's telephone rang and rang, and nobody picked up;
then the answering machine clicked on and a man's voice said,
"Hey, nobody's in right now, you know what to do." This didn't
startle Derrick; he'd been warned that Dawn's brother had
taped over her original, sexy message, thinking it wasn't right
for a girl to seduce her callers. "Go figure," Dawn had said
scornfully. Derrick swore he'd kill the brother if he ever got his
hands on him.

"Hey, Dawn," he said, and the mini-audience in the cubicles
around him gasped upon hearing the Other Girl's name. "It's
me, Rick . . . just thought I'd call to say hi, to hear your voice.
Are you home? If you are, pick up . . ."

He waited, and he could sense one of his colleagues standing
behind him. From the smell of stale cologne, he knew it was
Donald Bailey. Without turning around, he told Bailey to get a
life. Bailey let out a sharp laugh and sauntered away, although
Derrick knew that hell would freeze over before Bailey stopped
eavesdropping on him entirely. When nobody answered on the
other end of the line, Derrick said, "Well, that's okay, you're
not home. I just wanted to tell you how good a time I had last
night, and that I'd love to go out again tonight, if you're not
busy. Give me a call? You know my number. See you, baby."

"Oh, God," somebody moaned from the next-door cubicle. As Derrick hung up, he heard the sound of one of his workmates retching. "'See you, baby'! Somebody shoot me!"

"Eff off, guys!" Derrick yelled, and everyone around him burst out laughing.

Geraldine and Hope pushed the rewind button and heard Derrick's message running backward, a high-pitched, chipmunk voice. They played back Derrick's romantic message of love, and, when it was over, Hope grinned, and Geraldine felt a wave of happiness — tinged, curiously, with a trace of poignancy. She leaned into Hope's embrace, and Hope kissed her ear, saying, "Just a couple more days, and we'll ask Dawn to go all the way with him. That should do the trick."

Bertha Asterville inhaled the wonderful aroma of her cappuccino cake and pulled on her oven mitts. She reached in to remove the tray. The smell was mouth-watering. She wasn't sure if Graham Hanson was a big fan of coffee, but she figured he'd appreciate the gesture.

She placed the cake on the kitchen table to cool before icing it. The telephone rang. Bertha removed one mitt and reached for the black plastic instrument, one of those old rotaries that took forever to dial. Pulling the receiver to her face and untangling the cord with her mitted hand, she spoke into the mouthpiece and heard her next-door neighbour Della Rosenberg's voice. She was smelling cake, Della said, could she come over? Sure, Bertha replied genially, and Della asked who the cake was for, knowing Bertha was a very charitable lady. Graham Hanson, said Bertha, and Della clucked her tongue, tsk-tsk, isn't it a shame about that dear Felicity Hanson? Yes, Bertha agreed, yes, it was, poor Felicity, may she rest in peace. Do you think he's all right? Della asked, and Bertha hesitated, remembering how cool Graham always seemed when she spoke to him. She answered, I honestly don't know, Della, but if you're free, maybe you would like to come over with me? Well, I don't want to intrude, Della replied, but Bertha said, no, no, you wouldn't be intruding, in fact, you'd be very much welcome. Okay, Della said, seemingly without really thinking very hard about it, I will—which gave Bertha the immediate impression that her neighbour had been meaning to tag along anyway, and she hoped Della wouldn't be asking for half of the cake because it was the most scrumptious-smelling cake she'd baked in a while, and she wanted Graham to have every single slice of it, down to the very last crumb. Okay, then, why don't you come over? Bertha asked, and they said their pleasant goodbyes and see-you-soons. Then Bertha was back at the kitchen table, bent over with the icing bag filled with coffee cream in her hands, giving her bare cake a beauty makeover.

After school, Zack McPherson caught up with Carrie Taylor in front of her locker, where she was struggling to fit an oversized jumper into it without getting the sleeves caught in the door. "Hey, let me help you with that," he said as a manner of greeting, and proceeded to give her a hand before she had a chance to refuse. "Got it?"

"Yeah," she muttered. "It's in there."

"That was a huge jumper."

"Just in case I need it," she said curtly. "Winter's coming and all."

"You sure prepare early," he said, meaning for it to be a joke, but she didn't laugh.

"Thanks," she replied, and began to walk away.

"Hey, Carrie," he said, jogging after her, "come on, don't go just like that. Where are you off to?"

"Home. People go home when school's over."

"Hang out for a bit. Wentworth and I are going to the pizza place, and . . ."

"No, thanks. I've got other plans."

"But it's been so long since we last went out . . ."

"I've lost the mood for socialising. Must be my hormones or something."

"Come on, Carrie. Just a pizza, a couple of Cokes . . ."

She shook her head and kept walking. "I've got . . . things I have to do."

"Look," he said, stopping and pulling on her arm so that she'd stop also, "we miss you."

She stopped. "You what?"

"Pete, Alf, Joe and I . . . we miss you."

That made her laugh. "That's fuckin' hilarious, Zack. Leave me alone."

Now he frowned, and, with his expression serious, moved in closer to her, so close she thought for a moment he intended to kiss her. But he didn't. He stopped inches away from her lips, and when he spoke, she could smell the faint tang of spearmint on his breath. In a low, harsh whisper, he asked, "What did he do to you, Carrie? Joe, I mean. He did something, didn't he . . . ?"

Offended, she took several steps back, her eyes flashing. "He didn't do anything."

"Funny how he's been avoiding you . . ."

"He hasn't been avoiding me!"

"Funny, then, how you've been avoiding him."

"I've been avoiding the whole *lot* of you, it's not just Joe, this has nothing to do with Joe!" she shrieked, realising too late that she was a little too loud and a little too hysterical for the words to be true. Zack watched her, his expression twisted in concern, and she shook her head violently, as if he had a hold of her hair and she were trying to pull free. Stepping further backward, she exclaimed, "Why can't you leave me alone, Zack? Respect my privacy a little? Why the hell are you so nosy? Stop staring at me like that, McPherson! *Stop it!*"

Several students gawked in their direction. A small-sized girl with large, oversized glasses moved away from them as fast as her legs could take her, her expression revealing alarm.

Carrie glared large, deadly daggers at Zack, slicing him into shreds.

Swallowing hard, feeling his heart pound and his balls tighten with anxiety, he whispered, "Sounds to me like I ought to be asking *you* what the hell's wrong."

The tears came now, and she let out a frustrated cry. She'd so wanted to avoid a scene like this; that was why she'd avoided her parents, her friends, the father of her child. She didn't want to be questioned, didn't want to be blamed for any decision she was going to make. And now the pain unleashed itself in a torrent of tears, and she found herself sobbing, angry and hurt and exasperated and shit-awful tired, seeking the comfort of somebody's arms, anybody's arms, anybody who'd listen to her without thinking she was a whore who deserved whatever punishment she got.

As she let out a high-pitched wail of despair, Zack put his arms around her, pulling her close to him, letting her wet the front of his sweater. The other students in the corridor were turning away now, awkward and embarrassed, feeling sympathetic without even knowing what was going on.

"Sssh," Zack whispered as she sobbed against his chest, "it's okay. It's okay now, I'm here for you." And, at the back of his mind, he wondered again where Maggie was, why he hadn't seen her in four days, four freaking days, and why Joe was refusing to let them see each other. It made absolutely no sense, he thought as he stroked Carrie's dark hair—but he knew the common denominator between Maggie and Carrie Taylor was Joe Cooke . . . and one way or another, he was going to find out the truth.

Maggie Cooke tossed and turned on her bed, feeling hot and uncomfortable despite her window open and an autumn breeze blowing through the gaps in the rose trellis into her room. She knew Zack had been calling for her; she'd even seen him the day before, sitting on that bench in the field—the bench from where only minutes before she'd observed a young man walk away. She'd watched this young man for a while, wondering if it was Zack. It wasn't; it was somebody she'd seen before but never met, a dark-haired guy who stared about the field as if searching for someone. When he'd disappeared, she'd turned from the window, feeling sick with sadness and despair, knowing she had to talk to somebody soon about what she was facing and what she was feeling, but not knowing who else she could turn to.

Somewhere in the house, a door slammed, and it registered dimly in the back of her mind that Joe must be back from school. She heard footsteps, and she fleetingly wondered if her brother could be trusted to be told of what she was going through. *No — no way*, she quickly admonished herself; *Joe would tell Mum, and Mum would make a big stink out of it, and all hell would break loose all over again. That's the last thing any of us wants.*

She heard the footsteps approach her door, and waited for them to disappear past. But they didn't — instead, she heard a knocking, followed by her mother's worried voice: "Maggie? Maggie, sweetheart, are you home?"

Having A Blast

"I'll come by your place tonight, darling."

"I can hardly wait."

"Bye-bye, Derrick."

"Goodbye, Dawn."

A pause.

"Hang up."

"No," Derrick said, laughing, "*you* hang up."

"Uh-uh! You go first."

"You first," he insisted, and his colleagues, packing up for the day, rolled their eyes. Somebody gagged loudly in disgust.

"No way, I called, so *you* hang up first."

"What kind of logic is that?" Derrick demanded. "If you called, *you* should hang up; otherwise, the line won't disconnect."

"Nonsense," Dawn insisted, giggling, sending shivers down the boy's spine.

"I won't hang up until you hang up."

"Well, I've got news for *you*, mister — I won't until *you* do."

"Looks like we're going to be here all day then." Derrick snickered.

"Looks like it," she replied, and Derrick waited, listening to her breathe and enjoying every pointless, time-wasting moment of it, while his workmates coughed and choked and made puking noises in the background.

Chitra walked into the cosmetics section of the departmental store and headed straight for the counter where her dear friend Sanjeev worked as a promoter of men's products. She had just come from her office, and looked absolutely stunning in her dark blue top and matching pants, hugging her figure proportionately and causing many shoppers—both male and female—to turn and stare at her in admiration and/or envy. "Hey, Chit," Sanjeev greeted, smiling at her before turning back to his customer, a ruggedly muscular man with a chiselled jaw covered with five o'clock shadow, sniffing enthusiastically at a strip sprayed with a cologne sample and thinking it perfect for his live-in partner of four years. "So what do you think, sir?" Sanjeev crooned, sucking up full-time in the hope of sale. "Too tart?"

"Nothing's 'too tart' for Bernard," the big guy said, and grinned, a toothy leer that frightened Chitra to no end. "Smells good," he grunted, Neanderthal-like. "Wrap it up and put a little bow on it, Bernie would like that."

When he'd gone, Sanjeev leaned over to her and whispered, "We're surrounded by them, aren't we, darling?"

"Oh, you betcha," Chitra replied, and grinned.

"So Dawn's currently using *Immemorial*," Sanjeev said, looking at the display counter. "When do you think we should get her to switch?"

"As soon as possible. I spoke to Geri. She wants Dawn to go all the way with Derrick by this weekend. So we should get her to start using the other fragrance, get Derrick accustomed to it."

"Do you think this is going to work?" Sanjeev said, lowering his voice dramatically. "This whole crazy plan of ours—do you really think . . . ?"

Chitra smirked. "Come on, Jeev, it's *already* begun, surely you can see that. And when Dawn switches fragrances, it's the next step leading up to our much-anticipated climax."

Sanjeev giggled as he reached into the glass case for the new box of perfume. "This," he said, "is going to be a blast."

"A blast," Chitra agreed, and cackled. "That, my dear, is an understatement."

"So what's the story?" Zack asked, his arm draped loosely around Carrie's shoulders.

Carrie took a deep breath, held it. Zack waited, knowing she needed to take her time with whatever she wanted to tell him. He didn't want to hold Carrie too tightly in case Maggie looked out her window, saw him snuggling up to another girl, and took it out of context. A faded pink flower fell onto the seat next to him from the boughs overhead. Somewhere, a dog yipped. A couple of cars moved slowly along the road on their left.

Maggie, Maggie. Zack wondered if Joe had poisoned her mind against him. He hoped not; he truly wanted to get to know her better. He'd even respected her wishes on the night of their first date when he'd tried to go all the way with her. "I don't think I'm ready for this," she'd said softly as they'd snuggled in the back seat of his Corolla, and he'd nodded in understanding.

"It was Joe," Carrie spoke, momentarily startling him. She avoided his gaze, looking down at the grass. "Joe and I," she whispered, her voice nearly inaudible, drowned out by the rustling of the browning leaves and the sibilant whispers of wind blowing through the grass. "Zack," she attempted again, and he waited patiently.

She let it out: "I'm pregnant with Joe's baby."

"You haven't been to school in four days," Jessy said softly, sitting on the edge of Maggie's bed, smoothening the covers with the palm of one hand. "The school was so concerned they called me, and I came straight home. Are you all right?"

Maggie struggled to fight back the wetness that had seeped into her eyes. Battling to keep her voice steady, she whispered, "I'm—I'm okay, just—extremely tired."

"Honey." Jessy reached out and touched Maggie's forehead with the back of her hand. "You don't feel like you have a temperature." She looked intently into her daughter's eyes, and her heart broke upon seeing what was registered there: pain, sadness and silent suffering. "Is it Daddy?" Jessy asked quietly, and reached for her child's hand, clasping it between hers. "Is that what this is all about, sweetheart? You still miss Daddy?"

Maggie blinked, and the first rivulet rolled down her cheek, warm and wet. "I . . ." she began, and swallowed hard. Her throat was dry, her tongue thick. She licked her lips, tasting salt, and more tears came. "I wish I could stop thinking about him," she managed.

"Maggie," Jessy said softly, "you don't have to stop thinking about him. Just because he isn't here, just because he has chosen a life somewhere else . . ." Her voice trailed off, and she lowered her gaze to her daughter's quilt: multi-coloured floral designs against a bright blue background, ironically cheerful. "I'm so sorry," Jessy said when she found her voice. "I'm so sorry about Daddy and me, but it wasn't meant to be."

Maggie wiped her face with her free hand. "It's not your fault. It's Daddy's — he's the one who ran away."

"Don't say that, it's nobody's fault . . ."

"No, it's Daddy's," Maggie repeated, her voice taking on an edge. "You've been here all this time, struggling and trying to help us go on, while he's been out there . . ." She shook her head, and the tears continued, watering the bright flowers on the quilt. "It isn't fair, Mum," she whispered. "It's just not fair."

Jessy swallowed, a hard lump rising in her throat. "I know. But we're going to get through this, right? We are. We have. And we will. Whatever decisions your father has made — if they're making you sad, if they're making you cry, then I'm sorry. I'm so sorry he's hurt you. But you know what? It's all right to cry, it makes you stronger after." Jessy raised a hand to wipe the wetness away from her daughter's cheek. "Daddy makes me cry, too." She smiled weakly. "Maybe we should just cry together. You, me, and Joey," she said, using the nickname she'd not used in years.

Maggie wrapped her arms around her mother, crying into her blouse. Yet as Jessy hugged her, she had no way of knowing that Maggie's tears were, in actuality, not for her father or for her mother's suffering, but for a personal agony that tore into the very heart of her every time it crossed her mind.

Bertha Asterville and Della Rosenberg walked across the field towards Graham Hanson's, and they both turned to peer at the couple on the bench: the boy with the faded jeans and stonewashed t-shirt; the girl with the dark hair and makeup running down her face. "Ah, the spirit of youth," Della gushed, seemingly oblivious to the girl's unhappiness, and Bertha laughed, balancing the gorgeous coffee cream cake in her hands. "What do you think," Della whispered conspiratorially, "do you reckon they've been doing it?"

Bertha's jaw dropped. "Della!"

"Oh, lighten up, Bertha," Della said, as they walked past the couple. "It's not as if neither of us has ever done it."

"Yes, well, those are days *long* gone," Bertha said, and sighed wistfully.

They reached the end of the field and crossed the road towards the Hansons' home. *Or rather,* Bertha thought, *the* Hanson *home—only one of them is left.*

Della knocked on the sturdy oak front door. As Graham's footsteps sounded inside the house, Bertha pondered on something he'd told her when he'd dropped by. She'd asked how he'd been coping, and he'd said . . .

"Bertha, I'm perfectly fine. She was old, it was just her time to go."

That was a strange statement if she'd ever heard one. It made her think of all the other conversations they'd had since the funeral. Frequently he had mentioned Felicity's name—but now that Bertha thought about it, what if he *hadn't* been referring to Felicity, but had instead been saying the name of his late Aunt Phyllis? It was hard to differentiate between the two names, as he sometimes shortened Felicity to "Fel", which sounded similar to "Phyl"—especially where it came to the questionable hearing of old people. What if Graham had been saying "Phyl" in response to everybody else's "Fel", and nobody had noticed the difference because of the homonymous nature of the two names? That bizarre statement—*"it was just her time to go"*—gave Bertha the impression that Graham had *not* been talking about his late wife . . .

Another thought crossed her mind, and she frowned: *"She and I drifted apart a long time ago anyway; we definitely weren't as close as we used to be."* Now *that*, Bertha thought, was definitely suspicious. As far as she could recall, Graham and Felicity had always been close; they'd been *closer* than close; they'd practically had conjoined souls . . . !

Could it really be, Bertha wondered, the cake trembling almost perceptibly in her hands, *he doesn't realise Felicity has gone to God? Has he been thinking all this while that it's Phyllis who just died, not Felicity?*

The door swung open, and Graham stood there, smiling uncertainly.

"Graham," Bertha began—

—But she was cut off by Della's exclamation: "Oh, Graham, how *are* you?"

And before Bertha could do or say anything, the other woman threw herself through the doorway and flung her arms around Graham's neck, hugging him tightly as she declared, "I'm so sorry about Felicity's passing, Graham, how are you coping?"

CONFUSION IS THE
STATE OF MIND

———

"**J**oe's baby?" Of course! The idea of Carrie being pregnant
had previously crossed Zack's mind, and his initial reaction had
been a cynical *surprise, surprise.* But then the revelation finally
made an impact, and he found himself chortling in disbelief:
random, inappropriate spurts of laughter. "My God. What are
you going to do? Does he know?"

Carrie sighed. "I told him."

"How did he take it?"

"How d'you think?"

Zack groaned, leaning against the hard back of the bench,
and chuckled.

"We got into a huge fight," she told him. "I fell, and he
wanted to hit me, as if getting pregnant were *solely* my fault,
that fuck."

"I don't believe it." Zack shook his head and let out another
laugh, unwarranted as it was. "He's such a shit!"

"He told me whatever I chose, he'd want no part of it. So
if I got rid of it, he wouldn't pay for the procedure; if I kept it,
he'd not be involved as the father either."

Suddenly he felt anger, hot within him. Who the hell did
Joe Cooke think he was? How on earth could he treat Carrie
in such a callous manner? "So what did you do? What are you
going to do?"

"I've already decided," she replied quietly, and stopped.

He waited for a bit, then pushed gently: "What?"

"I'm going to screw him up. Screw him up real bad."

"What do you mean?"

"I'm going to tell his mum, get him into deep shit, and make sure Joe's involved in this baby's life whether he fucking likes it or not."

"The baby's—? So you've decided to keep it?"

She shook her head, noncommittal.

"And your parents . . . do they know?"

"No."

He laughed sombrely. "It's not something you can hide from them for long, you know."

"Don't be stupid; of course I'm going to tell them."

Zack fell silent, his emotions roiling within him. He figured this was why Joe had detached from his friends, and also why he didn't want Zack to spend time with Maggie—because of the proximity, the degrees of separation between Joe and Carrie. What a tangled web . . .

For a long time neither spoke. Across the field, a young man stood watching the bench, and Zack stared back. Whoever it was, he was too far away for Zack to recognise from this distance. After a while, the man walked away, his head low, looking forlorn. It didn't take long for Zack to forget about him and focus on the situation at hand. "Tell me what Joe said, exactly," he said.

She tried to recount what Joe had lashed out at her that night. She clearly couldn't remember every word verbatim, but what Zack heard was enough to turn that anger into a red-hot glow of rage within his chest. "That fuck," he swore. "How can he do this to you? What a *coward!*"

"Yeah, well," Carrie said scornfully, "he's everything like his father."

A new thought popped into his mind, and he felt every hair on the back of his neck and on his arms stand. He whispered, "Let's hope it's just a guy thing, this running away."

Carrie looked at him, not comprehending.

"Maggie," he explained. "I'm going out with Joe's sister."

"I know. Joe told me."

"She's been—ignoring me lately," Zack said. "I don't know, it's as if I'd hurt her, or something; she's not been picking up my calls, she's not been to school, I just don't know what the hell's going on. But enough about my problems!" he abruptly exclaimed. "Back to you, Carrie. Oh, Jesus. You're really going to do that? March right over to his house and demand that Joe take responsibility for what he has done? Maggie will be dragged into this, too, you realise? I mean, if you tell Joe, it'd upset him, and it'd upset his mum, and Maggie wouldn't be spared from any of this, you realise?"

Carrie leaned back, exhaling audibly. "Yeah. I do."

"And you're going to do it . . . ?"

"Yeah," she answered resolutely, "I am."

Zack gulped, but there wasn't anything to swallow. He thought fast, trying to clear his mind of the jumbled mess within. "Let me talk to him," he told Carrie. "See if I can drive some sense into him. Let's leave Mags and her mum out of this for now. Let me deal with Joe personally, one on one. I'll sort this out for you, I promise."

She looked at him, her eyes revealing confusion. Zack met her gaze, feeling weighed down by the drama of it all. "I'm sorry he's done this, but let me deal with him first. Before you say anything to anyone else, just let me try. Please?"

"But then he'd know I told you."

"Yeah, well, I guess he'll have to deal with that."

Carrie hesitated, before finally nodding.

"Thank you," he said gratefully. He'd have to speak to Joe someplace neither Maggie nor her mother would be within hearing range. The last thing he wanted was for Maggie to be adversely affected by the news.

"In the meantime, I'll psych myself up to tell my parents," Carrie murmured.

"How do you think they'd react?"

She sighed. "Oh, I'm sure they'd be *real* proud."

Matthew Leigh walked back to his car, having looked in the direction of the bench to see if his little buddy had turned up. He hadn't expected to see him this late in the evening; yet the sight of the couple sitting there, whispering intimately between themselves, made him disappointed. He walked with his hands in his pockets towards the car, where he waited for his sister to come back from—whomever's house she had gone to visit.

Tomorrow would be another day.

"Felicity's passing?" Graham repeated, his eyes wide and confused behind his glasses. "What are you talking about?"

Bertha balanced the cake on one hand and used the other to take Della's arm, drawing her away from the man. Bertha saw Della flush and look embarrassed. Della's mouth moved, but no sound came out.

"What in heaven's name do you *mean*, Della?" Graham exclaimed, and stepped back from the doorway to gesture to his wife, who was standing in the foyer behind him, looking just as puzzled. "Felicity's standing right there." Both ladies stared in silence. Graham looked at his wife, who shrugged in apparent bewilderment.

"I brought you a cake, Graham," Bertha said quickly, holding up the luscious cream sponge. "Cappuccino. I hope you like coffee."

"I do, thank you," Graham replied, and gave Della a strange look. The woman averted her eyes, baffled and mortified. As he took the cake from Bertha, both women observed his wrinkled hands were trembling under the feather-light weight of the dessert. "Why don't the four of us share this, make it a late tea?" He smiled, and the women shifted uneasily, their feet scuffling against the floor. Graham approached his wife, holding the cake out to her. "Honey, why don't you cut this up and put the kettle on . . . ?"

And, as the women watched in shock, Graham let go of the cake, letting it fall, tumbling base over surface, to the ground. It hit the wooden floorboards with a low *splat*. Cream and sponge scattered in a wide blotch across the floor. Della cried out, and Bertha shot her an urgent look, warning her not to react too openly, because Graham, poor Graham, was nodding and smiling at empty air, seemingly not realising that the cake now lay in a mess at his feet.

COMPLETE AND
TOTAL OBLIVION

The delusions were getting worse, there was no denying it. Graham walked into the kitchen, not looking back, and the women followed him, unable to keep their eyes off the coffee disaster decorating the floorboards. Entering the kitchen, they both stopped short and looked around in horror. A large pile of dishes and cutlery filled the sink, crusted with remnants of food. More food particles—some as large as a human fist—lay in chunks on the floor, while several puddles of liquid had coagulated into thick, sticky pools. There was the stink of sour food in the air. Graham, oblivious to it all, invited them to sit at the dining table.

Della and Bertha sat, the latter woman wondering how it had reached this point. She'd never imagined it to be like this! Graham had been unmindful of the cake falling to the ground; in his mind, Bertha realised with a cold jolt, he must have seen Felicity take it from him, and she was probably standing at the counter right now, cutting the non-existent cake into non-existent pieces with a non-existent knife! *Oh, my God,* Bertha thought, swallowing hard. *Dear Lord, how bad has it got?*

Graham came over, holding nothing in his hands, and placed empty air in front of them. Della looked at Bertha in fear and desperation, uncertain of what to do. Bertha returned her gaze, shaking her head, moving her lips soundlessly. *Graham,* she thought, feeling a tug upon her heartstrings, *Graham, oh, Graham, she's gone, can't you tell she's gone? Don't do this to yourself.*

"Go ahead," he urged them, "don't wait for Fel and me, eat up."

"Bertha," Della said pleadingly.

Bertha stood. "Graham," she said, her voice lowering to barely above a whisper, "you've got to listen to me."

Almost at once, he looked wary. "What is it?"

"I think you need to sit down." Bertha waved to the chair.

Graham cast a glance over his shoulder at the sink, where he'd left the tap running, the plates and dishes piled high, unwashed. He moved tentatively to the table. Keeping his eyes on Bertha, circumspect, he sat.

Bertha saw Della's helpless look of sympathy. She didn't want to do it, but she felt she had to—otherwise, God only knew how far from reality Graham would slip. She moved close to him, took his hand. "Graham, honey . . . I'm so sorry, but she's gone. Felicity passed away three weeks ago."

His reaction was immediate. "No!" he objected, pulling his hand away.

"Please," she whispered. Tears sprang to her eyes. "I'm so sorry. I really am, we both are," she said, gesturing to Della and herself, "but it's true. She passed away, Graham. She's not here."

"No!" he repeated. Bertha saw the blood drain from his face, leaving a pale, agonised pallor. He stood, pushed himself away from the table, and turned to the sink. "What kind of sick game are you playing, Bertha? She's there. She's right there, cleaning up!" He jabbed his finger in the direction of the basin, where the food-encrusted dishes bathed in the flow from the tap. "Della," Graham exclaimed, speaking loudly and urgently now, "you see her, don't you? You see her there? Felicity . . . ?" He turned back to the sink, where Felicity was watching him with an expression of incomprehension and alarm. He stormed over to the sink, reached for his wife's wrist, grabbing it, pulling her towards the table, towards the two accusing women. "Look," Graham insisted, holding up his wife's arm by the wrist. "She's right next to me. She's here. She's right here. Felicity, say something!"

His wife's mouth moved, and, when she managed to find her voice, she uttered, low and hoarse, "I—I don't know what to say."

"There you go! She's talking! She speaks! She's right here! What are the two of you trying to do to me?"

The two women saw nothing next to him. His fingers—the one supposedly holding her wrist—were curled around empty air.

Della looked at the floor, her own tears dropping now.

Bertha could only gaze upon Graham with distress, not sure what to do. Maybe this had been a mistake. Maybe she should have waited before telling him. Maybe she should have called Dr Rubinstein. He might have been able to deal with this better. Maybe this hadn't been her business, she hadn't the right to say anything. After all, who was she? Just the nosy neighbour with a squeaky voice who'd been infatuated with Graham for the longest time, even before her second divorce had reached a settlement. *No,* she told herself regretfully, *I've made a mistake. I shouldn't have said anything . . .*

"Mr Hanson?"

Graham's head snapped up, and both women turned to look at the kitchen doorway, where the girl's voice had come from.

"Michelle," Felicity spoke into Graham's ear.

"Mr Hanson, I just came for my scarf," said Michelle Leigh, walking into the room. Her eyes widened with bewilderment as she surveyed the messy kitchen, saw the anger on Graham's face, and the two traumatised-looking women by the table. She looked at the cake that lay in the middle of the corridor, like some sort of bizarre, messy conversation piece. "Oh," she whispered, her eyes registering her astonishment. "What's going on?"

"Michelle," Graham said, "I'm glad you're here." He was speaking quickly, frantically, more agitated than she'd ever seen him. He gesticulated to the empty air—to his wife, standing next to him. "Doesn't Felicity look pretty today? I told her to wear the bow—it's the same colour as your scarf, isn't it beautiful?"

Michelle gaped, not knowing how to respond.

"Honey," Graham said pleadingly. "Michelle?"

The girl's mouth moved, but produced no sound.

"Michelle!" Graham cried, his voice cracking. "Don't tell me you're in on this, she's right *here!*" He gestured at the empty space by his side, where Felicity, the love of his life, was crying, crying with the women, *because* of the women. "You can see her, can't you? You see her every time you come over. She's here right now, and she was here when you came over for dinner on Tuesday—"

No, Michelle thought, trembling with emotion, *no, I haven't. She wasn't here, Mr Hanson, it was just you, and it all seemed very strange and very frightening* . . .

It had grown worse since her last visit, she realised, looking at the mess all around them. His delusion . . .

"This is incredible," Graham exclaimed, and turned to look at nothing, his expression filled with stark incredulity. "Can you believe this, Feli?!" he raved, flailing his arms wildly as Felicity shook her head, sobbing quietly into her trembling hands, his voice hoarse and ragged with feeling. "I mean, can you *believe* this?" Without warning, he turned back to the three ladies and shouted, "Go away! Go *away,* leave me alone, *you're not welcome here!*"

Michelle, swallowing the lump of sorrow that had risen in her throat, whispered, "I'll—I'll just take my scarf."

"Graham," Bertha began, but stopped when she saw the new redness of his face, scarlet with anger and offence.

"Go. Just go."

Bertha moved to the kitchen doorway, torn between staying and leaving. Could she really leave it hanging like this? To what end? On the other hand, would it be beneficial for her to try and convince him of his loss? Again, to what end? What was she supposed to do—pretend she'd never said anything and, thus, allow him to go on with the illusion, or stay and attempt to talk him into believing her—into realising the sad, tragic fact that Felicity Hanson, God bless her soul, had passed away in her sleep about three weeks ago? Why couldn't he remember that day when he'd calmly called emergency services upon discovering she wouldn't get up, and had obediently and coolly led the police and paramedics into the bedroom? They'd been there—she and Della and Jessy Cooke from across the field, and their neighbour Mr Wong, as well as Mr Buckley from number 41, Mr Sobinski from number 46, and Mr Jensen, the grocer—gathered at the end of the driveway where the ambulance lights had flashed in the early-morning sunlight, red, bright red, spinning round and round, casting an eerie, dancing glow upon the bodies and faces of those who'd been there.

That he'd remained tranquil throughout the entire experience should have been their first clue. That he'd not shown any emotion during Felicity's funeral—*Felicity's, not Phyllis's*—should've been another. Why hadn't they noticed what was going on sooner?

Because, Bertha thought regretfully, *Graham Hanson has always been a strong-minded, rational man. That's why we never knew—he hid it so well from the rest of us.*

At the front door, Michelle and Della stepped out, but Bertha turned around to face the man. "Please," she whispered softly, "get some help. Call somebody, your best friend, your relatives, anybody. We're sorry, Graham, we truly are. Please call somebody. Don't stay home alone, it's—it's not good for you."

He shut the door with a loud bang behind her.

The three women stood on the porch, shaken and completely vexed. Della asked what they were going to do. Michelle Leigh was, by that point, already dialling Sarah Robertson's number on her mobile phone, grateful that they'd exchanged contact information when they'd met in the supermarket.

Graham stood in the foyer, glaring icicles at the door, his heart pounding furiously, his blood roaring in his eardrums. *How dare they?* he thought, and gritted his teeth in rage. *How* dare *they?* The nerve of them, barging in and proclaiming that Felicity was dead, accusing him of being delusional, of being unable to accept that his wife had moved on. Lord God, the women were crazy; they were *senile,* he thought vehemently. And they'd influenced that girl, too, little Michelle, their *daughter!* "Jesus!" he uttered, and then regretted taking the Lord's name in vain. His vision was unclear, and he blinked the dampness—the tears of indignation, shock and fury—out of them. They'd made him cry. Not only that, they'd made *Felicity* cry, and that was too much! Way too much!

She wasn't dead; he'd *know* if she was dead, he wasn't crazy. No; he was quite convinced that Felicity was alive and standing in the kitchen, probably trying to recover from the events that had just taken place. *She didn't deserve that,* Graham thought heatedly, and snorted air out through his nostrils, a bitter, resentful grunt. *And neither did I. They had no right. No right!*

He treaded blindly into cake on the way to the kitchen, not missing a step. After all, to him, the cake had been cut and served generously to his guests, who had thrown it back into his face, figuratively speaking. Bertha Asterville had always had a thing for him, he knew, but this time, she'd gone too far. To flirt openly in front of his wife was one thing; to concoct asinine and hurtful stories in order to get the man she couldn't have was another. He shook his head, trying to clear his mind of angry thoughts. "Dear God," he whispered to himself, and took off his glasses to rub at his tired eyes. He put them back on and stepped into the kitchen, unaware of the trail of cream and sponge he'd left in his wake.

"I'm so sorry, Felicity," he said aloud.

And stopped.

The kitchen was empty.

"Who are you waiting for?"

"Matt, please."

They sat in the front seats of the car. Matthew leaned his arms against the steering wheel, while Michelle peered anxiously out the window, waiting for Sarah Robertson to arrive. She didn't look in the direction of Graham Hanson's home. She wasn't keen on knowing what would happen once Sarah arrived, didn't want to be a witness to whatever would take place in the old man's house. She didn't think her heart could bear any more pain.

"Remember when we used to pray?" she asked her brother quietly.

"Oh, hell. Not you, too."

She gave him a puzzled look.

"Forget it," he muttered.

"I sometimes wonder if there's something to it," Michelle continued. "Praying."

"I don't pray," Matthew replied curtly.

She sighed and looked back out the window. "And maybe that's why we don't have a prayer," Michelle whispered.

"Felicity?"

The dishes she'd cleaned were arranged in a short pile by the side of the empty sink. The room smelled of the detergent his wife usually used. He looked around the kitchen, seeing the untouched slices of coffee cake on the otherwise spotless table, and wandered over to the door that led into the backyard, his shoes gliding across the clean, immaculately mopped floor. "Fel?" he called, and turned the knob, pushing the screen door open. Stepping out into the yard, the wind swirled around him, and he felt—for the first in a long, long time—a cold chill race down his spine. His sparse white hair fluttered about in the gust, and he squinted behind his glasses, trying to see if his wife had decided to wander into the garden. No, he couldn't see her. "Feli?" he shouted. "Honey, are you here?"

He moved down the path alongside his house, which linked the backyard with the front. The women, he saw to his relief, had left his yard. The older two were moving across the field on the other side of the road. Michelle wasn't with them. He let his eyes scan the garden. Felicity wasn't there.

Once more he squinted. In the distance, he saw the bench he and his wife sat on every morning during their post-breakfast walks, vying to see who'd be the first one to spot the vanishing moon. No, he couldn't have imagined those walks, as those crazy women had insisted. Felicity was real; she slept by his side every night, woke up with him every morning, constantly kept him company. His wife was with him; there was no reason for him to believe she wasn't.

Only—where *was* she?

Graham went back into the house through the front door, calling out his wife's name. He stepped into the bedroom, wondering if she'd decided to lie down. It was empty, and the adjoining bathroom was also unoccupied. He was about to walk out of the bedroom when something caught his eye that was rather unusual: Felicity hadn't made up the bed that morning. He stared at the rumpled sheets and the dented pillows, frowning. It was strange, but there was nothing sinister about it, despite the fact that he'd not earlier picked up on it.

Increasingly perplexed by Felicity's disappearance, he walked towards the kitchen, forced himself to take a deep breath. He winced. There was a sour scent in the air, the faint odour of garbage, or of decay . . .

When Graham stepped into the kitchen, he felt as if somebody had punched him in the stomach, knocking the breath out of him. The kitchen was a mess, with filthy dishes stacked high in an overflowing sink, and a disarray of crockery and cutlery displayed upon the counter- and tabletops. He stepped in, his mouth wide, his eyes wider, unable to believe what he was seeing, feeling his breath catch in his throat. *What a mess!* His right shoe stepped into a slippery patch, and he looked down in horror at the spillages on the floor, little puddles of grease and

sauce and congealed substances, decorated with the occasional
shard of broken glass and china. Suddenly terrified, he walked
on trembling legs towards the open back door. The garbage
bin under the sink was full and spilling over with decomposing
food—the breakfasts he had cooked for Felicity every morning,
the dinners she'd supposedly cooked for him . . . most of it—*all*
of it—uneaten, left to rot.

Graham felt nausea sweep over him, and he was overcome
by a strong sense of vertigo. The room tilted, and he let out a soft
cry—*"Feli!"*—as he staggered back towards the front section of
the house, for the first time noticing the grease-smeared dining
table and the mysterious disappearance of the untouched coffee
cake; the coffee cake that was *smeared across the corridor, oh, my
God, it's all there, it's been stepped in, spattered all over, sweet Jesus!*
Again, vertigo, a terrible light-headedness that forced bile into
the back of his throat and sent his heart pounding into overdrive,
overcame him, and he lurched for the front door, swallowing
the nausea and choking out his dead wife's name—

And it came back to him.

The morning of three weeks ago, when he'd woken up and
taken a cold shower, as he usually did, unmindful of the coolness
of the break of day. Afterwards, he'd gone to wake Felicity, *only
she'd refused to wake up, hadn't she? She'd refused to open her eyes, and
you knew, damn it, you knew!* He'd remained calm, called 911.
They'd come for her, and he'd collapsed into bed, worn out by
all the frantic activity. When he'd come to, she'd been there by
his side, and together they'd seen off their anxious neighbours
and friends.

So it had come to pass: despite having the memory of her
unconscious body in his mind, he'd kept seeing her, believed she
was alive, to the extent that the memory of her lifeless body had
been pushed into the deep, dark recesses of his mind, because
she is *here, she's alive, she* has *to be, I only have to look for her, good
God, where* is *she? (Lying in the coffin, buried six feet under, we had
the funeral just recently, the funeral where your cousin Jacob came up
to you and asked if you wanted to give an eulogy, and Jim Williamson*

came up to you and you stupidly asked him how he knew the deceased, thinking it was Aunt Phyllis when, goddamn it, it wasn't *Phyllis but Felicity, Felicity, Felicity!)*

No! No, no, no!

Felicity!

"Oh, my God!" Graham cried aloud, and slipped on a greasy patch of cappuccino cream and went sprawling to the floor on his hands and knees. "Oh, dear Jesus, dear Jesus, *help me!*" he wailed, as his glasses fell from his nose, washed off his face by tears of agony.

A Solid Stone in the Stomach

It was a quarter to twelve the following day. Matthew waited diligently on the bench for his little friend to show. He hoped the kid would turn up; he'd made another ham sandwich and was looking forward to seeing little Robby's face light up when he gave it to him.

While the previous few days had been relatively cool, today the sun was restored to its full glory. It was the kind of weather children played in, based on Matthew's limited knowledge of that category of people. He'd never been a young-person person. Kids were far more adorable when they were of the four-legged mutton variety. Children, he thought, were the epitome of irritation: whiny, snivelling little monsters whose favourite pastimes consisted of trite chatter and nerve-grating queries. If grown-ups had the propensity for driving Matthew round the bend, what more little sticky-faced mudslingers whose idea of popular culture involved a singing purple dinosaur and fruit dressed in bedtime clothing?

Brats, he thought, shaking his head, feeling a droplet of sweat trickle down his neck. Yet, the fact that he was sitting there perspiring with a sandwich in his lap meant Matthew held little Robby in a different regard from the smarmy, loud-mouthed ankle-biters he loved to hate. Little Robby got on his nerves, make no mistake, but he had also triggered Matthew's curiosity and — and — *what? Paternal instinct?*

Whatever it was, Matthew realised he wanted to learn more about the kid. He should at least *try* to listen to what the kid had to say, even if the notion of God displeased him. And he reminded himself now: *Don't be so quick to brush the little twit off. Listen to him.*

With his own reproach echoing in his mind, Matthew crossed his legs, shook his foot restlessly, and waited.

Waited.

And waited.

Derrick Weston looked at the computer on his work desk without seeing what was on the screen. His mind was on Dawn, and his heart was thumping in anticipation of meeting up with her yet again tonight. Every time they went out, he found out more and more about her, and he liked each new thing he learned. Dawn Parker, he had discovered, was a part-time college student, studying civil engineering ("What's that?" he'd inquired, and as she'd explained, he'd listened attentively, nodding, rapt, totally interested even though he'd had *no* idea what she was talking about).

The previous night, he'd dropped her off at the posh Lightview Condominiums, and she'd whispered into his ear, "I'd ask you up for a nightcap, but you know how it is." Yes, he knew—she lived with two brothers and a sister, and as such, privacy was hard to come by. "That's all right," he'd replied, and meant it.

"My brother, Jamie, and my sister don't get along. It's, like, they were born to be quarrelsome, and they usually go for each other's throats over the most insignificant things. They could both look at a white wall, and Jamie would go, 'It's a blue wall', while Sondra would argue, 'No, it's a green wall', when, for God's sake, a white wall is a white wall!"

Derrick had burst out laughing, and had kissed her again. Something had been different about the kiss the second time, and it now occurred to him: *She'd changed her perfume!* It had been subtle, but he'd noticed it, and *he liked it.* Whatever fragrance she'd switched to, smelling it on her had definitely been a turn-on. Maybe he'd find out the brand and buy some for her as a gift. Oh, was *that* an idea . . .

"Weston!"

He looked up and smiled placidly at his colleague, Donald Bailey.

"Oh, Jesus, Weston, snap out of it!" Bailey smirked. "We know you've found someone new and've gotten a little nookie; we're all freakin' happy for you, but it's time to get back to work!"

Derrick smiled broadly as Bailey walked away. A little nookie? No, that hadn't happened yet. In a way, he was glad: Dawn holding back meant he was getting to know her as a person, not just as a sexual object. And if he and Dawn were to do it *now*, it'd be so much the sweeter; he'd be making love to a girl he truly cared about, not simply hooking up with a stranger for the sake of getting over somebody else.

He still thought about Geraldine, but he'd moved closer towards accepting her thorny decision. He still had several hang-ups about Geri's relationship with Hope, but, for the most part, he was learning to let it go. If Geraldine and Hope could truly find happiness together, perhaps it wouldn't be impossible for him to acknowledge it. He hoped the day would come when he'd give them his sincere and unconditional blessings—but, he thought, that day was probably still a long way off.

His vision was usually foggy when he woke up, but today, Graham Hanson was in a deeper state of disorientation than usual. His head was incredibly heavy as he opened his eyes, blinking away the unconsciousness, and he found himself unable to sit up, unable even to move. Blinking hard, he managed to turn his head slightly sideways. Where *was* he? In his bedroom. Under the sheets, a pillow propped firmly under his head. Who was that, pounding against his temples? He winced, realising there was no-one; it was his own skull throbbing. *What's happened to me?*

He tried to speak, but his tongue was thick and his mouth was cotton-dry. He managed to lick his lips, but there was hardly any moisture. He tried again to sit upright, but his energy was sapped, and he could do nothing but remain on his back, breathing heavy and wishing that awful pain would stop.

Felicity. Where was Felicity?

Again, he tried to find his voice. It came out a hoarse croak; a sound that could barely carry halfway across the room. "F-Fel . . . ?"

Silence was the only response.

Graham closed his eyes, praying for respite, and told himself he was just tired. *Yes, that's right—I'm exhausted, I need my rest . . .*

And, before he knew it, sleep was returning to paint the edges of his vision, dark and soothing.

Quarter past one. He'd been sitting there for over an hour.

"Come on, kid," Matthew murmured under his breath. He was leaning against the back of the bench; when he pulled away, his skin was cool and damp with sweat. He'd eaten half his sandwich, and he thanked God (or *somebody)* that he'd had a magazine in his car, which he had thumbed through during his wait.

He contemplated leaving, but a part of him didn't want to just yet. Not when there was a chance of the kid coming by, although it had previously only taken the child a matter of minutes to show up. Maybe his mummy had got upset with him for going home late the other day and grounded him . . .

Matthew looked at his watch. He had to get back to the university for a class. A part of him was tempted to skip it, but a bigger part of him told him to go, learn what he had to learn, come back after.

Naturally, he listened to the smaller part.

Nevertheless, he got off the bench and headed to his car, deciding to take a drive around the block. Maybe he'd see the boy, playing in his driveway or something. It occurred to Matthew that he'd never actually seen the boy's house, even though he knew the general location of it, behind the bench, behind the tree, somewhere in the row of houses beyond. He got into his car, turned the engine on and thanked —*somebody*— for the wonderful invention that was the air-conditioner.

Joe Cooke had the feeling it was going to be a bad day. He felt it in his gut as he wandered semi-aimlessly along the corridors of the school, drifting through his classes without knowing what his teachers were going on about, His friends Wentworth and Richards had stopped talking to him, choosing instead to hang out with a group Joe didn't recognise. Carrie and Zack were not part of this new bunch.

He'd had the good fortune of avoiding Carrie entirely this Friday; maybe she wasn't even at school. *That* was a stroke of luck. But the perturbed feeling remained like a solid stone in his stomach, difficult to ignore. And his apprehension was realised when, after school, he heard Zack McPherson call out to him.

Joe kept walking, taking wide, brisk steps towards the exit, intent on heading home. Zack's footsteps were audible behind him, soles pounding against the tile of the corridor. "Joe! Joe, wait up, I want to talk to you!"

Well, I don't want to talk to you, Joe thought darkly, not breaking his stride. He shoved his way through the doors and jogged down the steps that led to the parking lot and the main gate. "Joe, come on!" Zack shouted behind him. Joe continued without heed —but stopped when he heard Zack's laboured breathing close behind his neck, and felt Zack's hand against his shoulder, stopping him in his tracks, pulling him back. "Joe —"

"Let me go, Zack." Joe spoke through gritted teeth, clenching and unclenching his fists repeatedly with his tongue pushed into his cheek—a sign he was trying to control his temper. Further provocation would likely cause Joe to spin around and deliver a knuckle sandwich right into his face, but Zack felt it was a risk he had to take. So he kept his hand firmly on Joe's shoulder. "I'm warning you . . ."

"I need to talk to you, Joe," Zack said softly. "It's about Carrie."

Joe tore himself away, the sudden movement making McPherson recoil in self-defence. Zack raised his eyes to meet Joe's ice-cold, red-hot gaze; saw blood rising to his cheeks. "I don't want . . . to talk . . . about Carrie. Got that?"

Zack raised his hands in surrender, or compromise. "I just want to chat. What's so wrong about that? I thought we were friends."

Joe snorted. "Friends, huh? Well, I don't speak to *friends* who go around fucking my sister!"

"What are you talking about?"

If anyone had asked Joe why he'd proceeded to say what he said, he would have had no idea. He'd chalk it up to it being one of those rash, spontaneous decisions, the kind his own father would make—one of the infamous Cooke deceptions. He looked Zack straight in the eye and said, "My sister's pregnant." Later, Joe would figure that with everything that was going on with Carrie, pregnancy had been foremost on his subconscious, which was why he'd blurted it without thinking.

But now, shock registered on Zack's face, and his mouth dropped open.

"Wha—what are you talking about? Maggie? Maggie's pregnant?"

"Why do you think she's ignoring you, McPherson?"

Zack shook his head in bewilderment. "You're talking crazy, Joe; she and I, we never even—*no*. We *didn't*. That can't be. How—how do you know?"

"Simple." He grinned unpleasantly. "She leaves her diary lying about."

He turned and walked away, leaving Zack rooted to the spot, sputtering in confusion and hurt. Joe made his way out of the school compound, his face hard as flint. He didn't know what Carrie had told Zack, but she *must* have said something; otherwise why would Zack want to confront him? He was tempted to head over to Carrie's and find out what she'd said, but it would imply he gave a damn about what was going on with the baby. No, confronting Carrie would be a bad move—it would indicate that the things she said and did *did* have an impact on his life, which he was desperate to prove untrue. So he decided to stick to his original course and go home. Go home and figure a way to keep Zack off his back, at least until he could work out what to do next.

Zack pushed his mobile phone so hard against his ear it actually hurt. The ringing tone bleeped on without anyone answering. "Damn it, Maggie!" he swore under his breath. "Pick up, pick up, pick up!"

Nothing.

Shit, he thought, hanging up. For a moment he stood there, not moving, his mind roaring with a thousand different thoughts at once. He forced himself to filter through the noise in his head, and zone in on the main issue. If it was true that Maggie *was* pregnant, then that would explain why she'd been acting distant and moody lately. And if it *was* true that the child was his, then—

He cut himself off with another thought: *No way.*

They hadn't done it. They *hadn't.* Again he recalled that night in the backseat of the Corolla—the last time he'd actually seen her—and how she hadn't been ready. So there was no way she was pregnant, unless—

Unless it wasn't his *baby.*

He tried to think what to do next. He could go over to the Cookes' and brazen Maggie out with the issue—but no, her brother would probably be there, and the last thing he needed was to get into another fight with Joe.

Go home, he told himself. Don't waste time and energy trying to sort it out now—go home, calm yourself, and think it through.

Defeated, he listened to the voice in his head, and slunk off towards the parking lot for his car.

ONE LAST DRIVE AROUND THE SQUARE

Matthew headed over to the shopping centre after circling the Square three times. He'd had no luck spotting the boy. He stopped at the supermarket where his sister worked to buy himself something to drink, and when he headed to Michelle's usual register, he was surprised to see another girl standing there. A glance at her nametag showed her name was Elizabeth Mann. "Hey," he said by way of greeting, "where's Michelle? Didn't she show up?"

"Oh, she's around, I'm just covering for her," the girl replied with an unsteady smile. "She got an urgent phone call, took an early break to answer it. One of her friends from school, I think."

Matthew nodded and paid for his can of soda. "Well, tell her her brother dropped by."

"Not a problem," Elizabeth Mann said, and Matthew nodded his thanks before walking away.

He decided to window-shop for a while. The sports shop was having a sale, all sportswear half off! *Who'd want to buy sportswear with half off?* he thought, and found himself grimacing at his own lameness. Jokes didn't come easily to him, although that wasn't to be mistaken for his rather deft churning-out of sarcastic remarks.

When he was younger, Matthew's solitary nature and his negative behavioural traits had not made him very popular, even though he'd been a good student. In school, he'd exceled at science-related topics—biology, chemistry, physics; when it came to the artistic side, he'd always floundered—drama, literature, English in general. He was the exact opposite of his sister—where he was non-artistic, she was dramatic, in a good way; where she was hardworking, he was lazy; where he was self-absorbed, she was selfless.

Part of what little Robby had said about his plan to become a lawyer had struck a nerve in Matthew, because it was exactly what Mr Leigh, senior, had said. "Lawyers defend the bad guys, Matt," Jonathan Leigh had once told him, following Matthew's announcement that he was going to college to pursue a law degree. "It's in the medical profession where we gain the most satisfaction, helping those in need. There's something gratifying knowing you have contributed to another person's well-being, and I'd love for you to experience that feeling, Matthew."

No, Matthew had responded. His mind was made up.

"What about your contribution to mankind?" Jonathan Leigh had demanded.

Get off your high horse, Dad, Matthew had said unkindly. He thought his father's altruism phoney, covering up for a mind that preferred cash over compassion. All that talk about helping other people and taking on a magnanimous attitude was a mantle for the money-lusting, profit-centric heart that beat inside Jonathan Leigh—a heart whose blood was also flowing in Matthew's veins. In many ways, Matthew was very much like his father—the main difference being that Matthew chose not to hide it with pretension. With Matthew, what you saw is what you got: *I* like the way I behave, *I* am comfortable with the way I think, *I* am confident in my opinions, *I* don't have to change for anybody—and if *you* don't like it, then you can go *fuck yourself,* because *I* don't give a rat's ass. Such was his philosophy. Michelle had taken on more of her mother's qualities, and that was fine, too, but why the hell did she have to impose those traits and beliefs upon others? *Stay away, sis,* he frequently warned her; *I don't have to listen to a damn thing you say.*

I am what I am, as the saying went. Who said that? Matthew didn't know. *Popeye?*

That point was, little Robby whatever-his-last-name-was had created in Matthew an interest in other people and, for once, thinking about others. Maybe it was pathetic that Matthew, at his age, should have to learn from a six-year-old the art of interacting, of *caring,* but it was progress. Baby steps.

Looking into the windows of the shopping outlets, the thought crossed his mind that if his father wanted him to be unselfish, he still could be, without having to become a doctor or a welfare worker or a philanthropist. All it took was a little cash in the wallet and a general knowledge of the likes and dislikes of the recipient of charity.

Matthew walked into a toy store.

"I'll come by tonight," Michelle Leigh said, speaking softly into the telephone. She was in the manager's office, where the call had come in for her earlier. Looking around uncomfortably, seeing Mr Fernandez staring at her with his bushy, caterpillar-like eyebrows raised, she whispered, "Everything will be okay. I'll come by tonight, and we'll talk it through, okay? Promise me you won't start crying, sweetie. It's not so bad. Everything will be all right, you'll see."

Quarter past four, and Matthew was back on the bench, holding a paper bag. At the store, he'd seen something he imagined would make little Robby happy: toy medical equipment. Cheap, plastic stuff—a stethoscope of sorts that the manufacturers claimed actually worked; a couple of tongue depressors that looked like Popsicle sticks; and a blood-pressure gauge, which, Matthew was certain, wouldn't actually work—otherwise, children would be strapping it on and pumping up each other's arms to bursting point, he thought with a grin.

Still, Matthew remembered the boy's passionate declarations about wanting to be a doctor, and he felt the gift would be a pleasant enough surprise for the kid. And even if he didn't like it, Matthew thought it was better than the toy courtroom-judge set he'd contemplated, complete with a bleached-white wig and plastic gavel painted brown to look like wood. It was amazing what toy producers came up with.

His watch struck half past, and now he was getting impatient. The fact that he'd stuck it out for so long proved his tolerance for other people had improved. But, as with everything, there was a limit, and little Robby's no-show impinged on the boundaries. Exhaling his frustration, he stood up and tossed the paper bag onto the hard seat of the bench. *Damn it,* he thought, shaking his head, *where the hell is that kid?*

Matthew headed back to his car and told himself, *One last drive around the Square. That's the most I'm willing to do.*

The roads were practically empty, so he moved at a snail's pace, taking note of the buildings and houses he passed by. A stretch of double-storey terrace houses lined the perimeter of the Square directly across from the bench and tree, and he didn't see anything or anyone of interest, save for a Hispanic woman rinsing out a pair of jeans, and a little Jack Russell terrier barking its furry little head off behind a closed gate. It was, he realised offhandedly, the dog he'd heard barking the first time he'd come to the field.

He turned the junction and hit the next road, driving past the main entrance of the Kiara apartment building. He continued, reaching the end of the road and turning right, so he was now on the road that ran behind the bench. He looked out the window and saw the tree and the back of the bench, shrouded in shade, and then turned to look left, at the driveways and porches of the houses there. Little Robby lived in one of the houses—at least, Matthew believed so, although he'd never actually seen the boy come out from any of the homes.

He reduced the pressure of his foot on the accelerator, bringing his car to an even slower crawl, peering keenly up the driveways of the houses, at the front porches. Some of the homes had extended porches, some had little ones that barely cast a shadow. A lady of African heritage stared at him suspiciously as he rolled by, and in another home, a young, plump Asian girl raised her eyebrows at him, signalling with a wave of her stubby fingers to ask if he needed any help with directions. He ignored her and moved on, scanning the houses. A couple of nondescript homes, followed by one with a front wall streaked with dark streaks of mould. Matthew grimaced and continued past —

And froze when he recognised a familiar face.

No, not one familiar face — two. A pair of blond-haired little girls, playing chase with each other in the driveway of the house next to the fungus-infected one. As Matthew brought the car to a halt, he realised they were the girls who'd turned little Robby away on the first day they'd met.

He turned the key in the ignition, felt the engine vibrate as it coughed and died, and got out of his car.

Felicity Robertson and Graham Hanson first met in the one-thousand, nine-hundred and fiftieth year of our Lord, when Felicity Robertson and her family moved into the newly constructed wooden house next to the Hanson property in a quaint countryside town far south of the city. Graham was sixteen; she a couple of years younger. He first set eyes on her as she attempted, valiantly, to heave a box full of family items into her new home on her own. He watched her balancing the cardboard box on the back of her bicycle, teetering and tottering as she tried to manoeuvre her way to the front of her house. Then she tried to lift the box, but the weight proved too much for her. Graham figured that somebody had helped her get it onto the bicycle, because it was clear the girl couldn't have managed on her own.

She was beautiful: fair-skinned, like a delicate porcelain doll, with rosy cheeks and dark blond curls that reflected the rays of the sun; back then, the sun hadn't hurt the skin like it does today. Graham observed this magnificent vision that was to be his next-door-neighbour with a feeling of awe and nervousness and excitement all at once. He himself wasn't unattractive, with his dark hair and chiselled features and his penetrating dark eyes. He was a little on the wiry side, but helping out with his father's carpentry was helping to build muscle. It was probably all the hefting of wood that his old man constantly ordered him to do. *"If the Lord God Jesus Christ could ascend the place of the Skull with thorns on His head and a heavy cross on His back, I don't see why you can't."* Words to live by.

Graham watched her, sitting on the wooden front porch of his father's house, as she ran into the house to get some help from some of her family members who were inside. They must have been too busy, because she came out alone. That was when he jumped to her rescue, startling her as he approached to give her a hand. She initially declined, but after another failed attempt at lifting the box, she conceded.

Thus became the starting point for the long and enviable relationship that Graham and Felicity Hanson had, a relationship that would last through thick and thin, through good times and bad, in sickness and in health, for sixty-two long years. Sixty-two years during which they'd enjoyed the peaceful solitude of each other's company, during which they'd greeted many new friends and bade farewell to some; during which they'd struggled through childlessness and depression and rejoiced in times of cheerfulness and celebration. It was sixty-two of the best years of Graham's life.

Now, lying in his bedroom, his eyes filled with grit, and his mouth and throat feeling as if he'd just swallowed sand, he wondered, weakly, if it was over. Sixty-two years of bliss come to an end, just like that. Because Felicity was—if his senses weren't betraying him—gone. Gone, after more than a half-century of companionship. *No, that cannot be,* he told himself, struggling to reach out with one arm to touch the sheets next to him, where he was certain he would feel the warmth of Felicity's body. *It cannot be.* His hand moved, ever slowly, weak, taking up the vestiges of strength within him. He spread his fingers apart, trying to touch, trying to reach, trying, desperately, to feel his wife's warmth.

Nothing.

Dear Jesus, nothing.

Please, he begged, squeezing his eyes shut and struggling to open them again. *Please, please.* He was so groggy. What had happened? What had gone wrong? Was he sick? Was he dying? *Please,* he thought again, and still felt nothing next to him.

With all of his strength, he willed himself to sit up. Miraculously he managed to do it, although a wave of dizziness hit him and caused him to shut his eyes briefly. When it faded, he raised his hands to his face and rubbed at his eyes, clearing the grit out of them; and when he blinked again, he realised the room was dimly lit.

Is it night-time? What day is it?

With difficulty, he swung himself around so his legs were hanging off the edge of the bed, and instinctively reached for the bedside table, where he usually left his glasses. They were there, thank God. He fumbled, his fingers trembling involuntarily, as he put them on. With clearer vision, his headache intensified for a moment and then abated. He squinted at the window, where he saw the reddish glow of the sky, signalling that it was either early morning or sometime in the evening. Now that autumn had come, it was really difficult to tell what time of the day it was.

He was hungry. But the thought of food made him remember, distantly, the brouhaha that had taken place in his kitchen with Bertha Asterville and Della Rosenberg. And thinking of them brought back remote images of a messy kitchen, and a cake all over the floor, *and Felicity . . .*

A dream. It was all a dream!

Yes, he told himself, feeling his entire body shake, *it was just a bad dream, that's all it was. I was asleep and I dreamed it, and Felicity is probably somewhere in the house, or outside, in the garden, or maybe she took a walk out to the field to sit on the bench like we always do . . .*

The sound of footsteps snapped him out of his wishful thinking. He turned to look at the door, where he saw the silhouette of a person, casting a shadow across the floor. The person hurried over to him and reached for the table lamp. The burst of light made him wince, and he blinked through a sudden veil of tears as he waited for his eyes to adjust. The person was touching him, touching his forehead, stroking his hands, and was whispering something in a soft, low voice that he imagined was supposed to be soothing, but which instead sounded terrifying.

It was only when his eyes adjusted that he realised he was staring at the face of his sister-in-law Sarah, with the silver hair and the sharp chin. And Sarah was whispering something about taking it easy and not burdening himself unnecessarily: you need to rest, darling, you mustn't exert yourself. *"I'm fine,"* he wanted to say, but his throat was too parched, *"tell me where my wife is and I'll be on top of the world again, you'll see."*

"You've been through a terrible strain," Sarah was murmuring, her breath smelling of pumpernickel, her skin like papyrus against his. "I'm sorry, Graham, but Dr Rubinstein says you need to rest as much as possible. He gave you some relaxants, and you've been sleeping for *hours.* Oh, my God, you must be hungry and thirsty, aren't you?" she exclaimed abruptly. "Stay here. I'll get you something to drink and some soup."

But, he wanted to protest, *I don't understand—*

She smiled at him, what he thought was a cajoling smile and not a reassuring one, and patted his hand. Then she left the room, walking slightly unsteadily as if she'd been drinking, leaving him staring vacantly at the spot where she'd stood.

HELPLESS AGAINST SUCH CIRCUMSTANCES

"Hi there."

The girls turned to stare at Matthew, their eyes wide as one alarming thought struck them: *A stranger!* A stranger was talking to them!

"You girls live here, huh?" he said, thinking he should start with some pleasant, if mindless, banter before moving on to the nitty-gritty. "It's a nice place."

The smaller of the two looked at her sister with obvious concern.

The big girl said smugly, "Our mummy tells us never to talk to strangers."

"Well, your mummy's right," Matthew said, thinking, *Little twat.*

Then, a woman's voice: "Can I help you?"

Matthew looked up and saw her standing in the doorway of the house, gazing at him with—understandably enough—wariness. She was like a mother bird ready to start pecking at the first sign of her chicks being in danger. Straightening, Matthew cleared his throat and called to her, "I'm looking for Robby."

"Robby?" The woman's eyes narrowed.

"Robby?" the younger girl echoed, her mouth forming a perfect O after.

"Yes. Does he live here?"

"No," the woman replied, starting towards the gate. "I'm afraid you have the wrong house. Robby and his mother live next door." She pointed with her right thumb at the house next to hers, the one with its front walls painted eloquently with streaks of black. The woman walked right up to the gate and looked Matthew in the eye. "You must be here to see the child after his bad fall."

An invisible fist slammed into Matthew's abdomen, the impetus of the non-existent blow knocking the breath out of him and causing him to take several seconds to recover. With his mouth momentarily agape, he gawked at the woman, speechless, uncertain if he'd heard right. Then he managed to move his tongue and form the words: "I—I beg your pardon?"

The woman didn't look too perturbed by his being perturbed. "The boy. Robby. Fell down the stairs a couple of nights ago; his crazy mother comes screaming and pounding on my front door at two in the morning, calling for an ambulance. They take their own sweet time getting here, bloody medics. It's like the boy's father all over again."

None of this made any sense to Matthew. He continued to stare at the woman until she felt uncomfortable and quickly excused herself, grabbing her daughters' hands and ushering them into the house. The door slammed shut behind her.

It took several minutes before Matthew slowly and numbly moved away from the gate, his heart thudding rapidly in his chest, palpitating, and his stomach filled with a thousand dancing butterflies, ready to pour out of his mouth. He swallowed hard, swallowing nothing, tasting a vile bitterness at the back of his throat, and wondered if the woman was speaking the truth. Had little Robby whatshisname fallen down the stairs? How? What had happened, and where the hell was he now?

What did that have to do with the boy's father?

He shuffled his way to the house next door, splashed with dark fungus all down the facade, and stood in front of the gate at the end of the driveway. There were two small yards on either side of the drive, and he saw the grass was long, overgrown, most of it brown owing to the dry weather. The gate was rough and jagged, and he winced, feeling splinters embed into his palm. Without really thinking about what he was going to say or do, he pushed at the gate, and it moved open with a low, loud creak—a sound that sent scurries of ice, like spider-legs, down his spine.

Matthew made his way towards the front door. When he reached it, he raised one hand and formed it into a fist. A sickly, sticky cold sweat sheathed his skin, and he hesitated, frightened of what might lie ahead of him should he knock and the door be opened. On the other hand, he wanted to know—he *needed* to know—if it was true, or if the woman next door had simply been making up stories. Only one way to find out.

He knocked, three hard raps, and waited.

For a long time there wasn't any sound from behind the door. But just when Matthew was about to turn away, he heard it: footsteps.

His body tensed with awful anticipation.

The woman who opened the door was stick-thin, wearing an ill-fitting sweater that hung off her frame like a tent. She was very young, but Matthew could see that the travails of life had affected and aged her. Her eyes were red-rimmed with dark sacs under them, and Matthew was struck with the feeling that the defects were probably permanent. She should have been pretty, but she'd been ravaged by burden and time, and now she looked sad, frail, pitiable. Her bleary eyes narrowed as she scrutinised Matthew. For a moment neither of them spoke. Then Matthew broke the silence by saying, "Uh . . . hi, I was just wondering if this is where I could find Robby?"

The woman's mouth moved silently, like a fish out of water. After several seconds, she whispered, "Rob's—Rob's not here. What do you want with him?" If she'd meant to sound stern and demanding, she'd failed; her voice was so feathery that Matthew had to strain to hear her.

"I'm a friend," Matthew replied, and realised it might sound suspicious, a twenty-four-year-old man proclaiming to be pals with a six-year-old boy. "We've been talking. On the bench, see?" he said idiotically, and pointed to the tree in the distance for visual effect. "I—haven't seen him in a while, I was just wondering if he . . . if he's okay."

"Are you Matty?" she asked, surprising him.

"Oh. Yeah. Yes, I am. Matthew Leigh." He held out his hand.

She brushed her fingers against his, nothing more. She looked down at the ground, her lips moving soundlessly, and Matthew watched her, feeling increasingly nervous and wishing his heart would stop racing so. When she looked up, her eyes were wet, and she whispered, almost inaudibly, "I . . . I always thought he'd made you up."

"Made me up?" He didn't know to laugh or remain serious. "What do you mean?"

"He makes up stories, many stories, all the time. You know—dreams and ambitions, and such. It's hard to distinguish what's real and what's not. He's a funny boy like that. Sometimes he talks about people who don't exist as if they really do, and sometimes he doesn't pay any attention to actual people who're right in front of his nose." She gave him a long, hapless look. Then she held the door wide open. "Why don't you come in?"

"Robby's an epileptic," the woman revealed, sitting in the dark, dingy living room. Matthew, sitting on a threadbare chair, shifted uncomfortably. He couldn't breathe, not just because of the mustiness of the room, but because of what she was telling him. His eyes danced around the living room: at the dank walls, decorated with several framed canvases of panoramic scenes, and a host of religious pictures, pictures and icons. In a far corner, a wooden table served as an altar, festooned with drying flowers, statues of saints and of the Virgin Mary, and several rosaries. No wonder little Robby was so passionate about his faith—he was surrounded by it all the time.

The woman went on quietly, "Most times he experiences petit mal seizures, where he loses touch with his surroundings, blacks out for a while. He doesn't actually fall to the ground or anything," she said with a chuckle, as if this were something amusing, "but . . . yes, he—goes through this. Absence seizures, that's what they're also called. Sometimes you think he's only sleeping, or staring blankly into oblivion, but he's not; he's really having one of his silent fits." She stopped and raised a hand to her mouth, rubbing her upper lip lightly, the rapid blinking of her eyes betraying how she was trying to stem her emotions "And sometimes," she went on after a while, "he actually has these convulsive fits, and . . . that can be really traumatic. For both of us."

She stopped there, and Matthew struggled to ask, "How long has this been going on?"

"Since . . ."

Matthew waited. His back, resting against the chair, was beginning to feel clammy and itchy, but he ignored it.

The woman looked at him with pain-filled eyes, and now the tears came, unhindered. Her mouth trembled for a moment before she coughed out, "Since his father—dropped him down the stairs two years ago."

Another indiscernible fist rammed into Matthew's solar plexus. He gritted his teeth, forcing whatever breath he had left out of him, causing him to feel a sharp pain in his chest. "Jesus," he murmured, and shook his head in disbelief. "Robby was—" He faltered, tried again: "Down the s-stairs?" He turned his head to look at the steps: a steep, wooden flight that stretched from the ground floor to the upper level, at least twenty steps in all. "H-how?" he demanded. "Why?"

"It was an accident. His father—he was carrying the boy when he slipped, I don't know why, I don't know how, but he did. My husband managed to stop himself from falling, but—but my Robby just went tumbling down." She stopped to sob into her hands, and Matthew could do nothing but watch her, feeling sick to his stomach. When she had composed herself, she added, "Robby hit his head, and that was when it all began. The seizures. And it's been going on ever since. I need some coffee."

The abrupt shift in subject disoriented Matthew, and he blinked, not understanding. The woman stood up, trembling on her bird-thin legs. "Coffee always helps me to calm my nerves. Something about the caffeine, I guess. Makes some nervous, and calms other people down. I'm one of the other people."

She wandered off into the kitchen, and Matthew leaned back in the itchy, scratchy chair, unable to fully comprehend all that he'd been told. His head spun, and he felt as if he were going to throw up. So where was the father now? he wondered. And, more importantly, *where's little Robby?*

The mother returned with a tray carrying a coffee pot and two mugs. Matthew didn't think he'd be able to swallow any of it, he was so nauseated. She placed the tray on the table between the two of them, but didn't make any move to serve it. She sat, and he waited, not knowing if he had to prompt her to speak further. A long while passed. Finally, to break the dreadful silence, he asked, "What about . . . your husband?"

The boy's mother looked visibly startled, as if she'd forgotten he was there. Recovering quickly, she licked her lips and whispered, "Rob — Robby's father couldn't deal with what he'd done, and . . ." A pause. She licked her lips again: a swift, uptight movement. "He — he decided to end it all not long after the accident."

"End it all?" Matthew repeated, although he knew what it meant, and didn't like it one bit.

She trained her eyes on the coffee pot. "He killed himself."

Matthew shook his head. It was all he could think to do.

The woman reached out and grabbed the handle of the coffee pot. She began to pour it into the mugs, her hand unsteady. "None for me," Matthew murmured, and the woman stopped after filling one mug, dark coffee dripping over the side. The smell of the beverage was rich and thick in the air — sickeningly strong, threatening to send Matthew's stomach into lurching mode. He gritted his teeth and struggled to remain calm. The woman raised her mug to her lips and took a tentative sip, and the silence began to get on his nerves. This was taking far too long—he need to know about little Robby's condition!

Clearing his throat, he said, "I heard—from somebody—that Robby had an accident a couple of nights ago. Is this true?"

She put her mug down. Her hand was noticeably shakier. "I'm—I'm afraid so."

"What happened?"

She looked to the top of the stairs, prompting Matthew to do the same. "He was on the top of the stairs. I don't know why, but he undid the latch of the gate . . ." She looked at Matthew and added a belated explanation: "I put a gate at the top, so if he's upstairs, he has to call for me to help him down. Just as a safety precaution. I don't know what got into him, but . . . he—undid the latch and began to make his way down, and—I don't know why it had to strike him right at that moment, but it did, and he had an absence seizure and went falling down." She shook her head and pursed her trembling lips together. Again, the tears began to flow, and Matthew could only avert his eyes so that he was looking anywhere but at the woman herself. "It was like—it was like that day all over again, when his father dropped him. I found him and I went ballistic and I was screaming all over the place. We don't have a phone. I couldn't afford the bill, so I went next door, to the Coulsens' . . ."

Matthew, struggling to keep himself under control, asked, "So where is he now?"

"The GH."

"How is he?"

Now the woman broke down, wailing softly, pathetically. "I don't know. G-God, I j-j-just don't know . . ." And she wept into her quivering hands, softly at first, then louder, and louder, until Matthew knew he had to get out of there.

"I—I should go," he said, but the woman was too caught up in her unleashing of emotion to hear him. He stood up and looked around anxiously, sniffled once, struggled to contain himself—*I've not cried in ages, no need to make a scene now*—and told her, "Thank you for your time. I'm really sorry." And without waiting for any further response, he hurried for the front door, his chest tight, his breathing laboured, his expression sombre, and his heart aching with a feeling he'd never before experienced.

Matthew hurried towards the reception of the general hospital, his heart pounding. It had taken him a good three-quarters of an hour to drive to the hospital, *fucking traffic jams! Why the hell did everybody have to be on the road at six in the evening, it didn't make any sense!* Sitting behind the wheel of his car, he'd prayed, prayed to whoever, *what*ever, something he didn't believe in, that Robby would be okay.

Now Matthew rushed over to three young women in white uniform who sat behind the counter. One of them, a pretty redhead with tanned skin and a round face, looked up from her computer as he approached. Breathlessly, he asked about little Robby—little Robby *what?* "Robby," he repeated, struggling to catch his breath. "Um—Robert something, a kid, six years old, he fell down the stairs." And then he remembered: "No, I'm wrong—it's not Robert, it's Robson. Robson something. Little guy, sandy-haired, freckled."

The receptionist's fingers flew across the keyboard, touch-typing for information. "Yes, here we are. Emergency dispatch, room three, Children's Floor, Robson—"

He didn't wait for her to finish, choosing instead to startle all three women by darting towards the elevators as fast as his legs could take him. He waited for what seemed like forever for the elevator to arrive. When the doors slid open, he shoved his way in, angering an elderly lady who was on her way out. Ignoring the old witch, he pounded on the button that closed the doors, and then pressed the button for—

The Children's Floor. Which was the Children's Floor? God *damn* it!

No—no, wait—the little markers were there, below the buttons. *Third floor: Paediatric.* Yes. That's the one. He pushed at it with one finger, then jabbed it repeatedly, as if that would make the lift ascend more quickly.

The doors slid open, and he went tumbling out, barely missing an orderly pushing a patient in a wheelchair. The orderly warned him to "steady on there, mate", but Matthew ignored him, sprinting towards the reception for the Children's Floor. A nurse in white looked up from her clipboard as he approached. She was short and plump and had dark, curly hair; her appearance was neither friendly nor unfriendly, just cautious.

"I'm looking for room three, um—Robson," he said, realising once again he hadn't caught the boy's last name.

"Are you a family member?"

"No. No, I'm a friend. Oh, God, please don't tell me I can't see him because we're not related. I mean, Jesus, I'm just want to see how he's doing, what's going on with him, you know? Come on, don't keep me out," he exclaimed, babbling, not caring.

The nurse looked at him, and her expression changed into one of empathy and concern. "I'm afraid Robson's in a bad way, Mr . . ."

"Leigh. Matthew Leigh."

"I'm sorry, Mr Leigh. You're welcome to see him, but I feel you should know that he's not in the best shape right now."

"I just need to see him. Please."

She nodded, an almost imperceptible movement, and began to walk in the direction of the rooms. "Follow me."

Matthew stepped into room three, mentally gearing himself to see the boy—and stopped short when he saw the pitiable creature in the hospital bed in front of him. His mouth dropped open, and he felt as if his heart had stopped. There, lying in the bed, surrounded by machines and wires and intravenous tubes, was little Robby. Matthew forced himself to move closer, and when he saw the boy's face, his legs nearly faltered, his heart jumping into his throat. "Sweet Jesus," he murmured unconsciously, "oh, my dear God . . ."

The nurse, Sister Marsha, stood next to him, placing a hand on his shoulder to keep him steady. She'd warned him that it wouldn't be pretty, but he hadn't expected this. Little Robby's head, from the forehead up, was wrapped in thick gauze, and one of his eyes had been plastered over. His lips were bloodied, the upper one badly torn, and there were sutures covering the length of his right cheek where the flesh had been slashed by the jagged edges of the steps. Matthew could hear the ragged breathing of the boy, each noisy exhalation driving a spike through his heart. Swallowing his pain, Matthew walked up to the edge of the bed, and saw the boy's right arm was in a cast, his knees were bandaged over, badly scraped, and one of his feet was also wrapped in gauze, like a mummy's foot. There were large patches of black-and-blue bruises where capillaries had been crushed, as well as several blotches of dark red where blood showed under the skin.

Matthew's mouth moved and he uttered gruffly, "Is he asleep?"

Sister Marsha whispered, "He's in a coma. Unconscious since they brought him in."

"When—when's he gonna get up?"

She hesitated, and Matthew knew the answer. "You don't know, do you? He might never wake up."

Sister Marsha shook her head sadly. "It could be tomorrow. It could be next week. Or it could be a long, long time from now, we don't know. The only thing we can do is to pray for the best, and keep him alive."

"Pray for the best," Matthew said scornfully, and actually laughed. "You religious people are just amazing, you know that? I mean, this boy is shitting on death's door and all you can do is say 'we'll leave it to God, let Him decide'. Well, looks to me like your God's not making the right decisions here, is

He? I mean, this is a little kid, what the hell did he do to *deserve* this?" He looked at little Robby again, and the tears welled up in his eyes, forcing him to blink them back, *I will not cry, I will not cry* . . . ! And he turned to the nurse and spat, "What the hell kind of merciful God would let this happen to a little kid, huh? I mean, just *look at him!* What the hell has he done? Merciful God, my ass! If God really does exist, then He's one hell of a vindictive bastard, that's what *I* think! Jesus Christ!"

The nurse's hand, which she'd placed on his shoulder, remained there. In fact, he felt her give him a little squeeze, as if she understood his trauma, his confusion; as if, in actuality, she'd also been struggling with her faith, secretively, hidden underneath the white tunic and crucifix hanging around her neck. Matthew turned back to little Robby and let out a soft cry — one of anger, of frustration, of total helplessness.

The nurse waited, and he muttered under his breath, "His father dropped him down the stairs when he was younger. Because of that, he began to experience seizures — epileptic fits. Then his father kills himself, and now this. Seems to me that this concept of a 'merciful, loving Father in Heaven' ought to be dragged into the street and shot, because I sure as hell can't see how *God* works in this situation here," he declared, uttering the word as if it were a curse. He laughed again, bitterly, brimming with resentment. "I don't get it. I just don't fucking get it."

Then, as Sister Marsha watched, he reached down and touched the boy's face ever so lightly, taking care not to hurt him any further. His voice dropped even further; the humming of the vent overhead threatened to drown him out. Now he spoke wistfully, the anger dissipating from his voice: "He said he wanted to be a bird. Wanted to learn how to fly, and be free from the constraints of our world, kind of like the main character in that William Wharton novel." He touched the boy's cheek again. "He also said everyone in the world should adopt a puppy, for puppies are the ultimate representation of love, innocence and playfulness. And he said . . ." He faltered, took a deep breath, tried again: "He said if everybody in the world could see in grey and not in colour, then we'd all be better off." He laughed softly, shook his head. "I think he got that from a movie somewhere, or a song on the radio or something, I'm not sure."

Sister Marsha nodded quietly.

Matthew moved away from her, going to the other side of the bed to look at the boy from a different angle. The kid didn't look any better from here. "We had a fight. The last time I spoke to him, I got angry and I stormed off, and Jesus God, I didn't get to say I'm sorry, we didn't even get to make up . . ." He shook his head ruefully. "Nurse, this kid—he's incredibly smart, I hope you'll be able to find this out for yourself someday. I mean, he—he had a big mouth, he could throw things back in my face without even blinking or thinking twice about it. He was really—smart. And—he had such a positive outlook on life, even in spite of . . ." He realised he was using the past tense, and his voice trailed off. He took a moment before adding, "Even in spite of all this shit he's had to experience at such a young age. It's like, all the corruption around him didn't pervert his soul one bit. I mean, if there *is* a soul. I don't know. But none of this affected him; he was still—so positive, except for his strong belief in God, it seemed almost obsessive to a point, I don't understand why . . ."

But of course he understood—he understood it now, standing by the child's side and touching him lightly. The boy was so unlike Matthew. While Matthew could live his life on his own, the kid couldn't do that. Little Robby could not depend on himself. His condition betrayed him, weakened him, and as such, it was only natural that he hung on to the purported ultimate source of strength: God. And seeing that his own father had betrayed him by hurting him and leaving him, it was no wonder that little Robby felt a strong need to hold on to *another* Father, even if it was one that he couldn't see, touch, smell or hear. The faith of children could be so strong and unwavering compared with that of grown-ups. Matthew could remember being like that once himself, until life had turned difficult and everything started falling apart.

Except . . .

Except nothing has fallen apart, has it?

The realisation made him flinch, as if he'd inhaled something nasty.

In comparison with Little Robby's life, Matthew was living in the lap of luxury. He'd never known misery, or sadness, or circumstances he was helpless against. He had his family, and even though he didn't have many friends—through his own fault—he still had a *handful* of them. Little Robby didn't have much in the way of a family, and the two girls next door seemed to be his only "friends", for lack of a better word. The kid had to battle against his seizures, absence or otherwise, and had probably been on medication for the past two years. He was probably undergoing some kind of treatment—brain examinations, or a special kind of diet, or whatever—

Diet. The word made him recoil again, and this time, Sister Marsha asked if something was the matter. Matthew recalled little Robby telling him about the food he ate: seemingly unhealthy, fattening stuff. But what if those foods had been *necessary*, as a means of controlling the child's condition? He knew, vaguely, that such a form of treatment existed; he'd read it in one of his father's medical textbooks years ago, back when they'd been on talking terms.

Looking at the nurse with wide and bemused eyes, he asked if a child's diet could influence the occurrence of epileptic episodes. Sister Marsha nodded. "Yes, I know of one. I'm not trained in the field, so I don't know very much about it, but there's the ketogenic diet, where the patient is weaned on high-fat, low-carbohydrate foods. This results in ketosis, which produces an anti-epileptic effect."

"That's it," Matthew murmured.

She looked at the boy, then raised her eyes to meet Matthew's. "Mr Leigh, do you think you might want a few moments by yourself? Maybe to speak to the child in private?"

Matthew raised his eyes to meet hers, nodding. "Yes. I'd — I'd like that. Thank you."

When she left, he turned his eyes upon the unconscious child again. He pursed his lips, trying to gather his thoughts. The only thing he could think to say now was "I made you a sandwich, kiddo"—which, after he'd said it aloud, sounded absurd. Still, he went with it: "And the other day I brought over some Chinese food, but you weren't there. I waited for you, but you didn't turn up, but I didn't know . . . I didn't know that this had happened. I'm sorry."

Again he felt overwhelmed, and had to fight the surge of emotion that threatened to burst out from him. *Don't cry. Big guys don't cry.*

"Hey, make sure that heart of yours doesn't stop beating, kid," he murmured, and nearly choked on the ball of misery that rose up in his throat. "I want to talk to you again," he managed to cough out. "And I mean soon. I want to hear more of what you want to tell me, even if it's all about God and Jesus and angels and saints and birds and doctors and whatnot, I don't care, I just want to hear you, you understand me, kid? You hear me, you little—" He stopped, took a deep breath—"You little brat?"

Then he staggered away from the bed, knowing he had to get out of there before the dam gave way within and the torrent was unleashed. He stumbled past Sister Marsha on the way out, managed to give her a vague, weak wave with one hand. Then he was back in the elevator, and back on the ground floor, and back in his car in the parking lot.

He leaned back against the headrest, breathing through his mouth, inhaling, exhaling, over and over, controlling himself, keeping himself composed. He didn't want to break down, not yet. Not when the boy relied on his strength, and not while there were several riddles regarding little Robby's family that still needed to be solved.

WRONG NUMBER,
PLEASE TRY AGAIN

———

Zack McPherson picked up his bedside telephone and dialled the Cookes' number. He had arrived at the conclusion that whatever Maggie was going through, he was going to be there for her, in a direct contrast with the way Joe was treating Carrie Taylor. Even if the baby wasn't his, if the father didn't want anything to do with it, he'd be there for her. And this was what he planned to tell Maggie: he'd confront her with it, and let her know he supported her.

He listened to the ringing tone, and hung up when it automatically disconnected. So much for that. The alternative course of action was to go over to the Cookes' house and speak to Maggie face-to-face. He wasn't sure how he was going to do it, especially if Joe was home. But he would, he decided with determination. And he'd do it tonight.

"How are you feeling?"

He spooned chicken soup into his mouth. It was warm, but it was too thick and gooey, far from the gourmet broth his wife always cooked. He swallowed, thinking it was as if he'd just swallowed a spoonful of phlegm, and whispered, "I've been better."

Sarah sat on a chair across from Graham, who was sitting up in bed, his back against the headboard. She leaned forward, her hands clasped together as if in silent prayer. She looked at her brother-in-law with concern. "I'm serious, Graham. Dr Rubinstein says . . ."

"I don't care what Rubinstein says, he's a quack."

Sarah laughed weakly. "He says you're anti-Semitic."

Graham forced another spoonful of goo into his mouth. He raised his eyes to Sarah's. "Did Felicity say where she was going?"

Sarah stared back at him, expressionless. Several seconds passed.

"Sarah?"

"Graham," she said quietly.

"Did Feli say . . . ?"

"Graham. Honey, you've not been listening to what I've been saying. Felicity isn't here anymore. She moved on three weeks ago. You were here, don't you remember?"

"No," he protested, too quickly. His voice hardened. "You're lying. She was right here. She was here yesterday, and she was here this morning, and she was here this evening when the girls came by, and she was—"

"Bertha and Della and Michelle were here yesterday, Graham," Sarah cut him off patiently. "When I arrived, you had passed out in the hallway. So I put you to bed and called Dr Rubinstein, who gave you some sedatives. You slept the whole night, all the way until now. It's Friday evening, Graham. The girls were here yesterday."

Graham shook his head obstinately. *Impossible*, he thought. *For years, I've needed only five hours of sleep, six at the most!* "So where *is* she?"

Sarah closed her eyes briefly, opened them again. She reached for him, and he recoiled. The tray with the bowl of soup, balanced on his lap, threatened to topple over, and he secured it with one hand. His other hand gripped the spoon tightly, blue-green veins prominent, knuckles white and showing. When she moved her lips to speak again, he exclaimed, "She's here! I know she is! I don't know why you're telling me she's not when she *is*, she *has* to be! I've seen her!"

"Graham, please . . ."

"We've been out talking, we've been out walking, we've been doing everything together, over the past three weeks —"

"She wasn't . . ."

"Why the hell are you here in the first place, Sarah? What sick mind game are you playing? Where's Felicity, what did you do to her?"

"I didn't do *anything* to her —"

"You're lying!"

"Graham, please *listen to me!* She passed away! I'm so sorry, honey, but she did, she's gone home to God, and you've got to accept that!"

"You hate me, don't you?" he countered harshly. "You've always resented the fact that I chose Felicity and not *you*, and this is how you're paying me back, isn't it?"

"No. No, this has *nothing* to do with any of that! I was young, I had a teenage crush; it was *nothing*. Graham, please open your eyes and *see* what's going on! I'm doing this for your own good —you have the rest of your life ahead of you, and I won't be able to live with myself if you chose to go on imagining that Felicity's still around when she's *not*. She's gone, Graham! She's with Jesus now, why won't you believe me?"

"Because you're lying!" Graham yelled hoarsely, and, in one quick, unexpected movement, tossed the tray onto the floor, sending the bowl and the soup spattering across the room. Sarah looked at the mess in dismay. "She's here, somewhere," he insisted, throwing the spoon onto the floor as well. "Why won't you tell me where she is? Felicity!" He raised his voice, looking in the direction of the bedroom doorway. "Felicity, where *are* you? Fel!"

Sarah sighed and stood. "I'm sorry, Graham."

He ignored her. "Felicity? I need you! Where are you?"

Sarah squatted to retrieve the spoon, bowl and tray. Then she left the room. Her brother-in-law continued to call for his wife, a woman who no longer walked the earth and hadn't done so in weeks. His voice, husky and overwrought, rang in her ears: "Felicity! Answer me! Fel! *Felicity!*"

When she checked on him twenty minutes later, Graham had, once again, passed out from exertion, in spite of the sleep he'd had. The act of living an illusion must truly be draining, Sarah pondered sadly. She slid to his side, avoiding the congealed puddle on the floor, and removed his glasses, placed them on the bedside table.

You poor dear. You've got to go on with the rest of your life. Please try to move on.

He looked as if he were peacefully sleeping. *Maybe he's dreaming of Felicity,* Sarah thought, and squatted to clean up the mess with a damp cloth.

But this is real life, Graham.

And we can't live our fantasies in real life.

Derrick was idly surfing the Internet when he heard a knock on the door. When he opened it, he wasn't surprised to see the foursome—Sanjeev, Chitra, Geraldine and Hope—who traipsed in blithely as if they owned the place.

"Don't you guys have lives?" Derrick greeted them.

"Don't *you?*" Hope shot back.

"As a matter of fact, Dawn and I are going out again tonight."

Chitra whooped: "All right, you go, boy!"

"We were about to ask you if you'd like to join us for a movie tonight," Geraldine said. "Which reminds me: Sanjeev, you've got to call the movie theatre and make the bookings. It's the weekend, you know how it is."

Sanjeev plodded away to use Derrick's phone.

"That's nice of you, but we've got our own plans," Derrick told Geraldine.

She opened her mouth to reply, but Sanjeev interrupted: "Hey, Rick, your phone's dead."

"What?"

"Your phone. You didn't pay the bill." Sanjeev reached down and plucked up a notice from the telephone company, a reminder that they hadn't yet received his payment. "Better get that sorted out as soon as possible. In the meantime, could I borrow somebody's mobile phone? Mine's out of whack."

"That's just great," Derrick groaned.

Chitra volunteered to make the reservations, plucking her mobile phone out of her back pocket before wandering away in the direction of the kitchen. Geraldine turned back to Derrick. "So how are you and Dawn doing? You two getting any closer . . . ?"

Derrick smiled stiffly. "We're fine, Geri."

"How fine?"

"Pretty fine."

"Brilliantly descriptive," Hope muttered.

Ignoring her, Derrick said, "What time do you guys have to be at the theatre?"

"Movie starts at eight," Sanjeev replied, "so around a quarter to. What will *you* two be up to?"

"Don't know. I'm meeting Dawn in front of *Interreactive*, but I doubt we'll be hanging out there tonight. I'm thinking of taking her up to the Point. We can take in the view of the city, should be pretty romantic. Or we might decide to come back here, spend some time together, see where the night brings us, you know? Hey, Chit, grab me a Coke when you're done, will you?" he shouted in the direction of the kitchen, before turning back to Geraldine.

"Yeah, sounds good," Geraldine said earnestly. "Well, we'd better get going . . ."

"Have a good time," Derrick said, as Chitra bounded back to them with a can of Coke in hand. "And if we get stuck for something to do, who knows? We might meet up with you guys after the movie, go for coffee or something . . ."

Sanjeev shot a look at Chitra, who nudged him without Derrick noticing. Hope was the one who responded, saying quickly, "Yes, well, we'll see what happens, come on, let's go, we're going to be late", before hurriedly ushering her companions out the front door.

Derrick and Dawn met as planned in front of the dance club, and the first thing Derrick thought was that she looked stunning. She wore tight red-leather pants and a matching jacket over a black top. On her feet were a pair of high-heeled stilettos, and a designer bag hung from one arm. She had straightened her hair, and it flowed down on either side of her face like a glimmering, blond river, parted neatly in the middle like Moses had the Red Sea. She looked *amazing.* When they embraced, he inhaled that marvellous, intoxicating fragrance, the new one she'd switched to. He relished the warmth of her.

"So what do you have in mind tonight, darling?" Dawn asked, whispering into his ear, her warm breath tickling his lobe.

"I don't know, honestly," Derrick said, and laughed. He took a step back to admire her again, and let out a wolf-whistle. She kissed him. It was like a drug: it created a euphoria that zipped to his brain and sent him on a wild and funky trip. He found himself drowning in the spell that Dawn Parker was casting by pushing his mouth against hers. She ran her sweet tongue into his mouth. Drowning. Drowning, and it wasn't frightening, it was *far* from it. It felt good. It felt absolutely refuckin'markable.

Later, he said, "The other guys are going out for a movie tonight."

"What are they seeing?"

He told her, and her eyes sparkled. "Oh, I've heard that's a really good one."

"Really? Well, we could join them."

A look of uncertainty crossed her features, but it quickly disappeared. "Nah," she replied. "We can go on our own another time."

"Well, if you're really keen on watching it, it might be fun to go as a group," Derrick said hesitantly. "I mean, they know we're together, it's not as if we have to act secretive or anything, right? And we can sit on our own in the back or something, so that we can do whatever we want . . ."

"Honey, that's sweet, but I'd really prefer to spend tonight with just the two of us." She planted a kiss on his cheek. "You said you'd bring us up to the Point. Let's do it."

"Sure thing." He returned the kiss. "Whatever you wish, my darling."

"Don't make me gag," she replied cheekily, and dodged out of the way as he tried to smack her on the bum.

The view from the Point was breathtaking but, of course, neither of them was doing much sightseeing. They were intertwined in the back seat, making out, going crazy with lust and passion. She sucked on his lips, and he moaned, feeling a pleasurable sort of pain course through him. With one hand he caressed her back; the other he moved up her neck, towards her hair—carefully, because she'd said she was very particular about the way her hair was styled, so it was pretty much off-limits. "Nothing personal," she'd told him, "it's just that the stupid shampoos and conditioners and hot-oil treatments and whatnot cost a packet, so it's kind of pointless for me to do it all up only to have my boyfriend tear it down again." Which made sense, in a queer sort of way.

Tonight, she didn't protest as he stroked her long, glossy hair with caution. She'd taken the effort to straighten it, so he didn't want to mess it all up.

After twenty minutes in the backseat, they decided to head back to Derrick's for the rest of the festivities.

Carrie Taylor got into her car, trying to stop crying. She sobbed vehemently as she struggled to get the key into the ignition. She couldn't see much through the veil of tears, and her hands were trembling so badly that she couldn't do it. She cried out in frustration after several seconds of fumbling around, and wiped her eyes with her arm violently. Blinking through the obscurity, she finally found the ignition and started the engine. Without even checking if there was anybody in the driveway, she stomped down on the accelerator, backing out of her family's property and onto the road. She wasn't sure where she was going, although she knew she had to get as far away from her house as possible. Her father's voice still screeched in her ears, and her mother's look of anguish was seared into her mind.

"*How could you have done this? We trusted you, Carrie . . . !*"

"*How could you have been so careless?*"

"*If you think we're going to stand here and listen to this . . .*"

"*You chose to act irresponsibly; now you deal with the consequences!*"

No encouragement. No support. Only condemnation.

She sobbed uncontrollably, wishing she hadn't told her parents about the baby. Wishing she could've foreseen the severity of their objection to the situation. And wishing she hadn't fooled herself into believing she could handle their reaction, no matter how bad it got.

Shit, it'd got really bad. She'd anticipated a negative reaction, but nothing like *this*. Not the hysterical screaming from her father, red-faced like an overripe tomato; not the look of extreme disappointment on her mother's time-aged features, the bloodlessness of her skin upon hearing that Carrie, their only daughter, was pregnant with child. If their neighbours had been within hearing range, she was certain they would have called the police by now.

She stepped on the accelerator, pushing it down as far as she could.

In her mind, she blamed only one person for the situation she was in: Joe Cooke. Without thinking it, she began to steer the vehicle in the direction of the Square. Whether he liked it or not, she was going to confront him, spill the beans and humiliate him in front of everyone. If it was all right for *her* to be degraded in front of her parents, surely Joe could put up with it, too. He deserved it a lot more than she did.

Dimly she remembered she'd promised Zack she wouldn't say anything until he'd spoken to Joe himself, and she didn't know if Zack had accomplished that yet. But right now, she wasn't concerned about her promises. Anybody could make promises; it was the *keeping* of promises that determined the quality of a person. And if this made her a bad person, screw it. She couldn't care less. All she was aware of was the boiling-hot anger within her, the flushing of her cheeks at the thought of how she'd let her parents down, and the deep, dark yearning to pay Joseph Cooke back for all the shit he'd thrown into her face.

They played around on the couch, just the two of them, in the privacy of Derrick's apartment. Derrick felt Dawn's fingers fooling around with his fly, and he grinned triumphantly, excited by what he knew was going to happen next.

Dawn didn't disappoint. She was really good at it.

Halfway through it, as she worked on him, he moaned and groaned and whispered, "How about it, babe? Do I get a shot tonight . . . ?"

She continued doing what she was doing, not answering, and he reached down to stroke her hair. When his fingers touched her head, she pulled away briefly and grinned up at him, saying, "Watch the hair, honey", before returning to the job.

"Sorry," Derrick said, and laughed, and moaned in delight, writhing in his seat.

When it was over—with him realising that they weren't going to go all the way tonight, at least not within the next half hour or so—Dawn grinned at him and excused herself to use the bathroom, while he cleaned up. Feeling thirsty, he went to the kitchen and reached for the refrigerator door. His eyes fell on an object lying on the counter next to the fridge, and he realised it was a mobile phone. Chitra's. She must've left it behind when she'd grabbed him the can of Coke earlier.

He was about to put it away when he considered that Chitra would probably worry if she discovered her phone missing. The best thing to do was to call someone to let them know Derrick had it with him. Of course, the gang was at the movies, so they likely wouldn't be able to pick up. Derrick told himself to leave a message, and began scrolling down the list of numbers in Chitra's phonebook.

Unbelievably, neither Geraldine nor Hope owned mobile phones, which proved to be both advantageous and otherwise at the same time. It meant they couldn't call each other to chat at all hours of the day. But it also meant that Derrick had not been able to get in touch with Geri as frequently as he'd have liked. *Get into the twenty-first century, girls.* He smirked to himself, continuing down the list. Who *were* all these people? There was an Ian something, a Jace, Jason, Jessica, Kelly, Liam, Lisa . . .

He finally reached Sanjeev's mobile number, clicked the "call" button, and listened for the ringing tone. He didn't get one; instead, there was a mechanical voice informing him that *the number you have dialled is currently unavailable . . .* Then Derrick recalled that Sanjeev's mobile phone was "out of whack". He figured Sanjeev had probably tried testing its durability again, only to have taken it too far. The last time he'd dropped it from the top floor of an apartment building. Derrick imagined that the latest experiment involved Sanjeev running it over with his car. Sanjeev was a bit quirky like that.

Derrick shrugged to himself. *Too bad; it's not like I didn't try.*

Then he scrolled up the list, thinking that he had one last shot. Geraldine hadn't mentioned if anyone else would be joining them for the movie, but he figured it wouldn't hurt to give it a try. So he located Jason's name—thinking it would be the same Jason as that gay guy upstairs—and pressed the 'call' button.

He listened for the ringing tone.

Ah, there it was, strong and steady—

And at the same time, a high-pitched bleeping noise rang out from the living room of his apartment, making him jump.

Derrick spun around, his eyes scanning the room, his heart pounding, jarred by the unexpected noise.

It sounded again. Shrill, electronic wailing.

At first he couldn't locate the source of the bleeping. He narrowed his eyes, looked around frantically, trying to find it—

And then, as it rang the third time, he located the source. It was on the coffee table in the middle of the living room.

Dawn's bag.

Dawn's bag.

Dawn's bag.

An ice-cold hand wrapped its fingers around Derrick Weston's heart as he stared in bewilderment at Dawn Parker's designer bag. In his ear, the ringing tone continued; from the gleaming leather bag, the high-pitched bleeping noise rang out.

He distantly heard the flushing of the toilet, and quickly pressed the "disconnect" button. Then, filled with a deep, deep fear that his worst fears were about to come true, he strode to the bathroom door and waited for Dawn to step out.

He heard Dawn's footsteps, followed by the rattling of the doorknob. The door swung open, and Dawn stepped out, trilling, "Was that my cell phone I heard, darling . . . ?"

Derrick Weston leapt at Dawn Parker.

A loud cry escaped his lips as he jumped upon her, and she shrieked in fright.

Then he was practically upon her, and he was reaching for her hair, her long, blond hair, as she screamed at the top of her lungs and staggered under his weight and began to pound against his shoulders with tightly curled fists. Derrick managed to wrap his fingers around the ends of her hair, and with one quick, frantic motion, he pulled. "Ohhh!" she screeched, and her knees buckled, sending them both crumbling to the ground like felled building blocks. "Derrick, what the hell are you *doing?*" she wailed, and cried out again as he yanked at her hair, feeling it give and knowing that his nightmares had encroached upon real life. "Derrick — *nooooo!*"

The hair slid off her head and ended up in a tangled mess around Derrick's hand.

"No! *No! Nooooo!*" Dawn screamed.

"I don't *believe* this!" Derrick bellowed, and threw the wig onto the floor. "Oh, my God, oh, sweet Jesus, what the *hell* are you trying to do to me?"

"Nooo! Nooooo!"

"Shut up!" Derrick yelled, and abruptly he felt his stomach heave. He shoved his way past Jason Marcel, and was two feet shy of the toilet bowl when his dinner made its way out of his stomach and all over the floor.

ALL HELL BREAKS LOOSE

Zack stopped the car in front of the Cooke residence, his countenance serious as he got out of the vehicle and made his way up the driveway towards the porch. The garage was vacant; Jessy Cooke probably wasn't home yet. He stopped at the front door, took a deep breath, and reached out to press the doorbell. Moments later, he heard approaching footsteps. He held his breath, praying it would be Maggie.

It wasn't Maggie.

"Don't slam the door in my face," Zack exclaimed.

Joe slammed the door in his face.

Seething, Zack ran off the porch and to the side of the house, where the roseless trellis rose to Maggie's window. Cupping his hands around his mouth, he shouted Maggie's name. The window was shut, but he hoped it wasn't soundproof. "Maggie!" he tried again, louder this time, not caring if he was disturbing the neighbours. "Maggie, it's me! Can you hear me?" It was such a silly question; the old joke came back to him the moment he'd uttered it: *"Can you hear me?" "No!"*

"Mags! It's Zack!"

Then —

His heart leapt to his throat when he saw the figure standing behind the glass. "Maggie!" he called again, and waved his arms frantically. He saw the window move, and fingertips appeared in the crack at its base. Then the glass was sliding upward, and Maggie, his beautiful Maggie, was staring down at him, her face expressionless.

"Zack?"

"I need to speak to you! Your brother won't let me in."

"Stay there, I'll come down."

"No, wait—in private! It's important!"

"Zack—I don't think—" she began, and shook her head. "I'll come down, okay?"

"Mags, open the door for me. We'll talk in your room!"

She hesitated, then shook her head again. "No, Zack, please, just stay there, I'll come down, we'll talk alone in the yard, okay? Please?"

Zack looked around quickly, saw nobody else within hearing range, and blurted, "I know about the baby!"

Maggie's face drained of blood instantly. Her eyes grew saucer-wide, and her mouth dropped open. "W-what—! What did you say . . . ?"

"Just let me in. Please!"

Without letting her respond, he darted back to the front porch and waited.

Waited.

And waited.

Maggie thought her heart was going to stop. She forced herself to take a few deep breaths. Deep shudders racked her body, and her mind spun with a million frantic, frightened questions. Who told him? How on earth could he have found out?

How could he have known about the baby?

The only persons who could have known about it were the doctor and nurses who had performed the procedure—the procedure she regretted with all her heart. But the medics were sworn to confidentiality, and they wouldn't have told, especially not Zack McPherson, of all people . . .

So who else could it have been? *Who spilled the beans?*

Then it struck her: *Michelle.*

No!

No, Michelle wouldn't have blabbed to anyone what Maggie had shared in confidence when they'd met up at

Nick's Place at the shopping centre—the day the waitress had eavesdropped and told her she'd best get rid of it. Michelle didn't even *know* Zack, why would she have told him about Maggie's pregnancy?

Maybe it was the waitress, Maggie thought, even though that made far *less* sense.

She sat on the edge of the bed with her head bowed, feeling the bitterness of bile as it pushed its way to the back of her throat. She was trembling—with fear, with revulsion at herself for having gone through with the abortion, and with shame. Shame at the whole situation that had further turned her world upside-down.

Michelle wouldn't have told, I trust her, I believe in her completely . . .

So—who else . . . ?

Chris?

Chris Hardman, her ex-boyfriend, the father of her ex-baby?

It didn't make sense. When she'd called Chris days earlier to let him know that she was carrying his child, he'd gone into shock and had uttered something about "not wanting to know about it" before hanging up. Maggie had been so upset. Further attempts to call him had proven futile; he refused to be involved. Which just went to show that men, Maggie thought, truly were disgusting, selfish pigs. She'd loved Chris—or so she'd believed—that she'd actually been stupid enough to have sex with him before he'd left the country with his family. They were both young, naïve. But they'd been careful—at least, they *thought* they'd been. However, accidents happen, and with this accident came the confirmation that Chris was, like most young men, irresponsible, egoistic and cowardly. The hurt and heartache of missing him had diminished somewhat following the disastrous phone call. Maggie's next step had been to call Michelle Leigh, her only reliable confidante in high school, who'd ultimately advised her to follow her heart. Maggie's heart had told her she should keep the baby, but her logical mind had told her otherwise: that she was too young and ignorant to be saddled with such a responsibility. Maggie had obeyed the rational part of her, not the emotional. So she and Michelle had gone over to the clinic on Monday—*slice and dice, into the vacuum it goes*.

Now Maggie absolutely regretted it. She didn't know why, but having got rid of it, she felt empty inside, not just physically, but spiritually, emotionally and mentally. It was why she'd been moping around and crying over the past few days. Ironically, Paul Cooke leaving his wife and family had proven to be a blessing—she could pretend that her grief was over her father, and not over the baby she'd lost. Perhaps it was to do with the way she'd been brought up, and how the abortion had clashed with every single one of her principles. At the age of thirteen, nearly three years ago, a teacher had given her class the task of developing a series of posters for a public campaign of any theme. Maggie had decided to do an anti-abortion campaign with the tagline *Pro-Choice is No Choice*, and had been awarded top marks for her effort. She'd studied the main forms of abortion, and had been disturbed by them—the sucking of the foetus into a vacuum cleaner-like apparatus, followed by the blades that sliced it into ribbons. Or the injecting of a concentrated, high-sodium saline solution. Otherwise, if the baby had already developed its brains and nervous system, the insertion of a metal rod into its skull while still in the mother's womb so that it would die before being brought out of the body—since killing it after birth would be murder. They were all horrible, she'd thought. *Horrible, horrible, horrible*.

She'd sworn, at that young age, that she'd never do it. She'd never have an abortion.

Sometimes, principles were hard to maintain.

Now, somehow, Zack had found out. The notion that Chris Hardman had spilled the beans was so ridiculous that she actually laughed out loud, and then sobbed into her hands, thinking she was going to be sick and wishing she would just drop dead there and then to save her any further shame and suffering. Meanwhile, Zack was calling out to her again. His voice floated through her half-open window, and she cringed, shook her head as if he could see her, willed him to go away. *Help me,* she cried out in silence, and at the same time: *Go away, Zack, I don't want to see you!*

"Maggie! Come on, Mags, please—"

Her room door flew open, and she jumped, letting out a shriek.

"What the hell, is he still out there?" Joe demanded, storming across the room to the window, not noticing Maggie's devastated, enraged expression. She got to her feet unsteadily, cursing herself for not realising she hadn't locked the door, and then turned to face her brother, who shoved the window all the way up and stuck his head out. "Get the hell out of here, Zack!" he yelled. "You're pissing me off. Get *out* of here!"

"Joe . . ." Maggie clenched her fists, fighting back tears of misery.

"Get out of here, Zack!"

"Joe, *please!*" she cried.

"I just want to talk to her," came Zack's voice, which was cut off by Joe's angry retort: "You're not welcome to talk to *anybody,* you fuckwit! Get the hell off our property!"

"Joe, Joe, don't," Maggie exclaimed, and now the tears came. She stood by her brother's side and tried to pull him away from the window, tugging desperately on one arm. Her brother refused to budge. "Joe, please," she begged, "you don't even know what he wants to talk to me about . . . !"

Joe turned to her, his face twisted in a scowl. "It's probably the baby thing."

She froze, a deep, penetrating coldness turning her blood into ice. *What?!* She stared at him with her eyes wide, her jaw practically hitting the ground.

Joe shook his head. "Don't look so shocked, sis. All I did was make up some sob story about you being pregnant, to get him off our backs. Sorry about that."

"You—" She shook her head, letting this sink in, trying to decipher what he'd said so it would make sense. "You mean he—"

"He thinks you're pregnant. I told him you were."

"Why—why would you do that?"

"I just said, to get him off our backs. What's your problem?"

"I don't understand," she whimpered.

He gave her an exasperated look. "I'm trying to keep him away from you, okay?"

"So you told him I was pregnant," she murmured numbly.

"It was the first thing that came to my mind."

"Oh, my God." Maggie backed away from the window. "Joe, you are absolutely incredible, you know that? You're just—*did you even think before you said it?*" she shrieked. Confused, Joe stared at her. She stuck a finger into his face, practically jabbing it against his nose as she sputtered vehemently, "You can't just *say* things like that! You can't go around telling people I'm pregnant—it isn't right!"

Joe laughed uncertainly. "W-what?"

"Maggie, open the door!" Zack's voice.

"You have *no* idea what's going on in my life, Joe, so you have no right to make such statements about me!" Joe's smile vanished as he realised his sister was being deadly serious. "For God's sake, why the hell would you *tell* him such a thing? Of all the things to say! You're incredible! You're—you're just *fucking* incredible!"

Now her brother frowned. "Hey, why are you getting so riled up? I was trying to protect you—"

"Don't protect me! I don't need your protection!"

Zack's voice: "Mags? What's going on?"

"You don't tell me who I can or cannot see, and you don't tell other people lies about me when you have absolutely no idea what I'm going through, you understand me, Joseph?"

Joe could only blink stupidly, confused at how the tables had unexpectedly turned on him. She was extremely and genuinely ticked off, he could see that; she would never address him by his full name otherwise.

Abruptly, she stomped away from him towards the open bedroom door.

"Where are you going?"

She didn't reply. Stormed quickly towards the stairs.

"Mags, don't let him in!" Joe called after her anxiously. "Maggie!" Suddenly filled with a sense of fear, he hurried after his sister.

What if Zack told Maggie about Carrie's baby?

The door flew open, and Zack staggered backwards as Maggie came barging out. She flew straight at him, and he opened his arms, startled as she enveloped him in an embrace. For a moment he stood there, taking pleasure in the feeling of her body against his. Then he drew his breath sharply as he realised she was crying. What was she saying . . . ? "It's not true. Zack, I'm — I'm not pregnant, it's not true!"

"It's — it's not?" he managed.

She pulled away, wiped her face with the back of one hand. "No. No, Joe made it up, just to keep you away, just to frighten you . . ."

"But I'm not frightened," he said, and took her hand, the one stained with tears. "I came over to let you know that I . . ." He hesitated, feeling foolish now. "I was going to say I support you one hundred percent. I mean, back when I thought you were . . . pregnant, which — you're not. It seems."

She stared at him, dumbstruck.

Then Joe barrelled out of the front door, shoved Maggie roughly aside, drew one arm back, and slammed a clenched fist into Zack McPherson's face, sending the other boy tumbling backwards off the porch and onto the driveway, his nose and mouth bloodied.

Derrick wiped his mouth, got up off the floor and lunged at Jason Marcel, who was still standing in the bathroom doorway. Jason, stuck in Dawn mode, let out a girlish scream as Derrick jumped upon him, bringing them both to the ground again. "You sick bastard!" Derrick screeched, his voice sounding surprisingly like Dawn's. "You son of a *bitch*, what the hell have you been *doing* to me? What's with this charade? Tell me! *Tell me!*" And without giving Jason a chance to respond, he began to pummel him in the face, socking him in his lipsticked mouth, slapping blushed cheeks and taking shots at mascara-ed eyes.

"Stop!" Jason cried, reverting to his regular voice. "Stop, don't hit me, I'll explain everything!"

"I don't *want* you to explain!" Derrick yelled, and sent a knuckle sandwich straight into Jason's right cheek, glancing off the thick layer of foundation.

"But-but-but you just *said!*" Jason protested.

"Shut up, bitch!"

Now Jason began to fight back, lashing out with his hands and attempting to scratch Derrick's eyes out with long, red—and silver-painted fingernails. "Get off me!" Jason screamed, kicking his stockinged legs wildly. "I said *get off!*"

"You tricked me!" Derrick ranted, riding Jason's abdomen like a jockey on a horse. "You made me fall for you! You—you—"

Without warning, he got off Jason and stumbled into the bathroom. Again, he was too late in reaching the bowl, and ended up throwing up for the second time all across the floor, creating a bigger mess.

Jason took the opportunity to run to his purse and rummage in it for his mobile phone. Fishing it out, he saw the words *1 Missed Call* on the screen, and, pressing a button, saw Chitra's name. He ignored it and began scrolling down his list of contacts for the mobile phone number he'd passed on to Hope—the contingency number to be dialled in the event of screw-ups in the plan, which was exactly the case at this moment. He connected the call and waited apprehensively, tapping one high-heeled foot against the beige carpet, watching the bathroom door with frightened eyes, wincing as he heard Derrick retch and throw up a third time. Nobody was answering. *Damn it,* he thought, *pick up, pick up!*

He heard Derrick groaning loudly. Then he watched in full-blown horror as Derrick appeared in the bathroom doorway, staggering, green-faced, one hand wiping vomit from his chin, another hand rubbing his tummy in a circular motion. Jason's eyes widened, and he felt his pulse rate quicken as the ringing tone droned on and on in his ears. *Come on, come on,* he thought frantically as Derrick advanced. *Pick up, pick up, pick up, for the love of God —*

"Put down the phone," Derrick hissed, coming closer.

"Come on, come on, pick it up, pick it up," Jason pleaded into the mouthpiece.

Derrick pointed a trembling finger at the mobile. "Jason, put the phone down. Drop it. Drop it now."

"Pick up!" Jason begged shrilly. "Please, pick —"

He heard a *click,* followed by Hope's bored voice: "Y'ello?"

At the same time, Derrick made a flying tackle for Jason's mobile, and Jason screamed as he shoved himself out of his attacker's way, hollering into the mouthpiece, *"Code blue, code blue, strategy has failed, I repeat, strategy has failed, target is on the rampage, target is on the rampage, code blue, stat!"*

Hope, instantly alert: "Where are you?"

"Two-A!" Jason replied breathlessly, and squealed as Derrick slapped the phone out of his hand, sending it flying across the room and bouncing off the wall.

"I'm going to kill you," Derrick growled as he moved in on the cross-dresser. "I swear to God, when I get my hands on you, I'm going to kill you dead . . . !"

Now they were staggering about in circles, Jason moving backward and Derrick moving forward, around the coffee table. Jason had his hands held out in a gesture of surrender, and he was sputtering, "Wait. W-wait! Look, for God's sake, calm down, I swear to you, there's a good reason for all of this, a logical explanation, a good, logical explanation. This is all part of a plan. It's a *good* plan, and I would tell it to you if you'd just calm down!" He swallowed hard and added quickly, "Come on, Derrick, if you were beginning to love Dawn, surely you can't hate *me*, because I *am* Dawn!"

This made Derrick stop in his tracks, which made Jason stop as well.

A moment of silence ensued, broken by Jason's hesitant voice: "Dawn and I are the same. If you were falling for her, you were falling for *me*."

"No," Derrick protested instantly. "No! I was falling for Dawn. I was falling for a woman, not—not *you!*"

"But she *is* me, and I'm her," Jason said softly. "That means—"

"No. Don't say it. I swear to God, if you say it, I'll kill you."

Jason looked forlorn and contrite, and he practically bowed his head as he whispered, "If you kill me . . . then you'll kill *her.*"

Matthew Leigh got out of his vehicle and headed for the house with the fungal infection, pushing the noisy gate open and getting more splinters embedded into his palm. Grimacing, he walked up the dirt-streaked driveway and prepared to knock on the front door. But he didn't have to, because little Robby's mother pulled it open and gestured for him to come in. "I saw you coming."

He stepped in, inhaling the sour odour of mustiness. "I went to see him."

"How is he?" she whispered softly.

"He's—been better. How come you're not with him?"

The woman seemed taken aback. "I—" she began, and stopped, looking uncomfortable. "I—I have to work. At the diner? Nick's Place? To make money, you know? And—I don't have a car. Driving all the way up to the hospital is difficult, and if I were to rely on public transport . . ." She laughed incongruously. "It would eat up all the money I make, you know? So . . ." She shrugged, as if that were a satisfactory explanation.

Matthew frowned. "But he's your son."

"I know. I know he is."

"You should—I'm sorry, but I think you should be by his side all the way through."

A dark look crossed her features, and she turned away to make her way through the living room and into the kitchen beyond. Matthew followed her, waiting for a response, knowing he was probably overstepping here, but not giving a damn. This was what had been bothering him since he'd left little Robby's home earlier: that the woman didn't seem to be overly concerned about her child's well-being. Sure, she'd been distraught, but . . .

"He's an epileptic, you told me," he said out loud, and the woman wandered over to the stove and began tinkering with the kettle. "Forgive me," he added, "but what were you doing about it?"

She fiddled with the knob on the stove, trying to get it to light up. For a long while she remained quiet, and Matthew was about to repeat himself when she whispered shakily, "He was on the diet."

"The ketogenic diet?"

She gave him a sideways glance. Adjusted the position of the kettle atop the stove. "Yes," she said. "That's the one."

Matthew dug his hands into his pockets, suddenly feeling chilled. "Well—I don't know much about it, but . . . if he's on the diet, shouldn't you be consulting an expert?"

She kept quiet.

"I mean, there are routines and plans to be adhered to, last I heard."

"What are you getting at?"

"I'm just wondering if you got the advice of a dietician or someone."

"Of course I did," she said, but her words lacked conviction.

Matthew shifted uncomfortably. "Well . . . that's good, then."

She watched the kettle, mindless of the adage. For a long time Matthew stood where he was in silence, knowing he had no right to be questioning the woman like this in her own home, realising that any further questions were probably going to get him kicked out, his welcome long overstayed. But he had to ask, he had to probe; otherwise the questions, the concerns and the anxiety, would remain with him. He'd earlier sat on the bench in the field, thinking about the complexity, the strangeness and the awfulness of the whole situation with little Robby, when a sudden suspicion had crossed his mind—a notion that was dreadful, shocking, but plausible. Plausible, and quite possibly the case. Now, standing in the kitchen with little Robby's old lady, he knew he had to find out if his painted scenario was accurate.

Matthew cleared his throat and whispered, "If he has fits . . ."

The woman visibly stiffened, even while her back was to him.

". . . How come you let him go out on his own?"

Graham sat up in bed, still feeling sick to his stomach, but less weak than he'd been earlier. Dimly he remembered the bowl of mucous chicken soup. He wondered if it had actually helped strengthen him.

He swung himself out of bed and pressed his soles against the cold floor, shivering as the chills made their way up his legs. His head throbbed, so he remained there for some time, on the edge of the bed, trying to suppress the nausea, closing his eyes in an attempt to will the ache away. He wasn't prone to headaches or migraines, so he wasn't sure of the best way to get rid of the pain. Maybe Felicity could make him one of her bitter drinks, those herbal concoctions he'd tasted many times throughout his married life, all the while not knowing what she put into it—a heady brew of Chinese roots and eleven secret herbs and spices, that kind of thing. As horrible as it had tasted, he sure could use a good dose of it right now.

He worked his jaw. "Fel?"

There was no response.

He cleared his throat, took a deep breath and croaked, louder this time: "Felicity?"

When silence greeted him, he reached for his glasses on the bedside table, put them on, and forced himself to stand up. A head rush threatened to topple him to the floor, but he managed to steady himself, praying for God to send His angels to keep him on his feet. He shuffled, ever so slowly, towards the bedroom door. Perhaps Felicity was in the kitchen. Cooking dinner. What time was it? He didn't know. He looked at his wrist. His watch wasn't there. "Felicity?" he tried again, and moved laboriously. The corridor beyond the doorway was dark. He successfully reached the doorway and peeked in both directions. The living room was on the right, and it, too, was dark. On his left was the kitchen, and he could see a glow emanating from it. Somebody had turned the kitchen light on. He began to move towards it. *Felicity, sweetheart, what have you been up to . . . ?*

"Felicity?"

He stepped into the kitchen. Looked around.

The air was fresh with the smell of detergent, and he saw everything was in its proper place. The floor had been mopped. This was good, wasn't it? This was a sign that Felicity had been busy while he'd been asleep—right?

But where *was* she?

Then, another thought: *Why did I fall asleep?* Strange, he never fell asleep at this time of the evening. At least, he *thought* it was evening. He couldn't be sure.

And chicken soup. Phlegmy chicken soup—why on earth had he eaten it? He tried to recall, but couldn't. He figured that Felicity must have cooked it for him, which was weird, because her cooking was definitely a lot better than that. Then again, if she'd spent all her time making the kitchen smell and look as good as this, maybe she'd been too tired or distracted to pay much attention to her cooking . . .

He heard the front door open and swing closed. *She's home. Felicity's home!*

He heard a woman's voice—Felicity's, no doubt!—and began to make his way towards the living room. *Felicity?* he called out, and then realised he'd only mentioned her name in his head, not out loud. Clearing his throat, he hurried into the living room, breaking into a smile of delight, exclaiming, "Fel!"—

It was the stranger. The woman he'd met at the supermarket.

The small-sized woman with honey-brown, curly hair, and a round, pleasant face: plump, red-cheeked.

Graham stared at her.

She was speaking into a mobile phone, saying, "Yes—yes, Doctor, that's not a problem. Tomorrow, then. That's fine, thank you." When she clicked off, she raised her eyes and saw him standing there, gaping at her in confusion and fear. "Graham!"

"Who are you?" Graham demanded, taking a frightened step backward. "How did you get into my house?"

"Graham—it's me, Sarah."

"Sarah?" No way. *No way, she's doing it again, she's pretending to be somebody she's not!* "Get away from me," Graham hissed, taking another tentative step back. "Get out of here! Go away, or I'll—I'll call the police! *Felicity!*"

"No," the woman named Sarah said softly, tossing her phone onto the couch, where it bounced against the seat. "No, Graham, you're mistaken. You're—you're imagining things again. I'm Sarah, Felicity's sister. Graham, you need help. I'm sorry, honey, but you really, seriously need professional help."

"I'm not crazy," he spat at her. "I'm *not!*"

"I didn't say you were. But you've been under a terrible strain—"

"Go away!"

"Dr Rubinstein has recommended a wonderful doctor friend of his who can help you," she said, and quickly added, to appease him, "who can help *us*. Graham, you've got to trust me, this is all for your own good. You can't go on living your life like this. You—*we*—have got to move on. Please understand, I'm not trying to hurt you or upset you. It's been very, very hard for both of us, but we've got to move on."

"*Get out of here!*" he roared, and she recoiled, taken aback by the outburst. "Go away! Get out of here! *Felicity!* Felicity, call the police, *call the police!*"

She held her hands out in front of her, trying to compose him. "Sssh! Sssh, Graham, please, calm down."

"I want you to get out of here. Now. *Now!* Felicity, where *are* you?" Then a new thought seemed to hit him, as his eyes widened further and his mouth formed a perfect O. Glaring intently at the woman named Sarah, he hissed, "What have you done to her? My Felicity. She's not here—you've done something to her, haven't you? *Haven't you?*" he demanded, advancing towards her. The woman shook her head, retreated, and Graham let out a frightened sob: "Oh, my God, oh, my God, what the hell do you want from us?"

"I h-haven't done anything," the woman whispered.

"But Felicity's not here! Where *is* she?! You must have seen her!"

"No, Felicity *isn't* here, but I had nothing to do with that."

"Who *are* you, anyway? And why would you hurt my wife?"

"You're not listening to me, Graham," she replied jerkily. "You're not—you're not well. Darling, I'm sorry, but you *have* to listen to me now—you're not well, and if you don't get help, you're only going to get a lot worse."

"Who *are* you?!"

She swallowed hard, fought back tears. "I'm Sarah. I'm Felicity's sister. Your sister-in-law. You've got to believe me."

"Where's Felicity?" he demanded.

They were going round in circles, figuratively and literally. The woman let out a drawn-out sigh, shaking her head. "She's gone, Graham," she said wearily. "She's gone home to God. I've told you this before, and I'm telling you again. She's gone. She's in the arms of our Lord now. She passed away, honey. I'm sorry, I know it's crazy and it hurts, but it's also *true.*"

"No!" he wailed, and shook his head vehemently, his eyes welling up with tears behind his glasses. "No, no, no! You're lying! I don't believe you! She's here! She's here somewhere, you just won't tell me where for God knows what reason, and *I don't believe you!*"

Exhausted, the woman named Sarah reached for her mobile phone. "I'm sorry. I'm sorry, darling, but I have to call Dr Francis now, okay? He's a very nice man, I just spoke to him. I'm going to ask him to come over, okay? Please?"

Graham spun around and began to run as fast as his elderly legs could take him, into the kitchen, his destination being the back door to get out of the house, since the stranger named Sarah Robertson was blocking his path to the front. Sarah watched him leave, not suspecting his intentions, and waited for Dr Raymond Francis, psychiatrist, to pick up on the other end.

"*Joe!*" Maggie shrieked in shock. Joe wiped his fist, stained with Zack's blood, against his shirt. "Joe, what the *fuck* is the matter with you, are you *crazy?*"

"I warned you!" Joe shouted at Zack, who was scrambling to his feet unsteadily, one hand rubbing at his mouth. Zack stared down at his fingers and saw the glistening redness. A look of hurt and anger danced across his features as he stared up at Joe. "I warned you, Zack!" Joe repeated harshly. "I told you to get away from us, to get away from my sister!"

"*Why?*" Maggie cried, and shoved at Joe's shoulder. He nearly fell over, but managed to catch himself. "Why? What's the problem? Why can't he talk to me? Why are you acting like such a—like such a—"

Joe gritted his teeth and spat out the words: "I—don't—want—him—*near* you!"

"He's just afraid because I know what he did," Zack put in, back on his feet. He touched his split lip with an already bloodied finger. "He told me you were pregnant in the hope that I would turn all chicken-shitty and run away. He's trying to get me out of here because he knows that I know."

A look of panic crossed Joe's features.

"What are you talking about?" Maggie demanded.

"He's scared, Mags!" Zack shouted, and laughed in spite of the blood running down his chin. "I know what your brother did to his girlfriend, and he's trying to stop me from saying anything!"

"Stop it," Joe snapped. "Stop it!"

Maggie turned to Joe, her pale face betraying her fear. "What?" she whispered sharply. "What did you do, Joe?"

Joe's response was to leap off the porch, aiming for Zack, who tried to dodge him but failed. Joe shoved Zack to the concrete and began to strike at his face with tight fists. Zack cried out, struggling desperately to defend himself. "You son of a bitch!" Joe screamed, as Maggie, rooted to the spot and disoriented by the explosion of tempers all around her, cried out her brother's name over and over again. A car's tyres squealed in the distance, but none of them heard it, too caught up in the cacophony of the fight. Joe was yelling profanity after profanity at Zack, who grunted and ordered him to stop, while Maggie screamed away on the porch, staring down at them, too stunned to do anything to break them up. Then Zack managed to push Joe off him, and the two boys wrestled fiercely, grasping each other's arms as each tried to keep the other off. They rolled around, kicking and thrashing, Zack gripping Joe's forearms tightly to restrain him from dishing out any more punches. The obscenities flew, and then Zack was on top of Joe, pinning him down against the hard cement, screaming that Joe had completely lost it, that he was absolutely crazy, spitting saliva and dripping blood as he yelled.

Suddenly, twin beams of headlights came upon them, bathing them in a warm glow. A car veered into the driveway, tyres wailing, hot rubber against concrete. The boys froze in mid-spar, their heads turned to stare at the vehicle, which stopped only inches away from where they lay. Maggie, too, clammed up and stared at the car with wide, terrified eyes. They looked like deer frozen in the middle of a road, seconds before being struck by an oncoming automobile.

The lights flickered off. The car door opened and the driver got out.

"Carrie!" Joe and Zack exclaimed at the same time.

Zack pulled himself off Joe, who remained on his back on the ground, panting and gasping loudly. It took several seconds for Joe to scramble to his feet as well, by which time Carrie reached him —

Only to slap him with all her might across his face.

The unexpected blow caused him to cry out and stagger backward, falling against the steps leading to the porch.

"Carrie —" Zack cried, and turned to look at Maggie. She stood transfixed on the porch, tears streaming down her face.

Carrie launched herself at Joe, who caught her by the wrists as she tried madly to hit him again and again and again. *"Fuck you, Joseph Cooke!"* she screamed at the top of her lungs, flailing and buckling like a wild horse. *"This is your fault! This is all your fault!"*

"Carrie, stop it. Carrie, calm down!" Zack moved in and managed to grab her around the waist. She thrashed like a bronco, making it hard for him to get a firm grip; but once he did, he pulled her away, grunting from the effort. "Carrie, please — !"

"It's — all your — f-fault!" Carrie roared, her voice cracking as she hurled the words at the pasty-faced Joe, sprawled upon the front steps. She was hyperventilating, choking and sobbing incoherently, occasionally managing to convey her frenzied message: "Everything! *E-Everything!* My p-parents—the baby—t-they know—they know, and it's—it's *all y-your fault!*"

The words spurred Maggie into speech: "What baby?"

Carrie turned away and began to sob loudly against Zack's shoulder. Zack swallowed hard, tasting the copper of blood. Looking at Maggie, he managed to whisper, "J-Joe's baby. Carrie's pregnant with—with Joe's baby."

"D-Don't," Joe sputtered, and let out a strangled sob.

"Joe doesn't want it," Zack whispered, moving one bloodied hand to gently stroke Carrie's hair as she wept and dry-heaved against him.

And Maggie, her face whiter than flour and her cheeks puffy from all the tears, turned to her brother with what Joe thought was the most devastating look of hurt and betrayal he'd ever seen.

Jessy Cooke smiled to herself as she drove her car onto her street, pleased that the meeting had gone so well. She'd scored the account for Mayson Limited, a soft drink manufacturer that would soon be launching its new range of beverages and had outsourced a company to handle its public relations. Jessy's expertise had led to Houssen & Dwight clinching the deal. A successful project would mean additional income, and she was grateful for the opportunity to move on with her life, to get over Paul once and for all.

Yes, she told herself as she approached her home, *things are definitely looking up now . . .*

Maggie managed to whisper hoarsely, "Is this true? Your friend. She's—she's pregnant?"

Joe snorted. "What's the big deal?"

"What did you tell her?"

He hesitated. Looked at Carrie, trembling in Zack's arms. Turned back to his sister and murmured, "A baby is the last thing we need. Not right now."

"So what did you tell her? Tell me!"

Joe shook his head, clamming up.

"*Joe!*" Maggie cried. "*Tell me!*"

"He said he didn't want to be involved." Zack was the one who answered. He ignored the ice-cold look that Joe shot him, and continued, "Told her she could get rid of it, or she could keep it . . . either way, he wouldn't be part of it."

"Get rid of it?" Maggie repeated, sotto voce. She let out an abrupt, cynical laugh and turned to address her brother. "It's that simple, isn't it? Get rid of it. Kill it off. It's an inconvenience, just chuck it out." Joe met his sister's gaze, his expression perplexed, confused, and she laughed again, out of place as it was. "What are you thinking, Joe? Let me guess: you're thinking a woman's body is no big deal, it's something to be used and abused and kicked around and trashed about. You're thinking, it's just a foetus. Get rid of it. No worries. No problems. You're thinking, she's just *carrying* it; it's not even a baby yet; there are no feelings attached to it. And, oh," she said, as if a new thought had just occurred to her, "if she *is* attached to it, who the hell *cares*, right, Joe? She's just someone to sleep with and knock up and make full use of before chucking aside and moving on to the next victim, isn't that right? Tell me, Joe! Isn't that what you're thinking? *Isn't* it?"

Joe stared at her, confounded.

"You have no idea," Maggie hissed through gnashed teeth, "what it's like. It's so fucking easy for you, the man, to tell us what to do, to simply say, 'Go to the doctor, get rid of it'. But you have no idea what we're feeling, what we're thinking, what the emotional and psychological after-effects of doing it are. You have no idea—but you've no intention of finding out, either, do you? It's 'Do it or I'm running away', as simple as that, isn't it, Joe? Huh? Come on, *answer me!*" she bellowed, and he shrank away from her. "You're such a bastard, Joe! If you think that you can treat your friend like this, get her pregnant and then run away, thinking she can just get rid of it, then you're an even worse human being than I ever figured you to be! Jesus Christ, Joe, how the *hell* can you be putting her through this?! Do you have any idea what *I've been through?*" she screamed.

Her last words made Joe's eyes pop wide open, the whites visible all around, even though his left eye was swollen owing to the bash-up with Zack. "W-what have you been through?" he coughed out.

A second car pulled in behind Carrie's, the headlights momentarily illuminating their surroundings. Nobody paid heed to it.

"I was pregnant," Maggie revealed, and Joe gaped at her, speechless. "I got rid of it."

The headlights clicked off; the engine was killed.

"What?" It was Zack who said it.

At the same time, a female voice called out, "What's going on?"

"You were—what?" Joe cried breathlessly.

"You cannot do this to her," Maggie responded shrilly, furiously. "You can't expect her to do this, not by herself. If she chooses to get rid of the baby, you've got to stand by her side, support her through this. If she wants to keep it, you've got to help her out. For God's sake, Joe, you can't run away! You can't leave her in the lurch like this! *Think*, Joe! Think of somebody else apart from yourself, for *once* in your *goddamn* life!"

Jessy Cooke took in with shock the scene that was unfolding before her—the bedraggled girl crying hysterically in a bruised and bloodied Zack McPherson's arms; her daughter, white-faced and teary, screaming at her son, who was sprawled on the steps, also beaten up. "What's going on?" she repeated loudly. And then Maggie's words hit her, struck her hard in the back of the head, and she turned to look alternately at Maggie and Joe, Zack and Carrie, whispering, "What—what is this? What's happening? Maggie, what the hell are you talking about? What baby?"

Maggie could only reply shakily, "Ask Joe."

"Joe . . . ? What's your sister on about . . . ?"

"N-nothing, Mum," Joe replied, just as tremulously. "She's . . . n-nothing."

"It doesn't *look* like nothing!" Jessy exclaimed.

"Mrs Cooke."

Joe's head snapped up, and he glared in horror as Carrie pulled away from Zack, wiping her face with her hands. Jessy turned to face the girl with unkempt hair who had make-up streaked all down her face, and Carrie, ignoring Joe's pleas for her to shut up, whispered, "I'm pregnant, Mrs Cooke. I'm pregnant with your son's baby."

How come you let him go out on his own?

Little Robby's mother spun around on her heels, her nostrils flaring, her eyes wide with indignation. "Just what are you getting at, Mr Leigh?"

He held both hands out, palms facing her. "Calm down, I'm just asking . . ."

"Well, I don't appreciate your line of questioning."

"I'm sorry," he said, and let his arms fall back to his side. "But, you know, it all seems very—strange." As strange, he thought, as her overly defensive reaction.

"*What* seems strange?" she countered, and Matthew heard the challenging tone in her voice. She stalked over to a cabinet, pulled the door open roughly and grabbed a jar of coffee.

"Just that," Matthew replied. "The fact that you let him go out unsupervised."

She turned back to the stove, grabbed a cloth, and used it to remove the kettle from the flame. Softly, she replied, "I didn't think he'd come to any harm."

"But he's an epileptic."

"I *know*," she snapped.

"And you just let him go out."

"For God's sake!" she cried, and slammed the kettle back down. Spinning around, she glared at him with a deeply affronted expression, shaking her head in anger. "Look, I don't know what the hell you're accusing me of, but I really don't like it. I think you should leave."

Matthew pursed his lips, telling himself that he *had* to say what he'd planned. His mind—the calculative, scientific mind that his father was incessantly telling him to put to full use—began to see the pieces of the puzzle fitting into place, forming the whole picture. Suddenly he knew, almost for sure, that the complete image in his head was accurate, that it *had* to ring true. Quietly, he prodded, "I'm sorry, but if *my* son were prone to fits, I wouldn't let him wander about on his own."

"That's enough," she seethed, and Matthew saw she was trembling slightly—with guilt? Fear? Anger? Or a mix of all three? "I want you to leave, right now."

"How come you've never come out to look for him?" Matthew replied, his words neither harsh nor accusatory, simply quiet—a tactic that proved even more interrogatory than speaking with loud, strident tones. "I've been sitting with him on that bench practically every day, often for hours, and sometimes he falls asleep. Maybe he goes off on one of his absence seizures, I don't know. But it's funny . . . you—you've never come looking for him."

"Get out of here!" she yelled, her face taking on a shade of red.

"The roads. What if he had a seizure on the roads?"

"I said get out!"

"I mean, if he'd fallen on the roads, anybody—"

"What the hell are you trying to do?" she screamed, and this time, her entire body shook with fury. "Get the hell out of my house, or I'll call the cops, I swear to God!"

"You'll call the cops. With what?" Matthew replied softly. "You don't have a phone."

"You have *no* right to be speaking to me this way, accusing me of—of—"

"I wasn't accusing you of anything. I was just wondering. Maybe you have your reasons. I'm curious to know what they are."

She closed her eyes, and Matthew saw the tears dribbling down her cheeks. She squeezed her fingers shut and lowered her arms to her sides, trembling. She chewed on her lower lip, obviously trying to contain herself, while Matthew watched her and felt the red-hot ball of rage grow bigger and bigger within him. He told himself that he, too, had to remain calm. No sense in both of them losing control. Swallowing, he said, "Aren't you going to visit Robby? He's in the hospital. Do you know he's in a coma? Maybe he'll wake up. If you turn up. If you show your face."

She struggled to speak, coughing the words out roughly: "I told you: I can't. It's too—difficult."

"Too difficult," Matthew repeated dully "Right." He paused. Then: "Do you want him to die?"

She snapped her head up, staring at him wide-eyed with shock. "*What?*"

"Do you want him to die?"

"I don't want him to die!" she quickly replied, terrified.

"You don't want him to die?"

"I don't want him to die!"

"No?"

"I don't want him to die! For God's sake, he's my son, I don't want him to die!"

Matthew nodded. "Right. Okay. I believe you."

"He's my son," she whimpered, and shook her head vehemently. "No, I don't want him to die. He's my son."

"Yes. Okay. I know. I believe you."

"He's my son," she repeated miserably, and raised one hand to her mouth as her lips quivered and the tears began to gush. Sobbing loudly into her palm, she cried out, "He's my son. He's my son."

"And it's not his fault," Matthew whispered quietly, "is it?" She didn't reply. She couldn't; she was crying too hard.

Matthew shut his eyes, exhaled loudly. "It's not Robby's fault that your husband killed himself, you know. Robby had nothing to do with it." He turned away so that he wouldn't have to look at the mother, knowing if he were to keep his eyes on her, he'd eventually lose control and slap her for what she'd done, for what he suspected — and knew — she'd subjected little Robby to. He fixed his gaze on the floor, the knot of anger in his belly dissipating, turning into grief, into anguish. *I will not cry.* He had to support himself by leaning against the row of cabinets behind him, and he folded his arms across his chest, feeling colder by the minute.

"I don't know what you were trying to do, but it seems to me like you didn't really care if Robby was run down in the middle of the street, or climb a tree and have a seizure and fall to the ground. Seems to me like you wanted it to happen, you were *hoping* he'd fall, that he'd be hurt, because somehow it would justify your husband killing himself." He stopped, not anticipating a reply. He didn't get one; only her whimpers of remorse rang in his ears. "I don't know what you've been telling him, but Robby seems to think his father was a monster who didn't love him. I don't know if he thinks this because of anything *you've* said, but if he does, then — that's pretty horrible of you, isn't it?"

She bawled like a baby, covering her face with both hands. It took Matthew a while to realise she was trying to speak, but was too overcome to form any words. He thought he heard her utter, obscurely, the word 'mistake'. "Mistake?" he repeated, as the mother wept. "Yeah, okay, that *was* a mistake, punishing Robby for something he wasn't responsible for. You're right." He nodded, even though she couldn't see him. "Tell me," he went on, still looking at the floor, at the thick layer of grime that dusted the boards, "how did you feel when he fell down the stairs? When he *actually* got hurt? Huh? Tell me, please." Through his veneer of politeness, some of the fury that was boiling within him began to rear its ugly head. Struggling against the scorching passion within, he looked at her and repeated, harsher now: "He fell. He hurt himself. He's in the hospital! How do you feel? Do you regret it? Or do you still think he deserved it? A boy. A little boy! Six years old, for the love of God! How the hell could he have been responsible for your husband's death? And now that he's actually in the hospital—now that some of your dreams have come true—how do you feel? Does it feel good? It doesn't, does it? Doesn't feel as great as you always thought it would—*does* it?"

Her legs buckled, and she sank to the floor on her knees, weeping helplessly.

Sighing, Matthew averted his eyes again, refusing to look at her. Feeling like a real bastard for all he'd thrown into her face, but thinking, at the same time, that an irresponsible parent like her surely deserved it.

"So tell me," Derrick Weston said, "what the hell was this fabulous plan of yours?"

Jason, glamorously garbed in drag, eyed him warily. "Promise you won't kill me."

"Depends on what you tell me."

Jason thought about this briefly. Then he sighed and lowered himself onto the couch. He used his right foot to kick off his left high-heel, vice-versa with the other stiletto. "Oh, that's a relief," he breathed, and leaned into the softness of the couch, the fabric still stained with—"Hey, man, you didn't clean up right," he said, and looked at Derrick.

Derrick saw the dark spatters on the fabric and knew he needed to run to the bathroom again. *Dear God*, he thought as he scurried out of the living room, *he had his lips on me! He touched me intimately! He did so many things to me! We kissed! Oh, God, I tasted his spit! No! No! Noooo!* And then his stomach heaved and whatever was left inside him ceased to remain inside him. The coagulating puddle on the floor became ever wider as he threw

up, his mind filled with nauseated, noxious thoughts of Dawn/
Jason's tongue in his mouth and the memory of Jason/Dawn's
sweat on his lips.

Outside, Jason began to unbutton his dress, removing the
bra and the rubber breasts that he'd purchased from an adult
store in the city. Plucking them away from his chest—they
were like little suckers; they stuck to your body and had to
be eased off with a hollow *pock!*—he thought about how much
Derrick had wanted to touch them, to see them, to taste them.
But that would've given the game away because, as hard as the
manufacturers had tried, they'd failed to create a pair of boobs
that looked, felt, smelled and tasted the same way a woman's
actually would. So the breasts had been out of the question.
Jason was glad to get rid of them, although he decided he'd
keep the bra as it was a fabulously delicate, lacy item from the
Victoria's Secret catalogue.

The front door flew open and the Dream Team thundered
in. Sanjeev, Chitra, Hope and Geraldine ran to Jason's side,
demanding to know what had transpired. They saw the wig
was gone; Jason's hair, cropped short, still held a couple of the
bobby pins he'd used to secure the fake hair in place. Sanjeev
pulled them out adroitly, while Chitra looked around the
apartment, demanding, "Where the hell *is* he?"

"Oh, my God, you're hurt," Geraldine gasped, touching
Jason's bruised face gingerly.

"How did he find out?" Hope wanted to know.

"I don't know. I—I went into the bathroom to relieve myself,
and when I walked out, he just leapt at me . . . !"

"Hey, my phone! Thank God!" Chitra exclaimed, picking
it up off the floor.

Jason turned to her. "Did you leave it here?"

"Yeah. I must've left it on the—" She clicked on the
"last-dialled-number" button and saw Jason's name. Her voice
trailed off as the realisation hit her. "Oh, shit. He didn't."

"Ooh, I think he did," Jason murmured.

"Why didn't you turn your mobile *off?!*"

Jason bowed his head sheepishly.

"Well, it looks like the plan's gone bust," Sanjeev said, eyeing Jason's bra, "no pun intended. So where *is* he?"

A loud retching noise from the bathroom.

"Oh," Sanjeev said.

"What are we going to do?" Jason demanded.

Hope, looking as bored as ever, popped her chewing gum loudly and said, "Looks like we don't have much of a choice, sweetums. It's time for . . . the confrontation!"

Jason gasped. "Not the confrontation!"

Hope nodded gravely. "Yes. The confrontation."

Derrick's voice, from the bathroom doorway, reeking with sarcasm and bile: "Ah. The Famous Five reunite." His face was chalky, wet with the water he'd splashed on; his eyes were narrowed with anger; his lips were twisted into a grimace that indicated he wanted answers, and he wanted them *now*. None of the Famous Five decided to greet him; they each figured any pleasantries would be duly ignored. "So tell me," Derrick said coldly, "what's this big conspiracy you people have plotted against me, huh? Come on, tell me."

Nobody said anything.

"Don't everyone start talking at once!" Derrick spat heatedly, and violently shook his head. "Far out!"

Geraldine was the first to answer: "Okay. Okay, I know you're upset, you're probably thinking this is the craziest thing we've ever done, but . . . believe me, we had—*have*—your best intentions at heart."

"Really," Derrick said flatly. "Yeah, all right, I'd love to hear it. I mean, it can't be too complicated, can it? It sure seemed easy enough for Jason to get all dolled up and pretend to be something he's not, going out there like some namby-pamby limp-wrist fairy fruitcake in a tight mini-skirt and frilly pink panties and high stiletto heels and Jesus, are those fake boobs?" He laughed, a high-pitched giggle that goose-pimpled the skin and hurt the ears. "You people are *insane*. Insane, I tell you!"

"You haven't even heard the plan yet," Sanjeev said.

"I don't *want* to hear it!" Derrick yelled, suddenly switching to full-out anger. "You have *no right* to make me look a fool like this! You have no right to play around with my emotions, to toy with me, to trick me into thinking I was falling for a person who actually doesn't exist!"

"But that's the point," Hope spoke up, and popped gum loudly. "If you could fall for Dawn, doesn't that mean you could just as easily fall for Jason?"

It took several seconds for the words to register, and when they did, Derrick could only ogle at the group. "What??"

"Did you find Dawn desirable?" Geraldine asked.

Uncertain, he stumbled over his response: "I—well, yes. I mean, I didn't—"

"Hence, you found Jason desirable," Geraldine said.

"Huh? No. No way. I was attracted to the woman. To Dawn. Not to Jason."

"But Dawn *is* Jason, that's what I've been trying to tell you," Jason said, addressing himself in the third person for added dramatic effect. "It's always *been* me. When you kissed Dawn, you were kissing me. When you tasted her, you were tasting me. And you liked it. You enjoyed it. You were turned *on* by Dawn. Which means," he said, breaking out in a wide, delighted grin, "you were turned on by *me*."

"No!" Derrick shouted, and felt his stomach lurch again, although he was sure there was nothing left in him to throw up. "No way, for God's sake, I was turned on by the *woman!*"

"Who was a man," Hope said.

"Who is Jason," Geraldine added.

"And if you liked Dawn, you could so easily like Jason, because, after all, they're one and the same," Sanjeev said smugly.

"Huh? N-no! *No!*" Derrick said, tottering on his feet.

"Honey, I think you need to sit down," Hope said. "Chit, why don't you get him something to drink?"

"Good idea," Chitra said, and skipped away to the kitchen.

"What are you loonies trying to do, huh?" Derrick demanded desperately. "What sick game *is* this?"

"Think about it, man," Jason said, and wandered over to Derrick's side to put an arm around his shoulders. "Imagine *Dawn* putting her arm around you. Can you smell my cologne? It's Dawn's perfume. You like it, don't you? Well, good news, buddy, it's actually a very masculine scent, and *you liked it.* I also notice you're not pulling away from me," Jason added, prompting Derrick to pull away from him, "which could imply that you actually *like* having me stand so close to you."

"You know what this means, don't you?" Geraldine said.

Derrick looked at her, soundless, terrified.

"You're bisexual," Hope said. "Just like we *all* are."

He found his voice at last: "What?! No! No, I'm straight!"

"Doesn't seem that way," Jason said, checking out his intricately manicured and varnished nails.

"Honey, it's no big deal; everybody's bisexual, it's the ratio that counts," Hope said, Cheshire cat-like, grinning from ear to ear. "The question now is, what's your ratio like?"

"No," Derrick said, and shook his head. "No. I'm not listening. This is crap. This is complete and utter bullshit."

"Is it?" Geraldine said.

Chitra appeared with a glass of Scotch and Coke, and she held it out to Derrick, who didn't even look at it. "You guys are talking crazy!" he shouted. "Look, I've told you what I think about this whole sexuality thing, and you know where I stand!"

"Oh, *we* know where you stand," Hope said. "The question is, do *you* know where you stand?"

"*What?*"

"How come you don't find us exciting?" Hope said, gesturing to Geraldine and herself. "I mean, we're lesbians, babe. We're going at it hot and heavy in front of you, and you're not the least bit interested. Seems to me like *that's* a little suspicious. Most straight guys find the lesbo thing very, very enticing. How come *you* don't?"

Derrick's jaw moved frantically, and he sputtered, "I just—it's—it's not right!"

"Ah, there you go," Jason said. "It's not right. It's a sin. It's wrong. Regardless, even if it *is* wrong, many straight guys find it *hot*. Girl-on-girl action, all dildos and pussies, you know what I'm talking about? I mean, *I* find it *bleargh*, but I'm gay; what does that say about *you*? Maybe it's because of your sexuality—you're covering up your predisposition of being gay by insisting oh-so-adamantly that it's a sin and a crime and blah-blah-blah."

"I don't have to stay here and listen to this!" Derrick shouted.

"Well, actually, it's *your* home," Sanjeev reminded him quietly.

"Shut up!"

"So maybe you're gay," Jason said, and returned to looking at his nails. "That's why you liked Dawn. Deep down inside, there was this masculinity about her that intrigued you, and your subconscious knew all along that Dawn was a guy in drag, only your *conscious* mind refused to let you believe it. Sounds plausible to me. You liked me. You *like* me. You're gay, man. Gay and unhappy. Very sad."

"No!" Derrick shouted, his eyes dancing from one person to the next: Geraldine to Hope to Jason to Sanjeev and back. Chitra was standing next to him, out of his direct vision. "God, I don't believe you're standing here feeding me this load of crap! I can't take this! I need a drink, *shit,* I desperately need a drink . . . !"

"Hello!" Chitra held out the glass. "Scotch and Coke."

He grabbed it from her and chugged it down.

Chitra smiled at the others, and they smiled back.

Graham hurried into the backyard, looking around, squinting through his glasses for any sign of his wife. He couldn't see her, but he knew in his heart of hearts she was around

somewhere, she *had* to be. He didn't call out, didn't want that
Sarah-wannabe in the living room to know he'd run away. So
he ran along the side of the house to the front yard, his heart
thumping in anticipation of seeing Felicity, perhaps kneeling
in the soil in the middle of some late-night gardening activity,
which would've been unusual, but not improbable.

The garden was empty.

"Felicity?" he whispered, now at the end of the driveway.
He stood at the gate and looked both ways, seeing nobody
familiar. "Fel, where are you, can you hear me?"

Looking back towards the house to make sure the Sarah
impersonator wasn't watching him, he reached for the gate,
pulled it open with a low creak, and made his way out of the
yard, onto the pavement. *Felicity,* he continued to cry out in
his mind, *where are you? Let me see you, tell me where you are!
Felicity . . . !*

Michelle Leigh hurried from the bus stop towards the Cookes'
home, wishing that Dan Michaels hadn't chatted her up after
work and delayed her from visiting Maggie as she'd promised.
No, that wasn't exactly true; she was *very* glad that Dan had
approached her: she'd had her eye on him since he'd first shown
up at the supermarket to apply for the position of a part-time
cashier. His having asked her out was a reason for her to jump
in the air and perform cartwheels all down the aisles of the
supermarket. But her mind had been preoccupied with the
issues surrounding her: Mr Hanson's state of mind, and her
friend struggling to cope with an abortion.

Michelle hated the idea of killing off an unwanted baby,
but she also thought Maggie too young to handle such
responsibility. Even if Jessy Cooke were to be supportive, the
social implications, she imagined, would likely be too much
for Maggie to handle. The people here were a nice, friendly
bunch, but many of them were conservative, especially the
older residents. Look at how many people were talking about

Jessy and Paul's separation—although in all fairness, nobody had ever liked Paul; Michelle herself had always had the creepy feeling he was checking her out whenever she visited . . .

A part of her wished she could have spoken to Mr Hanson about Maggie's pregnancy. Still, she was certain he would've talked her into talking Maggie into keeping the baby. *"Look at Felicity and me, unable to have our own,"* she could imagine him saying. *"A baby is to be cherished, even if at present you deem it to be more of an encumbrance than a blessing. What if you could never have another child ever again? What if you were physically and physiologically unable to have any more children? Think of how sorry you'd be, for what you had, and for what you chose to give up—the regrets would surely far outweigh any difficulties you'd have out of keeping the child."*

She sighed and hurried down the road, stopping short only a couple of doors down from the Cookes'. She could hear voices—heated, violent voices. She ventured closer and saw five people in the driveway, including Maggie's mum. They were screaming at one another.

Michelle figured it was best not to show her face just yet.

Hoping that everything would be all right, she turned and made her way across the road to the field, deciding to take a longer stroll.

Jessy Cooke told herself she'd been foolish all along. With the revelation that Joe had got his girlfriend pregnant, she realised with a horrible, sinking feeling that her conviction about life getting back on track had only been a desperate attempt at seeing the glass half full, at covering up her wounds with words and thoughts of restitution. But it had only been a superficial layer that flaked apart the moment something came along to throw everything out of order. Something like this. Like her supposed grandchild, in the womb of this girl she'd never met, Carrie Taylor.

Jessy could only look at her son despairingly, and Joe returned the gaze, his face caked with blood. It occurred to her how much she'd taken it for granted that her children were dependable enough to clean up their own messes. She told herself this would not have happened if she'd only taken the time to be more involved in their lives after the separation from Paul. Maybe the websites were right—parents were prone to abandoning their responsibilities during and after a break-up. If she'd been more responsible, she would've been more conscientious in monitoring Joe's activities, and maybe Carrie would not be pregnant today.

God, she'd been so intent on rebuilding her life after the breakdown of her marriage that she'd completely neglected her role in the lives of Maggie and Joe. The realisation struck Jessy now, and it made her heart break into a million pieces. Sure, she'd taken the time to speak to them, to ask them if everything was all right; but as a parent, shouldn't she have done *more*, dug a little deeper, found out what exactly was going on with her children? Yes, she should have. No, she hadn't done it, because she'd been selfish, so desperate to prove that she didn't need Paul, that she could live without him, that she could rebuild the household and live with Joe and Maggie happily ever after without Prince Charming. It had been doomed to fail right from the start, and this was the consequence of her irresponsibility, her foolhardiness in thinking that Joe was mature enough to look after himself. It was all her fault, she fingerpointed, and began to cry. *All my fault.*

"Mum." Maggie's voice, from the front porch. "Mummy, don't cry."

Joe, seeing the tears pour down his mother's face, began to climb to his feet, but he seemed to lack the strength, and he stumbled, fell to his knees. "Mum—" he whimpered, and now his own salty wetness dripped down his cheeks, stinging the open wounds. "Mum, I'm—I didn't mean to—"

"He told me to get rid of it," Carrie spoke up, adding fuel to the fire. Zack patted her back gently, whispered something in her ear, but she didn't respond. "He—he told me that he doesn't want a-anything to do with the baby."

"Carrie, shut the *fuck* up!" Joe screamed.

Zack whispered something in her ear again. This time, she acknowledged him with a nod. He spoke aloud, directing his words to nobody in particular, his speech partially garbled from his injuries: "I think—we shouldn't be here right now. I'm—I'm sorry. This was just . . . something that got out of hand." Then he turned, and Carrie let him lead her away from the house, down the driveway and out the gate.

Jessy watched them as they walked away. Then she turned back to Joe, her expression ever more wounded. Dear God, this was what it had come to. Joe lowered his gaze to glare at the driveway, his tears dripping, creating a dark smudge on the cement. His fists clenched and unclenched, and Jessy realised he was trying to control himself, trying to control his temper, he had always been such a hard-headed, hot-blooded young man, always looking for and getting into trouble. Maybe she should have taught him the meaning of moderation and patience and tolerance when she'd had the chance. Instead, what had she done? Dwelled on her failed marriage. Focused on herself, just herself, while her husband's traits and characteristics grew within her son and took control of his actions, his decisions. *Running away; Joe, you're running away, just like your father . . .*

She moistened her lips, tasting salt. Her voice, when she spoke, was a barely audible whisper, hoarse with anxiety and quavering with emotion: "J-Joe, don't—don't be like Daddy, okay? Please? This is just like your father—" She shook her head, blinked tears out of her eyes. "You're acting just like your father. Please. Please, d-don't . . ." Then she fumbled, and she stumbled towards the porch, up the steps, brushing past her son, who called for his mother and was ignored. Jessy teetered past Maggie, sniffling and sobbing, and staggered through the front door and into the house, leaving brother and sister out on the porch.

For a long while neither of them spoke. Joe stared at the open gate where Zack and Carrie had just walked out. His clenched fists and tongue literally in cheek indicated to Maggie that he was on the verge of blowing up. Swallowing hard, trying to clear her throat of the lump that had risen in it, she whispered, "Joe, listen . . ."

But Joe wasn't in any mood to listen, and he startled her by climbing to his feet and stalking down the driveway.

"Joe!" she called out. "Where are you going?"

He strode to the end of the drive, where their mother's Datsun was parked. Pulled the driver's door open and got in, slamming it loudly behind him.

"Joe!" Maggie cried, frightened now for her brother's safety. "Joe! Hey, don't!" The engine roared to life. "Come back! *Joe!*"

She could only watch helplessly as the car swerved backward out of the driveway, tyres squealing against the tarmac as Joe stepped on the accelerator and sent it roaring down the road.

Jason Marcel stood next to Derrick Weston and slung his arm around his shoulders. "So tell me, Derrick, can I kiss you?"

Derrick pulled away. "No!"

"You sure?"

"Yes!"

"It'd be Dawn kissing you."

"No. No, it wouldn't!"

"You liked it when Dawn kissed you, didn't you? Hmm?"

"Well—yes, but that's because—"

"So if it's okay for Dawn to kiss you, why isn't it okay for *me?*"

"Go on, Dick, let him plant one on ya," Hope said cheerfully.

"No! That's sick!" Derrick shouted, pulling away further. "That's really sick! That's wrong, sinful, sinful, sinful—"

"Sinful because you're gay and you're denying it?" Hope suggested.

"Sinful because you want to, but you can't bring yourself to?" Jason added, smirking.

"Sinful because you know you want to do it, but cannot admit to it?" Geraldine said.

"Sinful because," Sanjeev spoke, and stopped, realising he had nothing further to add.

"No! No! No! Sinful because—it's a sin!"

"Pathetic," Hope muttered.

"Come on, man," Jason said warmly, "give it a shot. Think of me as Dawn, what's so bad about that? If it was all right for you and Dawn to swap spit, I don't see what's so bad about you and *me* doing it. After all, as we've established, Dawn and I are the same person. You like her, you like me. You're turned on by her, you're turned on by me. You wanna do her? Then you wanna do me."

"My God," Chitra said quietly, "why didn't any of us see it before?"

"See what?" Derrick asked in a tight, frightened voice.

Chitra looked him in the eye and said, "You're gay."

"What? No—no, I'm not—!"

"Yes, you are," Sanjeev agreed enthusiastically, and grinned at his bemused friend. "You're gay. Gosh, I wonder why we've never seen it before, but *crikey*, it's so obvious! Derrick Weston is gay! Amazing!"

"I don't know what you're talking about!" Derrick yelled, and suddenly a wave of dizziness struck him, and he found his vision getting blurry, almost as if the effects of the alcohol he'd just consumed had kicked in ten-fold. "Whoa," he gasped, and reached out to steady himself—reached out and found only Jason, good old Jason, standing by his side.

"Whoa," Jason imitated him, and grinned. "Steady on there. I know you're excited . . ."

"I'm not—I'm not excited!" Derrick swallowed hard. "I just—got a little giddy all of a sudden, I don't know why—"

"You're giddy with excitement!" Hope shrieked with joy. "You're finally realising that we're right, that you *are* gay, that's why you're all disoriented, the realisation has hit you smack on the head, wham, bam, thank you ma'am, you're gay, and you're accepting it!"

Chitra let out a cheer and began to clap her hands with childlike exuberance. Sanjeev reached out and thumped Derrick playfully on the back, which didn't help his dizziness one bit. Derrick moaned and shut his eyes, leaning against Jason, *who was warm, pleasantly warm,* and he imagined *Dawn's midriff against his arm.* The thought assailed him and he pulled away, only to experience another bout of unsteadiness. He raised his hands to rub his temples, whimpering, "What's going on?"

"You're gay," Hope repeated cheerfully.

"You're gay," Geraldine agreed, nodding earnestly.

"Oh, yeah, buddy, there's no doubt about it, you're gay," Sanjeev concurred.

"I'm not! I'm not gay!" He spun to face Chitra, his expression melting into an accusatory scowl. "Chit—the drink. You put something in my drink, didn't you? You must have—why else—why else would I be feeling . . ."

"You're just coming to terms, that's all," Chitra said softly, encouragingly. "You're dealing with it. Accepting. *Acceptance.* It's the first step."

Derrick groaned and began to make his way towards the front door. "I need—I need to get out of here, get some fresh air . . ." He stumbled over an ottoman and nearly went sprawling, but Jason, ever the protector, saved him again by wrapping his arms around his waist to secure him. "Whoa!" Derrick cried out, and, on his feet again, murmured, "I really need to get out of here . . ."

They waited until he was out the door. Then Sanjeev turned to Chitra and demanded, "How many of those little pills did you put *in* there?"

"Three," she said. "Too many?"

Hope grunted. "Nah, won't do him any harm. Will only make him easier to convince."

"I don't know," Jason said, moving towards the front door. "I popped one into his vodka the other night, and that was enough to convince him to take me home and let me give him a BJ."

"And the effects lasted until the next morning," Hope remembered. "That's how we got him to believe that he'd asked Dawn to be his girlfriend, the gullible fool."

"Where are you going?" Geraldine asked Jason.

"Just making sure he's okay. With three of those little babies . . ."

"You might want to change into something manly first," Hope said flatly.

"Oh. Right."

"I think Derrick's clothes might suit you," Geraldine suggested.

Jason made his way towards Derrick's bedroom, murmuring something under his breath about hoping to find dirty laundry.

Hope slid an arm around Geraldine's slender waist and said, "Well, darling, tonight we're going to find out once and for all if your suspicions are right."

"I'm right," Geraldine replied confidently. "I know I am. He's just covering up. He looks at women and finds them gorgeous, a vision of beauty, but it's all a lie. He's trying so hard to believe he's straight, it's not even funny. But tonight, we'll do it." She leaned in to give her girlfriend a peck on the cheek. "We'll break his outer shell and get the inner Derrick to climb out of the closet."

Mass Destruction

———

"Whoa, mate, wait up," Jason said, jogging up to Derrick, who was halfway out of the main entrance of the apartment block. The drug must have made Derrick's movements slower than usual, because Jason had had time to change into men's clothing *and* wash the make-up off his face before heading downstairs.

Derrick didn't acknowledge him. They walked to the edge of the pavement. Jason reached out to touch Derrick's shoulder, keeping him back. "Hey, you know what, darling? I think it's best we stick to the pavement instead of trying to cross the road, okay?"

Derrick turned to him, his eyes cloudy. "Yeah, okay," he murmured, his words slightly slurred, "but I'm not gay."

"Sure. Sure."

They began to walk along the pavement, moving side by side in silence. Derrick inhaled and exhaled loudly, taking in the cool, crisp air of the night. Jason looked around. There weren't many people around, which wasn't surprising since it was a Friday night. In fact, the area was surprisingly quiet, with only the occasional barking of a dog and the chirping of cicadas in the field breaking the silence. *Nice,* Jason thought, grinning to himself. Walking with a cute guy in a quiet, peaceful square. Not a bad way to spend the weekend, although the physical stuff they'd been up to earlier had also been pretty enjoyable . . .

"Who's that?" Derrick mumbled, pointing straight ahead of them.

Jolted out of his thoughts, Jason saw a tottery figure in the darkness, and he squinted, trying to see if it was someone familiar. "Don't know. Probably one of the neighbours."

Derrick moaned. "What did you people *do* to me?"

"You're gay, that's all."

"What?"

"Nothing."

They continued to shuffle down the pavement.

"So tell me," Derrick mumbled, "you don't live with your sister and brothers, do you?"

"No. No, I don't."

"And when I dropped you off in front of the Lightview Condos . . ."

"The others gave me a ride back here," he replied, gesturing to the Kiara building.

"You people are sick," Derrick grumbled.

As they walked towards the other person, they saw it was an elderly man, moving at a surprisingly fast speed for someone his age, squinting behind thick glasses and mumbling something neither of them could decipher; a name, Jason thought. The stranger's eyes widened when he saw them, and, before either of them could say anything, the old man asked, "Have you seen her? My wife, Felicity? Have you seen Felicity? I can't find her."

Derrick's mouth worked, but he didn't reply. Jason was the one who responded, "No, sorry, sir, we don't *know* your wife."

"Felicity. She's—she's somewhere, I've just got to find her," the man whispered huskily. "If you see her—please—tell her I'm looking for her."

Jason blinked uncertainly. "Okay."

The old man moved on, his bare feet making no sound against the cool pavement, leaving Derrick and Jason to stare at each other. Derrick, rubbing his left temple with one hand, queried, "What the hell was *that* about?"

"He could be senile," Jason said, not unkindly, and put his hand on Derrick's right shoulder, guiding him forward. If

Derrick minded the contact, he didn't let on. Jason let his hand linger, saying, "Poor old man, he's probably living in some sort of dream world. A shame, really."

In the Hanson home, Sarah called Graham's name, wandering from room to room in search. He was nowhere to be found, she realised with a sinking feeling, and considered calling Dr Francis again to urge him to hurry up. The good doctor had agreed to come over and see to Graham, but if he wasn't in the house, they had a bigger problem on their hands than just a confused man in need of help. They'd have a *missing* confused man — and a missing confused man was a man who could easily get into trouble.

So she prayed he was somewhere in the house as she stuck her head into the bedroom and looked around. Empty. *Oh, Lord, please don't say it's so* . . . Into the bathroom she went, only to find it vacant. Then she checked the kitchen, where earlier in the evening she'd cleaned up the mess on the floor and on the countertops and in the sink. The smell of disinfectant and other cleaning agents was still in the air, but she barely noticed it because her eyes were on the back door.

Oh, no. Sweet Jesus.

And when she wandered out into the backyard and saw the footprints in the soil, she knew it was just as she'd feared.

Further down the pavement, Derrick moved away from Jason, whose hand was becoming too warm against his shoulder. In the distance, they heard the roar of an engine, the squeal of tyres against the road, but neither of them paid much attention: Derrick was too preoccupied with trying to control his nausea; Jason was too preoccupied with trying to control his lust. "I need to sit down," Derrick mumbled.

"Hmmm?" Jason said softly.

"I need to sit down, feeling too dizzy."

"You're gay. Do want to head back . . . ?"

"No, I need air."

"Where do you . . ."

Derrick gestured vaguely in the direction of the field, which was one big blur to him at this point. He blinked rapidly, trying to clear his vision, and mumbled something about the bench under the tree.

Jason looked across the road. Saw the tree in the distance, and said, "Can't do it, sweetheart. There are people sitting on it."

"Can't we shoo them off . . . ?"

Jason laughed. "No, I don't think so. It's not *our* bench."

"It could *well* be our bench," Derrick muttered enigmatically.

Jason stared at him, an eyebrow raised.

"What?" Derrick said.

"Nothing," Jason replied, and smiled. "Come on. Let's see if we can get those two to move."

Joe stomped down on the accelerator, his anger so hot and intense within him that he was breathing loudly and noisily. In his mind, the words he absolutely *hated* to hear continued to taunt him: *"You're just like your father! You're just like your father!"* To hear Carrie say it had been bad enough, but for his own *mother* to throw the words into his face—and not for the first time . . . that was too much. It was unbearable.

He gripped the steering wheel tightly. His insides churned, bubbled with rage, as he told himself Carrie had gone too far this time. The stupid, fucking slut! How *dare* she?!

"Bitch!" he screamed aloud in the confined space. "Bitch, bitch, bitch, bitch, *bitch!*"

He made a sharp right-hand turn, and, in the course of manoeuvring the curve, the car's headlights illuminated the couple on the bench.

It was only for a mere fraction of a second, but it was enough.

In that split-second of light, Joe saw Zack and Carrie.

And Zack was whispering intimately into her ear, his arm draped around her shoulders.

His temper was running amok now, overriding all rationale and causing him to behave crazily, driven by white-hot wrath. All he could see was Zack and Carrie, Carrie and Zack, both responsible for the demolition of his relationship with his mother and sister, both to be blamed for the mass destruction of his social and familial life. In his fury—the same violent anger he had inherited from his no-good, morally corrupt, hot-headed father—he acted solely on instinct, not giving a fuck about what he was doing and the consequences thereafter.

He wanted to hurt them. To hurt them bad.

So he gave in to his passion, and allowed his adrenaline and ire to soar into overdrive, superseding all sense of judgement and control . . .

Matthew Leigh stepped out of little Robby's home, holding the front door so that it slid closed silently. He stood on the stoop and took a deep breath, his emotions roiling within him, turbulent, pushing at the dam that he'd erected to keep his feelings in place.

As the door shut he could still hear little Robby's mother sobbing in the back of the house, and he prayed *(to whom? God? Does He even exist?)* that she would truly repent and rectify the errors of her ways. He knew he'd had no right to break her down like that, to hurt her without lifting a finger, driving a stake through her heart by confronting her with the truth. But he'd felt compelled to; little Robby's life had ended up the way it had because of her.

He walked down the driveway, his hands deep in his pockets. His legs felt as if they were made of jelly. In fact, his entire body shook, and he bit his lower lip, thinking, *Robby, you little twat, how the hell did you drag me into this mess?* He wasn't sure what he was going to do next. He would visit the hospital, certainly, but as for the boy's welfare when—if—he woke up . . .

Matthew told himself to worry about that later. At the moment, all that mattered was that he'd tried to drive some sense into little Robby's mother, cruel as his approach might have been. He needed to go home, maybe get his sister to pray for the boy. As he pushed the gate open, careful to avoid the splinters, the thought occurred to him that he could easily do the praying himself. But that would mean having to reopen the ol' religious can of worms, having to come to terms with the notion that, perhaps, there *was* a higher force governing everybody's lives somewhere out there. No. Praying was much too tiring, too much work; maybe he could kneel by his bedside and think something like *God, I don't believe in you, but if you're real, then maybe you could look out for that little shit lying in the hospital, because he's an amazing little sunnovabitch.*

He made his way towards his car, and then changed his mind; he didn't want to drive just yet, he was in no state to. Instead, he walked away from his vehicle, thinking how strange life was: about three weeks ago what had weighed most heavily on his mind was that he'd been unable to find the right library book for his university assignments; now, it all seemed so trivial. Maybe his studies would seem more important if he were focusing on something other than law. Something like—medicine. Then maybe he would be able to help people like little Robby, who suffered from fits he couldn't control, and who was now lying helpless in a hospital bed with tubes and wires running out of his tiny, frail body.

And maybe it would help Matthew to put others first for a change.

He shook his head and forced himself to stop thinking, realising that the dam within was already crumbling, *big guys don't cry*, the flood waters on the cusp of breaking through. He walked on, heard the roar of a car engine somewhere in the area, paid no heed to it.

"Matt!" He froze. "Matt, wait up!"

Matthew turned. His sister was hurrying towards him. He sighed, thinking he didn't have the strength to talk to her right now. He didn't have the strength to talk to *anybody* right now — although he would've given his right arm for five minutes on that bench with the annoying little brat Robby, talking about how sour milk resulted in runny shit and shit like that.

Zack McPherson and Carrie Taylor sat on the bench, his arm around her, his mind on Maggie. Her confession about her terminated pregnancy had shaken him, and he found himself very much affected by the notion of a fifteen-year-old having to go through something like that all on her own. Well, perhaps she hadn't been entirely on her own, but who had she turned to? He didn't know, even though Joe had obviously picked a bad time to make up the fake pregnancy.

Zack looked at Carrie, wondering how they'd been dragged into such a mess. His mind flitted to Joe, and how he'd thought they were friends, which just went to show how volatile friendships are, and how somebody you consider a buddy could easily turn around and stab you in the back. He had never previously encountered any bad blood with Joe, which was part of what made this all so sad. This whole situation with the double pregnancies and the abortion and the uncertainty of the future — it was one big, messy mistake, but mistakes can be fixed by taking the proper measures. To err, after all, is human, which meant, despite all that had happened, there was no reason for them not to be able to deal with the consequences and move on. For heaven's sake, they were young; they had the rest of their lives ahead of them. If they couldn't deal with the present, how could they deal with the future, when they were older and more jaded and cynical, when *everything* posed a problem, and when these adolescent issues paled in comparison? (Then again, he reflected, these weren't issues that *every* teenager necessarily went through. They were being forced to grow up before their time—Maggie and Joe especially, with the double whammy of their parents' separation.)

"Imagine," he said aloud, keeping his voice at a minimum, "if we get through this, how much stronger and more experienced we'll be in the future." Carrie snorted loudly into a tissue, and Zack hugged her, saying, "I know it's one hell of a cliché, but it's true."

"Why do people always talk about the future when what we have to deal with is the here and now?" she asked wretchedly.

Zack looked at her in the darkness, uncertain if the question had only been rhetorical, but deciding to give his two cents anyway. "I guess it's because if the future looks bright, then it's a *reason* for us to deal with the here and now." He grimaced at the metallic taste of blood in his mouth, touched his lower lip, winced. "Otherwise," he added carefully, "if it's all bleak, what's the point in making the present work? Might as well just give up. Give in. Drop dead."

"Yeah, well, that's what I feel like doing," she responded, and sniffled. "Drop dead, I mean." She paused, blew her nose loudly.

Silence ensued for several seconds. Then, as an afterthought, Zack said, "On the other hand, how would we know whether or not the future will be bright if we were to give in right now and drop dead? By dropping dead, we'd be ending the *possibility* of a future. There would *be* no future, bleak or otherwise."

"Hmph," she grunted in response.

"Can I just say," Zack added, "that I've never seen you so furious before. Y'know. When you confronted Joe. Hell hath no fury, huh?"

Carrie opened her mouth to reply, but a noisy car punctuated the silence of the neighbourhood, cutting her off. They looked up to see a vehicle turn sharply around one corner of the Square. For a moment they were both lit up by the car's headlights; then they were back in darkness, and Carrie turned back to Zack. Again she worked her lips to say something, but they were distracted by footsteps in the distance, and they looked up to see two figures approaching the bench. Zack stiffened, and Carrie pushed herself closer against him, uncertain, chary. He gave her shoulders a gentle, protective squeeze, although he wasn't sure himself if these guys were going to be trouble, and, if they were, whether he had the fortitude to stand up to them after all he'd been through tonight.

The newcomers stepped up to them. Zack saw, in the dim moonlight, there they were just two regular, harmless-looking young men, one of whom had his arm casually slung over the other's shoulder. "Hey, guys, sorry to interrupt," the one with the short, closely cropped hair said, "but my friend over here isn't feeling too well, pigged out on drinks and got himself sick to the stomach. We were just wondering if we could have a sit-down."

The other boy looked at them with glazed eyes, blinked a few times and told his partner, "Maybe we should leave them alone, Jason. Think they want privacy or something."

"You're gay," the guy named Jason said, which made Zack and Carrie stare at them, bemused. "Come on, Rick, you're the one who wanted to sit down." Jason looked at the two on the bench, cocked a thumb at his friend, and repeated, "He's gay."

"Fuck you, I'm not."

"He's just coming to terms," Jason said, as Zack and Carrie nodded numbly.

"Jason, for God's sake—"

Zack cut them off by chuckling weakly and saying, "Look, no offence, guys, but—we're in the middle of something here. Sorry."

The guy named Rick grumbled, "Told you they want privacy."

"Yeah, well," Jason said, grinning at the couple, "they don't know what they're missing."

"What's that mean?" the one called Rick murmured. Jason laughed aloud at some secret gag that only he understood, and Zack figured it was probably a gay joke.

Graham Hanson left the pavement to cross the road. Pebbles and bits of gravel dug into the soles of his feet, but he didn't pay any attention to the pain. All he could think about was the possibility that Felicity had decided to take a solo walk to the bench in the field, and was possibly sitting there right now, listening to the silence of the night *(if not for that screeching car)*, taking stock of her life . . .

And on the other side of the field, Sarah Robertson continued to scout around for him, calling his name, catching the attention of several neighbours in their front yards, asking them if they'd seen him. Some of them had, and pointed in the general direction of Graham's passage; others who had only just stepped out of their houses said they hadn't heard anything, except for that terrible driver who probably thought he was in the Grand Prix or something —

Bertha Asterville looked out the window upon hearing the horrendous squeal of a car's tyres, wincing as the noise sent chills up her spine. *The drivers of today,* she thought wistfully, and moved to the front door, slipping her feet into a weathered pair of slippers, old but comfortable.

She wandered to the end of the driveway, leaned over to look to her left and right, up and down the sidewalk. Her eyesight — impeccable for a woman of her age, an attribute she was particularly proud of — made out the silhouettes of several people wandering about; other residents of the Square. But it was a solitary form stepping off the pavement that caught her eye, and she felt her pulse quicken, recognising the person at once. There was no mistaking it: Graham Hanson had a profile that was inimitable, even shrouded in darkness. *What on earth is he doing by himself at this time of night?* She remembered the scene in his house two days ago. *I hope he's okay.*

"Graham!" she called, and the figure, halfway across the road, froze to a stop. "Graham, it's me, what are you doing?"

There was another ghastly screech of tyres, the loud roar of an engine. Bertha jumped, seeing the car careening round the corner, its headlights briefly sweeping across the field, illuminating the couple seated under the tree and the other two figures accompanying them . . .

Felicity?

Graham froze in his tracks, hearing the woman's voice calling to him.

It's her — where is she?

He was dimly aware that he was standing in the middle of the road. To be more precise, he was of closer proximity to the grassy area than the pavement, which meant he was in the middle of the lane that skirted the perimeter of the field . . .

"Graham, it's me, what are you doing?"

"Feli?" he cried, but it came out as a gravelly whisper. Clearing his throat and looking around anxiously in the darkness, he tried again: "Fel? Where are you?"

The car that tore around the corner should have, by right, passed him by in its own lane — only the driver decided to make a detour and veer across to the wrong side of the road, intending to drive the vehicle straight into the field — and straight into the stationary, hunched-over figure of seventy-eight-year-old Graham Hanson, lost and preoccupied, spotlighted like a performer in the middle of a very brutal stage.

"**M**att," Michelle said breathlessly, jogging up to her brother. "What are you doing here?"

Matthew shrugged.

"Matt, are you okay? What's going on? I saw your car back there, what's wrong?"

"I'm fine," he said curtly.

"Did your car break down or something?"

"No. I'm okay. I'm just—walking."

They moved on in silence for a moment. Somewhere in the distance, a woman's voice could be heard, calling out for someone. Matthew, with his hands still in his pockets and his gaze still fixed firmly upon the sidewalk, asked, "What about you? What are *you* doing here?"

"I was just—" Michelle began, and then stopped as the angry blast of the car engine that Matthew had heard earlier grew louder. Tyres screeched, searing against the road, and Michelle snapped her head up to stare right ahead. Her eyes widened as they fixed upon the dark but all-too-familiar figure in the middle of the road, lit up by the headlights of the oncoming vehicle.

"Matt!" she gasped—and as the car began to swerve off-course, she realised all at once what was going to happen. "Mr Hanson—*look out!*"

"Jesus!" Matthew exclaimed, seeing the car make its deadly detour, ready to ram into the old man.

"*Oh, my God!*" Michelle screamed.

Matthew burst into a sprint and ran as fast as he could into the middle of the road, wincing as the sudden movement sent a stitch of pain up his side, barely hearing his sister screaming his name.

The car ploughed forward, only feet away from Graham Hanson, the heat of its headlights strong against his skin. If the driver saw the person in his path, he was certainly making no effort to stop the vehicle. *Christ*, Matthew thought, and it seemed to him as if everything were moving in agonisingly slow-motion: the car soaring towards the old man, towards *both* of them; Matthew's legs moving as if he were stuck in melted tar, or as if he were running in water, leaden, weighed down; the old man's realisation that doom was impending as he raised his hands in front of his face in a helpless and hopeless gesture of self-defence.

In that split second before he shoved the old man out of the way, Matthew's senses heightened, and everything registered with ten times the force they normally would have—the smell of burning rubber assaulting his nostrils; the heat of the headlights; the stinging sensation of pebbles sent flying in their direction by the spinning, wailing tyres; the screams of his sister in his ears, mixed with the terrified shrieks of the other woman and the loud moan of defencelessness from Graham Hanson; the shrill bay of that blasted thrice-barking dog somewhere in the neighbourhood; the roar of his own blood at his temples, pulsating with every ear-splitting beat of his heart.

And then there was the bone-jarring impact as Matthew Leigh hurtled himself at the old man and made contact, sending Graham Hanson sprawling to the side of the street where the tarmac ended and the grassy field began. Graham cried out in pain as he felt his skin being scraped off where he hit the road. His head struck the ground, but thankfully, his skull hit mostly grass and earth, although that was enough to render him unconscious.

Matthew screamed in anguish as most of his epidermis was scraped off against the tarmac—and then let out a greater cry of agony as the front of the car slammed into his right leg. He heard something go snap, and then felt his joint give as excruciating pain soared through him. His forehead bounced off the road, and he whimpered, convulsing, as everything went a deep, terrifying shade of red, and then a stark black.

In the car, Joe Cooke sat with his eyes wide and his mouth locked in a silent scream of terror, his hands held out in front of his face in the same way the old man had raised his in a futile attempt at warding off the looming tragedy. The sight of Graham Hanson in the middle of the road had rendered Joe into a state of immobility, almost as if his nerve endings had been cut off and he was unable to move any part of his body. Suddenly he saw everything with a cruel, mocking precision and sagacity: the consequences of what he had planned to do, the deadliness of his actions for all the people involved.

With this petrifying realisation, ice took place of his blood and froze him into a state resembling catalepsy. He was unable to think, unable to move, unable to make a sound, unable even to breathe. All he could do was watch the imminent disaster, stuck in that helpless stance of defence with his hands held out in front of his face to fend off the impending blow—

Straight into the field, headed for the bench, for the four people that were gathered under the tree . . .

If only he could move his arms, turn the wheel, step on the brakes, do something, *anything*—

But he didn't; *couldn't*.

He could only gape in heart-stopping panic as the car sped towards its target.

"**W**hat the hell—!"

Zack and Carrie looked up in horror as the twin headlights of the car danced across them, lighting up the area under the tree. The tyres made scraping sounds against the grassy ground, interspersed by the roar of the engine as the automobile sped towards them, aimed straight at them, directly at the bench—

It was Jason who cried out, and Zack was momentarily pinned in place by the lights. Then, as Carrie let out a frightened shriek, he was spurred into action, and his first instinct was to get her out of harm's way, shoving her off the wooden seat, screaming, "Carrie, move! *Move!*" She staggered, stumbled, fell off the bench, and Zack was frantically helping her to her feet, pushing her, telling her to get away from the tree, *quickly!*

"What's that psycho *doing?*" Jason yelled, as the car rapidly approached, five metres away, four, three—

"He's going to hit it!" Zack cried, grabbing Carrie's hand and pulling her away from the shaded area. She stumbled and nearly fell again, but he caught her, kept her on her feet. "*Look out!*" he bellowed, impulsively shielding Carrie from the possibility of any debris hitting her—the same instinct that caused Jason, across from them and also out of the shaded area, to shove Derrick to the ground, protecting him, keeping him safe.

The car slammed into the bench. Metal against wood, a horrifying crunching sound, mixed with the *twang* of dented metal and the tinkle of broken glass. The wooden seat splintered, cracked apart upon impact, chips, splinters and dust flying. The collision slowed the movement of the car some, but it wasn't enough to stop it from ramming with full force into the tree. There was a sickening crash as the front of the vehicle smashed against the tree trunk, folding like an accordion, the windscreen shattering into a million pieces, the stench of gasoline and timber and burned rubber hot and thick in the air. The explosion of sound caused all four of them to cry out and recoil, their every bone jarred by the intense brunt of the crash.

It all happened within a matter of seconds, and when it was over, the silence was deafening.

Slowly Zack turned to look, and groaned in shock at the scene that only seconds ago had been one of calm. Now the bench lay in large, jagged pieces under the wreck of the car, which looked as if it were trying to climb the tree, its front half tilted upwards against the bark, partially wrapped around the trunk. One of the headlights was still on, and it shone a flickering beam of yellow light up into the boughs, illuminating the leaves and flowers above. Glass, dust, splinters and other fragments littered the ground around them, and the mixture of noxious odours made all four of them wheeze.

Jason gradually got to his feet, unsteady, helping Derrick up. Zack turned to Carrie and asked if she was all right. She nodded yes, and he helped her stand. Somewhere in the distance they could hear voices—girls screaming, people shouting—and they knew the neighbours were up and about. Carrie wandered cautiously towards the wreck, moving to its rear, and when she saw the make—Datsun—and the registration plate, she let out a strangled cry. Zack, Jason and Derrick turned to her, startled, as she ran to the driver's door, took one look at the lifeless and mangled figure in the seat, and began to scream and wail at the top of her lungs. "Joe!" she screamed, and began to pull at the driver's door. It wouldn't give.

Zack reached for her shoulders, stunned. A violent tremor ran through him, and he could only stutter, "C-Carrie, don't—please, don't—"

"Joe! Oh, my God, Joe! *Joe!*"

"What's going on?" Jason demanded, his voice reflecting his own fear. "Who *is* he?"

"Joe! *Joe!*" She kept on pulling at the door, but it was so bent out of shape that it refused to open.

Somewhere across the field, they heard more screams, and Zack, struggling to breathe, didn't need to turn around to know that Jessy and Maggie were running towards them.

"Carrie, don't," he whispered, and pulled a struggling, buckling Carrie away from the car. "We can't do anything, we've got to get help—"

Jessy Cooke reached them, screaming her son's name hysterically, tearing at her hair. Zack's eyes fell on Maggie, saw that she could only gape at the wreck in silent, ashen-faced horror, and he was suddenly filled with a grief so deep and intense that he broke out in tears as he dragged Carrie away from the smashed car.

"Joey!" Jessy shrieked at the top of her lungs, her voice cracking with hysteria. She started to pull with all her might on the handle of the damaged door, and grew increasingly frenzied as she realised she wasn't able to open it, wasn't able to get her son out of the car. "Joey!" she screeched, "*Joey, Joey, Joey!*" Jessy pulled and pulled and pulled, moaning and screaming and weeping, while her daughter chanted numbly in the background, "Mum, don't, Mummy, Mummy, don't, don't"—breaking her nails, bloodying her fingers, not knowing, not caring, not feeling it, sensing only the excruciating anguish of knowing her only son lay bloodied and broken in the driver's seat.

At the other end of the field, Bertha Asterville crouched shakily next to Graham Hanson, while Michelle Leigh bent over the inert body of her brother, whimpering into her hands, whispering his name, wanting to touch him, to wake him, but not daring to lest she hurt him further. She could see the dark patches of blood all over his body, and his right leg was bent at an awful angle, clearly broken.

And somewhere in another part of the pitch, Sarah Robertson hurried towards the scene of the crash, shocked beyond comprehension, praying with all her might that Graham hadn't had anything to do with it.

It didn't take very long for all the residents of the Square to rush to the field, excited and astonished by the drama that had unfolded in their sleepy area. Bertha and Michelle were suddenly engulfed by agitated neighbours, and many more made their way across the grassy expanse to the site of the accident, where a single, solitary headlight shone towards the sky, like a beacon announcing where the tragedy had taken place, lighting up the tree.

"**M**-Michelle?"

The paramedic, crouched next to Matthew's side, held the oxygen mask in his hands, having removed it from Matthew's face.

Michelle, squatting on the other side of her brother, reached out and took his bloodied hand. "Matt," she whispered. "I'm here. Everything's going to be okay."

He moved his lips soundlessly and ran his tongue along them, but his mouth was dry. Breathing raggedly, he whispered, "What happened?"

"You saved Mr Hanson. He's going to be okay, too."

It seemed to take a long time for him to understand this. Then he nodded, a barely perceptible movement, and choked out, "What—what about the car? The d-driver?"

She looked in the direction of the tree, where the crowd of people gathered. Two ambulances were parked in the middle of the field, red lights swirling. Turning back to her brother, she gave his hand a gentle squeeze and murmured, "He—he crashed. Into the tree."

"And—and the bench . . . ?"

Michelle blinked at the unusual question. She shook her head. "It's gone, too."

His jaw worked again, and when he spoke next, his voice was hoarse, quivering, high-pitched with emotion and slightly unintelligible: "We sat there." She watched numbly as tears began to fill his eyes, tears she'd not seen for many, many years. A violent sob escaped him and his entire body shook as he repeated, "We—we s-sat there. A-And we talked. And he told me—he told me about his dreams, and . . . and the birds, and—and, oh God, so many things . . ." Another sob, and he began to weep, having difficulty forming the words to convey all that he was feeling, the dam having given way at long last, allowing everything to gush forth in a massive, incoherent flood.

Michelle reached out and touched his face, wiping the tears off his wounded cheeks.

"We t-talked," he managed, and wailed like an injured animal, a shrill, keening sound that tore through the very heart of her.

He continued to cry as the paramedics lifted the stretcher and put him into the back of the waiting ambulance.

Jason, Derrick, Hope, Sanjeev, Geraldine and Chitra stood in the distance, watching the throng that had gathered in the field, keeping their eyes on the medics and police who rushed back and forth, barking excitedly into handheld radios. Jason grasped Derrick's hand firmly in his, and if Derrick minded, he didn't show it. The others saw this and were pleased, although they didn't say anything. Derrick himself was a little blurry-eyed, but the crash had jolted some life into him, so it wasn't as if he was too out of it to realise how intimately Jason was touching him.

"It's incredible, isn't it," Geraldine spoke softly. "Incredible and terrible."

Hope held her by the waist, pulling her close. "Did the driver make it?"

Jason was the one who replied: "Don't know. Can't imagine he did, though."

"Makes you wonder, doesn't it," Derrick murmured, "how incredibly short life is."

"Short," Jason concurred, nodding. "Makes you think maybe you've just got to *go* for certain things and not shy away, you know what I mean?"

Derrick looked at him, expressionless.

"It really *is* short," Jason whispered.

"It is," Geraldine agreed, and Hope nodded, too.

"That's why we've got to savour every moment, make the most of it," Sanjeev clichéd. "I mean, if you don't experience something new now, what if you *never* get the chance to experience it . . . ever?"

Everyone looked at him before turning their attention back to the scene. The six of them became quiet then, and stood there for another good ten minutes or so, silent spectators in a noisy crowd of restless, excited neighbours.

ALL GOOD THINGS . . .

Graham Hanson opened his eyes and found himself in a bed. He knew at once he wasn't in his bedroom. The lights were too bright, and they were fluorescent. He didn't have fluorescent lighting in his home. Blinking, he stirred, moving his right leg. There was something on his forehead, and he raised a hand to it. It felt like fabric. Fabric and cotton. Then he saw there was some of it on his hand, too. Gauze, he realised.

"You're awake."

It was a woman's voice, familiar, with a cheerfulness that somehow conveyed sadness and relief at the same time.

He didn't have his glasses on, so he couldn't see who it was. She moved to his side. "How do you feel?"

"S-Sarah," he whispered.

Sarah Robertson smiled, pleasantly surprised by his ability to place her. "Yes. Yes, honey, it's me. It's Sarah. Hang on a minute, I'll help you sit up, okay?" She turned to press a button by his bedside, and there was a buzz followed by a mechanical whirr as the upper half of the bed began to rise, bringing his body into a sitting position. It stopped automatically at a comfortable angle, and Graham raised his other hand—Band-Aided, but not bandaged—to rub his eyes, murmuring something about how he'd thought only nurses were authorised to raise the beds. Sarah chuckled softly. "You must be thirsty; let me get you some ice chips."

"How—how long have I been out?" he croaked. She passed him a paper cup. He took it gratefully and tipped it towards his mouth.

"Not long," she answered his question. "It's Saturday morning now. Do you remember what happened last night?"

He passed the cup back to her. "I—I think so. I was looking . . ." He grimaced, shifting his position. "I was looking for Felicity."

Sarah tensed, wondering if he was going to ask about his wife again. Anticipating it.

Graham shut his eyes and leaned back against the raised half of the mattress. Speaking in hushed tones, he smiled and said, "I met her last night."

She held the cup in both hands. "You did . . . ?"

"Yes. And she was beautiful." Now he looked straight at her, his eyes strangely clear in spite of the fact that he'd just woken up, had been given painkillers, *and* he wasn't wearing his glasses. His smile was serene as he murmured, "I understand now. I finally understand what you've been trying to tell me. And I remember. Felicity passed away. She was old; she hadn't been in the best of health; she died in her sleep. I remember all that now. I mean, I knew it before, but somehow I forgot, and now I remember again.

"I saw her last night," Graham said quietly, his smile not wavering. "Right after that car came at me, and someone—someone pushed me out of the way, didn't he? My guardian angel. Pushed me out of the way, and I landed on the roadside, and everything went black. I think I nearly died. I think I *did* die." He paused. Looked up at the ceiling, at the harsh, white lights, then flickered his eyes to look at his sister-in-law. "Did I, Sarah? Did I die?"

Her lips trembled, and she gathered her strength to reply, "Let's just say your heart stopped. For a while. But the guys brought you back, got your ticker ticking again."

Graham's smile widened, full of quietude. "That's when she told me."

Sarah couldn't help it: tears began to run.

"I know I wasn't dreaming. I know I really saw her. She gave me this really, really warm embrace, and she said . . ." He chuckled wistfully at the memory. "She said it's not my time. I still have some years left, and she told me to be patient, it won't be too long, but for now, I still have my friends, I still have my health. And that's when I realised. I *really* realised. You were right, Sarah. What you've been saying all this time . . . you weren't trying to hurt me, you weren't conspiring against me, you were trying to help, you were trying to get me to accept the reality that she's gone.

"I don't know how it happened, Sarah—how I got so . . . convinced. I really, really believed she was with me. She was even talking to other people, and they responded to her. Or maybe I just *believed* they responded; maybe they just said things that were coincidentally related to what Felicity had said. Or maybe they never even *said* anything, and I imagined it all. It's hard to figure it out."

"Then don't," Sarah said, moving to his side to stroke his hair gently, careful not to touch the bandaged area. "Don't figure it out. It's in the past now. Think of how wonderful it would be to meet up with Fel again, and use that as motivation for you to make the most out of the rest of your life before you reunite with her."

He nodded, shutting his eyes, the smile still there. "Yes. That sounds like a very good idea. She's gone, but it's not the end. There'll never be an end. All good things don't necessarily *have* to end."

Touched, Sarah leaned over and kissed him on his forehead. "No," she whispered, and laughed with tears in her eyes. "No, you're right, they don't have to."

FLUSHED WITH TRIUMPH

Derrick awoke with the most awful, skull-splitting headache he'd ever had in his life. It was almost as if he'd got extremely drunk the night before, although the only alcohol he'd consumed had been the Scotch and Coke. Grimacing, he struggled to roll over in bed, writhing, agonised, as he made the effort.

"Morning."

The voice caused Derrick to cry out in shock and bolt upright, resulting in a detonation of TNT inside his skull. He groaned and rubbed the back of his head, feeling the queasiness rise. "Sorry, honey, didn't mean to startle you," Jason Marcel whispered. He touched Derrick's left shoulder gently. "You okay? You're probably having a splitting headache right now, aren't you? Bloody pills, they do that. And you're gay."

Derrick couldn't answer. Just kept on wincing and rubbing.

"Listen," Jason said, sitting up. "Thanks for last night. That was the best, man."

Derrick turned to stare at him. His expression revealed that he had no idea what Jason was talking about.

"You did it, buddy," Jason said, patting Derrick's shoulder affectionately. "You got to fourth base with Dawn."

"What?!" Derrick shrieked, and pain rocked him.

"Remember? After the car crash, we spoke to those flippin' reporters, and then you were so upset, you asked me to bring Dawn back and we did it."

Against his better judgement: *"What?!"*

"Now *that* could get annoying," Jason reproached, and grinned. "You're pretty good, for a beginner. Well done."

"Good—good at *what*? What did we do?"

Jason's grin became a full-fledged leer. "Come on, surely you don't need me to say. Just make sure you brush your teeth thoroughly, all right?"

Derrick could only gawk at his companion with his eyes wide open, his face draining of blood.

"And you liked it. From the way you were moaning . . ."

"Stop."

"You liked it. You did. Although you know what I think? I think you only like it when you're with Dawn, not with me."

"Stop!"

"So this is what I'm thinking," Jason said, looking at his nails for no reason, "you and I aren't an item, but you and *Dawn* are. How about that?"

Derrick was too busy hyperventilating to respond.

"You know you want it. You're gay," Jason said.

Without warning, the bedroom door flew open, and Sanjeev and Chitra burst in, arm-in-arm, smiling broadly. "How's the merry couple?" Chitra chirped.

"Derrick! You look radiant, absolutely radiant," Sanjeev gushed.

"Dawn told him to exfoliate," Jason said, and caressed Derrick's arm lightly. "You see what happens when you listen to Dawn's advice?"

Geraldine skipped in cheerfully. "Hey, what's this I hear about Rick and Dawn becoming an official item?"

Derrick glared at her, his mouth moving without a sound, his mind conjuring the words that he was so desperately trying to speak: *Mind game. This is one bloody mind game! What are they trying to* ". . . *do* to me?!" he shrieked, only the last three words bursting forth from him. He flung himself out of bed, ignoring the agony within his skull. "I know what you're doing! You're playing some kind of sick, psychological mind game, and I don't like it! I *hate* it! You sick bastards! I'm not gay! I'm not gay! I don't like Dawn, I don't like Jason, and I don't like Dawn!" he cried, seemingly not aware of what he was saying.

Jason flung the covers aside and crawled out from under them. Clad in Minnie Mouse boxers, he muttered, "Well, that's great. That's just great. Fine. Whatever." And he began to make his way to the door.

"Whoa," Geraldine uttered, "Jason . . ."

"No. No, forget it, I'm not going to hang around in a dead-end relationship."

"No!" she exclaimed, and ran to his side. "Come on. You're not in a dead-end relationship. There's so much more ahead of you guys —"

"Not if he's not interested," Jason said, and reached for his shirt, which was hanging behind the door. "Sorry, darlings, I can't hang around like this. I've got bigger fish to fry."

Chitra rushed to Derrick's side, giving him an imploring look. "Come on, Rick, you can't let Dawn leave like this!"

Derrick snorted. "He's not Dawn."

"Yes, but if you let *Jason* leave, you're letting Dawn leave, too," Sanjeev pointed out.

"Can't hang around," Jason said regretfully, and pulled on the shirt. "Sorry, people."

"Derrick, you and Dawn are great together, you *know* that!" Chitra cried. "Remember how happy Dawn made you after Geraldine and Hope got together? You're gay. Don't you want to feel that happiness again? She's right there. She is. But Jason's about to go, and if Jason goes, she goes."

Mind game, Derrick thought, but suddenly he couldn't think straight — in all aspects of the word. His foggy mind began to picture the nights he'd spent with Dawn: in his apartment, in his car, in restaurants and coffee shops and movie theatres; nights that had been fabulous, the most wonderful times of his romantic life. He'd thoroughly enjoyed Dawn's company. But that was, of course, before the whole charade had been exposed — now it was simply shocking. And yet, when he thought about it, the idea of Dawn standing in his room right now was still a turn-on—assuming that it was the version of Dawn with the tight clothing and the boobs and the hair . . .

And the idea of Dawn being upset and threatening to walk out was *devastating.*

"No," he murmured, "I'm not gay . . . !"

Jason heaved a sigh, shook his head, and walked out.

Geraldine whirled around. "Are you just going to let her leave?"

"You're letting Dawn go," Chitra chided.

"Don't be crazy, man, you know you want her," Sanjeev said.

Derrick shook his head without much force, not just because of the migraine, but also because he was unclear what he wanted. He muttered, "I can't."

"Yes, you can," Geraldine insisted. "She's there. You're gay. Don't let her go."

"She's a good catch, Derrick," Chitra added. "Think about it."

"If she walks out of her and finds somebody else, you'd have blown it for the rest of your life," Sanjeev pushed. "Think about it, Rick. Think of what we were saying last night—grabbing opportunities, making the most use of this limited time on earth that we have. She could walk out of here, get into a car and end up like that poor bastard last night, knock on wood. Or you could step off the pavement and get struck down by a bus. *Don't take the risk,* Derrick. If you want Dawn, if you're willing to look past her imperfections and see her as the person you've always dreamed of being and the person with whom you can spend the rest of your life, then go for it. Fucking *go for it.* Don't lose her, Rick. You'll regret it forever, I swear to God you will!"

"I—I can't," he uttered weakly.

"Of *course* you can!" the three of them yelled.

"Go!" Geraldine shouted.

"I can't!"

"Oh, fuck you!" Geraldine spat, and gave Derrick a rough shove towards the door. He squealed as he stumbled, pain bursting through his entire body, and fell against the doorjamb, regaining his balance. He turned back to look at her with a pained expression on his face. She turned away in a huff, not caring.

Hope jogged into the room, her jaw busy working on her usual wad of chewing gum. Her expression was bleak as she said, "My God, Dawn's crying. She's out in the living room, and she's crying." She turned to Derrick and socked him on one arm. "You made her cry, Dick!"

"What? No, I—"

"She's crying her eyes out now. I think she's really hurt."

Derrick felt a stab of guilt. The wall that he'd built around himself to protect against sexuality-themed confrontations began to crumble, pieces of it chipping off and falling to the floor of his psyche. Swallowing hard, he unconsciously raised one hand and placed it upon his chest, on his heart, trembling at the thought of—

"You remember hurt, Rick?" Chitra said sharply. "The same emotion you felt when Geri dumped you? Only that time it hadn't been hurt per se, had it, Rick? Because you weren't really in love with Geri, you were only *convincing* yourself that you were. But this time, it's different, Rick. Dawn *loves* you, she genuinely does, and you love her too, you *know* you do. If your forced love for Geri hurt so bad, can you imagine what kind of pain Dawn is experiencing right now?"

"Forced love? What are you *talking* about?"

"It's okay," Geraldine said gently. "I know you weren't really in love with me. You only made yourself believe it because you couldn't admit to being gay. But you *are* gay. And you like Dawn. And Dawn's out there, hurting, crying because of you. Can you seriously go on with the rest of your life knowing that you made such a sweet, sensitive, beautiful woman as Dawn *cry?*"

Crumbling. Crumbling.

"She tried to save you last night," Geraldine added. "She said when the car was about to hit the tree, all she could think about was your safety. *Yours.*"

Derrick whimpered.

"Go get her," Hope said, jerking a thumb in the direction of the doorway. "Go heal those wounds."

The wall of resistance and denial shattered into a million pieces of redbrick chunks. Letting out a soft cry, Derrick tore out of the room. "Dawn—!"

Then he stopped short, drawing in a sharp breath—

Jason was leaning against the kitchen counter, his expression serious and his eyes sad.

Derrick felt a wave of relief, and he chuckled softly. "Oh, my God."

"What took you so long?" Jason whispered, and made a strange movement with his shoulders, something resembling a shrug, as Derrick moved towards him.

Sanjeev, Chitra, Hope and Geraldine marched proudly up the stairs towards apartment 3B, flushed with triumph: the victors of an intricate and protracted battle against a man's personal oppression and denunciation of self.

"I told you," Geraldine said smugly. "See? I was right. It's all over. Derrick's truly himself now."

"And the great thing is, neither of them is going to be lonely," Sanjeev said.

"Well, they're only a couple as long as he's going out with Dawn Parker," Hope reminded them. "Otherwise, Jason Marcel is just a—very, very close friend."

"It's a strange kind of relationship," Chitra reflected.

"But not unheard of."

They reached the apartment, and as Hope fished out her keys, she said, "Hopefully this will end the religious debates once and for all."

"Yeah, well, I'm not a hundred percent unruffled, you know," Geraldine reminded her. She gazed at Hope, who smiled warmly, a smile of understanding, of compassion and love. "But I'm getting there," Geri added. "I'm getting there."

HOPING BEYOND HOPE

"Matt."

"Dad."

A tense moment of silence followed.

"How're you feeling, son?"

"I've—been better." He felt like shit, but he wasn't going to let his father know it.

Jonathan Leigh stood by his son's side. A long period of silence ensued, and Matthew's mother Moira stroked his hair, her touch soothing. He hadn't been comforted by his mother in a long, long time, and with each brush of her fingers, the pain in his head eased. It was as if mothers have some sort of magical touch that could miraculously heal all afflictions. At least, that's what Matthew thought, lying there, hurting, his right leg numb following the corrective surgery that the doctors had performed on him overnight. It was going to be a while before he could walk again; hours of physical therapy lay ahead of him, but he figured he could deal with it. With his mother there, soothing him, he could deal with almost anything.

The main reason for his line of thought was, of course, the knowledge that little Robby had probably not experienced his mother's touch for a long, long time. And now, the kid was out cold, on the children's floor of this very hospital. *How ironic,* he thought, and sighed. How tragic.

Jonathan cleared his throat loudly and said, "You're going to be in here for a while, Matt. I think they've told you."

Matthew nodded. "Yeah. I know."

There was another awkward moment of silence.

"That old man is going to be all right, son," Jonathan finally said softly, almost bashfully. "That was a—a remarkable thing you did there."

Matthew managed a weak laugh. "It was my pleasure."

Moira smiled. "We're proud of you, Matt."

"Thanks, Mum."

Jonathan didn't meet his gaze. "I've let the university know that you're going to be unavailable for quite some time. They understand, but some of your tutors are worried that you might fall behind . . ."

"I'm already falling behind, Dad," Matthew cut him off gently, and he was speaking the truth. "It's okay. I'll—I'll deal with it."

His father finally looked at him, his expression unreadable.

"In fact, I don't know if I'm even going to go back," Matthew added after a while.

His mother's fingers stopped in mid-stroke. "What?"

Matthew shut his eyes, took a deep breath, let it out slowly. He wasn't sure how much he could contribute to mankind, but if helping sick children like little Robby was in his list of options, he sure wasn't going to ignore it. He had so much going for him, he realised now. And he wasn't going to let all his strengths slip through his fingers in the name of laziness and apathy.

"I just might decide to be a doctor," he said softly, and his father stared at him, not comprehending. Matthew nodded, and his mother's fingers moved again, tender, loving. "Yeah," he murmured, and shut his eyes, complacent, certain. "I just might."

He thought of little Robby, lying so helpless in his little hospital bed on the third floor. Thought of how the boy led such a shit-arsed life and yet had seemed so unjaded, still innocent and hopeful, perhaps even hoping beyond hope. *(But with God there's no such thing as 'beyond hope', is there? That's what I used to hear every Sunday, back then. No such thing as hopelessness; everything is possible with the hand of God . . .)*

Matthew hadn't yet reverted to being a believer, but one thing was for sure: he'd been damned lucky to have come this far in his life. Even with a broken leg and his multifarious injuries—at least Matthew wasn't comatose. Little Robby, on the other hand, had had it bad all the way to unconsciousness. Matthew was going to be all right. It wasn't fair.

Lying in the hospital bed, Matthew began to wonder if the kid had been right in his beliefs. Because right now Matthew felt blessed, very much protected. He might not believe in guardian angels, but it sure looked like they believed in him.

Little Robby's mother surprised him by making an unannounced visit to Matthew's room.

She still looked as frail and haggard as she had that week when he'd intruded on her privacy and debunked her deep, dark secret. If anything, she looked even more fragile, like a delicate china doll, a woman desolated by circumstance.

She didn't have much to say. She didn't comment on the way he'd lashed out at her in her own home, didn't bring up that visit at all.

All she said, upon stepping in and making him look up from his comic book, was, "I just left the diner . . . thought I'd hop on a bus and come here. To see my son." Matthew stared at her, feeling a stirring within him; a sensation that he'd later come to acknowledge as sympathy. She didn't meet his gaze—the non-slip floor, a bland beige colour, seemed to be more interesting than Matthew's bandaged and plastered body. "Still nothing," she shared. "Still in his dreamland, wherever that is."

Matthew didn't answer.

"I'm praying," she said, "that he'll come back."

A pause. Matthew waited, thought it seemed as if she were one waiting for him to say something. He watched her, and she raised her eyes fleetingly, and then lowered them again.

Then she said, "I think — it'll be better after this. If he wakes up."

Now Matthew spoke, correcting her: "*When* he wakes up."

This time, she looked up at him. "You think so?"

"If you're praying," Matthew replied, and left it at that.

She nodded. It was a tense, agitated movement. "Yes. Yes, I am. Are you?"

Another pause. Then, something that resembled a smile danced across his lips, and he whispered, "Ask. Seek. Knock."

"Yes," the mother responded at once, understanding. "I — I know." And, still nodding her head, she turned to walk out of the room.

Matthew's voice made her stop in her tracks: "Hey, lady . . ."

She waited, her back to him.

"What's your last name?"

She turned around and smiled weakly.

She told him.

Matthew nodded with an appreciative look on his face. "I see," he said. "Thank you," he said. And, "Goodbye," he said, as the woman shuffled away.

AN EXCERPT FROM THE
DIARY OF MAGGIE COOKE

The past few weeks have been an absolute blur. After Daddy left I thought the worst was behind us, but apparently that was just the tip of a whole crazy iceberg.

Mum and I have been to the hospital every day, visiting Joe, hoping he'll come out of the coma soon. There was so much that had to be done on him—the broken ribs, a punctured lung, to name just two—and there's so much more that remains in the air. We don't know whether or not he's going to come to, but I'm hoping every day that he does, because, jerk or not, Joe didn't deserve to end up like this.

Zack and I are still seeing each other, although it is obvious that he still cares for Carrie very much. And why shouldn't he? I care for her too, since she is going to be the mother of my niece or nephew. I'm just grateful that her parents have seen things a little more clearly now and are supporting her through this difficult time. This is another thing Joe has to deal with when he wakes up—what's he going to do with the baby? Mum says there's no way he's not going to be involved. But Mum says a lot of things right now, not knowing what the future will hold, not knowing if Joe will even—

The other day Mum received a cheque from Daddy. She didn't tell me how much, but I figured from the way she reacted that it would be enough to help us through this, even if just for the moment. I don't know where Daddy is, he hasn't made any other form of contact, hasn't even been in to see Joe. But I figure he must know about the accident, I mean, the media was having a field day! I have the strongest feeling that Mum, Joe and I might never see Dad again, which is sad, but, in a way, a good thing. I think what Joe did that night was mainly because he'd been driven by Dad's temper, the kind of anger that causes you to react first and then think later.

So what about Zack and me? Don't know. He's been very supportive through all of this, and I still get all teary-eyed thinking that he was ready to help me when he thought I was pregnant, even though I wasn't (anymore). Maybe not all boys are bad. Not all boys are like Joe or Chris or—Dad. There are some good ones out there.

I still think getting rid of my baby was the biggest mistake. I also think Michelle feels guilty for talking me into it, although I've reassured her that the decision was largely mine, since it is, after all, my body. We're okay, Michelle and me. Her brother's in the hospital, too, interestingly enough. When I go over to visit Joe, I sometimes go over to Matthew's room to say hello. He's always been a little sullen, but since the accident, something about him is different. I don't know him well enough to say what, but Michelle claims her brother is a better man now. I don't know.

Mum is still devoted to her job, although she's been taken off the Mayson project, by her own choice. It's funny; since the accident, Mum seems to have changed, too, but not for the worse as you might imagine—no, she seems stronger now, more resolute. It's like she suddenly believes in herself when she never used to. Don't ask me why. Or maybe I'm just imagining it. But anyway . . .

Her bosses have been so understanding. They're allowing her to go on paid leave because of Joe's accident. But Mum, bless her, has turned down their offer, opting instead to work in half-shifts, coming home in the afternoons to spend time with me so we can really get to know each other. If you ask me, her boss Mr Dwight has a thing for Mum, the way he grants her all these exceptional working arrangements. And she has always spoken highly of him. Hmmm. I wonder . . .

Mum was naturally upset to learn about my abortion. Can't blame her, since I will forever be upset about it myself. I swear, when I'm older and out of school, I'm going to get more actively involved with this anti-abortion business. I think it's very important for everyone to learn about why abortion is not to be taken lightly. Don't get me wrong; everyone's still free to make their own decisions in life, free will and all that, but there's something to be said for education and awareness. I think most women abort their babies without really knowing what they're doing. If they do know and are certain about it, that's their decision; I'm not going to be one of those placard-carrying folks who camp outside of abortion clinics and swear at proponents. But at the same time, I'm not going to condone abortion if it's viewed as "the quickest way out". I was looking at my Pro-Choice is No Choice posters the other day. Really made me think. Maybe getting rid of the baby was the most convenient thing to do, but convenience shouldn't be a factor when it comes to another human life. But it's easy for me to say these things when I've already gone through with the procedure. If I were now bloated, four months pregnant, maybe I'd be thinking otherwise. Sometimes as much as you try not to be a hypocrite, you inevitably wind up being one. It's a bitch of a situation, really.

Anyway.

As you might expect, they're no longer going to have their silly residential meetings here anymore. Mum thinks these meetings are trivial and pointless, more of a social gathering than anything else, and it's nice to see she's finally come to her senses and realised that! Joe and I have been saying that for yonks!

They cleaned up the field the other day. The tree's all bruised and chipped, poor thing. The bench is gone. Maybe that's good. I don't know. I know Joe used to meet his friends on that bench, and that was probably where he'd first gotten involved with Carrie. It is definitely ironic that this whole drama also ended with Joe and Carrie and the bench.

Poor Carrie. Poor Joe.

Poor bench.

EPILOGUE

CONVERSATIONS ACROSS THE HANDS OF TIME

Matthew Leigh surveyed the area and nodded in approval. "It's looking good, isn't it?"

"I wanna sit," the boy next to him said, tugging on the older guy's pants leg.

"It says 'wet paint', you twit."

"Don't call me a twit. *You're* the twit."

"I'll call you whatever I want. And don't make fun of me, I'm older than you."

"I wanna sit!"

"If you sit, your butt's going to stick to the seat."

"Aw! Come on!"

"No."

"Can we sit in the car, then? Maybe get some milkshakes?"

Matthew sighed long-sufferingly. "Fine. I'll buy. As usual."

"You're not goin' to make me pay you back, are you?"

"No."

"You did the last time."

"I was being mean."

"You *always* mean, mister."

"Whatever, get in the car."

"How long would it takes for the paint to dry?" the child asked.

"I don't know," Matthew said, as they walked across the grass to the side of the road where his vehicle was parked. "I guess it depends. If the birds poop on it, they're going to have to do it over. They've already pooped on it twice, you know."

The boy rolled his eyes and sighed. "Stupid birds."

"So how did it go?" Jason asked, stretching lazily. "Did you tell her? Did you come out to your mum?"

"I did," Derrick replied. "It was hell."

"What happened?"

Derrick leaned against the headboard. "Oh, you know. The usual—screaming, ranting, carrying on like a madwoman. Then I finally calmed down and told her."

"Snort. You dick."

"Seriously, though, she was shocked, but surprisingly accepting. I think, somehow, mums just know."

"Even when their sons don't," Jason muttered.

Derrick ignored him. "Geri's mum freaked out, too, when Geri told her, but she's all right now."

"Shock therapy notwithstanding."

"Indeed."

Jason propped his head up with one hand, his elbow sinking into the pillow. "So, you think your mum will tell your dad?"

"Without a doubt."

"How do you think he'll take it?"

"I don't know. Maybe he's gay, too. Maybe it's hereditary."

"That's hilarious."

"Yeah, well . . ."

"Or maybe," Jason said with a twinkle in his eye, "your mum will take off her wig and remove her fake boobs, and say, 'Son, there's something you should know—' . . . *Ow!*" he cried, recoiling and laughing as Derrick tried to pinch him. "That hurt!"

"You deserved it."

"Did not!"

"Did too. You need a good spanking."

"Well, wait until morning," Jason replied cheekily. "That's when Dawn comes."

"My back hurts," Carrie grumbled.

Jessy Cooke looked at the girl fondly. "It's all part of the joy, isn't it?"

Carrie sighed in response.

Sitting at the dining table, Maggie looked up from her laptop and said, "What about Zoey? If it's a girl?"

"It's a girl," Carrie replied at once. "I just know it."

"Zoey. Rhymes with Joey," Jessy said quietly. "I think your brother would like that."

There was a moment of silence. Then Carrie groaned. "Hurry up, baby! Come into the world already!"

"That's when the *real* pain begins," Jessy retorted, and laughed at Maggie's affronted expression. "I'm just kidding, honey." She turned to Carrie and touched the girl's cheek affectionately. "Sweetheart, I know it feels insufferable right now, but enjoy this while it lasts. Pretty soon your child will be here, and she—or he—will be growing up." She paused, and tilted her head wistfully. "They'll grow up real quickly."

"I know," Carrie said softly.

"If you could help it," Jessy added, as her daughter met her gaze with a sad smile, "you wouldn't want them growing up at all."

"You know, it's strange, Zack," Maggie said later, "I know this is a form of self-torture, some sort of masochistic endeavour, but I still imagine the hospital calling us up one day and saying, 'We've got good news. Joe is awake'. And that's bad, because every day I wake up wondering if today's going to be the day, only to wind up disappointed and thinking, oh well, maybe tomorrow."

"But it's not impossible, Mags," Zack said, rubbing her back in soothing circles.

"I know. Still, almost six months on, and . . ."

"Some people stay in a coma for years. This isn't to say it will happen to Joe, but—I don't know. Michelle's brother's strange little friend came out of it, so . . . God knows."

"God knows," Maggie repeated, and even though she knew he meant it rhetorically, she smiled at him and gave him a gentle peck on the cheek. "That's exactly right."

"More coffee?"

"Bertha, I'm stuffed."

"You've only had one cup and a slice of cake."

"*Coffee* cake. I'm on a high now!"

"Seriously."

"I *am* serious, that's the frightening thing."

She sighed. "You're incorrigible."

"And you drive me round the bend. It looks like we just have to put up with each other."

"What time is Michelle supposed to come over?"

"About eight," he replied.

"She's such a good girl, and so dedicated to the work. Not to mention, you've got *such* a story to tell."

Graham smiled. "I can't argue with you there." He stood and reached for his walking cane. His hip still ached dully, which was why he preferred to use a walking aid, but he was otherwise doing just fine. Turning to his companion, he said, "Think you might want to take a walk?"

"What am I going to do with my cake?" she protested feebly.

"Leave it. We'll walk off the calories and caffeine, and come back for more!"

As the sun began to set, the old couple made their way across the grass to the single, solitary bench, its new coat of paint gleaming in the orange light of dusk. A dog barked a repeated pattern of three high-pitched yaps in rapid succession. Somewhere, not too far away, a doctor-to-be laughed sarcastically with a loquacious little boy who had just turned seven. A recently divorced woman, empowered by circumstance, spent precious time with her daughter and the girl who would shortly be the mother of her grandchild. Two young couples embraced, learning to live and love each other and themselves.

And the elderly couple sat on the bench, enjoying the peacefulness of their surroundings, comfortable with each other.

Watching the sun disappear, confident that a brand new day lay ahead.

ABOUT THE AUTHOR

Nick Choo graduated from Murdoch University in Western Australia with a Masters of Arts in Journalism and Creative Industries, and has worked as a writer, illustrator and copy editor with media companies in Kuala Lumpur and Singapore. His books have been published by iUniverse and Marshall-Cavendish (Malaysia). Nick is also an accomplished playwright, composer and musician, whose musical and theatre works have been performed in Malaysia and Australia.

Made in the USA
Las Vegas, NV
23 January 2022